Maid of the Mist by John Oxenham

John Oxenham was the pseudonym used by William Arthur Dunkerley for most of his fiction works including poetry. For journalism he went by the name of Julian Ross.

Dunkerley was born on November 12th 1852 in Manchester. He attended Old Trafford School and Victoria University, both in Manchester.

He married in America and lived they for a short time before returning to these shores, this time to Ealing in West London becoming both the Deacon and teacher at Ealing Congregational Church in the 1880's.

In 1913 he wrote a bestselling book of poems entitled 'Bees In Amber' followed by 'All's Well" in 1916. As a journalist he was a major contributor to Jerome K Jerome's Idler magazine.

In 1922 he moved to Worthing in Sussex and became the town's Mayor.

He died in Worthing on January 23rd, 1941.

Index of Contents

BOOK I

FOR A WOMAN'S SAKE

I

At sight of where the chase was leading, most of the riders reined in their panting horses and sat watching those in front with anxious faces.

The Old Roman Road—so called, though with possibly somewhat doubtful claim to antiquity so remote—had an evil reputation. At best of times it was dangerous. More than one of them had sacrificed a horse to it at some time or other. Some had come near to sacrificing more.

After several hours in the field, wound up by a fast five-and-twenty minutes' run which had led round Endsley Wood and the coppices almost to Wynn Hall, and then back through Dursel Bottom, and up Whin Hill, it was too much to ask of any horse. Besides, it meant the end of the run in any case, for that old fox, if he failed to shake them off elsewhere, always made for the Roman Road and always managed it there.

The hedge on this side was as thick and matted a quickset as ever grew. The sunk road had no doubt originally been a covered way from the old fort up above. It was indeed more of a trench than a road, with a sheer descent from the quickset of ten good feet, a width of about as much, and a grass slope on the other side at a somewhat lower level.

The leap was therefore by no means impossible if your horse could rise to the hedge and cover the distance and the extra bit for a footing.

But what was the good? The bottom of the old road was always a muddy dribble from the fields above, and up and down it went several flocks of sheep whenever they changed pasture. And the wily old fox knew the effect of these things on scent as well as any hound or huntsman. So, when it was his day, and he had had enough of them, he made for the Old Roman Road, and then went home with a curl in his lip and a laugh in his eye.

But there were riders among them to whom a ride was nothing without a risk in it, and the Roman Road a standing test and temptation. It was two such that the rest who had got that length stood watching, some with tightened faces, none without anxiety. For a leap that is good sport when one's horse is fresh may mean disaster at the end of the run. Even old Job, the huntsman, and young Job, his son, who acted as whipper-in, watched with pinched faces and panted oaths between their teeth. Pasley Carew, the Master, lifted his foam-flecked black to the hedge, and the dull crash of his fall came up to them, horribly clear on the still autumn air.

Wulfrey Dale, the Doctor, on his big bay, cleared hedge and road with feet to spare, flung himself off as soon as he could pull up, and ran back to help.

It was as bad as it could be. Carew lay in the road, smothered in mud and obviously damaged. His horse had just rolled off him, and the Doctor saw at a glance that one of its forelegs was broken. It was kicking out wildly with its heels, flailing clods out of the steep bank and floundering in vain attempts to rise.

Carew, on one elbow, was cursing it with every oath he could lay tongue to, and with the pointed bone handle of his crop in the other hand was hammering the poor brute's head to pulp.

"Stop it, Carew!" shouted Wulfrey, sickened at the sight, as he jumped down the bank. "Damn it, man, it wasn't her fault!"

"— her! She's broken my back."

"You shouldn't have tried it. I told you you were too heavy for her. Stop it, I say!" and he wrenched the crop, all dripping with hair and blood, out of the other's hand, and with difficulty bit off the hot words that surged in his throat. For the man was broken and hardly responsible.

It was a hard age and given to forceful language. But never in any age are there lacking some to whom brutality to the dumb beast appeals as keenly as ill-treatment of their fellows.

Wulfrey Dale was of these, and a great lover of horses besides, and Carew's maltreatment of his broken beast cut him to the quick.

With another quick look at the useless leg, and a bitter word which he could not keep in, at the horror of the mauled head, he drew from his pocket a long knife, which had seen service on many a field, opened it, pressed down the blinded tumbling head with one hand, and with the other deftly inserted the blade at the base of the skull behind the ears and drove it home with all his force, severing the spinal cord.

"Poor old girl!" he said, as, with a quick sigh of relief, the great black body lay still.

Then he turned to Carew and knelt down to examine into his injuries.

"No need," said the broken man. "Curse it all! Get a gate. My back's gone. I've no legs,"—and the others, having found their roundabout ways, came flocking up, while the dogs still nosed eagerly up and down the road but got no satisfaction.

Young Job plied his whip and his tongue and carried them away. His father looked at Carew, then at the Doctor, who nodded, and the old man turned and hurried away to get what long experience of such matters told him was needed.

"Take a pull at this, Carew," said the Doctor, handing him a flask. And as he drank deeply, as though to deaden the pain or the thought of it, Dale beckoned to one of the group which stood a little aloof lest the broken man should take their anxiety for morbid curiosity.

"Barclay, will you ride on and break it to Mrs. Carew?"

"Is it bad?"

"Yes, his back's broken."

"Good God!" and he stumbled off to his horse, and with a word to the rest, mounted and rode away.

Old Job came back in a minute or two with a hurdle he had rooted up from the sheep-fold, and they lifted the Master on to it and carried him slowly and heavily home.

II

Carew was on the front door steps as they came up the drive. The Doctor went on in advance to speak to her.

"Dead?" she jerked breathlessly, as he strode up.

"Not dead. Badly broken. He may live," and her tightened lips pinched a trifle tighter.

She was a slight, extremely pretty woman of three and twenty, white-faced at the moment with the sudden shock; in her blue eyes a curious startled look—anxiety?—expectancy? Even Dale, who had known her all his life, could not have said. All he knew was that it was not quite the look one found in some wives' faces in similar circumstances, and this was not the first he had seen.

She looked scarcely more than a girl, though she had been married five years. That was due largely to the slim grace of her figure. Her face was thinner than he had known it, less eloquent of her feelings, somewhat tense and repressed, and her eyes seemed larger; and all that, he knew, was due to the fact that it was to Pasley Carew to whom she had been married for five years, for he had seen these changes come upon her gradually.

They had played together as boy and girl, when he was just little Wulf Dale, the Doctor's son, and she Elinor Baynard, living with her mother at Glynne. As youth and maiden they had flirted and even sweet-hearted for a time. But Mrs Baynard of Glynne had no intention of letting her pretty girl throw herself away on a mere country doctor's son, however highly she might esteem both father and son personally.

Wulf had at that time still to prove himself, and even if he did so, and eventually succeeded his father in the practice, it meant no more than a good living at the cost of constant hard work.

Elinor, she was sure, had been gifted by Nature with that face and figure for some better portion in life than that of a country doctor's wife, and so she saw to it that the feelings of the young people should not get too deeply entangled before it was too late.

As for Elinor herself she was very fond of Wulf. She liked him indeed almost well enough to sacrifice everything for him. But not quite. If he had only been in the position and possessions of Pasley Carew of the Hall, now, she would have married him without a moment's hesitation, and she would undoubtedly have had much greater chance of happiness than was vouchsafed her.

If, indeed, Wulf had ardently pushed his suit he might possibly have prevailed on her to marry him in spite of her mother, though whether Wulf without the possessions would have satisfied her eventually may be doubted. But Wulf, two years older than herself, had no intention of marrying at twenty, even if his father would have heard of it.

He was a gay, good-looking fellow, with the cheerfullest of humours, and on the best of terms with every man, woman and child, over all the country-side. Moreover he was an excellent shot, a fearless rider, good company at table, an acceptable and much-sought-after guest,—whenever circumstances and cases permitted of temporary release from duties with which no social engagements were ever allowed to interfere. Marrying and settling down were for the years to come.

As his father's assistant he had proved his capabilities. And when the old man died, Wulf stepped up into the vacant saddle and filled it with perfect acceptation to all concerned.

His ready sympathy, and his particular interest in and devotion to everyone who claimed his services, endeared him to his patients. They vowed that the sight of him did them as much good as his medicines, but he made them take the medicines all the same.

He had also lately been appointed Deputy-Coroner for the district, in order, in case of need, to relieve Dr Tamplin—old Tom Tamplin who lived at Aldersley, ten miles away. So that matters were prospering with him all round. All men spoke well of him, and the women still better.

A practitioner from the outside, with a London degree and much assurance, had indeed hung out his large new brass plate in the village about a year before, and lived on there in hope which showed no sign of fulfilment. For everyone knew and liked Wulf Dale, and Dr Newman, M.B., clever though he might be and full worthy of his London degree, was still an outsider and an unknown quantity, and the way of the medical outsider in a country district is apt to be as hard as the way of the transgressor.

So Elinor Baynard, for the sake of her bodily comfort and her own and her mother's worldly ambitions, married Pasley Carew and became Mistress of Croome, and learned all too soon that it is possible to pay too high a price even for bodily comfort and the realisation of worldly ambition.

Worldly ambition may, indeed, be made to appear successfully attained, to the outside world; but bodily comfort, being dependent more or less on peace of mind, is not to be secured when heart and mind are sorely exercised and bruised.

Jealous Jade Rumour even went the length of whispering that it was not heart and mind alone that had on occasion suffered bruising in this case. For Carew was notoriously quick-tempered and easily upset—and notoriously many other things also. His grooms and boys knew the feel of his hunting-crop better than his reasons for using it at times—though doubtless occasion was not lacking. As to his language!—it was said that the very horses in his stables lashed out when he began, as though they believed that, by much kicking, curses might be pulverised in mid-air and rendered innocuous.

Now a wife cannot—Elinor at all events could not—kick even to that extent under the application of sulphur or riding-whip. Nor can she legally, except in the extremest case, throw up her situation, as the stable-boys could, but did not. For the pay in both cases was good, and for the sake of it the one and the other put up with the discomforts appertaining to their positions.

Pasley Carew's redeeming characteristics were a large estate and rent-roll, sporting instincts, and extreme openhandedness in everything that ministered to his own pleasures.

He ran the hounds and was a fine rider, though over-hard on his horses, with whom he was never on terms of intimate friendship. He esteemed them solely for their carrying capacities. He preserved, was a good shot, and free with his invitations to the less-happily situated. He was a jovial host and a hard drinker as was the fashion. He enjoyed seeing his friends at his table and under it. He was not a hard landlord, and this, and his generosity in the matter of compensation for hunt-damage, secured him the good-will of the country-side and palliated all else.

Morals were slack in those days, and no one would have thought for a moment of affronting Carew by calling him a moral man.

On the whole, Elinor paid a somewhat high price for the bodily comfort from which—according to the Jealous Jade—sulphurous language and an occasional blow were not lacking, and for the satisfaction of a worldly ambition which, if the gradual shadowing of her pretty face was anything to go by, had not brought her any great peace of mind.

III

Wulfrey Dale was a very general favourite. With men and women alike, quite irrespective of their station in life, his manner was irresistibly frank and charming. With the women it might be said to be almost unfortunately so.

He was so absolutely and unaffectedly sympathetic, so exclusively and devotedly interested in every woman he met, that it is hardly matter for wonder that in many quarters impressionable hearts beat high at his coming, and thought tenderly and hopefully of him when he had gone. That, too, in spite of the fact that their owners knew perfectly well that it was simply Wulf's way, as it had been his father's before him, and that neither of them could change his nature any more than he could change his skin or the colour of his eyes.

He took a deep and genuine human interest in every man, woman and child with whom he came into contact, and showed it. With men and children it made for good-fellowship and extraordinary confidence. The older folk all trusted young Wulfrey as they had all their lives trusted the old Doctor. The children would talk to him as between man and man, and with an artlessness and candour which as a rule obtained only among themselves. With the women it led in some cases to little affections of the heart—flutterings and burnings and barely-self-confessed disappointments, for which their owners, if honest in their searchings after truth, had to acknowledge that the blame lay entirely with themselves.

It was a time of hard drinking, hard riding, and quite superfluously strong language, but none the less, among the women-folk, of a sentiment which in these days of wider outlook and opportunity we should denominate as sickly. The blame was not all theirs.

So far Wulf had shown exceptional interest or favour in no direction, that is to say in all, and so none could claim to say with any certainty in which way the wind blew, or even if it blew at all.

Not a few held that Elinor Baynard's marriage with Pasley Carew had so wounded his affections that it was probable he would never marry, unless—. And therein lay strictly private grounds for hope in many a heart.

For a heart-broken man, however, Wulfrey managed to maintain an extremely cheerful face, and his manner to Elinor, whenever they met, was just the same as to other women.

If it had in fact been somewhat different it would not have been very surprising. For it needed no professional acumen to recognise that her marriage with Pasley had not fulfilled her expectations.

She was, indeed, Mrs Carew of Croome, mistress of the Hall and all such amenities—and otherwise— and luxuries of living as appertained to so exalted a position, winner of the prize so many had coveted, and—wife of Pasley Carew. And sometimes it is possible she wished she were none of these things because of the last.

For Carew made no pretence of perfection, or even of modest impeccability, never had done so since the day he was born, never would till the day he must die, would have scorned the very idea. Was he not a man,—rich and hot-blooded, able and accustomed all his life to have his own way in all things, easy enough to get on with when he got it, otherwise when thwarted?

And Wulfrey Dale had seen the freshness of the maiden-bloom fade out of Elinor's pretty face, in these five years of her attainment, had seen it stiffen in self-repression, and even harden somewhat. Her eyes had seemed to grow larger, and there were sometimes dark shadows under them. Without doubt she had not found any too large measure of the comfort and happiness she had looked for. At times, mind acting on body, her health was not of the best, and then she sent for Wulfrey to minister to her bodily necessities, and found that he could do it best by allowing her to relieve her mind of some of its burdens.

They had always been on such friendly terms that she could, and did, talk to him as to no other. Her mother was worse than useless as a burden-sharer. Her only counsel was not to be too thin-skinned, and above all to present a placid face to the world. Which, as medicine to a sorely-tried soul, was easier to give than to take, and proved quite ineffective.

Wulfrey, on the other hand, gave her tonics, and, to the fullest limits of his duty to Carew, his deepest sympathy in her troubles and vexations, and his friendly advice towards encouragement and hope of better times, when Pasley's hot blood would begin to cool and he would settle down to less objectionable courses.

At times, under stress and suffering from some more than usually immoderate outbreak on her husband's part, she would let herself go in a way that pained and surprised him, both as friend and doctor. He doubted if she always told him all, even at such times. More than once she had seemed on the point of still wilder outbreak, and it was all he could do to soothe her and bring her back to a more reasonable frame of mind.

On one occasion she openly threatened to take her life, since it was no longer worth living, and it took Wulfrey a good hour to wring from her a solemn promise not to do so without first consulting him. So over-wrought and alternately excited and depressed was she that there were times when, in spite of her promise, he would not have been greatly surprised by a sudden summons to the Hall with the news that its mistress had made a summary end of her troubles.

His mind was sorely exercised on her account, but it was only the effects that came within his province. The root of the trouble was beyond his tackling. He did, indeed, after much debate within himself, bring himself to the point of discussing the matter, in strictest confidence, with the parson, one night. But he, jovial sportsman and recipient of many bounties from Pasley, including the privilege of subsiding under his table whenever invitation offered, genially but flatly refused to interfere between man and wife.

"No good ever comes of it, Doctor. You know that as well as any man. It's only the intruder suffers. They both turn and rend him like boars of the wood and wild beasts of the field. Take my advice and leave 'em alone. These things always straighten themselves out in time—one way or the other. Deuce take the women! They're not blind kittens when they marry. They've got to take the rough with the smooth. Another glass of punch before you go!"—was the irreverent Reverend's final word on the matter. And Wulfrey could do no more in that direction.

IV

It was under such circumstances that they carried Pasley Carew home to Croome on the hurdle; under such circumstances that Elinor met them on the steps and asked Wulfrey, with that curious, startled look in her eyes which might be anxiety and might be expectancy.—

"Dead?"

And Wulfrey, subconsciously wondering whether she really had got the length of hoping for her husband's death, and subconsciously feeling that if it were so it was not much to be wondered at, though undoubtedly greatly to be deplored, had answered her, somewhat sternly, "Not dead. Badly broken. He may live,"—for the shock of the whole matter, and the extreme discomfort of having had to sever that poor Blackbird's spinal cord, were still heavy on him.

Elinor shot one sharp, searching glance at his face, and turned and went on before the bearers to show them the way.

The staircase at Croome was a somewhat notable one, wide enough to accommodate hurdle and bearers with room to spare, so they carried the Master right up to his own bedroom and as gently as possible transferred him to his bed.

The explosive fury of his outbreak against Fate and Blackbird, in the first shock of his fall, had been simply a case of vehement passion disregarding, and momentarily overcoming, the frailty of the flesh. Exhaustion and collapse followed, and as they carried him home he lay still and barely conscious.

He came to himself again as they placed him on the bed, and after lying for a moment, as though recalling what had happened, murmured in a bitter whisper, "Damnation! Damnation! Damnation!" and his eyes screwed up tightly, and his face warped and pinched in agony of mind or body, or both.

As Wulfrey bent over him, and with gentle hands assured himself of the damage, Carew looked up at him out of the depths; horror, desperation, furious revolt, hopelessness, all mingled in the wild gleam that detected and scorched the pity in Wulfrey's own eyes, and gave him warning of dangers to come.

"— it all! It's no good, Dale," he growled hoarsely. "I'm done. — that horse! Give me something that'll end it quick!"

"Don't talk that way, man! You know I can't do that. We'll pull you through."

"To lie like a log for the rest of my life! I won't, I tell you. — it, man, can't you understand I'd liefer go at once?"

"I'll bring you up a draught and you'll get some rest," said Dale soothingly.

"Rest! Rest! A dose of poison is all I want, — you! Don't look at me like that, — you!" to his wife, who stood watching with her hands tightly clasped as though to hold in her emotions. She walked away to the window and stood looking out.

"Carew, you—must—be—quiet. You're doing yourself harm," said the Doctor authoritatively.

"Man, I'm in hell. Poison me, and make an end!"

"Not till tomorrow, anyway. I'll run down and get that draught. We'll see about the other in the morning."

Mrs Carew turned as he left the room, and followed him out, and the sick man sank back with a groan and a curse.

"Will he die?" she asked quickly, as she closed the door behind them.

"Not necessarily. But if he lives he'll be crippled for life."

"He would sooner die than live like that."

"We can't help that. It's my business to keep him alive. I'll run down and mix him a draught which may give him some rest. You'll need assistance. He may go off his head. He's a bad patient. I'll send you someone up—"

"Not Jane Pinniger then. I won't have her."

He knitted his brows at her. "It was Jane I was thinking of. She's an excellent nurse, both brains and brawn, and he may get violent in the night."

"I won't have her here," said Elinor obstinately, and he remembered that gossip had, not so very long ago, been busy with the names of Pasley and Jane, as she had at other times occupied herself with Pasley and many another. Undoubtedly Elinor had had much to bear.

"All right! If I can find anyone else—" he began.

"I won't have Jane Pinniger here,"—and he went off at speed to get the draught and find a substitute for Jane if that were possible.

His doubts on that head were justified. He sent his boy up with the draught, and started on the search for a nurse who should combine a modicum of intelligence with the necessary strength of mind and body.

But his choice was very limited. Old crones there were, satisfactory enough in their own special line and in a labourer's cottage, but useless for a job such as this. There was nothing for it at last but to go back to the Hall and tell Mrs Carew that it was Jane or nobody.

"Nobody then," said she decisively. "I will manage with one of the girls from downstairs, and young Job to help."

"Young Job is all very well with the dogs—"

"He will do very well for this too. We may not require him, but he can be at hand in case of need," and he had to leave it at that.

V

Carew suffered much, more in mind even than in body. The thought of lying there like a damned log, as he put it, for the rest of his days filled him with most passionate resentment, and drove him into paroxysms of raging fury. He cursed everything under the sun and everyone who came near him, with a completeness and finality of invective which, if it had taken effect or come home to roost, would have blighted himself and all his surroundings off the face of the earth.

Even his wife, and the maid who took turns with her to sit within call, accustomed as they were to his outbreaks, quailed before the storm. Young Job alone suffered it without turning a hair, and paid no more heed to it all, even when directed against himself, than he would to the yelping of his dogs.

Wulfrey Dale came in for his share, chiefly by reason of his quiet inattention to the sufferer's impossible demands for extinction.

But he found his visits to the sick-room trying even to his seasoned nerves. What it must all mean to the tortured wife he hardly dared to imagine.

Once when he was there, Carew hurled a tumbler at her which missed her head by a hair's-breadth. Dale got her out of the room, and turned and gave his patient a sound verbal drubbing, and Carew cursed him high and low till his breath gave out.

"Has he done that before?" the Doctor asked the white-faced wife, when he had followed her downstairs.

"Oh, yes. But I'm generally on the look-out. I was off my guard because you were there. Oh, I wish he would die and leave us in peace."

"He'll kill himself if he goes on like this."

"He'll kill some of us first. He's wanting to die. It would be the best thing for him—and for us. Can't you let him die?" and a tiny spark shot through the shadowy suffering of her eyes as she glanced up at him.

"You know I can't. Don't talk like that!" he said brusquely, and then, to atone for the brusqueness, "I am sorely distressed for you, but there is nothing to be done but bear it as bravely as you can. What about your mother? Couldn't you—"

"It would only make him worse still, if that is possible. Pasley detests her. Oh, I wish I were dead myself. I cannot bear it," and she broke into hysterical weeping, and swayed blindly, and would have fallen if he had not caught her.

A woman's grief and tears always drew the whole of Wulf's sympathy. And he and she had been almost as brother and sister all their lives—till she married Carew.

"Don't, Elinor! Don't!" he said soothingly, as with her shaking head against his breast she sobbed as though her heart were broken.

Mollie, the maid, came hastily in, without so much as a knock, her red face mottled with white fear.

"He's going on that awful, Ma'am, I vow I daresn't stop in there alone with him. It's as much as one's life's worth when he's in his tantrums."

"Get your mistress a glass of wine, Mollie, and then find young Job and send him up. I'll go up and wait with Mr Carew till he comes."

He led Mrs Carew to the couch and made her lie down there, and explained matters to the girl by asking her,

"Does he throw things at you too?"

"La, yes, Doctor, at all of us, if we don't keep 'em out of his reach. He do boil up so at nothing at all," and she went off in search of young Job, who was passing a peaceful holiday hour in the company of thirty couple of yelping hounds.

VI

Dale was confronted with the problem with which every medical man comes face to face during his career.

Here was a man who, both for his own sake and still more for the sake of those about him, would be very much better dead than living; who wanted to die, and, as he believed, make an end; who begged constantly for the relief of death;—and yet, against his own equally strong feeling of what would be best for all concerned, his doctor must do his very utmost to keep his patient alive and all about him in torment.

Wulfrey wished, as devoutly as the more immediate sufferers, that he would die. He wished it more ardently each time he saw Mrs Carew, and wholly and entirely on her account.

Her white face, which grew more deathly white each day, and her woful eyes, which grew ever more despairing in their shadowy rings, were sure indexes of what she was passing through. Dale wondered how much longer she would be able to stand it.

He gave her tonics, and his most helpful sympathy and encouragement. And at the same time, by the irony of circumstance and the claims of his profession, he must do everything in his power to perpetuate the burden under which she was breaking.

But the whole matter came to a sudden and unlooked for end, on the seventh day after the accident.

Wulfrey was hastening up to the Hall to clear this, the unpleasantest item, out of his day's work, when he met young Job coming down the drive with a straw in his mouth and three couples of young hounds at his heels.

"Wur comen fur you, Doctor," said young Job. "He's dead."

"Dead?" jerked the Doctor in very great surprise, for his patient had been more venomously alive than ever the night before.

"Ay—dead. An' a good thing too, say I, and so too says everyone that's heard it."

"But what took him, Job? He was going on all right last night."

"'Twere the Devil I expecs, Doctor, if you ask me straight. He were getten too strampageous to live. Th' air were so full o' fire and brimstone with his curses, it weren't safe. 'Twere like bein' under a tree wi' th' leeghtnin' playin' all round."

"And Mrs Carew? ... Who was with him when he died? Tell me all you know about it," as they hurried along.

"I come up at ten o'clock as ushal, an' the missus met me at door wi' her finger to her lips. 'He's sleeping, Job,' she says, an' glad I was to hear it. 'I'll go an' lie down, Job, for I'm very tired,' she says, and she looked It, poor thing. 'Knock on my door if you need me, Job,' she says, and she went away. He were lying quiet and all tucked up, an' I sat down an' waited for him to wake up and start again. But he never woke, and when the missus came in this morning she went and looked at him, and she says, 'Why, Job, I do believe he's dead,' and I went and looked at him, and, God's truth, he looked as if he might be. But I couldn't be sure, not liking to touch him, and I says, 'No such luck, ma'am, I'm afraid,'—polite like, for we all knows the time she's had wi' him, and she says, 'Go and fetch Dr Dale.' So I just loosed these three couple o' young uns—they're all achin' for a run,—an' I'm wondering who'll work th' pack now he's gone, if so be as he's really gone, which I'm none too sure of. Th' Hunt were best thing he ever did, but he were terrible hard on his horses."

Dale hurried into the house and up the stair, and into the sick-room, the windows of which were opened to their widest, as though to cleanse the room of the fire and brimstone which had seemed over-strong even to such a pachyderm as young Job.

Carew lay there on the bed, at rest at last, as far as this world was concerned, startlingly quiet after the storm-furies of the last seven days and nights.

Dale was still standing looking down at him, full of that ever-recurring wonder at the quiet dignity which Death sometimes imparts even to those whose lives have not been dignified; full too of anxious desire to learn how it had come about.

The tightly-clenched hands and livid rigidity of the body suggested a startling possibility. He was bending down to the dead man to investigate more closely when a sound behind him caused him to look round, and he found Mrs Carew standing there. Her face was whiter, her eyes heavier and more shadowy, than he had ever seen them.

"He is dead," she said quietly.

"One can only look upon it as a merciful release—for all of you. How was it?"

"He wanted to die," she began, in the dull level tone of a child repeating an obnoxious lesson. Then the self-repression she had prescribed for herself gave way somewhat. Her hands gripped one another fiercely and she hurried on with a touch of rising hysteria, but still speaking in little more than a whisper. "You know how he wanted to die. He was asking you all the time to give him something to end it. But you could not. I know—I quite understand—being a doctor, of course you could not. But there was something he kept—for the rats, you know, in the stables. And he told me where it was and told me to get some. So I got it and gave it him in his sleeping-draught, and—"

"Good God! Elinor!..." he gasped. "... You never did that!"

"Yes, I did. Why not? He wished it. We all wished it. It is much better so," and she pointed at the dead man on the bed. "It is better for him ... and for all of us. I only did what he told me."

He stood staring at her in blankest amazement, and found himself unconsciously searching her face and eyes for signs of aberration. Her face was wan-white still, but had lost the broken, beaten look it had worn of late. The shadow-ringed eyes were perfectly steady and had in them a curious wistful look, like that of a child expecting and deprecating a scolding.

"Do you know what it means?" he asked at last, in a hoarse whisper.

"It means release for us all," she said quickly, and then more quickly still, "Oh, Wulfrey, I couldn't help thinking—hoping that—sometime—not for a long time, of course,—but sometime—when we have forgotten all this—you might—you and I might—"

"Stop!" he said sternly. "Were you thinking that when you did this?" and he pointed to the bed.

"Not then—at least—no, I think not. I just did what he told me to do. But when I saw he was really dead—"

He stopped her again with a gesture, and broke out with brusque vehemence, "Is it possible you don't understand what you have done? Do you know what the law will call it?"—

"The law? No one needs to know anything about it but you and me—"

"The law will want to know how this man died—"

"But you can tell them all that is necessary. It was Blackbird falling at the old road that killed him. If he hadn't broken his back he wouldn't have been lying here, and if he hadn't—"

"He might have lived for twenty years," he said, breaking her off short again with an abrupt gesture. "The law requires of me the exact truth. Do you understand you are asking me to swear to a lie? I would not do it to save my own life."

"He took it himself—"

"He could not get it himself, and the law will hold you responsible for supplying it."

"Oh—Wulfrey! ... You won't let them hang me?"—and he saw that at last she understood clearly enough the peril in which she stood if the whole truth of the matter became known.

Hang her they most certainly would if the facts got out, or coop her for life in a mad-house, which would be infinitely worse than hanging. And the thought of either dreadful ending to her spoiled life was very terrible to him.

She stood before him, little more than a girl still, woful, wistful, with terror now in her white face and shadowy eyes, and he remembered their bygone days together.

"Go back to your room, and rest, if you can. And say nothing of all this to anyone. You understand?— not a word to anyone. I must think what can be done," he said, and she turned and went without a word.

VII

Wulfrey Dale thought hard and deep.

He must save her if he could.

How?

For a moment—inevitably—he weighed in his mind the question of his own honour versus this woman's life.

With a few strokes of the pen he could probably bury the whole matter safely out of sight along with Carew's dead body. But those few strokes of the pen, certifying that this man died as the result of his accident, were as impossible to him as would have been the administration of the poisoned draught itself.

Moreover—though that weighed nothing with him compared with the other—there was in them always the possibility of disaster, should rumour or tittle-tattle cast the shadow of doubt upon his statement; and an idle word from Mollie or young Job might easily do that. The neighbours also had made constant enquiry after Pasley since his accident, and had been given to understand that he was progressing as well as could be expected. His sudden death might well cause comment. Indeed, it would be strange if it did not. That might lead to investigation, and that must inevitably disclose the fact that he died from strychnine poisoning.

The Dales had never been wealthy, but their standards had been high, and Wulfrey had never done anything to lower them. He could not sell his honour even for this woman's life.

He pitied her profoundly. He understood her better probably than any other. He knew how terribly she had suffered, and could comprehend, quite clearly, just how she had fallen into this horrible pit. But cast his honour to the dogs for her, he could not.

Then how?

And, pondering heavily all possibilities, he saw the only feasible way out.

It meant almost certain ruin to himself and his prospects, but, if it came, it would be clean ruin and he would feel no smirch.

It involved a false statement of fact, it is true, but of a very different cast and calibre from the other, and one that he himself felt to be no stain upon his honour.

As a matter of pure ethics a lie is a lie, and of course indefensible. I simply tell you what this man did and felt himself untarnished in the doing.

And the very first thing he did was to go straight home to the little dispensary which opened off his consulting-room, and alter the positions of some of the bottles on the shelves; and from one of them he withdrew a measured dose which he tossed out of the window into the garden.

Then he sat down at his desk and quietly wrote out a certificate of the death of Pasley Carew, of Croome Hall, Gentleman, through the administration of a dose of strychnine in mistake for distilled water, in a sleeping-draught compounded by Dr Wulfrey Dale. And he thought, as he wrote the word, of the awful pandemonium Pasley Carew, Gentleman, had created in his own household these last seven days.

He enclosed this in a covering letter to Dr Tamplin, the coroner, in which he explained more fully how the mistake had occurred. The bottles containing the strychnine and the distilled water stood side by side on his shelf. He had come in tired from a long country round. Had remembered the draught to be sent up to the Hall. As to the rest, he could not tell how he came to make such a mistake. But there it was, and he only was to blame. He could only express his profound regret and accept the consequences.

Then, having completed his documents, instead of galloping off to see his waiting patients, he sat down before the fire and let his thoughts play gloomily over the whole matter. His man was off delivering medicines, and would not be back till midday. Time enough if Tamplin got his letter during the afternoon. As to his own patients, he had run rapidly over them in his own mind, and saw that there was no one vitally demanding his attention. He could not go his rounds and say nothing, and the thought of carrying the news of his own default was too much for him. As soon as the matter got bruited about, he thought grimly, there would probably be a run on Dr Newman's services, which would greatly astonish and delight that gentleman and would compensate him for all his months of weary waiting.

It was a good thing for Elinor, he thought, as he sat staring into the fire, that he was not married. If he had had a wife and children, they must have gone into the scale against her, and she must certainly have been hanged.

Quite impossible to bring it in as an accident on her part. That he had seen at a glance. The jury would be composed of neighbours, and in spite of the placid face she had turned to the world, it was well enough known that she and Pasley had not lived happily together. And though the fault of that was not imputed to her, every man's thought would inevitably jump to the worst, and condemn her even before she did it out of her own mouth, which she most certainly would do the moment she opened it to explain matters.

No, this was the only possible way. If the cost was heavy, he was more capable of bearing it than she. In any case he could not hand her over to the hangman. That was out of the question.

He could pretty well forecast the consequences. His practice would be ruined, for who would trust a doctor capable of so fatal a mistake? He would have to go away and start life afresh elsewhere. It would have to be somewhere where he was quite unknown, or this thing would dog him all his life. Some new country perhaps,—say Canada or the States. Gad, it was a heavy price to pay for a foolish woman's lapse!

He would not be penniless, of course. His father had laid by a considerable sum in the course of his long and busy life. If necessary he could live in quiet comfort, without working, for the rest of his days. But it was hard to break away like this from all that had so far constituted his life. A heavy price to pay for mere sentiment—but not too heavy for a woman's life!

There was no doubt of his having to go. The question was whether he should go at once, or wait till there was nothing left to wait for.

It would be dismal and weary work waiting. But going would feel like bolting, and he had never run from trouble in his life. As a matter of fact he had never until now had any serious trouble to face, but now that it had come he found himself in anything but a running humour.

If there had been anything to fight he would have rejoiced in the mêlée and plunged into it with ardour. But here was nothing to be fought. By his own deliberate act he was labelling himself untrustworthy, and no uttermost striving on his part could rehabilitate him. For the essence of healing is faith, and a doctor who has forfeited one's confidence is worse than no doctor at all.

VIII

In the afternoon he sent off his man on horseback with the letter to Dr Tamplin, and towards evening he came galloping back with this very characteristic reply:

"MY DEAR WULFREY,

Shocking business and I'm sorely grieved about whole matter. Humanum est errare, but a doctor's not supposed to. Good thing for us we're not always found out. Could you not bring yourself to certify death as result of the accident? I consider it a mistake to admit the possibility of such a thing, so d—d damaging to the profession. And have you considered the matter from your own point of view? Cannot fail to have bad effect. Perhaps give that new fellow just the chance he's been waiting for. — him!

Think it over again, my boy, from all points, and be wise. I return certificate. Your man will tell you all about my fall. My cob stumbled over a stone last night and broke me a leg and two ribs. I'm too heavy for that kind of thing and he's a — fool! But it was very dark and we're neither of us as young as we were. For all our sakes I hope you'll come through this all right. We can't spare you. And it might come to that. Remember what silly sheep folks are.

Yours truly,
THOMAS TAMPLIN."

Just like the dear, easy-going old boy, fall and all, thought Wulfrey, and the advice tendered and the course suggested did not greatly surprise him. But he had to make allowances for the old man's age and easy-goingness, and his lack of detailed knowledge of all the circumstances of the case,—how almost impossible it would be to ascribe Carew's death to the accident, even if he could have brought himself to do so.

The old man's own shelving would add greatly to the unpleasantness of the situation, for, as deputy-coroner, he would have to call a jury himself, and submit the matter to their consideration and himself to their verdict.

However, there was no way out of that, so he set to work at once and sent out his summonses, calling the inquest for ten o'clock the next morning, at the Hall; and to relieve Elinor as much as possible, he gave orders to the undertaker at Brentham to do all that was necessary, and sent her word that he had done so.

Early next morning, before he was up, young Job was knocking on his front door, with half the pack yelping and leaping outside the gate.

"Well, Job? What's it now?" he asked, from his bedroom window.

"That gal Mollie says you better come up and see th' missus—"

"Why? What's wrong with her?"

"I d'n know, n' more don't Mollie. She thinks she's had a stroke."

"Wait five minutes and I'll go back with you," and in five minutes they were crunching through the lanes, all hard underfoot with frost that lay like snow, and white and gay with hedge-row lacery of spiders' webs in feathery festoons, and, up above, a crimson sun rising slowly through the mist-banks over the bare black trees.

"What makes Mollie think your mistress has had a stroke?" asked the Doctor. "What does Mollie know about strokes?"

"I d'n know. 'Sims to me she've had a stroke,' was her very words. She've just laid on her bed all day an' all night without speakin' a word, Mollie says,—eatin' noth'n, and drinkin' noth'n, which is onnat'ral; an' sayin' noth'n, which in a woman is onnat'ral too."

"She was quite worn out with nursing Mr Carew."

"Like enough. He wur a handful an' no mistake. Th' house is a deal quieter wi'out him. But who's goin' to run th' pack?—that's what bothers me."

"Don't you worry, Job. Someone will turn up to run the pack all right."

"Mebbe, but it depends on who 'tis. Why not yourself now, Doctor?"

"That's a great compliment, Job, and I appreciate it. But," with a shake of the head, "I'll have other work to do," and he wondered grimly where that work might lie.

Mollie took him straight up to Mrs Carew's room, where she lay just as she had sunk down on the bed when he sent her away the previous morning.

"She's nivver spoke nor moved since she dropped down there yes'day," whispered Mollie impressively. "I covered her up, but she took no notice. An' I brought her up her dinner and her supper but she's never ate a bite."

"Get me a cup of hot milk with an egg and a glass of sherry beaten up in it, Mollie," he whispered back. "And I'll see if I can induce her to take it. You did quite right to send for me," and Mollie hurried away with a more hopeful face.

Elinor lay there with her eyes closed and a rigid, stricken look on her white face, a picture of hopeless despair. But Wulfrey's quick glance had caught the flutter of her heavy lids, and the gleam of terrified enquiry that had shot through them, as they came into the room, and he understood.

He bent over her and whispered, "I have made it all right, Elinor. You need have no further fears—"

"They will not hang me?" she whispered, and looked up into his face with all the terrors of the night still in her woful eyes.

"No one will know anything about it unless you tell them yourself. You will eat something now, and then you had better lie still. Get some sleep if you can or you will make yourself ill. If you fell ill you might say things you should not, you know."

She struggled up on to one elbow. "You are quite sure they will not hang me?" she whispered again.

"Quite sure, unless you are so foolish as to tell them all about it."

"I have felt the rope round my neck all night. Oh, it was terrible in the dark. It was terrible ... terrible—" and she felt about her pretty white neck with her trembling hands.

"Forget all about it now. I have made all the necessary arrangements. There will have to be an inquest. It will be held here—-"

"Here?" she shivered.

"At ten o'clock this morning. You are too ill to be present, so you will just lie still. It will not take long. And I have done everything else that had to be done."

"It is very good of you," she murmured, with a forlorn shake of the head.

She did not ask by what means he had saved her from the consequences of what she had done. Perhaps she dared not. Perhaps she believed he had, after all, forsworn himself for her sake, and refrained from questioning him lest it should only add to his discomfort. Anyway she was satisfied with the fact. She was not going to be hanged. That was enough.

Mollie came in with her deftly-compounded cup.

"Drink it up," said the Doctor. "I will look in again later on," and he went away to prepare the household for the coming meeting in the big dining-room.

IX

The sixteen jurymen, whom Wulfrey had summoned in order to make quite sure of a legal panel, came riding up in ones and twos, with faces tuned to the occasion, disguising, as well as they could, the vast curiosity this sudden call had excited in themselves and all their various households.

That there was something gravely unusual behind it they could not but feel. They were all friends and neighbours; many of them had witnessed Carew's accident and had been constant in their enquiries as to his progress. The news of his death had come as a surprise and a shock, and such of them as happened to join company on the road discussed the matter by fits and starts, and surreptitiously as it were, but did not venture below the surface. Their women-folk at home had done all that was necessary in that respect for the fullest ventilation of the subject, without in any degree rendering it more savoury or comprehensible.

Every man had felt it his bounden duty to be there, and so it was sixteen keenly interested faces that confronted Wulfrey when he took the chair at the head of the table and stood up to speak to them.

His face was very grave, his manner noticeably quiet and restrained and very different from its usual jovial frankness.

"This painful duty, doubly painful under the circumstances, as you will understand in a moment, has fallen to me in consequence of Dr Tamplin being laid up through the fall of his horse yesterday. I am sure you will not make it any more painful for me than it is. I shall not trouble you long. The matter is unfortunately clear and simple. Our friend, Mr Pasley Carew, died the night before last from the effects of a dose of strychnine, administered in a sleeping-draught in mistake for distilled water which was in the bottle alongside it on the shelf in my dispensary."

His eyes ranged keenly over the startled faces round the table at which they had all of them so often sat,—under which some of them had not infrequently lain.

Every face was alight with startled surprise. Not one of them showed the remotest sign of questioning his statement.

Indeed, why should they? A man does not as a rule confess to so grave a lapse unless it is absolutely unavoidable, unless the truth must out and there is no possible loophole of escape.

Not many men would fling away their life's prospects from simple pity for a woman. For love—yes, without a doubt, and count the cost small. But from simple pity, in remembrance of the time when the greater love had been possible? ...

But no such idea found place in any of their minds. His eyes searched theirs for smallest flicker of doubt, but found none. Whatever the women at home might have suggested as extreme possibilities, these men accepted his word without a moment's hesitation. Elinor was perfectly safe.

"He was in great pain and could only get rest and relief by means of opiates. How the mistake occurred I cannot explain, except that the bottles of distilled water and of strychnine stand alongside one another on my shelf, and that I had come in very tired that night and the sleeping-draught was prepared hurriedly. I deplore the results more than any of you possibly can, and of course I must accept the consequences. I have not judged it necessary to make any post-mortem examination. I was called by young Job early yesterday morning, and when I got here Carew was dead and the symptoms were those of poisoning by strychnine. I was amazed and horrified, but when I hurried back home I saw at once how the mistake might have been made, and—and—well, there the matter is and you must bring in such verdict as you deem right. You can see the body if you wish. You can examine the servants. Mrs Carew, I am sorry to say, is quite broken down with the shock. She has been, I am told, practically unconscious for nearly twenty-four hours and has only just come to herself. But if you would like to see her—"

"No, no." "No need whatever," said the jurymen deprecatingly.

Dr Wulfrey sat down and dropped his head into his hands, then got up again heavily and said, "You will discuss this matter better without me. I will leave you—"

"Couldn't you possibly say he died as result of the accident, Wulf?" asked one—Jim Barclay of Breme.

They all liked the Doctor. With some he had been on terms of very close friendship. Some of them had known him all his life and his father before him.

"Ay, couldn't you?" chorussed some of the others.

"If I could I should have done so," he said quietly. "But it wasn't so and I couldn't say it was."

"Say it now, Wulf," urged his friend. "And I swear none of us will let it out. Isn't that so, gentlemen?"

"Ay, ay!"—but somewhat dubiously from the older members, who saw that after this revelation of the actual facts to themselves their relations with the Doctor could never be quite the same again, however they might succeed in hoodwinking the world outside.

They knew him, they liked him, but—well, at the back of their minds was the thought that if Dr Wulf could make a mistake in one case, there was no knowing but what he might in another,—that he might at any time come in tired and pick up the wrong bottle,—that, whatever risks one might accept on one's own account for old friendship's sake, one's wife and daughters should hardly be put into such a position all unknown to themselves. And more than one of them wondered what he would do if he should happen to be taken ill that night—send for Dr Wulf or the new man down in the village?

Dale diagnosed their symptoms with the sensitiveness born of the equivocal nature of the new relationship in which his confession placed him towards them.

"It is like your good-heartedness to suggest it, Barclay," he said to his impetuous friend, "but it cannot be. I can only do what seems to me right," and he left them to talk over their verdict.

"Gad! but I'm mighty sorry this has happened," said one old squire who had known Wulf from the year one. "Many's the time I've sat at this table—"

"And under it," interjected one.

"Ay, and under it, and I never expected to sit round it on Pasley Carew. I'd give a year's rents to have him back, even if he was all in pieces and raging like the Devil."

"Same here. Whatever we decide it'll get out, and it's bound to tell against Dr Wulf."

"He's bound to suffer,—can't help it,—it's human nature. Suppose you took ill tonight now, Barclay. What would you do?"

"What would I do? I'd send for Wulf Dale of course, and I'd have same faith in him as I've always had."

"Of course, of course,"—but even those who said it had more the air of wishing to placate Barclay, who had a temper, rather than of any deep conviction as to their own course should the unfortunate necessity arise.

"Well," said Barclay, with the manner of a volcano on the point of eruption. "All I can say is that if any man I know goes ill and does not send for Wulf Dale, he'll have me to reckon with if the other man doesn't kill him."

"Hear, hear!" from various points about the table.

"Well, we've got to decide something and make an end of the matter," said one. "Barclay, you write out what you think and I've no doubt we'll all agree to it."

"I'm going to write nothing," said Barclay, whose strong brown hand was more accustomed to the hunting-crop than the pen. "I say 'Accidental Death,' and keep your mouths shut."

They all said 'Accidental Death' and promised to keep their mouths shut; and Wulfrey, when he was called in, thanked theta soberly for their good intentions, but added to their verdict,—"as the result of strychnine poison administered in mistake for distilled water in a sleeping-draught prepared by Dr Wulfrey Dale."

X

Jim Barclay, who was a bachelor, kept his bed next morning with an alleged bad cold,—-a thing he had never been troubled with in all his born days, and ostentatiously sent his man galloping for Dr Wulfrey as though his master's life depended on it.

Wulfrey smiled at the message, understanding the staunch friendliness which lay behind it, and went.

"Well, what's wrong with you?" he enquired of the burly patient, when he was shown up to his bedroom.

"Just you, my boy. Haven't slept a wink all night for thinking of the whole — mess. Wulf, my lad, I'm afraid you'll have a deuce an' all of a time of it. Thought I'd show 'em there was one man thought none the worse of you. —! —! —! Can't any man make a little mistake like that? Trouble is, most of those other fools have got a pack of yelping women-folk about 'em, and they're all on the quee-vee and as keen on the scent as any old—," and he launched into comparisons drawn from the kennels into which we need not enter. "They all promised not to blab, and they'll none of 'em tell any but their wives under promise of secrecy, and it'll be all over the country-side in a week."

"I know it, old man. I've just got to stand it," said Dale soberly.

"What's in your mind then?"

"I'll just wait quietly and see what comes. I can't expect things to be as they were before."

"And if things go badly? — it all!"

"Then I'm thinking I'll go too."

"Where?"

"Oh, right away. America maybe, or Canada. It's a big country they say and just beginning to open up. I shan't starve anyway, wherever I go."

"But,—to leave us all and all this? — it all, man! The place won't be like itself without you. — Pasley Carew!"

"It wasn't his fault, you know—"

"It was his — fault putting Blackbird at that — Old Road after the run we'd had, wasn't it? I told him he was two stone too heavy for her. But he always was a fool."

"He was to blame there undoubtedly. But the rest I take to myself. If folks go to the other man I can't blame them. I shall go nowhere unless I'm sent for."

"You'll have a — long holiday," growled Barclay.

"Well, I can do with one."

"I've half a mind to have a smash-up just to keep your hand in."

"If you do I'll—I'll turn the other man on to you."

"If he puts his nose in here he'll go out faster than he came, I wager you."

It was comforting to have so whole-hearted a supporter; but one patient, and a sham one at that, does not make a practice, and Dale very soon felt the effects of the course he had chosen.

He adhered resolutely to the decision he had come to to visit none of his patients unless he were sent for. It would be neither fair to them nor agreeable to himself. It might do more harm than good.

As to Mrs Carew,—he had visited her immediately after the inquest, and told her briefly that all was right and she need have no further fears. There was nothing wrong with her which a few days' rest and the relief of her mind would not set right. All the same he rather feared she might send for him, and he debated in his own mind whether, if she did so, he should go or send her messenger on to Dr Newman. It appeared to him hardly seemly that the man who had accepted the responsibility for the death of the husband should continue his attendance on his widow.

She did not of course as yet know the facts of the case as outsiders did. He was somewhat doubtful of the effect upon her when she came to a clear understanding of the matter. On the whole, he decided it would be better if possible not to see her again. What he had done for her had been done out of pity, but it was not the pity that sometimes leads to warmer feeling. All that had died a natural death when she married Carew.

He attended the funeral with the rest. It would only have made comment if he had not. And Jim Barclay and most of the others were at pains to manifest their continued friendliness and confidence.

Whether the full facts had got out he could not tell, but, rightly or wrongly, imagined so, and for the second time in his life he found himself ill at ease among his neighbours.

The day after the funeral, young Job and a bunch of lively dogs came down again with an urgent message from Mrs Carew requesting him to call.

"Is your mistress worse, Job?" he said.

"She be main bad, Doctor, 'cording to that gal Mollie, but what 'tis I dunnot know. Mebbe she's just down wi' it all. Have ye heard ony talk yet as t' who's going to tek on th' pack?"

"Mr Barclay will, I believe. He's a good man for it."

"Ay, he may do. Bit heavy, mebbe, an' he's got a temper 'bout as bad as Pasley's."

"Bit hot perhaps at times, but he's an excellent fellow at bottom."

"All that, and his cussin' ain't to compare wi' Pasley's, which is a good thing. I c'n stand a reasonable amount o' cussin' myself and no offence taken, but Pasley did go past th' mark at times. Th' very hosses kicked when he let out. An' Jim Barclay he is good to his hosses, an' he only cusses when he must or bust. Ay, he'll do, seein' you won't tek it on yourself, Doctor."

"It's not for me, Job. A doctor's time is not entirely his own, you know."

"Ah!" said Job, and picked a twig from the hedge, and stuck it in his mouth, and trudged on in solemn silence.

"We wus rather hopin', feyther an' me," he grunted after a time, "you'd mebbe have more time now fur th' pack an' would tek it on."

"Why that, Job?"

"Well, y' see, it'll mek a difference this. It's bound to mek a difference. Folks is such silly fools 'bout such things—"

"What things?"

"Why, that there strychnine. 'S if anyone couldn't mek a li'l mistake like that. Might have sense to know ye'd never let it happen again. Even th' leeghtnin', they say, never strikes twice i' same place. Though sure 'nuff it did hit th' old mill one side one day and t'other side next day. But even then 'twere opposite sides. But folks is fools."

"So you know all about it."

"Ay, sure! 'Twere that gal Mollie told me, an' it were Mrs Thelstane's gal Bet told her. None o' us think a bit the worse o' you, Doctor, you b'lieve me. But some folks is fools—most folks, if it comes to that.... An' as to Pasley—well, he were a terror now'n again. Th' Hall's like Heaven wi'out him."

They went on again in silence for a time. But there was that in young Job's mind which had to come out.

"If 'twere me, Doctor, askin' your pardon in advance for bein' so bold, what I'd do would be this. I'd just sit quiet till they done yelpin' and yappin' 'bout it all, then I'd marry th' missus,—we all knows you was sweet on her once,—and settle down comfortable at th' Hall and tek over th' pack an' mek us all happy."

"That's out of the question, Job."

"Is it now? ... Well, I'm sorry. Wus hopin' mebbe a word of advice from a man what's old enough to be your feyther, an's known you since day you was born, might be o' some use to ye. We'd like you fain well for Master, both o' th' Hall an' th' Hunt."

"You're a good old chap, Job, and so's your father, but you'll both be doing me a favour if you'll stop any talk of that kind."

"No manner o' use?"

"No use at all."

"Well, I'm main sorry. An' so's feyther, I can tell ye."

Mrs Carew was sitting in a large chintz-covered armchair before the fire in her bedroom, when he was taken up to her by Mollie, who favoured him with her own diagnosis as they mounted the stairs.

"She's that bad again. Can't sleep and off her food. Ain't had hardly anything all day or yes'day. Just sits 'fore th' fire and mopes from morn'n till night. 'Taint natural for sure, for him 'at's gone weren't one to cry for, that's cert'n.... No, she don't complain of any pain or anything. Just sits and mopes and cries on the quiet 's if her heart was broke. Sure she'd more cause to cry before he was took than what she has now."

When he entered the room he did not at first see her, so sunk down was she in the depths of the great ear-flapped chair.

She made no attempt to rise and greet him. When he stood beside her and quietly expressed his regret at finding her no better, she covered her face with her hands and sobbed convulsively.

She looked little more than a girl, slight and frail and forlorn, as she crouched there with hidden face, and he was truly sorry for her. It was impossible for him to keep the sympathy he felt entirely out of his voice.

"What can I do for you, Mrs Carew?" he asked quietly, and the forlorn figure shook again but made no response.

"You are doing yourself harm with all this," he said gently again. "And there is really no occasion for it, that I can see."

Her silent extremity of grief—her utter discomfiture was pitiful to look upon. It touched him profoundly, for he penetrated the meaning of it. She was overwhelmed with the knowledge of the sacrifice he had made for her—and with pity for herself.

All he could do was to wait quietly till the feeling, roused afresh by his presence, had spent itself.

"Oh, I did not know," she whispered at last, through the shielding hands. "I did not know you would do that.... You have ruined yourself.... You should have let them hang me."

And there and then, on the spur of the moment, he leaped up a height which he had not even sighted a second before.

He had, by the sacrifice of his prospects, saved her from the legal consequences of her act. That was irrevocably past and done with, and he must pay the price. But she was paying a double due—remorse for what she herself had done, bitter sorrow at the ruinous price he had paid for her safety.

He had saved her life. Why not save her the rest?—her peace of mind, all her possibilities of future happiness.

In any case it would make no difference to him. For her it might mean all the difference between darkness and light for the rest of her life. And she looked pitifully helpless and hopeless as she lay there sobbing convulsively in the big chair.

He saw the possibility in a flash and gripped it.

"Hang you? Why on earth should anyone want to hang you?" he asked, with all the natural surprise he could put into it.

"You know,"—in a scared whisper. "Because I got him the poison—"

"Come, come now! Let us have no more of that. I was hoping a good night's rest would have ridded you of that bad dream."

"Dream?" and she looked up at him wildly. "Ah, if I could only believe it was a dream!" and she shook her head forlornly.

"Why, of course it was a dream. You were over-wrought with it all, and your mind took the bit in its teeth and ran away with you. What you've got to do now is to try to forget all about it."

"Forget!"

"How I came to make such a mistake I cannot imagine, but when I got home I saw at once that there was an extra dose gone out of my strychnine bottle instead of out of the distilled water, and that explained it at once."

"You? ... You made the mistake?" she looked up at him again, eagerly, with warped face and knitted brows, and a wavering flutter of hope in her eyes.... "You are only saying it to comfort me."

"I'm trying to show you how foolish it is to allow yourself to be ridden by this strange notion you've got into your head."

"Strange notion? ... Did he not beg me to get him that stuff he used for the rats? And did I not get it for him? And he took it. And then—" she shivered at the remembrance of what followed when her husband took the draught.

"All in that horrible dream when your mind was running away with you—"

"And did you not come and tell me they would hang me unless I kept my mouth shut? And I lay all that dreadful night with the rope round my neck—"

"All in your dream. I'm sorry. It must have been terribly real to you."

"A dream?" and she stared wistfully into the fire, hex hands clasping and unclasping nervously. "If I could believe it!"

"You must believe what I tell you, and forget all about it and recover yourself."

"And you?" she said after a pause.

"I shall be all right. Don't trouble your head about me."

"If I did not do it," she said, after another long silent gazing into the fire, "then there would be no need for you to hate me—"

"No need whatever,—all part of that stupid dream."

"And ... sometime perhaps ... you would think better of me ... as you used to do. Oh,—Wulfrey! ..."

If it had all happened as he had almost persuaded her to believe, he might have fallen into his own pit.

For, under the stress of her emotions,—the wild hope of the possibility of relief from the horror that had been weighing her down,—the letting in of this thread of sunshine into the blackness of her despair,—the sudden joy of the thought that it was not she who needed Wulfrey's forgiveness, but he hers;—the shadows and the years fell from her, and she was more like the Elinor Baynard he had once been in love with than he had seen her since the day she married Pasley Carew.

"We must not think of any such things," he said quickly, but not unkindly. He was very sorry for her, but he was no longer in love with her. "At present all we've got to think about is getting you quite yourself again. I will send you up some medicine,—if you won't be afraid to take it—"

"Oh, Wulfrey! ..." with all the reproach she could put into it, and anxiously, "You will come again soon?"

"If you get on well perhaps. If you don't I shall turn you over to Dr Newman," and he left her.

"She ain't agoing to die, Doctor?" asked Mollie, as she waylaid him.

"No, Mollie. She's going to get better."

"Ah, I knew it'd do her good if you came to see her," said the astute handmaid with an approving look.

"Get her to eat and feed her up. She's been letting herself run down."

"Ah, she'll eat now maybe, if so be 's you've given her a bit of an appetite," said Mollie hopefully; and Dr Wulfrey went away home.

XI

But even two patients hardly make a practice, and though from the stolid commoner folk calls still came for 'th' Doctor's' services, upon the better classes a sudden blessing of unusual health appeared to have fallen, or else—

Dr Newman bought a horse about this time, and, though he did not as yet cut much of a figure on horseback, it enabled him to get about as he had never had occasion to do since he settled in the village, and it seemed as though, in his case as in others, practice would in time make him passable.

Wulfrey watched the course of events quietly and with a certain equanimity. His mind was quite made up to go abroad, but he would not go till he was satisfied that that was the only course left to him.

Everybody he met was as friendly as ever, the men especially, but sickness was a rare thing with them at any time, and their women-folk seemed to be getting along very well, for the time being without medical assistance, so far at all events as Dr Wulfrey Dale was concerned.

Mrs Carew was better. Whatever she really believed as to the actual facts of her husband's death, she apparently accepted Dale's statement, to the great relief of her mind and consequent benefit to her health. She sent for the Doctor as often as she reasonably could, and sometimes without any better reason than her desire to see him. Until at last he told her she was perfectly well and he would come no more unless there were actual need.

"But there is actual need, Wulfrey. It does me good to see you. If you don't come I shall fall into a low state again."

"If you do I shall know it is simple perversity and I'll send Dr Newman to you."

"Mollie would never let him in."

Which was likely enough, for Mollie's mind was quite made up as to the only right and proper course for matters to take under all the present circumstances.

The March winds brought on a mild epidemic of influenza.

Dr Newman and his new horse were ostentatiously busy. Wulfrey saw that he had waited long enough, and that now it was time to go. No one could accuse him of running away. It was his practice that had found its legs and walked over to Dr Newman.

He made his arrangements at once and by no means downcastly. The hanging-on had been trying. It was new life to be up and doing, with a new world somewhere in front to be discovered and conquered.

He packed his trunks, gave Mr Truscott, the lawyer, instructions to dispose of his house and everything in it except certain specified articles and pictures, arranged with his bankers at Chester to collect and re-invest his dividends, drew out a couple of hundred pounds to go on with, told them he was going abroad and they might not hear from him for some time to come, and went round to say good-bye to Jim Barclay and Elinor Carew.

"Where are you going?" asked Barclay, when he heard he was off.

"Wherever the chase may lead," said Wulfrey, in better spirits than he had been for many a day. "I shall go first to the States and Canada and have a good look round. If any place lays hold of me I may settle down there."

"For good and all?"

"Possibly. Can't say till I see what it's like. I want you to take Graylock and Billyboy till I come back. You know all about them. There's no one else I'd care to leave 'em with and I don't care to sell them."

"They'll miss you, same as the rest of us."

"For a week or two, maybe. Dr Newman is getting into things nicely, but you might give him a lesson or two in riding, Jim."

"— him, I'd liefer break his back!" was Barclay's terse comment. "You'll let me know where you get to, Wulf, and maybe I'll take a run over to see you, if you really find it in your heart to settle out there. I'll bring the horses with me if you like."

"I'll let you know. Fine sporting country, I believe,—bears, wolves, buffaloes, game of sorts."

"Well, good-bye and God bless you, my boy! Remember there'll always be one man in the old country that wants you. I'd sooner die than have that new man poking round me. I'll send for old Tom Tamplin, hanged if I don't."

Wulfrey rode on to the Hall.

"Going away, Wulf? Where to and for how long?" asked Elinor, anxious and troubled.

"That depends. I've not been up to the mark lately and a good long change will set me up."

"But you will come back?"

"I have really no plans made, except to get away for a time and see a bit of the outside world."

"I was hoping ... you would stop and ... sometime, perhaps..." and the small white hands clasped and unclasped nervously, as was her way when her mind was upset.

"The change I am sure will be good for me. And you are quite all right again. You are looking better than I've seen you for a long time past."

"I'm all right," she said drearily, "except that I have bad dreams now and again. I cannot be quite sure in my own mind—"

"Now, now!"—shaking a peremptory finger at her. "That is all past and done with. Bad dreams are forbidden, remember!"

"I can't help their coming. They come in spite of all my trying at times. And they are always the same. I see Pasley lying on the bed, raging and cursing, and ordering me to go and get him—"

"It's only a dream of a dream. I was hoping you had quite got the better of it. You must fight against it. Now I must run. Got a lot of things to do yet, and I'm off first thing in the morning. Good-bye, Elinor,— and all happiness to you!"

BOOK II

NO MAN'S LAND

XII

Wulfrey Dale, as he strolled about the Liverpool docks and basins, felt very much like a schoolboy who had run away from home in search of the wide free life of the Rover of the Seas.

He had, however, one vast advantage over the runaway, in that he had money in his pocket and could pick and choose, and there was no angry master or troubled parent on his track to haul him back to bondage.

He had no slightest regrets in the matter. Under all the circumstances of the case, he said to himself, he could have done nothing else. Elinor, left to herself, would undoubtedly have paid with her life, either on the gallows or in a mad-house, and that was unthinkable. The inexorable Law would have taken no account of the true inwardness of the case. He had saved her because he understood, and because the alternatives had been too dreadful to think of.

As to the cost to himself,—the long blue-green heave of the sea, out there beyond the point, made little of that, changed it indeed from one side of the account to the other, and presented it, not as a loss, but as very substantial gain.

Out beyond there lay the world, the vast unknown, the larger life; and the windy blue sky streaked with long-drawn wisps of feathery white cloud, and the tumbling green waves with their crisp white caps, and the screaming gulls in their glorious free flight, all tugged at his heart and called him to the quest.

And these cumbered quays, with their heaps of merchandise, and the jerking ropes and squeaking pulley-blocks that piled them higher and higher every moment,—the swaying masts up above and busy decks down below,—the strange foreign smells and flavour of it all,—the rough tarry-breeks hanging about and spitting jovially in the intervals of uncouth talk,—all these were but a foretaste of the great change, and he savoured them all with vastest enjoyment.

He inspected, from a distance, the great clippers that did the voyage to New York in twenty to twenty-five days, stately and disciplined, in the very look of them, as ships of the line almost.

There were ships loading and unloading for and from nearly every port in the world. It was like being at the centre of a mighty spider's web whose arms and filaments reached out to the extremest ends of the earth. He had never felt so free in his life before.

He was in no pressing hurry to settle on either his port or his ship, but in any case it would not be on one of those great packet-boats he would go. His fancy ran rather to something smaller, something more intimate in itself and less likely to be crowded with passengers whose acquaintance he had no desire to make.

He wandered further among the smaller craft, with a relish in the search that was essentially a part of the new life. He developed quite a discriminating taste in ships, though it was only by chatting with the old salts who lounged about the quay-walls that he learned to distinguish a ship from a barque and a brig from a schooner. His preferences were based purely on appearances. The sea-faring qualities of the various craft were beyond him.

But here and there, one and another would attract him by reason of its looks, and he would return again and again to compare them with still later discoveries, saying to himself, "Yes, that would do first-rate now, if she should happen to be going my way. We'll see presently."

He came, in time, upon a brig loading in one of these outer basins, and even to his untutored eye she was a picture,—so graceful her lines, so tapering her masts, so trim and taut the whole look of her.

"Where does she go to?" he asked of an old sailor-man, who was sitting on a cask, chewing his quid like an old cow and spitting meditatively at intervals.

"Bawst'n, 'Merica, 's where she's bound this v'y'ge, Mister, an' ef she did it in twenty days I shouldn' be a bit s'prised, not a bit, I shouldn'."

"Good-looking boat! What does she carry?"

"Miskellaneous cargo. Bit o' everything, as you might say."

"And when does she sail?"'

"Fust tide, I reck'n, ef so be's her crew a'n't been ganged. Finished loading not ha'f an hour ago she did."

"Does she take any passengers?"

"Couldn' say. Passenger boats is mostly down yonder."

"I know, but I like the look of this one better than the big ones."

"Well, you c'n ask aboard."

"Yes? How can I get on board?"

"Why, down that there ladder," and Wulfrey, following the direction of a ponderous roll of the old fellow's head and a squirt of tobacco-juice, came upon some iron rungs let into a straight up-and-down groove in the face of the quay-wall. By going down on his hands and knees, and making careful play with his feet, he managed at last to get on to this apology for a ladder and succeeded in climbing down it, over the side of the ship on to its deck.

The deck, dirty as it was with the work of loading, felt springy to his unaccustomed feet. It was the first ship's deck he had ever trodden. The very feel of it was exhilarating. It was like setting foot on the bridge that led to the new life.

As he looked about him,—at the neatly-coiled ropes, the rope-handled buckets, the blue water-casks lashed to the deck below one of the masts, the masts themselves, massive below but tapering up into the sky like fishing-rods, the mazy network of rigging, four little brass carronades and the ship's bell, all polished to the nines and shining like gold,—the worries and troubles of the last few months fell from him like a ragged garment. Elinor Carew, and Croome, and Jim Barclay, and even Graylock and Billyboy, the parting with whom had been as sore a wrench as any, all seemed very far away, things of the past, shadowy in presence of these stimulating realities of the new life.

He walked aft along the deck towards a door under the raised poop, and at the sound of his coming a man came out of the door and said, "Hello!" and stood and stared at him out of a pair of very deep-set, sombre black eyes.

He was a tall, well-built fellow of about Wulfrey's own age, black-haired, black-bearded and moustached, and of a somewhat saturnine countenance. His face and neck were the colour of dark mahogany with much sun and weather. He wore small gold rings in his ears, and Wulfrey set him down for a foreigner,—a Spaniard, he thought, or perhaps an Italian.

"I was told you were sailing tomorrow for Boston," said Wulfrey. "I came to ask if you take passengers."

The man's black brows lifted a trifle and he took stock of Wulfrey while he considered the question. Then he said, "Ay? well, we do and we don't," and Wulfrey rearranged his ideas as to his nationality and decided that he was either Scotch or North of Ireland, though he did not look either one or the Other.

"That perhaps means that you might."

"Et's for the auld man to say—"

"The Captain?"

"Ay, Cap'n Bain."

"Where could I see him?"

"He's up in the toon."

"If you'll tell me where to find him I'll go after him."

The other seemed to turn this over in his mind, and then said, "Ye'd best see him here. He'll mebbe no be long."

"Then I'll wait. What time do you expect to clear out?"

"We'll know when the old man comes."

"Perhaps you would let me see the rooms, while I'm waiting."

The dark man turned slowly and went down three steps into the small main cabin. His leisurely manner suggested no more than a willingness not to be disobliging.

It was a fair-sized room, with a grated skylight overhead, portholes at the sides, seats and lockers below them, and a table with wooden forms to sit on. At the far end were two more doors.

"Cap'n's bunk and mine," said his guide, with a roll of the head towards the left-hand door, and opened the other for Wulfrey to look in at the narrow passage off which opened two small sleeping-rooms.

"You are then—?" asked Wulfrey.

"Mate."

"You're Scotch, aren't you? I took you at first sight for a foreigner."

"I'm frae the Islands.... Some folks hold there's mixed blood in some of us since the times when the Spaniards were wrecked there. Mebbe! I d'n know."

"And Captain Bain? He's Scotch too, I judge, by his name."

"Ay, he's Scotch—Glesca."

"If he'll take me as passenger I'll be glad. This would suit me uncommonly well."

"Ay, well. He'll say when he comes," and whenever his black eyes rested on Wulfrey they seemed to be questioning what it could be that made him wish to travel on a trading-brig rather than on a passenger-liner.

However, he asked no questions but pulled out a black clay pipe, and Wulfrey pulled out his own and anticipated the other's search for tobacco by handing him his pouch. They had sat silently smoking for but a few minutes when a heavy foot was heard on the deck outside, and there came a gruff call for "Macro!"

"Ay, ay, sir!" and the doorway darkened with the short burly figure of a man whose words preceded him, "Tom Crimp'll have 'em all here by ten o'clock an' we'll— Wha the deevil's this?"

"Wants to go passenger to Boston," explained the mate, and left Wulfrey to his own negotiations.

"If you're open to take a passenger, Captain Bain, I've fallen in love with the looks of your ship."

"What for d'ye no want to go in a passenger-ship? We're no a passenger-ship," and the Captain eyed him suspiciously.

"Just that I dislike travelling with a crowd, I've been looking round for some days and your ship pleases me better than any I've seen."

"Where are you from, and what's your name and rating!"

"I'm from Cheshire. Name, Wulfrey Dale. Rating, Doctor."

"An' what for are ye wanting to go to Boston!"

"I'm going out to look round. I may settle out there if I find any place I like."

"Are ye in trouble? Poisoned ony one? Resurrectionist, mebbe?"

"Neither one nor the other. I've no work here. I'm going to look for some over there."

"Can ye pay?"

"Of course. I'm not asking you to take me out of charity."

"That's a guid thing."

"How much shall we say? And when do you sail?"

"Et'll be twenty guineas, ped in advance, an' ef ye want ony victuals beyant what the ship provides, which is or'nary ship's fare same as me and the mate eats, ye'll provide 'em yourself."

"Understood! And you sail—"

"To-night's flood, ef the men get aboard all safe. They're promised me for ten o'clock."

"I'll pay you now and go up for my things."

"An' whaur may they be?"

"At Cotton's, in Castle Street."

"Aweel! Juist keep a quiet tongue in your heid, Doctor, as to the ship ye're sailing on. The 'Grassadoo' doesna tak passengers, ye ken, an' I dinna want it talked aboot."

"I understand. I've only got a box and a bag, but I'll have to get a man to carry them."

"Ay—weel!" and after a moment's consideration, "You wait at Cotton's an' we'll send Jock Steele, the carpenter, up for them at eight o'clock. Ye can coach or truck 'em as far as he says and carry 'em between you the rest."

So Wulfrey paid down his twenty guineas, and Captain Bain stowed them away in his trouser pocket, and buttoned it up carefully, with a dry, "Donal' Bain's word's his only recipee. You be here before ten o'clock and the 'Grassadoo' 'll be waiting for you."

"That's all right, Captain," said Wulfrey. "And I'm much obliged to you for stretching a point and taking me."

"It's me that's doing it, ye understand, not the owners. That's why."

XIII

The 'Grace-à-Dieu' justified Wulfrey's inexperienced choice. She was an excellent sea-boat, fast, and as dry as could be expected, seeing that she was chock full to the hatches, as Jock Steele informed him, while they carried down his baggage.

But after his first four hours on board his personal interest in her character and performance lapsed for three full days. He had stood leaning over the side watching the lights of Liverpool as they dropped away astern, and then those of the Cheshire and North Welsh coasts, and felt that now indeed he had cut loose from the past and was in for a great adventure.

It gave, him a curious, mixed feeling of depression and elation. He felt at once homeless and endowed with the freedom of the universe. He had burned his boats, he said confidently to himself, and was going forth to begin a new life, to conquer a new world. And he set his teeth and hung on to the heaving bulwark with grim determination.

But the sense of elation and width of outlook dwindled with the sinking lights. The feeling of homelessness and helplessness grew steadily upon him. He had taken the precaution of stowing away a good meal before he set foot on board, and he lived on it for three days.

He had never been bodily sick in his life before, but sick as he now was he was not too far gone to note the wretched peculiarity of his sensations, and to muse upon them and the ridiculousness of the provision he had made, at the Captain's suggestion, to supplement the usual cabin fare.

He could not imagine himself ever eating again, as he lay there in his heaving bunk, with nothing to distract his mind from the unhappy vacuums above and below but the heavy tread of feet overhead at times, and the ceaseless rush and thrash of the waves a few inches from his ear, and the grinning face of the cabin-boy who came in at intervals to ask if he would like anything yet.

But by degrees his head ceased to swim if he lifted it an inch off the pillow. By further degrees he found himself crouching up and clinging like a cat while he gazed unsteadily out of the tiny round porthole at the tumbling green and white water outside. Still further determination got him somehow into his clothes, and he dared to feel hungry and empty without nausea. Then he crawled out to the deck, feeling like a soiled rag. But the brisk south-west wind cleaned and braced him, and presently he nibbled a biscuit and found himself as hungry as a starving dog.

After that he very soon found his sea-legs, and by the fourth day he was a new man, eating ravenously to make up for lost time, and keenly interested in all about him.

So far they had had favourable weather and made good way. But Captain Bain was a fervent believer in the inevitability of equinoctials, and prophesied gales ahead, and the worse for being overdue.

Wulfrey learned, from one and another, chatting at meals with the Captain or Sheumaish Macro, one or other of whom was generally on deck, or with Jock Steele the carpenter, who also acted as boatswain, that the 'Grace-à-Dieu' was French-built which, according to Steele, accounted for the fineness of her lines.

"We build stouter but we cannot touch them for cut. She's as pretty a little ship as ever I set eyes on and floats like a gull," was the character Steele gave her. And he should know, as he'd made four voyages in her since their owners in Glasgow bought her out of the Prize Court, and she'd never given them any undue trouble even in the very worst of weather.

The crew, again according to Steele, were a very mixed lot, a few good seamen, the rest just lubbers out of the crimp house.

With Captain Bain and Sheumaish Macro, the mate, he got on well enough, but found both by nature very self-contained and manifesting no inclination for more than the necessary civilities of the situation.

"And why should they?" he said to himself. "I'm an outsider and they know nothing more about me than I've told them myself. Another fifteen or twenty days and we part and are not likely ever to meet again."

He made one discovery about them, however, which disquieted him somewhat. They were both heavy drinkers, but they usually so arranged matters, by taking their full bouts at different times, as not to bring the ship into serious peril.

Wulfrey's eyes were opened to it by the fact of his not being able to sleep one night. After tossing and tumbling in his bunk for a couple of hours, and finding sleep as far off as ever, he dressed again sufficiently to go on deck for a blow. As he passed through the cabin he found Captain Bain there with his head sunk on his arms on the table, and, fearing he might be ill, he went up to him. But he needed no medical skill to tell him what was the matter. The old man was as drunk as a lord and breathing like an apoplectic hog. So he eased his neck gear and left him to sleep it off.

Macro was on deck in charge of the ship. Wulfrey simply told him he had been unable to sleep, but made no mention of the Captain's condition. And the mate said,

"Ay, we're just getting into thick of Gulf Stream and it tells on one."

Another night he found Steele in charge, and on the growl at the length of his watch, and gathered from him that both Captain and mate had on this occasion been indulging in a bit drink and were snoring in their bunks.

He could only hope that Captain Bain's prognosticated equinoctials, which were now considerably overdue, would not come upon them when both their chiefs were incapacitated. And his only consolation was the thought that this was not an exceptional occurrence but probably their usual habit when well afloat, and that so far no disaster had befallen them.

So, day after day, they sped along west-south-west, making good way and sighting none but an occasional distant sail. Then they ran into mists and clammy weather, and sometimes had a wind and drove along with the swirling fog or across it, and sometimes lay rocking idly and making no way at all.

Wulfrey gathered, from occasional words they let fall between themselves, and from their answers to his own questions, that this was all usual and to be expected. They were getting towards Newfoundland where the Northern currents met the Southern, hence the fog, and it was too early for icebergs, so there was no danger in pressing on whenever the wind permitted.

Their seventeenth day out was the dullest they had had, heavy and windless, with a shrouded sky and a close gray horizon and, to Wulfrey's thinking, a sense of something impending. It was as though Nature had gone into the sulks and was brooding gloomily over some grievance.

Captain Bain stripped the ship of her canvas, and sent down the topmasts and yards, and made all snug for anything that might turn up. All day and all night they lay wallowing in vast discomfort, and Wulfrey lost all relish for his food again.

"What do you make of it, Bo's'un?" he asked, as he clawed his way up to Steele on the after deck, where he was temporarily in charge again.

"Someth'n's comin', sir," said Steele portentously, "but what it is beats me, unless it's one o' them e-quy-noctials the skipper's bin looking for."

In the night the fog closed down on them as thick as cotton wool; and, without a breath of wind, the long seas came rolling in upon them out of the thick white bank on one side and out into the thick white bank on the other, till their scuppers dipped deep and worked backwards, shooting up long hissing white jets over the deck, and making everything wet and uncomfortable. Every single joint and timber in the ship seemed to creak and groan as if in pain, and Wulfrey, as he listened in the dark to the strident jerkings and grindings and general complainings of the gear, and pictured the wild sweeps and swoops of the masts away up in the fog there, wondered how long it could all stand the strain, and how soon it would come clattering down on top of them. Once, when a bigger roll than usual flung him against the mainmast and he clung to it for a moment's safety, the rending groans that came up through it from the depths below sent a creepy chill down his spine. It sounded so terribly as though the very heart of the ship were coming up by the roots.

Sleep was out of the question. His cabin was unbearable. Its dolorous creakings seemed to threaten collapse and burial at any moment. If they had to go down he would sooner be drowned in the open than like a rat in its hole. And so he had crawled up on deck to see what was towards.

The only comfort he found—and that of a very mixed character—was in the sight of Captain Bain and the mate, sitting one on each side of the cabin table with their legs curled knowingly round its stout wooden supports, which were bolted to the floor, and which they used alternately as fender and anchor to the rolling of the ship.

They had made all possible provision against contingencies. They could do no more, and it was no good worrying, so now they sat smoking philosophically and drinking now and again from a bottle of rum which hung by the neck between them from a string attached to the beam above their heads.

Wulfrey stood the discomforts of the deck till he was chilled to the marrow, then he tumbled into the cabin, and annexed a third leg of the table and sat with the philosophers and waited events.

"It's hard on the ship, Captain," he said, by way of being companionable. But the Captain only grunted and deftly tipped some rum into his tin pannikin as the bottle swung towards him on its way towards the roof. And the mate looked at him wearily as much as to say, "Man! don't bother us with your babytalk," and it seemed to him that they had both got a fairly full cargo aboard.

However, he decided it was not for him to judge or condemn. They knew their own business better than he did. There was no wind, no way on the ship, and all they could do was to lie and wallow and wait for better times. And the fact that they took it so calmly reassured him somewhat.

The cabin was so full of fog and tobacco-smoke that the light from the swinging oil-lamp could barely penetrate beyond the table. It made a dull ghastly smudge of yellow light through which the bottle swung to and fro like an uncouth pendulum, and he sat and watched it. Now it was up above his head between him and the mate; now it was sweeping gracefully over the table; now it was up above the Captain, who reached out and tipped some more rum into his pannikin.

He watched it till it began to exert a mesmeric influence on, him and his head began to feel light and swimmy. He knew something about Mesmer and his experiments from his reading at home. He experienced a detached interest in his own condition and wondered vaguely if the bottle would succeed in putting him to sleep. He tried to keep his eyes on it, but they kept wandering off to the Captain, on whom it had already done its business, though in a different way.

He was dead tired. It was, he reckoned, quite six-and-thirty hours since he had had any sleep. What time of night or morning it was he had no idea. This awful rolling and groaning and creaking seemed to have been going on for an incalculable time.

What with the heavy unwholesomeness of the atmosphere, and the monotonous swing of the bottle, and the lethargic impassivity of his companions, he fell at last into a condition of dull stupidity, which might have ended in sleep but for the necessity of alternately hanging on to and fending off the table, as the roll of the ship flung him away from it or at it. And how long this went on he never knew.

He was jerked back to life by a sudden clatter of feet overhead and a shout. Then he was flung bodily on to the table, and found himself lying over it and looking down at Captain Bain, who had tumbled backwards in a heap into a corner. The rum-bottle banged against the roof and rained its fragments down on him. The lamp leaned up at a preposterous angle and stopped there.

"We're done," thought Wulfrey dazedly, and became aware of fearsome sounds outside,—a wild howling shriek as of all the fiends out of the pit,—thunderous blows as of mighty hammers under which the little ship reeled and staggered,—then grisly crackings and rendings and crashes on deck, mingled with the feeble shouts of men.

Then, shuddering and trembling, the ship slowly righted herself and Wulfrey breathed again. Outside, the howling shriek was as loud as ever, the banging and buffeting worse than before.

Macro unhooked his long legs from the table and made for the door. The Captain gathered himself up dazedly and rolled after him, and Wulfrey followed as best he could.

But he could see very little. The fog was gone. The fierce rush of the gale drove the breath back into his throat and came near to choking him. Huge green seas topped with snarling white came leaping up over the side of the ship near him. A man with an axe was chopping furiously at the shrouds of the fallen main-mast amid a wild tangle of ropes and spars. As they parted, the ship swung free and went labouring off before the gale under somewhat easier conditions, and Wulfrey hung tight in the cabin doorway and breathed still more hopefully. He had thought the end was come, but they were still afloat, though sadly shorn and battered. What their chances of ultimate safety might be was beyond him, but while there was life there was hope.

XIV

For three days life to Wulfrey was a grim experience made up of damp discomfort, lack of food and rest, and growing hopelessness.

Both their masts had gone like carrots, leaving only their ragged stumps sticking up out of the deck. "An' if they hadn't we'd bin gone ourselves," growled the carpenter to him one day. Where they fell the sides of the ship were smashed and torn, and the hungry waves came yapping up through the gaps, most horribly close and threatening.

Three men had been washed overboard in that first fierce onrush. The rest crouched miserably in the forecastle, and no man on board could remember what it felt like to be dry and warm and full.

Meals there were none. When any man's hunger forced him to eat, he wolfed sodden biscuit and a chunk of raw pork, and washed it down with rum.

So ghastly did the discomfort become, as the wretched days succeeded the still more miserable nights, that at last Wulfrey, for one, was prepared to welcome even the end as a change for the better.

Observations were out of the question. In these four days they never once saw sun or moon or star, nothing but a close black sky, gray with flying spume. The great seas came roaring out of it behind them and rushed roaring into it in front of them, and where they were getting to, beyond the fact that they were driving continuously more or less west-by-north, no man knew.

Captain Bain and the mate and the carpenter had done all that could be done since the catastrophe, but that was very little. An attempt was made to rig a jury mast on the stump of the foremast, but the gale ripped it away with a jeering howl and would have none of it. With some planking torn from the inside of the ship they barricaded the seas out of the forecastle as well as they could. It was the carpenter's idea to fix these planks upright, so that their ends stood up somewhat above the top of the forecastle, and so great was the grip of the gale that that slight projection sufficed to keep their head straight before it and afforded them slight steerage way.

So they staggered along, dismantled and discomfited, and waited for the gale to blow itself out or them to perdition, and were worn so low at last that they did not much care which, so only an end to their misery.

And the end came as unexpectedly as the beginning. From sheer weariness they slept at times, in chill discomfort and dankest wretchedness, just where they sat or lay. And Wulfrey was lying so, in a stupor of misery, caring neither for life nor death, when the final catastrophe came.

Without any warning the ship struck something with a horrible shock that flung everything inside it ajee. Then she heeled over on her starboard side, baring her breast to the enemy.

The great green waves leaped at her like wolves on a foundered deer. They had been chasing her for three days past and now they had got her. She was down and they proceeded to worry her to pieces. No ship ever built could stand against their fury. The 'Grace-à-Dieu' melted into fragments as though she had been built of cardboard.

Wulfrey, jerked violently out of the corner where he had been lying, rolled down towards the door of the cabin as the ship heeled over. As he clawed himself up to look out, a green mountain of water caught him up and carried him high over the port bulwarks which towered like a house above him, and swept him along on its broken crest.

He could swim, but no swimmer could hope to save himself by swimming in such a sea, and he was weak and worn with the miseries of the last three days.

He had no hope of deliverance, but yet struck out mechanically to keep his head above water, and his thrashing arm struck wood. He gripped it with the grip of a drowning man and clung for dear life.

It was a large square structure, planking braced with cross-pieces, almost a raft. He hung to the edge while the water ran out of his mouth and wits, and then, inch by inch, hauled himself cautiously further aboard, and, lying flat, looked anxiously about for signs of his shipmates, but with little hope.

He could see but a yard or two on either side, and then only the threatening welter of the monstrous green seas, terrifyingly close and swelling with menace.

Nothing? ... Stay!—a white gleam under the green, like a scrap of paper in a whirlpool, and a desperate face emerged a yard or so away and a wildly-seeking hand.

The anguished eyes besought him, and, not knowing what else to do, he gripped two of the cross-pieces of his raft and launched his legs out towards the drowning man. They were seized as in a vice, and presently, inch by inch, the gripping hands crept up his body till the other could lay hold of the raft for himself. And Wulfrey, turning, saw that it was the mate, Sheumaish Macro, whose life he had saved.

They drew themselves cautiously up into such further safety as the frail ark offered and lay there spent. And Wulfrey, for one, wondered if the quicker end had not been the greater gain.

XV

Sleeping and eating anyhow and at any time, they had lost all count of time this last day or two. It was, however, daylight of a kind, but so gray and murky and mixed with flying spume that they could see but little.

Neither man had spoken since they crawled up on to the raft. Death was so close that speech seemed futile. They both lay flat on their stomachs, gripping tight, and peering hopelessly through nearly closed eyes, expectant of nothing, doubting the wisdom of their choice of the longer death.

"God!" cried Macro of a sudden, as they swung up the back of a wave. "Where in — ha' we got to?"

And Wulfrey got a glimpse of most amazing surroundings.

Right ahead of them the sea was all abristle with what, to his quick amazed glance, looked like the bones and ribs of multitudinous ships, the ruins of a veritable Armada.

Now it was all hidden, as they sank into a weltering green valley with tumbling green walls all about them. Then the solid green bottom of their valley was ripped into furious white foam, and stark black baulks of timber came lunging up through it, all crusted with barnacles, festooned with hanging weeds, and laced with streaming white. They looked like grisly arms of deep-sea monsters reaching up out of the depths to lay hold of them. They seemed intent on impaling the frail raft. They seemed to change places, to dart hither and thither as though to head it off, to lie in wait for it, to spring up in its course. It was frightful and unnerving. Wulfrey shut his eyes tight and set his teeth, and waited for the inevitable crash and the end.

A great wave lifted them high above the venomous black timbers and, swinging on its course, dropped them as deftly as a crane could have done it, into the inside of a mighty cage.

Wave after wave did its best to lift them out and speed them on. Their raft rose and fell and banged rudely against the ribs of their prison. Up and down they swung, and round and round, bumping and grinding till they feared the raft would go to pieces. But the tide had passed its highest and the storm was blowing itself out, and they had come to the end of the voyage.

"We're in hell," gasped the mate, as he clung to the jerking cross-pieces to keep himself from being flung off, and to Wulfrey's storm-broken senses it seemed that he was right.

XVI

All that night they swung and bumped inside their cage, with somewhat less of bodily discomfort as the wind fell and the sea went down, but with only such small relief to their minds as postponement of immediate death might offer.

Wulfrey lay prone on the raft, grimping to it mechanically, utterly worn out with all he had gone through these last four days. He sank into a stupor again and lay heedless of everything.

The tide fell to its lowest and was rising again when dawn came, and though the huge green waves still rolled through their cage, and swung them to and fro, and sent them rasping against its massive bars, they were as nothing compared with the waves of yesterday.

It was the sound of Macro cracking shell-fish and eating them that roused Wulfrey. He raised his heavy head and looked round. The mate hacked off a bunch of huge blue-black mussels from the post they were grinding against at the moment, opened several of them and put them under his nose. Without a word he began eating and felt the better for them.

Presently he sat up and looked about him in amazement, and rubbed the salt out of his smarting eyes and looked again.

"Where in heaven's name are we?" he gasped.

And well he might, for stranger sight no man ever set eyes on.

"Last night I thocht we were in hell," said Macro grimly. "An' seems to me we're not far from it. We're in the belly of a dead ship an' there's nought but dead ships round us."

Their immediate harbourage, into which the friendly wave had dropped them, was composed of huge baulks of timber like those that had tried to end them the night before, sea-sodden and crusted thick with shell-fish, and as Wulfrey's eyes wandered along them he saw that the mate was right. They were undoubtedly the mighty weather-worn ribs of some great ship, canting up naked and forlorn out of the depths and reaching far above their heads. There in front was the great curving stem-piece, and yon stiff straight piece behind was the stern-post.

But when his eyes travelled out beyond these things his jaw dropped with sheer amazement.

Everywhere about them, wherever he looked, and as far as his sight could reach, lay dead ships and parts of ships. Some, like their own, entire gaunt skeletons, but more still in grisly fragments. Close alongside them a great once-white, now weather-gray and ghostly figurehead representing an angel gazed forlornly at them out of sightless eyes. From the position of its broken arms and the round fragment of wood still in its mouth, it had probably once blown a trumpet, but the storm-fiends would have no music but their own and had long since made an end of that.

Close beside it jutted up a piece of a huge mast, with part of the square top still on and ragged ropes trailing from it. Alongside it a bowsprit stuck straight up to heaven, defiant of fate, and more forlornly, a smaller ship's whole mast with yards and broken gear still hanging to it all tangled and askew. And beyond, whichever way he looked—always the same, dead ships and the limbs and fragments of them.

"It's a graveyard," he gasped.

"Juist that," said the mate dourly, "an' we're the only living things in it."

And presently, brooding upon it, he said, "There'll be sand down below an' they're bedded in it. When tide goes down again maybe we can get out."

"Where to?"

"Deil kens! ... But it cann't be worse than stopping here."

The slow tide lifted them higher and higher within their cage, hiding some of the baleful sights but giving them wider view over the whole grim field. They sat, and by way of change stood and lay, on their cramped platform. They knocked off shell-fish and ate them. So far, so water-sodden had they been of late, they had not suffered from thirst, but the dread of it was with them.

Then, slowly, the waters sank, and all the bristling bones of ships came up again.

"Can you swim?" asked Macro abruptly at last.

"I can. But I feel very weak. I can't go far I'm afraid."

"We can't stop on here."

"Where shall we go?"

"Over yonder. They're thickest there and they stand out more. Mebbe it's shallower that way."

"I'll do my best to follow you. If I can't, you go on."

"Nay. You gave me a hand last night. We'll stick together, and sooner we start the better.... Stay ... mebbe we can—" and he began pounding at the end planks of their raft with his foot to start them from the cross-pieces.

"'Twas the roof of the galley," he explained, "and none too well made. It got stove in last voyage and we rigged this one up ourselves. My wonder is it held together in the night."

He managed at last with much stamping to loosen four boards.

"One under each arm will help," he said, "An' we can paddle along an' not get tired."

He let himself down into the water, shipped a board under each arm, and struck out between two of the gaunt ribs, and Wulfrey followed him, somewhat doubtful as to what might come of it.

But the mate had taken his bearings and was following a reasoned course. Over yonder the wrecks lay thick. There might be one on which they could find shelter—even food. But that he hardly dared to hope for. As far as he had been able to judge, at that distance, they were all wrecks of long ago and mostly only bare ribs and stumps.

To Wulfrey, from water-level, the sea ahead seemed all abristle with shipping, as thick, he thought to himself, as the docks at Liverpool. But there all was life and bustling activity, and here was only death,— -dead ships and pieces of ships, and maybe dead men. The feeling of it was upon them both, and they splashed slowly along with as little noise as possible, as though they feared to rouse the sleepers who had once peopled all these gruesome ruins.

"See yon!" whispered Macro hoarsely, as he slowed up and waited for Wulfrey to come alongside, and following the jerk of his head Wulf saw the figure of a man grotesquely spread-eagled in a vast tangle of cordage that hung like a net from a broken mast.

"We had better see," said Wulfrey, and kicked along towards it, the mate following with visible reluctance.

It was the body of Jock Steele, the carpenter, livid and sodden, and many hours dead.

"I would we hadna seen him," growled Macro.

"He'll do us no harm. He was a decent man. I'm sorry he's gone. Is there any chance of any of the others being alive?"

"Deil a chance!"

"Still, we are—"

"You had the deil's own luck and it's only by you I'm here. Let's get on," and they splashed on again.

Past wreck after wreck, grim and gaunt and grisly, mostly of very ancient date, all swept bare to the bone by the fury of the seas, all with the water washing coldly through them. Now and again Macro growled terse comments,—

"A warship,—from the size of her. See those ribs, they'll last another hundred years. And yon's a Dutchman. They build stout too. Mostly British though, bound to be, hereabouts."

"Have you any idea where we are, then?"

"An idea—ay! I've heard tell o' this place, but I never met anyone had been here. They mostly never come back. They call it what you called it a while ago—'The Graveyard.'"

"And where is it?"

"Sable Island, if I'm right,—'bout one hundred miles off Nova Scotia."

"And is there any island?"

"Ay,—on the chart, but I never met any man had been there. We're looking for it. There's no depth here or all them ribs wouldn't be sticking up like that. They're stuck in the sand below. Must be over yonder where they lie so thick.... An' a fearsome place when we get there, with the spirits of all them dead men all about it—hundreds of 'em,—thousands, mebbe."

"Do ships ever call there?"

"Not if they can help it, I trow. It's Death brings 'em and he holds 'em tight.... Hearken to that now!"— and he stopped as though in doubt about going further.

And Wulfrey, listening intently, caught a faint thin sound of wailing far away in the distance. It rose and fell, shrill and piercing and very discomforting, though very far away.

"What is it?" he jerked.

"Spirits," breathed Macro, and his face was more scared and haggard even than before.

"Nonsense!" said Wulfrey, with an assumption of brusqueness for his own reassurance, for this dismal progress through the graveyard was telling sorely on him also, and the sounds that came wavering across the water were as like the shrieking of souls in torment as anything he could imagine. "There are no such things. Don't be a fool, man!"

"Man alive!—no spirits? The Islands are full o' them, an' this place fuller still. Yes, indeed!"

But it was obviously impossible to float about there for ever. The water was not nearly so cold as Wulfrey had expected, but the strain of the night and of the preceding days of semi-starvation had told on him, and he was feeling that he could not stand much more. He set off doggedly again towards the thickest agglomeration of dead shipping in front, and the mate followed him with a face full of foreboding.

They went in silence, paying no heed now to the things they passed on the way, though the apparently endless succession of dead ships and the parts of them was not without its effect on their already broken spirits.

"Gosh!" cried Macro of a sudden. "I touched ground or I'm a Dutchman! Ay—sand it is," and Wulfrey sinking his feet found firm bottom.

"Better keep the floats," suggested the mate. "Mebbe it's only the side of a bank we're on."

They waded on, breast-deep, and presently were out of their depth again. But the feel of something below them, and the certainty that it was still not very far away, were cheering. In a few minutes they were walking again, having evidently crossed a channel between two banks. And so, alternately walking and swimming, they drew at last towards the jungle of wreckage; and all the time, from somewhere beyond it, rose those piercing, wailing screams which Macro in his heart was certain came from the spirits of the dead.

Here the water was no more than up to their knees and shoaling still, and they came now upon more than the bones of ships,—chaotic masses of masts and spars and rigging piled high and wide in fantastic confusion, and in among them, tangled beyond even the power of the seas to chase them further, barrels and boxes and crates, some still whole, mostly broken; rotting bales, and pitiful and ridiculous fragments of their contents worked in among them as if by impish hands.

"Gosh, what wastry!" said Macro at the sight. "There's many a thousand pounds of goods piled here,—ay, hunderds of thousands, webbe."

"I'd give it all for a crust of bread," said Wulfrey hungrily.

"An' mebbe there's that too. If any o' them casks has flour in 'em we needn' starve. It cakes round the sides wi' the wet, but the core's all right."

Then, beyond the gigantic barrier of wastry, rose again that shrill screaming and shrieking, louder than ever, and Macro said "Gosh!" and looked like bolting back into the sea.

Wulfrey, determined to fathom it, hauled himself painfully up a tangle of ropes and clambered to the top of the pile and saw, about a mile away, a narrow yellow spit of sand, and all about it a dense cloud of sea-birds, myriads of them, circling, diving, swooping, quarrelling.

One moment the vast gray cloud of them drooped to the sea and seemed to settle there, the next it was whirling aloft like a writhing water-spout, every component drop of which was a venomous bundle of feathers shrieking and screaming its hardest in the bitter fight for food. And the harsh and raucous clamour of them, each intent on its own, had in it something fiendishly inhuman and chilling to the blood.

"It's only sea-birds, man," he cried to Macro. "Come up and see for yourself," and the mate, with new life at the word, hauled himself up alongside and stood staring.

"My Gosh! ... I never saw the like o' that before," he said at last. "There's millions of 'em. They're fighting ... over our shipmates mebbe.... We needn' starve if we can get at 'em," a sentiment which somehow, in all the circumstances of the case, did not greatly appeal to Wulfrey, hungry as he was.

"If they all set on a man he wouldn't have much chance," he said, with a shiver. "They could pick him clean before he knew where he was."

"It's only dead men they feed on," said Macro, quite himself again, since it was only birds they had to deal with and not disembodied spirits. "There's land. Let's get ashore," and they crawled precariously along over the wreckage, which sagged and dipped beneath them in places, and in places towered high and had to be scaled as best they could, and at times they had to wade or swim from pile to pile.

Amazing things they chanced upon in their course, but were too intent on reaching land to give them more than a passing glance or a shudder. More than once they came on bones of men, jammed in tight among the raffle, and slowly picked by the sea and the things that lived in it till they gleamed white and polished and clean. And their grinning teeth, set in the awful fixed smile of the fleshless, seemed to welcome them as future recruits to their company.

"Ah—ah! So you've come at last!" they seemed to say, as they laughed up at them out of holes and corners. "We've been waiting for you all these years and here you are at last."

There were, too, bales and boxes of what had been rich cloths and silks and satins and coarser stuffs, worried open by the fret of the sea and reduced to sodden slimy punk, and casks and barrels beyond the counting.

"Wastry! Wastry!" panted Macro. "We'll come back sometime, mebbe."

But, for the moment, their only craving was for dry land, to savour the solid safety of it, and get something to eat if they could, and a long long rest.

With desperate determination they dragged their sodden and weary bodies through the shallows beyond, and blind fury filled them with spasmodic vigour as they saw what the sea-birds were feeding on.

Over each poor body the carrion crew settled like flies, and tore and screamed and quarrelled. The two living men dashed at them with angry shouts, and the birds rose in a shrieking host amazed at their interference. But only for a moment. They came swooping down again in a gray-white cloud, with raucous cries and eyes like fiery beads, and beat at them with their wings, and menaced them with already reddened beaks. And they looked so murderously intentioned that the men were fain to bow their heads and run, with flailing arms to keep them off.

And so at last to dry land, and grateful they were for the feel of it, even though it seemed no more than a waste of sand but a few feet above tide-level. That last tussle with the birds had drained their strength completely. They dropped spent on the beach and lay panting.

Their flight had set their chilled blood coursing again, a merciful sun had come up above the clouds that lay along the horizon, and in spite of their hunger and the fact that their very bones felt soaked with salt water, they both fell asleep where they lay.

XVII

Wulfrey was wakened by a sharp stab in the neck, and when he sat up with a start a huge cormorant squawked affrightedly at the dead man coming to life again, and flapped away, gibbering curses and leaving a most atrocious stink behind him.

The mate was still sleeping soundly, and Wulfrey, for the time being more painfully cognisant of the gnawing emptiness within than of the miracle that permitted him any sensation whatever, sat gazing anxiously about and revolving the primary problem of food.

Out there among all that mass of wreckage it would be strange if they could not find something eatable,—cores of flour barrels, perhaps pickled pork, rum almost certainly; and the clammy void inside him craved these things most ardently. But he could not, as yet, imagine himself venturing out there again to get them. Later on perhaps, but for the present the land, such as it was, must provide, for him at all events. He felt that he simply had not the heart or the strength to make the attempt.

Let me say at once that the trying of these men, which came upon them presently, was not in the matter of ways and means. It was of the spirit, not of the flesh. But yet it is necessary to show you how they came through these lesser trials of the flesh only to meet the greater trials of the spirit later on. And even these smaller matters are not entirely devoid of interest.

Many birds came circling round expectantly, and swooped down towards the dark figures lying in the sand, and went off in shrill amazement when they were denied. And Macro at last stretched and yawned and sat up, staring dazedly at Wulfrey.

"Gosh, but I'm hungered," he said at last, as that paramount claim emphasised itself. "Anything to eat?"

"I'm wondering. Plenty of birds, and very bad they smell. I've seen nothing else."

The mate got up heavily and found himself sore and stiff. He stood looking thoughtfully about him.

"What about all that stuff?" and he jerked his head towards the graveyard wreckage.

"I couldn't go again yet."

"Nor me either.... Ground's higher over yonder," he said. "Let's go and see," and they set off slowly over the sand.

The level of high water was thickly strewn with seaweed and small wreckage. The slope of the shore was so long and gentle that no large object could come in unless it were first broken into fragments outside.

The mate kicked over the sea-weed and found some which he put into his mouth.

"Any good?" asked Wulfrey anxiously, hungrier than ever at sight of the other's working jaws.

"Better'n nothing," and he rooted up another piece and handed it over. Wulfrey found it tough and pungent of the sea and, after much chewing, capable of being swallowed, but the most he also could say for it was that it was just that much better than nothing.

They each picked up a piece of wood with which to root in the tangle, and, bending and picking and munching, made their way slowly towards the hummocks in front.

These were a low range of sandhills, some of them as much as thirty feet high, and on the seaward side, which they climbed, they were sparsely clothed with coarse slate-green wire-grass about a foot in height, which bristled up like porcupines' quills and helped to keep the loose soft sand together. They pulled some up to see if the roots looked edible, and found them spreading far and wide below ground in a matted tangle of white succulent-looking tendrils, which proved as tough and unsatisfying as the sea-weed, but had the advantage of a different flavour.

Grubbing along, they climbed heavily through the yielding sand to the top of the nearest hummock. Macro, arriving there first, jerked a gratified "Gosh!" and floundered down the other side whirling his stick, and Wulfrey was just in time to catch the amazing sight of the whole surface of the little valley beyond in violent motion.

He thought at first that something had gone wrong with his eyes, for everywhere he looked the sand seemed to be jumping and skipping and burying itself in itself. And then from the innumerable little flecks of white, bobbing spasmodically all over the place, he perceived that these were rabbits, and the mate was in among them, knocking them on the head as fast as his stick could whirl. By the time Wulfrey reached him he was sitting in the sand, skinning one with his knife, and half a dozen more lay round him.

"Better than roots and seaweed," he said, as he hacked the first in pieces and stuffed some into his mouth and handed some to Wulfrey. "There's millions of 'em. We won't starve," and he started skinning another.

Raw meat was a novelty, to Wulfrey at all events but baby-rabbit flesh is eatable, even raw, and it put new life into them both.

The little valley in which they sat was like an oasis in the sandy desert outside. For here, among the wire-grass grew innumerable small creeping-plants and that so sturdily though so modestly that, in spite of the vast horde of rabbits, the whole place was carpeted with green, and right in the centre, where the ground was lowest and the undergrowth thickest and darkest, was a considerable pool of rainwater, which they found brackish but drinkable.

"All we want now is shelter and fire, and we'll live like kings and fighting-cocks," said Macro, when he had time for anything but rabbit-flesh, and lay back comfortably distent.

"And where shall we find shelter and fire in this place?"

"Man! There's more'n we'll ever need in all our lives, over yonder. But it'll keep.... I'm not for going back there this day anyway. To-morrow, mebbe,—" he said drowsily, and presently they were both fast asleep again. And the rabbits came out at sunset and hopped about them, and sniffed them with quivering noses and disrelish, and the heavy dew fell on them, but they never woke. For Nature had now got all she needed for the reparation of the previous waste, and she was busily at work making good while they slept.

XVIII

Morning broke dull, and heavy. The air was mild but full of moisture, and they were chilled with their long sleep in the open.

"Gosh! but I'd like to feel dry again," said Macro, as they sat munching raw rabbit for breakfast. "D'you feel like going out yonder?"

"I feel three times the man I was yesterday. But should we not go on further first? There may be someone living on the island."

"Not a soul but us two, I warrant you."

"But since we're here there might be others."

"That's so. There might be, but not likely. It's just luck, deil's own luck, 'at those screeching deevils out yonder aren't picking us to pieces like the rest."

"Say Providence, and I'll agree with you," said Wulfrey, who saw no need to ascribe to the devil so obviously good a work as far as they were concerned.

"Ca' it what you like, not one man in a thousand comes alive through what we came through. And I'm not forgetting that but for you I'd no be here myself. We can take a bit look round, but I'm sore set on a covering of some kind and a fire, and some rum would be cheerful. It's in my bones that we'll find all we want out there, and more besides."

So, after breakfast, they set off, carrying a couple of rabbits for provision by the way.

Looking round from the top of the highest hummock, they saw the great twisting cloud of sea-birds hovering over the distant wreckage, and the shrill clamour of their screaming came faintly to them on the still air. They had cleaned up what the sea had stranded on the spit and had had to go further afield.

From this vantage point they could to some extent make out the lie of the island. It ran nearly west and east and the narrow sand-spit on which they had landed was the extreme western point. Where they stood, the land was about a quarter of a mile in width and it stretched away in front further than they could see, in vast stretches of sand with a line of hummocks all along the northern side. It seemed very narrow, just a long thin wedge of sand, with illimitable gray sea on each side, as far as their eyes could reach. Right ahead, and about a mile away, was a great sheet of water, whether lake or inlet they could not tell. The hummocks ran along its northern side, and a narrow strip of sand divided it from the sea on the south.

"We'd best keep to the ridges," said Macro. "Yon spit on the other side may only end in the sea," so they tramped on along the firm beach on the seaward slope of the line of hummocks, and every now and again climbed up to see what was on the other side. When they found themselves abreast of the sheet of water they went down and found it salt and very shallow. It stretched away in front as far as they could see, but Macro thought he could see more sand hummocks at the far end.

Every here and there, when they climbed the ridge to look over, they came on little basins like their own, comparatively green and populous with rabbits. But never a sign of human life or habitation, not a tree or a shrub, not an animal except the rabbits.

"A God-forsaken hole," was the mate's comment, as they stood, after a couple of hours' trudging, looking out over the interminable ridges in front, and the great unruffled sheet of water below, and the gray slow-heaving sea beyond on both sides, and the gray sky enclosing all.

"There's nought here and never has been. Let's go back and get to work."

"That lake, or inlet, or whatever it is, seems to narrow over there. Suppose we see where it goes to," suggested Wulfrey.

"Only back into sea, I reckon."

However, they tramped on along the beach, and next time they looked over the ridge the land below had broadened out. The water had shrunk to a mere channel which ran, they saw, not into the sea but into a still larger lake beyond, unless it in turn should prove to be a long arm of the sea running all through the middle of the island. They could follow the low sand-spit which divided it from the sea on the south side, and the long line of hummocks on the north, till they faded out of sight in the distance.

Right in front of them spread the largest valley they had yet come across, and the coast ridges ran down into the middle of it and ended in the highest hill they had seen, and between the hill and the lake lay a number of large ponds.

"We must get up there," said Wulfrey.

"No manner o' use," growled the mate, who found tramping through the sand very tiring, and was eager to get back and attack the wreckage for shelter and fire and food and rum.

"Stop you here then, Macro, and I'll go on. If there's anything to see I'll wave my arms. You might skin those rabbits too. I'm beginning to feel empty again."

He struck straight across the valley to the ponds, and was delighted to find them fresh and much better to the taste than their own little pool. Then he climbed the hill, which was not far short of a hundred feet in height. And then Macro, who had been watching him intermittently as he hacked at the rabbits, saw him wave his arms in so excited a fashion that he picked up the rabbits and ran, wondering what new thing he'd found now that set him dancing in that fashion.

And when at last he panted heavily up the yielding side of the hill and saw, he gasped "Gosh!" with all the breath he had left, and sat down open-mouthed and stared as if he could not believe his eyes.

Beyond the end of the valley, the great lake stretched away further than they could see, and in a deep bend on the north side of it lay two ships.

"Schooners, b' Gosh!" jerked Macro, as soon as he could speak; and eyed them intently. "How in name of sin did they get there?" and his eye travelled quickly along the sand-spit that shut out the sea, in search of the break in it through which the schooners must have entered. But no break was visible. Still it might well be that this great inland lake joined the outer sea somewhere over there, beyond their range of sight, and that this was a harbour of refuge, though he had certainly never heard of it before.

"We must find out about 'em," he said at last, and they set off at speed towards the ships to which his eyes seemed glued.

"Not a sign of a man aboard either of 'em," he jerked one time, as he lurched up out of a rabbit-hole. "Nor ashore either."

And to Wulfrey also there was something strange and uncanny in the look of them. The absence of any slightest sign of life anywhere about imparted to them something of a lifeless look also. And their masts were bare of sails, spars, or even cordage, just bare poles sticking up out of the hulls like blighted pine trees. The sea outside had a long slow heave in it, but the water of the lake was smooth as a pond, not a pulse in it, not a ripple on it, and the two little ships lay as motionless as toy boats on a looking-glass sea.

Macro was evidently much exercised in his mind. He never took his eyes off the ships. So intent was he on them that he stumbled in and out of rabbit holes without noticing them, and the "Gosh!" that jerked out of him now and again was provoked entirely by the puzzle of the ships.

So they came at last round the curve of the land and stood opposite the nearer of the two, which lay about a hundred yards out from the shore of bare sand, and neither on ship nor shore nor water had they discovered any sign of life.

"Schooner a-hoy!" bellowed the mate through his funnelled hands. And again. "Schooner a-hoy!"

But no sudden head bobbed up at the hail, and but that they were whole and afloat the ships looked as dead as those others out past the point.

"Gosh, but it's odd!" and he looked quickly both ways along the shore and over his shoulders, as though he feared some odd thing might start up suddenly and take him unawares. "What's it mean?"

"There's no one there. They're deserted."

"Deserted? Man alive! Who'd desert ships afloat like that? What in — does it mean?" his native fears of the unnatural and inexplicable getting the better of him.

"We'd better go and see," said Wulfrey.

"Swim?"

"I suppose so. I don't expect we can wade."

The mate shook his head. He had evidently no liking for the job, keen as was his desire to get to the bottom of it.

"Let's feed first anyway," he said, and produced the rabbits, which he had held on to in spite of his surprise and many stumblings. So they sat in the sand and ate raw rabbit, with their eyes on the ships all the time.

"They're dead ships like all the rest," was the sum of Macro's conclusions. "But how they got there beats me flat."

"They're afloat anyway and they'll be better to sleep in than the sandhills."

"Ay—mebbe,—if so be's there's no dead men aboard—or ghosts."

"There's no ghosts anyway. If there are any dead men we'll bury them decently and occupy their bunks."

At which the mate gave a shiver of distaste and chewed on in silence.

"Isn't it possible there's an opening to the sea over yonder?" asked Wulfrey, with an eastward jerk of the head.

"Mebbe, but I don't think it. There's no seaweed here, and no move in the water, and no tide-mark. It's dead level. But what if there is?"

"Why, then they might have got in that way, and then some storm blocked the opening and they couldn't get out."

"Mebbe. We can find out by travelling along yon spit till we get to the end of it. I'd liefer do that than go aboard."

"We'll sleep better on board than on the sand."

"Man, ye don't know what ill things may be aboard yon ships! There's a wrong look about 'em," which was undeniable, but still not enough to commend the chill sand to Wulfrey as a resting-place when shelter and possibly bunks might be had on board.

"It seems to me," he said, as they finished their meal, "that it doesn't matter much how they got there. We can perhaps find that out later. There they are, and if they're habitable we want to make use of them. I'm going to swim out to this nearest one and find out what's the matter."

"If you go I go," grumbled the mate uncheerfully.

"It's evident there's no one aboard or anywhere about, and it's absurd to sit here looking at them," said Wulf, and began to peel off his clothes, which had got almost dry with walking. "No good getting them wet again," he explained. "I've been all of a chill for the last five days. I'll fasten them on to my head."

"We'll be coming back."

"We might decide to stop there all night. Better take what's left of the meat."

"Gosh!" with a perceptible shiver of distaste again.

However, he peeled also, and by careful contrivance with belt and braces they bound their bundles on to their heads and stepped into the water.

"Phew! It's cold,—colder than the sea," said Wulfrey through tight-set teeth, as they struck out.

"'Tis that," and the mate's teeth chittered visibly, between the chill of the water and distaste of the adventure.

"Temperature ought to be same ... if sea comes in," sputtered Wulfrey.

"'Tisn't, all same. It's cauld as death."

They ploughed along till they reached the nearer ship, and swam round it in search of entrance, and failing other means laid hold of the rusty anchor-chain, which peeled in ruddy flakes at their touch. By the time Wulf tumbled in over the bows he was streaked from head to foot with iron-mould, and presented so ghastly an appearance that Macro's jaw fell as he came up the side, and he looked half inclined to drop back into the water.

"Man! You look awful. I tuk you for a ghost," he gasped in a whisper.

"You're nearly as bad yourself, but I took the cream of it. Now let us see what's what."

The mate's experienced eye showed him at once that the condition of the ship was not due to storm or accident. She had been deliberately stripped of everything that could be turned to account elsewhere. She was bare as a board,—not a rope nor a spar was left. The hatches were closed and looked as though they had not been touched for years.

They came to the fore-hatch leading down to the fo'c's'le, and he hauled it up with some difficulty and looked suspiciously down into the darkness within.

"Below there!" he cried, in a repressed hollow voice. But only the echoes answered him.

They passed the main-hatch leading to the hold, and went along, past a grated skylight thick with green mould, to the covered gangway leading to the officers' quarters. The doors were closed and bolted with rusty bolts. There could not by any possibility be anyone below, not anyone alive, that is.

Macro wasted no breath here, when they had managed to undo the bolts, but he visibly hesitated. Wulf stepped down into the cabin, and he followed.

Just bare walls, nothing more. Table, stools, lamps, everything movable or unscrewable had been carried away. In the four small rooms adjacent there were just four empty bunks and not a thing besides.

"Gosh, but it's queer!" whispered Macro. "Mebbe they're all lying dead in the hold."

"We'll make sure," and they went up on deck again, and with some labour, for the wood had swelled and stuck, got up the main hatch and dropped down into the hold.

But that was bare like the rest. The ship was as empty as a drum.

"Not so much as a rat, b' Gosh!" said the mate, with recovered spirits, seeing no sign of dead men or ghosts.

"What do you make of it?" asked Wulf.

"She's been stripped bare, that's plain. But why, beats me."

"Anyway, there's no objection to our stopping here now, I suppose. Bare bunks will be drier than the sand over there."

"That's so.... And I'm thinking that if we can bring over some of the stuff from that big pile out yonder we can make ourselves mighty comfortable here."

"We can start on that tomorrow. We've done enough for one day."

"We'll make a raft, like old Robinson Crusoe, and bring the stuff right down to the spit yonder," said Macro, waxing quite cheerful at the prospect. "Then we'll make a smaller raft to bring it aboard here."

"We'd better walk along that spit tomorrow and see if there's any opening to the sea."

"We can do that, but I doubt there's not, else this water wouldn't be so cold, and there'd be some movement in it. It's all dead like everything else."

They spent the rest of the daylight poking into every corner of the ship, and in the dark fo'c's'le Macro made a find of surpassing worth.

He had rooted everywhere, with a natural enjoyment in the process, and come on nothing but bare boards. "But you never know," he said, and went on rooting. And in the blackest corner his foot struck something loose which slid away and eluded him. He went down on his hands and knees and groped till he found it, and then gave a triumphant shout which brought up Wulfrey in haste.

It was a small round metal box such as was used for carrying flint and steel and tinder, well-worn and battered, but tightly closed, and the mate's fingers trembled with anxiety as he opened it with his knife.

"Thanks be!" he breathed deeply, for there in the little battered box lay all the possibilities of fire,— warmth, cooked food, life—all complete.

And—"Thank God!" said Wulfrey also. "That's the best find yet."

"If it'll work it's worth its weight in Guinea gold. But it's old, old," and he poked the tinder doubtfully with his finger, "as old as the ship, and that's older than you or me, I'm thinking. It's dropped out of some old pocket and rolled out of sight. We do have the deil's own luck."

"Providence!" said Wulfrey. "Can't we make a fire and roast some rabbit? I'm sick of raw meat."

"Where'd we make it? Galley-stove's gone with all the rest, and galley too for that matter.... Wouldn't do to set the ship afire.... There's only one safe way. Soon as we've got a bit of a raft together we'll bring over sand enough to make a fire-bed in the hold. Then we can roast all the rabbits in the island."

"What about the cover of the big hatchway there? Wouldn't that carry one of us and sand enough."

"Might. And there's wood enough and to spare in the skin of her down below. But it'll be dark in an hour."

"Come on. Let's get it overboard. I'll go. Can you rip up a board for a paddle?"

The hatch-cover was slightly domed and had four-inch coamings all round, and when let upside down on to the water made a sufficiently effective raft for light freight. Macro dropped down into the hold and ripped up a board and jumped it into pieces, and Wulfrey lowered himself gingerly down on to his frail craft and set off for the shore, with roast rabbit in his face.

"Ye'll have to look smart or ye'll be in the dark," Macro called after him, as he leaned over the side watching his clumsy progression.

"Ay, ay! I'll shout if I get lost," and the mate went down to break up firewood and shred filmy shavings in default of sulphur sticks.

Wulfrey, wafting slowly ashore, lighted on a colony of rabbits intent on supper, and was able to capture a couple in their panic rush for their holes. Then he hastily loaded his float with all the sand it could safely carry and set off again for the ship in great content of mind.

The transfer of his cargo to the deck of the ship was a much more difficult and precarious job than getting it alongside. He tried throwing it up in handfuls, but that proved slow work and more than once came near to spilling him overboard. And finally, as the night was upon them, he took off his coat and sent up larger parcels in it; and so at last Macro cried enough, and having shown him how to wedge his float in between the rusty anchor-chain and the bows, so that the wind should not drift it away in the night, he helped him up over the side.

It was an anxious moment when the first sparks shredded down into the ancient tinder. But they caught and glowed, and with tenderest coaxing lighted the mate's carefully-prepared matches, and these the chips, and these the faggots, and the mighty cheer and joy of fire were theirs.

They slept that night in great comfort, replete with roasted meat, roofed from winds and dew, and grateful both, each in his own way, for the marvellous encouragement of this first day on the island.

Though their beds were but bare boards, they had no fault to find with them, but slept like tops. And Macro's black head was so full of the wonderful possibilities of that vast pile of wastry out beyond the point, in conjunction with this amazing find of the ships, that there was no room left in it for any thought of ghosts or evil spirits.

XIX

Over their last night's fire they had made provision of roast meat for breakfast, and after it they paddled precariously across to the other schooner, a couple of hundred yards away, and explored it thoroughly. But it was in exactly the same condition as their own, so they closed all the hatches again and then, after a short discussion, decided to leave the solution of the puzzle of the ships for the present and devote the day to the salvage of any necessaries they could discover among the wreckage.

They paddled across to the southern spit which divided the lake from the sea, and found it a bare hundred yards in width, and at its highest point not more than ten feet above high-water level. They walked briskly along the side of the narrow channel that joined the two lakes, on past the first one, and in a couple of hours reached the sandy point where they had landed two days before. Out above the piles of wreckage the gray cloud of sea-birds swung and whirled, and their shrill screamings rose and fell with the varied fortunes of their quest.

"Screeching deevils!" was the mate's comment on them, and presently, "It'll be a long pull back with a log of a raft. It must be six or seven miles, I reckon."

"Perhaps we'll strike a boat among the wreckage."

"Ah—p'r'aps. We do have the deil's own luck."

It was almost dead low water. The storm of the previous days seemed to have exhausted the elements for the time being. The sea was smooth, with no more movement than the long slow heave which curled, as it neared the shore, into great green and white combers of exquisite beauty, rushing up the beaches in a dapple of marbled foam, and back into the bosom of the next comer with a long-drawn sibilant hiss.

There was a soft south-west wind and even a cheering touch of the sun, and as their work was like to be of the wettest, and dry clothes were a luxury, they left them above tide-level and went out stripped to the fight, their only weapon the mate's sailor's-knife in the belt which he buckled round his waist. But, in view of the screeching deevils already in possession, they forethoughtfully armed themselves with the weightiest clubs they could pick out of the raffle of the beach. For in that countless predatory host, although its components were but birds, there was menace passing words. It made them feel bare and vulnerable, and Macro cursed them heartily as he went.

They reached the pile without any difficulty, and the mate's keen eye raked round for the likeliest stuff for a raft. It was no good acquiring cargo till they had a craft to carry it.

There was no lack of timber, however, and cordage was to be had for the cutting, and with these the skilled hands of the seaman soon constructed a raft large enough for their utmost probable requirements. Then he turned with gusto to the more satisfying joys of plunder, and developed new and startling sides to his character.

Wulf laughed, but found him surprising, as the cateran spirit of his forebears came uppermost with this tremendous opportunity.

He climbed up and down and in and out of the high-piled wreckage like a hungry tiger, bashed in boxes and cases with a huge club of mahogany which had once adorned the cabin-staircase of a ship, and raked over their contents with the avidious claws of a wrecker of the evil coasts. Now and again strange ejaculations broke from him. More than once, in the wild glee of pillage and unexpected booty, he shouted snatches of weird runes and chanties which Wulf supposed were Gaelic. At times he stood and shook his fist at the screaming birds that swooped about him, and cursed them volubly. And once, Wulfrey, on the raft below, knitted his brows and watched him with doubtful perplexity as, in the disappointment of his hopes respecting one great case which had resisted his efforts and finally yielded nothing of consequence, he attacked another with shouts of fury and a Berserk madness that scattered chips and splinters far and wide. An incautious cormorant swooped by him. With a stroke he sent it spinning, a bruised and broken bundle of feathers, and it fell with a dull flop into the sea.

The man seemed demented, drunk with a rage for plunder and the destruction of everything that stood between him and it. His great club whirled, and the blows flailed here and there without any apparent regard to direction. The lust of slaughter and demolishment burst from him in volcanic fire and fury. For the moment he had reverted to his elemental type.

To the cooler head below he looked dangerous. Wulfrey's amused amazement gave place to doubt and a touch of anxiety. He could only hope that his companion was not often subject to fits such as this.

But the Berserk madness was not wholly without method, and presently plunder of all kinds came raining down on the raft.

Heralded by a sharp "Below there!" came a roll of linen and one of woollen cloth, a bale of blankets, more rolls,—this time of silk and satin and velvet, all more or less damaged by the sea, though they were the pick and cream of his salvaging, and all no doubt dryable.

"Good heavens! What does he want with these?" thought Wulfrey, but piled them up obediently.

Then, following the unmistakable course of the marauder up above, and clawing the raft along to keep in touch with him, down came on his head a bulging little sack, which felt like beans but proved to be coffee, and presently, after a pause, necessitated by packing arrangements up above, a series of soft bundles made up in crimson silk and tied with slimy rope.

Then, after another pause punctuated by shouts and crashes, down came a rattling heap of rusty cooking utensils all slung together with more slimy rope, a rusty axe, four broken oars. Till at last the raft became so crowded that there was barely standing room left on it.

"Steady, above there! We're full up. I can't take another pound, and I doubt if we can get this all home safely."

"Just this, man!" and Macro appeared up above with a small keg in his arms, and let himself and it carefully down on to the raft, with every appearance of a return to sanity.

"Man!" he said, with the afterglow of it all still in his face. "That was fine. We'll come again."

"We've got to get all these things home first."

"Easy that. This wind'll carry us fine," and he set to work with a couple of the broken oars and a blanket, and contrived a sail of sorts. Then, taking another oar and thrusting one into Wulfrey's hands, he propelled the clumsy raft along the side of the wreckage till it got clear, and the wind caught their sail and wafted them slowly towards the island.

"A grand grand place, yon!" he broke out again.

"There's stuff enough there to load a hundred ships.... Gosh, I've forgotten the pork!" and he uprooted the sail and began paddling back to the wreckage. "I stove in the head of a barrel and was smelling at it when I spied the wee keg."

"Was it eatable?"

"I've eaten worse."

"Couldn't we get it next trip?"

"Man, my stomach's been crying for it ever since I set eyes on it. 'Sides, those deevils of birds will finish it in no time. See them! They're at it now. Och, ye greedy deevils!"

He clambered up the pile with his oar and laid about him lustily, The birds rose up from the meat like a dense cloud of flies, and screamed and raved at him, and swooped at him with vicious eyes and beaks and claws, so that in a moment he became the centre of a writhing, fluttering, shrieking mass which threatened to annihilate him completely.

He flailed blindly at them with his oar, smashing them by dozens. But they were too many for him. He shouted for help, and when Wulfrey scrambled up he found him in very sore case, fighting blindly and streaming with blood.

"Come away, man!" shouted Wulfrey, and thrashed away at the nightmare of whirling birds. "Come away before they end us!" and in a moment he found himself the centre of a similar shrieking mass, dazed and blinded with their numbers and their fury. The terrified glimpse he got of their cold glittering eyes and gnashing beaks, and the compressed venom of their overwhelming assault, were too much for him. It was like fighting single-handed against all the fiends out of the pit.

He hurled his oar overboard, put up his arms to protect his eyes, and staggered to the edge of the pile, acutely conscious of jags and pecks and rips innumerable on his bare arms and shoulders. As he flung himself down into the water and dived under, a plunge alongside told him that Macro had done the same. A raucous swarm of birds followed them, but on their disappearance fluttered off to more visible chances above.

"Man! but that was awful!" gasped the mate hoarsely. "They nigh ate me alive."

"Let's get aboard or they'll be at us again. There's my oar," and he swam quietly to it and they climbed back on to the raft.

"An' never ae piece o' pork," lamented Macro. "The poaching deevils!"

"Be thankful you're alive, man! It was a close touch that."

"'Twas that. I'm bit all over. I'd like to end 'em all with one crack."

Fortunately the birds were too busy quarrelling up above to give them more than cursory attention. A few came whirling and swooping after them with greedy eyes and ravening beaks. But it was only in their multitudes that they were formidable and they soon gave up a chase that offered no easy prey.

The men, shaken and trembling, clawed along the pile till they caught the wind again, when Macro readjusted his masts and sail, and they drifted slowly back towards the island.

"Ye deevils! Ye scratching, scrawming, skelloching deevils!" breathed Macro deeply, every now and again, and shook his fist at the twisting column of birds behind. "I wish ye had ae neck and me ma hond on it."

Their weighty progress was of the slowest. When they drew alongside the yellow spit Macro plunged overboard and waded ashore for their clothes, and they drifted on along the low southern beach. But it was well after mid-day before they came abreast of the stark little ships which stood to them for home.

Then they made busy traffic transporting their salvage to the shore and carrying it across the bank to the edge of the lake. And when that was all done Macro unlashed the raft and they carried it over piece by piece, and roughly put it together there and loaded up again.

"It'll all come in for firing," said the mate. "We can't go on burning our own inside all the time."

It was no easy work propelling their rough craft with broken oars. Moreover Macro insisted on taking the hatch-cover in tow. But the spirit of accomplishment was upon them and the weight they dragged was a comforting one.

All the way, as they joggled slowly along, the mate never ceased enlarging on the wonders of the wreckage, nor forgot his one disappointment, which evoked resentful curses each time he thought of it.

"Man, but we're doing fine! A roof we've got, and fire, and things to eat.—There's flour in yon bundles,—just the cores of half a dozen casks. And yon bag's coffee, but we'll need to roast it and grind it. And the wee keg's rum, unless I've mistook it. An' there's enough stuff out yonder to last us for a thousand years. But, blankety-blank-blank-blank!—my stomach's crying after yon pork that them screeching deevils took out of our mouths, as you might say. Blankety-blank-blank 'em all—every red-eyed son o' the pit among 'em! But we'll try again, and next time I'll not broach the barr'l an' they'll know noth'n about it."

"Maybe they'll attack us all the same. It was the most horrible situation I was ever in. One felt so utterly helpless."

"Ay, blank 'em! There was no end to 'em.... They'd have ate me alive if you hadn't come and helped me tumble overboard. Blank 'em! Blank 'em! Blank 'em!"

"What on earth are all these things for?" asked Wulfrey one time, kicking a roll of crimson silk with his heel.

"Blankets to sleep on,—better than boards. The others for their gay gaudery,—the bonny reid and blue o' them. They mek me feel good and warm just to look at 'em. I just couldna leave them. Man, they're grand!"

They hoisted all their stuff on board, and found themselves hungry and thirsty with the heavy day's work. There were but the scantiest remnants of their breakfast left, and Macro undertook to chop wood and make a fire, scour some of the rusty cooking-utensils, and make flour-and-water cakes as soon as he had some water, if Wulfrey would go across for it and some fresh meat.

So he set off on the hatch-cover with a good-sized kettle, and was back inside an hour with water from the ponds by the hill and a couple of young rabbits, and found that the mate had not been idle. He had transferred a sufficiency of sand to the cabin to make a hearth at the foot of the steps, and had broken up wood enough to last for a week. He had spread out all the blankets, scoured most of the rust off a frying-pan and a small kettle and a couple of tin pannikins, and had opened the keg and sampled its contents and found it French cognac of excellent quality.

In the best of spirits he skinned the rabbits and set them roasting, with an incidental commination of thae screeching deevils that had robbed them of the pork which would have been such a welcome accompaniment. Then he compounded cakes of flour and water and fried them deftly, and set a kettle to boil wherewith to make hot grog, and boastfully promised coffee for the morrow when he had time to roast and grind it.

They both ate ravenously, and found great content in the taste of hot food and drink once more, after all these days of clammy starvation, and then they slept. And Wulfrey dreamed horribly all night of fighting helplessly with legions of screeching birds, and several times fought himself awake, and each time found Macro actively engaged in the same unprofitable business.

XX

In spite of his torn shoulders and unrestful night, Macro was for setting off again first thing next morning for more plunder. That huge pile of wastry drew him like a magnet. He hungered and thirsted to be at it again.

But Wulfrey flatly refused. They had enough to go on with, and he claimed at least a day to recover from the effects of the last excursion. And as Macro declined to tackle the job single-handed he was fain to agree, though with none too good a grace.

"This weather mayn't last. We'd best get all we can while we can," he urged.

"The stuff will be there tomorrow. Most of it's been there for years, you said."

"Ay, but man, there's mebbe things out of the 'Grassadoo,' that'll be spoiling for want of finding."

"They'll not spoil much more in one day. You're more used to this kind of work than I am, you see. I must have a rest."

Macro consigned rest to the bottomless pit, but after relieving his feelings in that way, consented at last to an easy-going exploration of the southern spit, to see if their lake opened into the sea, though he expressed himself satisfied, from his observations, that it did not.

First, however, out of the larger raft he constructed a smaller one, which bore them better than the hatch-cover and was more manageable, and the hatch they hauled on board again and fitted into its place, so as to keep the ship dry in case of bad weather. Then they paddled across to the spit and set off along it, both scrutinising the lie of the land carefully.

For a good hour they trudged through heavy sand, the sea swirling with long soft hisses up the yellow beach on their right hand, and on their left the placid water of the lake without a pulse in it. The dividing bank was nowhere in all its length more than a hundred yards wide, nor more than ten feet high at its crown.

More than once Macro stood and studied it in places, and when in time they came to long ridges of hummocks which stretched as far in front as they could see, he stood again, looking back from the top of the first they climbed, and said, "I'm thinking there's no opening this end. Mebbe it was on the level there. But this stuff shifts so in a gale you never know where you are."

Presently they came on the shallow rounded end of the lake, with higher sandhills beyond it, which ran along both sides of the island further than they could see. In between lay a vast unbroken stretch of level sand, and when they climbed to the top of the highest hill, they saw this sandy desert dwindle in the far distance to a point, with the sea on each side of it, like the one at the other end of the island.

"There's not a sign of anybody else," said Wulfrey.

"If there'd been anyone they'd bin living on them ships. We've got it all to ourselves, that's certain. And what's more, we'll have it all to ourselves till Kingdom come. No one else'll ever come, 'cept dead men.'"

"Those two ships came."

"Twenty, thirty years ago,—mebbe more. Must have bin an opening then and it's got silted up. They couldn't have got washed over the spit."

There were several more large fresh-water ponds close to these larger hills, and rabbits everywhere. They secured a couple and tramped back the way they had come.

Macro seemed to accept the whole situation and outlook with the utmost equanimity. They had very much more than they had had any right to expect; more was always to be had for the fetching from that wonderful pile out yonder; what that pile might yield in the way of richer plunder remained to be seen, and he was the man to see to it.

But Wulfrey had been cherishing a hope that the great lake would prove an inlet from the sea, a harbour of refuge into which other ships might be expected to run at times. And the fact that it was not, that no relief was to be looked for in that direction and that this desolate sandbank, bristling with wrecks, must necessarily be shunned by all who knew of it, weighed more and more heavily on him as he thought about it.

They were alive, where all their shipmates had perished. They were provided for beyond their utmost expectation. For all that he was most deeply grateful. But the prospect of passing the rest of his life on this bare bank troubled him profoundly and reduced him to silence and the lowest of spirits.

XXI

They woke next morning into a dense white fog, so thick that they could not see across the deck. Macro, intent on plunder, hailed it as an excellent screen from possible attack by the other pillagers of the wreck-pile, and though Wulfrey had his doubts, he would not counter him again.

His knowledge of human nature suggested to him the almost impossibility of two men living alone, in intimacy so close and exclusive, and with so little outlet for their thoughts and energies, without coming to loggerheads at times. He determined that, so far as in him lay, the provocation thereto should not come from him.

So far he had not only had nothing to complain of in his companion's presence, but, on the contrary, had found himself distinctly the gainer by it in every material way. But the strange wild outbursts, to which he had given vent when they were at the wreckage before, warned him of hidden fires below, and suggested the advisability of non-provocation of the under-man, if it were possible to avoid it.

So they paddled across to the spit, which they could not well miss, and set off on foot for the point, steering by the sullen lap and hiss of the waves as they stole softly up out of the fog on their left hand. There was a clamminess in the air which commended the idea of clothes to them while they worked on the pile. So they made their things into tight bundles, and carried them above their heads as they waded out neck-deep to their store-house. The shrill cries of the birds came dull and thin through the fog, more ghostly than ever from their invisibility. Now and again an inquisitive straggler fluttered down at them out of the close white curtain, and whirled back into it with a terrified squawk when it found they were alive.

They climbed the pile cautiously, but the birds seemed mostly at a distance; and when they had flung down sufficient timber Macro proceeded to construct another raft, while Wulfrey poked about up above on his own account.

And as he climbed about among the chaotic mass of barrels, boxes, cases, bales, he came to understand the wild craving to get at them, to bash them open and learn what they contained, which had possessed the mate that other day. There might be anything hidden there—goods of all kinds for the easement of their present situation. There might even be treasure of gold and jewels. It was impossible to say what there might not be. And though gold and jewels were absolutely useless to them, placed as they were, and with no prospect, according to Macro, of rescue or relief, the possibility of such things lying hidden in untold quantity all about him stirred him strangely.

He recognised feelings so abnormal to himself with no little surprise. He felt as a penniless small boy might feel if he were given the freedom of a great shop full of boxed-up toys and told to help himself. He wanted to smash open very closed case he came to, to see what was inside it.

The water lapped and clunked dismally in the hollows below, and at times he had to climb almost down to it, and then up the further side, to get across faults in the pile. In one such black gully, on what was usually the leeward side of the pile, he had stepped cautiously from ledge to ledge, and laid hold of a projecting spar and was hauling himself up the other side, when he came face up against a dark little cranny between two great cases. And in the niche sat the skeleton of a man, all huddled up and jammed together, but grinning at him in so ferociously jovial a manner, as though he had been expecting him and was rejoiced at the sight of him, that Wulfrey came near to loosing his hold and falling into the water. He scrambled hastily past, and saw grinning faces in every dark corner for the rest of the day, and some of them were fact and some were only fancy. For the tumbled pile of wreckage was like a huge trap for the catching of anything the sweeping gales might bring it.

He heard Macro's voice, dulled by the mist, calling to him, and he answered but knew not which way to go to get to him. It was only by constant shouting and long and precarious scrambling that they came together again.

"We'd best keep close in this fog," said the mate, "or one of us'll be stopping the night here. Found anything?"

"A dead man—"

"Any of ours?"

"No, he was only bones."

"It's full of 'em. They're no canny, but they'll not harm us. Where'll we begin?"

"One place is as good as another. Here, I should say, and quietly, or those fiends of birds will be at us again."

"Bear a hand with this, then," laying hold of a newly-stranded barrel. "That's pork out of the 'Grassadoo,' so it'll be all right," and heaving and hauling, they managed to get the barrel down on to the raft.

As they poked about the pile in the mist, it was evident they had struck a spot where a good portion of the contents of the 'Grace-à-Dieu' had lodged. Macro, having superintended the loading, recognised many of the marks and in some instances could recall their contents.

"Women's fallals," he said, with a scornful crack at one large case. "If they'd been men's, now, they'd have come in handy.... Boots and shoes, if I remember rightly,"—nodding at another case. "We'll soon see," and with a chunk of wood he stove in one side and hauled out a handful of its contents.— "Women's troke again! Mebbe we'll find some men's stuff in time.... I've seen yon chest before.... Old Will Taggart's, I think," and he stove it open, and went down on his knees and raked over the contents. "Seaman's slops, not much account.... A new pipe and a tin of tobacco! Thanks be! We'll take that ... and another flint and steel. Always useful! ... Clothes not much good, but we might be glad of 'em later on.... Yon's a box of tea and it'll be lead-lined inside. Should be more about. We had two hunderd aboard.... Glory! yon barrels are hard-tack. These ones are flour. If we work hard and get 'em ashore before the weather breaks again we'll live in clover.... What's this now? ... 'Duke of Kent'"—and he hauled up a stout wooden box by one handle out of a raffle of cordage and ragged sail-cloth. "Name of a ship—or name of a man? That's no a ship's box."

A deft blow under the lock and the box lay open, displaying a number of uniforms, richly decorated with gold braid and lacing, all more or less damaged by water, but otherwise in good condition.

"Duds enough to keep us going for a couple of years if so be as they fit," said the mate exuberantly, and Wulfrey laughed out at the idea of their peacocking about their sandbank rigged out in court costumes.

"He was Governor-General of Canada," he said. "I remember hearing he lost his baggage on the journey."

"We'll be Governor-Generals here when we're needing a change.... Nothing but his clothes," as he ran his hands all over the box. "Mebbe we'll find more of 'em lying about. Man! what a place it is! It'd take a man a lifetime to work through all the stuff there is here."

They worked hard and carried home a huge load, but as there was no wind they had to paddle all the way, and even Macro acknowledged to being a bit tired before they got all their plunder across the spit and on board, the transit across the lake on the smaller raft necessitating three separate journeys. He was in the highest of spirits however, and keen to be back at the pile next day. As for Wulfrey, hardening though he was with all these unusual labours, he found himself almost too weary to eat.

The fog lay on them like a white pall for six days. Macro predicted that it would go in a storm, and was urgent on salvaging all they could before it came.

So, day after day, they went out to the pile, and came back loaded at night till they had stuff enough in their hold to keep them in comfort for many months to come.

They had meat and drink, clothes and firing, and comfortable quarters. What more could any man want, unless it were to get away from it all? And that, the mate asserted, time after time, was the unlikeliest thing that could happen.

"We're here till Kingdom come," was the burden of his tune. "So we may as well be comfortable. And we've had the deil's own luck. We might ha' been living on rabbits and roots, and sleeping on the sand. Man! be thankful at being tired to such good purpose!"

"I'm thankful enough and tired enough, and we've got stuff enough for a year. I'm going to take a rest."

"I'm for the pile again tomorrow. If you won't come I'll e'en make shift alone," and Wulfrey let him go alone.

XXII

The smothering white fog lay thick on them for six days and then disappeared in the night. The morning broke dull and heavy, with a gusty wind from the south-west, and they could hear the waves breaking on the spit with a sound like the low growl of a menacing beast.

"I'm off to the pile," said the mate.

"Better take a day off. You've been working too hard."

"Not me. I cannot sit here while all yon stuff's crying aloud to be picked up."

"Well, I'll be on the look-out, and come across to give you a hand from the spit when you get there."

"I'll lash you up a bit float that'll bring you over, before I go. And you'll mebbe have some food ready against I get back. It's hungry work out there."

"I'll be ready for you. If you load up too heavily you'll not get back at all."

"I'll see to that. Wind's fair, it'll bring me home all right."

So Wulfrey had the day to himself, and had time, which the labours of the previous days had not permitted him, to consider the situation in all its aspects.

So far they had been marvellously favoured, without doubt. Ten days ago they were swinging up and down on the galley-roof inside the cage of the dead ship's ribs, possessed of nothing but their bare lives, and those but doubtfully. And here they were, provided for in every respect, with comforts which shipwrecked men had no right to expect, and with unlimited further stores to draw upon. They could live without fear....

But what a life, after all. Eating, drinking, sleeping,—raking over the wreckage for possible plunder that was useless to them,—rambling among the rabbits and the sandhills. Quarrelling in time, maybe. Perhaps it was a good thing there was a ship for each of them.

He was not himself of a quarrelsome disposition. The mate, he thought, might be difficult to put up with if he took a crooked turn. But it would be the height of folly for two men, bound together by ill-fortune, and to this bare bank for all time, to fall out. Every circumspection within his power he resolved to exercise, and so far, indeed, his companion had given him no cause to mistrust or doubt him.

But he had a somewhat discomforting feeling that he knew very little of the real man that lay beneath that saturnine exterior, that there might be elemental depths there which would surprise him if they came to be revealed. This Macro that he knew was to him something in the nature of a sleeping volcano, outwardly quiet but full of hidden fires.

He could imagine no likely grounds for dispute between them. Each worked for the common good, and so far they had shared all things equally and without question. But how would it be as the weeks dragged into months, and the months into years?

So far the rifling of the wreckage had afforded the mate all the outlet he needed for his activities. In ministering to the cravings of the riever spirit that was strong in him it had also supplied their wants in overwhelming abundance. The longer it kept him busy the better, and if it yielded him plunder of value he was entirely welcome to it.

Wulfrey could not imagine his discovering anything out there which could by any possibility lead to any serious difference between them. And yet, in spite of all that, from little glimpses he had caught at times of the strange wild, hidden nature of the man, he was not without doubts as to his absolute congeniality as a sole companion for the rest of his days.

In short he had a vague feeling that, if by any chance they came to loggerheads, Macro might prove an extremely unpleasant person to be shut up with, within bounds so limited as this great bank of sand.

He recognised such feelings, however, as unnecessarily morbid, and ascribed them to the general murkiness of the outlook and over-weariness from the exertions of the last few days. So he tumbled overboard on to the new raft and paddled to the nearer shore, and set off for a brisk walk over the sandhills and along the beach, in search of a more hopeful frame of mind.

Why could they not build a boat? Macro said the coast of Nova Scotia was but a hundred miles or so away. A hundred miles was no great affair, and there was wood among that pile enough to build a thousand boats. So far, indeed, they had not come upon any tools except the rusty axe, for tool-chests probably sank at once on the outer banks where the ships went to pieces.

Still, he would suggest it to Macro. It might prove a further outlet for his energies. If he should by chance find plunder of value out there he might, when he was satiated, favour the idea of an attempt at escape. In fact, plunder without any attempt to utilise it would be absurd.

The opportunity of making his own position clear, and thereby obviating any cause for dispute, occurred that same day.

When, in the afternoon, he saw the mate coming slowly along before the wind, he paddled over to the spit to meet him and found him in great spirits.

"Man! it's been a great day, and if ye'd been there ye'd have had your chance. I lit on some graand things. Wait while I show you—"

"Let's get 'em all aboard first. They'll keep, and I'll be bound you're tired and hungry."

"Hungert as a wolf, but finding siccan things takes the tired out o' one," and his black eyes sparkled over his finds, and he must go on telling about them as they worked.

"It was down under where we found yon Duke o' Kent box. I spied another, and then more, mebbe there's, more yet down below."

"More fancy coats?"

"Ah!—and some with jewelled stars on 'em and swords with fancy hilts. I'll show you when we get aboard."

"You didn't come across any tools, I suppose?"

"Tools? No. What would we want tools for?"

"I was wondering if it might not be possible to build some kind of a boat and get across to Nova Scotia."

"We're safer here than trying that, I'm thinking."

"When you've got all there is to be got out there you'll want to get home and enjoy it—"

"Man! It'd take a hunderd years to go through it all. It's bin piling up there since ever this bank silted up."

"Oh well, we don't want to stop here a hundred years, that's certain. What's the good of it all if you can't make any use of it?"

"It's graand to handle anyway."

And when they had eaten, he opened some of his bundles and displayed his treasures,—a jewelled 'George,' roughly cut from some Garter-knight's court-coat, several smaller decorations, all more or less ornamented with precious stones, three dress-swords with mountings, in ivory and gold, a small wooden box lined with sodden blue velvet in which were half a dozen rings, some of which from the size of the stones and the massiveness of their setting, seemed to Wulfrey of considerable value.

"They're worth something, all those," said Macro, as he handled them with loving exultation.

"Ay, if you could get them home and turn them into money. I don't see what use they're going to be to you here," said Wulfrey, fiddling his own string again.

"They're fine to have anyway."

"I'd sooner have another pipe and some more tobacco than the whole of them."

"Ye can have that too," and he rooted in another bundle and produced both. "They're oot a dead man's chest and they're wet. But he's no use for 'em and they'll dry. So there ye are. Ye dinnot care for jewels?" and he looked at Wulfrey wonderingly.

"As to that, I don't say I wouldn't pick them up if I came across them, but I've no hankering for them."

"Ye've plenty money of your own, mebbe."

"As much as I need—if ever I get ashore."

"Ah! It meks a difference, ye see. I never had any to speak of, and these bonny sparklers pluck at the heart o' me."

"You're welcome to all you can get, as far as I'm concerned—"

"Ay, man, they're mine, for I found 'em."

"But they're no use to you unless we can get away from here. Get ashore and you can turn them to account. Now why couldn't we build some kind of a boat and get across to Nova Scotia? There's wood enough and to spare out yonder—"

"Ay, there's wood, but ef we had the tools 'twould still be no easy matter. An' then ye've got to reckon wi' the weather. 'Twould be a bad move to spend our time building a boat only to go to the bottom in her with all the gear we'd gathered. We're safe here, anyway. Mebbe some day a boat'll come ashore not so broke but we can patch her up.... How'd ye like to be afloat in a home-made boat a night like this?"

For while they sat, eating and talking, the day had darkened, and now and again there came a menacing whuffle down the open hatch, and the little ship was filled with a tremulous humming as the rising wind played on their bare masts, and the growl of the spit had deepened into a long hoarse roar.

"It'll be a bitter bad night I'm thinking. I saw it coming away out yonder. Mebbe it'll add some to our pile of stuff. Mebbe it'll bring us a boat."

"We will not hope for either," said Wulfrey soberly, "for that means more deaths out yonder—"

A long shrill scream outside sent a creepy chill down his spine for a moment. He glanced apprehensively across at Macro in the flickering light of the fire, and saw his face livid, his eyes like great black wells, his jaw dropped.

"The spirits o' the dead!" jerked the mate. "There's a hantle o' them out there.... They're mebbe after me for these things...." and he rocked himself to and fro, where he sat on the floor, and muttered strange words,—"An ainm au Athar, 's an Mhic, 's an Spioraid Naoimh,"—in the name of the Father, and of the Son, and of the Holy Ghost.

The weird shrieking waxed louder and shriller. Wulfrey got up and climbed the steps, and found the stormy twilight gray with that vast cloud of birds, all fleeing blindly before the gale and each one screaming its loudest.

It was a fearsome, blood-curdling clamour, an ear-splitting pandemonium, a whirling Sabbat, as if all the demons of the pit had broken loose and clothed themselves in wings and shrieks and deadly fear.

"It's only those damnable birds," he bent and shouted gruffly down to Macro, vexed with himself at his own momentary fright.

But the mate was not for accepting any such simple explanation as that.

"Man!" he said hoarsely. "Birds ye may think 'em, but I know better. It is spirits they are,—spirits of all the dead that ever died in this dread place,—a great multitude—their bones are white out there, but the spirits of them cannot rest. A Mhoire ghradhach! 'Twas under the Dark Star we were born, and here we'll die and leave our bones to whiten in the sand, and the spirits of us will go screeching and scrauchling wi' the rest. Come away, man, and shut the doors tight or they'll be in on us!"

Wulfrey had never seen anything like it. Those myriads of fluttering wings looked as though the whole gray sky had come tumbling down in fragments. It was like a snowstorm on a gigantic scale, every whirling flake a bundle of wildly screaming feathers.

He stood watching for a time and listening to the growing thunder of the rollers on the spit. He imagined their crashing in white foam-fury among the stark ribs of the dead ships out there on the banks.

He shivered as he recalled the chill horrors of their own undoing and deliverance. It was wonderful beyond words, with that in his mind, to be standing there, safe and warm, and well provided, and his heart was full of gratitude.

"God help any who are out there this night!" he said to himself, and closed the doors on the storm-fiends, and squatted on the floor over against the mate, who sat rocking slowly to and fro in great discomfort and muttered Gaelic seuns as a protection against the unholy things that wandered outside.

All night long their little ship was filled with the hum of the shuddering masts, broken now and again with the creaking and jerking of their rusty cable. And whenever Wulfrey, warm in his bunk with many blankets, woke up for a moment, he heard the deep thunder of the waves on the spit, and the howl of the wind, outside, and the thrashing of the rain on deck; and he thanked God for warmth and shelter, and lay listening for a moment, and then rolled over and went to sleep again.

The storm lasted three full days, during which they never once left the ship. They had all they needed, and fresh water was obtainable in any quantity by slinging an empty keg outside one of the scupper-holes through which the rain drained off the deck.

Macro's gloomy humour lasted, off and on, as long as the storm. The birds had mostly hidden themselves in sheltered nooks among the sandhills. But every now and again the evil in them, or maybe it was hunger, would stir them up and set them whirling and shrieking round the ship, and sometimes lighting on it in prodigious numbers, and the mate would curse them long and deep and fall once more to his spells and invocations. The fury of the storm did not trouble him, but the screaming of the birds seemed to touch the superstitious spot in his nature and set all his nerves jangling.

It was during one of the lull times that he astonished Wulfrey by hauling out his rolls of silks and velvets, and with an elemental, almost barbaric, delight in their rich colourings, he cut them into long strips, which he fixed neatly to the walls of the cabin by means of wooden pegs. The gorgeous results afforded him the greatest satisfaction, which nothing but the wailing of the birds could damp. Whenever their shrill clamour broke out the darkness fell on him again. He hurled uncouth curses at them and no arguments availed against his humour.

To Wulfrey, on the other hand, the birds and their dismal shriekings were but an incident, the fury of the storm a wonder and a revelation.

All through that former time of stress, which had ended in their undoing, his powers of observation and appreciation had been dulled by his fears of disaster. Then, the howl of the gale and the onslaught of the seas had been like hungry deaths close at his heels. But here, in the perfect security of the land-locked lake, he was free to watch and to wonder.

At times, indeed, it seemed to him that the terrible force of the wind might lift them bodily, ship and all, and hurl them into the turmoil beyond. Then he remembered that many such storms must have swept the island and still the ships were there.

The waves that broke on the spit seemed to him higher than tall houses, and the weight of them, as they curled and crashed on the sand, made the whole island tremble, he was certain. The uproar was deafening, and at times great lashes of white spray came hurtling over into the lake, and scourging it into sizable waves of its own.

When Wulfrey woke on the fourth morning he was conscious of a change, and running up on deck he found the sun shining in a pale-blue, storm-washed sky, and nothing left of the gale but the great green waves breaking sullenly on the beach beyond the spit.

He stripped and plunged overboard, and climbed up again full of the joy of life and physical fitness.

XXIII

The days crept into weeks, the weeks into months, with nothing to break the monotony of their life but visits to the wreckage, an occasional skirmish with the birds, rabbit-hunts, rude attempts at fishing, which met with so little success from lack of anything approaching proper material that they gave it up in disgust, and rambles among the sandhills.

They got along companionably enough; the mate's only complaint,—and that not untinged with satisfaction, and obviously prompted more by a desire for his help than from any wish to halve his spoils—that Wulfrey showed so poor a spirit in the matter of plunder, and so shamefully neglected the opportunities of a lifetime.

For himself, if he could have found safe lodging out there, he would have lived on the wreck-pile, to save the time and trouble of going to and fro. The riever spirit of his forefathers was kept at boiling-point by the possibilities of fortune which lurked there. The search in itself at once satisfied and stimulated the natural craving for booty which rioted in his Highland-Spanish blood, and he never tired of it.

He came back laden every time with things for the common good, and rarer pickings for his private hoard, over which he exulted like a chieftain returned from a successful foray.

Wulfrey was on the whole not ungrateful to the pile for affording him such distraction. He discussed the latest additions to his treasure-trove with him, as they sat by the fire of a night, and speculated with him on their probable origin and value, and the higher he assessed this the more the mate's black eyes glowed.

He would sit watching Wulfrey as he turned the latest find over and over, and weighed it in his hand, and polished a bit of it to get at its basic metal, and mused on its shape and endeavoured to arrive at its history. And at such times there was in the sombre black eyes something of the look of an uncertain-tempered dog whose lawful bone is in jeopardy.

Once or twice, Wulfrey, glancing up as he passed an opinion, caught that curious suspicious look bent on him, and was amused and annoyed at it, and also somewhat discomfited. Did the man think he coveted his useless little gauds?—useless in their present extremity, though some of them doubtless valuable enough if they could be sold. Why, he esteemed a dryable twist of tobacco infinitely more highly than any silver candlestick or shapely silver cup that the other could fish up from the depths. It seemed to him just as well that the plunder-fever had attacked only one of them, for he doubted if his companion would willingly have shared with another. For the fever grew with his finds.

Once they came within an ace of a quarrel, and though it blew over, the seeds remained.

Where the mate hid his spoil, Wulfrey neither knew nor cared nor ever troubled his head about. He would no more have occupied his thoughts with it than he would have taken more than his proper share of the food or tobacco.

But increase breeds suspicion, and suspicion clouds the outlook. Among other things, Macro one day brought home a small crucifix and some strings of beads, which he believed to be of gold, while Wulfrey, from their hardness to the touch of the knife, pronounced them only brass. They were all curiously carved or cast, however, and, whatever the metal of which they were made, he expressed his admiration of the workmanship.

A night or two later, to his amazement, Macro came out of his own cabin more black-a-vised than he had ever seen him, and asked abruptly, "Where's that cross?"

"What cross?"

"You know what cross. Yon gold cross I showed you two nights ago. Where is it?" and he lowered at Wulfrey like a full-charged thunder-cloud.

"I know nothing of your cross, man. I suppose you put it with the rest of your things."

"I did that, and it's gone. Where is it?"

"Don't speak to me like that, Macro. I won't have it. I know nothing about your cross or any of your plunder. I've told you before, it is nothing to me. If I wanted it I'd go and get it for myself."

"It was there with the rest and it's no there now. And—"

"—!" cried Wulfrey, springing up ablaze with indignation. "Do you dare to think I would touch your dirty pilferings?" and it looked as though the next instant would find them at grips.

But the mate had broken out in the sudden discovery of his loss. Wulf stood full as tall as himself. He looked very fit and capable, and looked, moreover, as the mate's common sense told him, as soon as it got the chance, the last person in the world to tamper with another man's goods—even though he might be the only one circumstantially able to have done so.

"It's gone anyway," he growled. "But it's no good fighting about it."

"That's not enough. Your greed for gain has blinded you. Till you come to your senses I've nothing more to do with you," and for two days not a word passed between them.

Each prepared his own food as and when he chose, and ate it apart from the other. The mate hung about as though loth to leave Wulfrey in sole charge at home, and the atmosphere of the little cabin was murky and charged with lightning.

On the third day Wulfrey ostentatiously set off for the wreck-pile by himself. He was running out of tobacco and would not have accepted any from the mate if it had been offered.

He waded out, made a rough raft on Macro's lines, and smashed open such seamen's chests as he could discover, for it was always in them that they found tobacco.

He got several small lots, and a couple of new pipes, and a flint and steel, charged his raft with a keg of rum and a case of hard-tack, and managed to get it all back to the spit and to the ship single-handed.

As he came up the side, the mate met him, with the missing crucifix in his hand.

"The little deevil of a thing," he said, with quite unconscious incongruity, "had slipped down a crack, back o' the locker, and I were wrong to think ye could have taken it."

"Well, don't play the fool again," said Wulfrey shortly. "If your greed for other folk's goods hadn't blinded you, you would understand that a gentleman does not stoop to stealing."

"I've seen some I wouldn't trust further'n I could see 'em, and then only if their hands were up over their heads. But ye're not that kind, an' I was wrong. So there 'tis, an' no more to be said. What have ye found?"

"Pipes and tobacco. That is all I went for."

After his two days of enforced silence Macro was inclined to expand, but found his advances coldly received. Wulfrey's pride was in arms and the insult rankled.

By degrees, however, the storm-cloud drifted by, and matters between them became again much as they had been, with somewhat of added knowledge, on each side, of the character of the other.

The mate had learned that the Doctor, quiet as he might appear, was not a man to suffer injustice or to be meddled with. And Wulfrey had got a further warning of the possibilities of trouble should he and the mate come to serious differences.

It seemed absurd that two men, stranded, perhaps for life, on this bare sandbank, should be unable to live together in amity. Yet, his experience of men told him that it was just such enforced close intimacy—the constant rubbing together of very divergent natures, with nothing in common between them but the necessities entailed by their common misfortune—that might, nay almost certainly must, come to explosion at times, unless they both set themselves sedulously to the keeping of the peace.

If any actual rupture took place between them, he foresaw that the mate might develop phases of character which would be exceedingly awkward and difficult to deal with. Freedom from all the ordinary restraints which civilisation imposed upon the natural inner man might easily run to wildest licence.

At bottom this man was just a wild Highland cateran with a dash of Spanish buccaneer, hot-blooded, avid of gain under circumstances so propitious, insatiable. The chance of a lifetime had come to him and he was exultantly set on making the most of it. He was like a cage-bred wolf set down suddenly into the midst of an unprotected flock of sheep. There was his natural prey in profusion and there was none to stay him. To be dropped unexpectedly on to this enormous pile of plunder was like the realisation of a fairy tale. No wonder he was inclined to lose his head.

It was fortunate, thought Wulfrey, that they were built on different lines, and that the plunder-pile made absolutely no appeal to himself beyond the necessaries of life.

He determined, as far as in him lay, to walk warily and to avoid, as far as possible, any just cause of offence on his side.

BOOK III

BONE OF CONTENTION

XXIV

They had been three months on the island, and in all that time had never sighted a living ship, though the remains of newly-dead ones were never wanting after bad weather.

It was evident that the men of the sea avoided Sable Island as if it were a pestilence, and came there only when it no longer mattered to them whether they came there or not.

Macro was, by degrees and with never-lessening enjoyment, amassing a very considerable treasure. If ever the chance of getting back to land arrived, and he could get his plunder home, he would have no need to follow the sea for the rest of his life. But, whether or not that crowning good fortune should ever be his, this gathering of spoil was a huge satisfaction to the very soul of him, and he desired no better.

The only flies in his big honey-pot were those rival depredators the birds. He had many a battle royal with them, and came home at times scratched and clawed and furiously comminative, consigning birds of all shapes and sizes to everlasting perdition. Spirits or no spirits, in the day time, and in the prosecution of his work, he would fight them valiantly or trick them cleverly.

But in the black storms that swept over them at times, when the great waves crashed like thunder on the spit, and the sandhills and hummocks melted away under Wulfrey's wondering eyes and built themselves afresh in new places, when the shrieking hosts came whirling round the ship and the sky was full of their raucous clamour, then the darkness came on Macro and he fell again to his seuns, and knew them, beyond all doubt, for things of evil.

When the odds out there on the wreck-pile were too much for him, he learned by experience how to fool them. He would smash furiously at them with his club, shouting in wild exultation as the bashed bodies went tumbling into the sea. If that did not discourage them, and their venom persisted, he would drop quietly into some adjacent hole amid the wreckage where they could not get at him, and wait there till they whirled away after easier prey.

So keen was he on adding to his store that, when their commissariat needed replenishing, Wulfrey found it necessary to accompany him and to insist on his attending strictly to this more important business, or at times they would have gone short. For the rest, Wulfrey left him to the satisfaction of his cravings and interfered with him not at all.

One memorable morning, which broke sweet and clear after two days of stress and storm, the mate set off as usual to find what the gods had sent him; and Wulf, leaning over the side, watched him paddle across to the spit, and land there, and stride away towards the western point from which they always waded out to the wreckage.

But on this occasion, before he disappeared in the distance, he stopped and stood looking out over the sea, and the next moment Wulfrey saw him wading out towards something which only caught his eye when thus directed to it,—something which bobbed up and down among the waves with a glint of white at times.

He saw Macro reach it and lift his arms in a gesture of amazement. Then he bent over it and presently came staggering back up the shore bearing a white burden over his shoulder. It looked at that distance so very like a body that Wulfrey tumbled over on to his raft, and paddled across to the spit, and ran along the shore to where the mate was kneeling now alongside his find.

It was the body of a woman, pallid and sodden, with her long dark hair all astream, her white face pinched and shrunken and blue-veined, with dark hollows round the closed eyes, and colourless lips slightly retracted showing even, white teeth. She was clothed only in a long white nightdress, which the water had so moulded to her shapely figure that it looked like a piece of fair white marble sculpture. In life she must have been beautiful, Wulfrey thought, as he stood panting, and gazed down upon her.

"Dead?" he jerked.

"Ay, sure! She were lashed to yonder spar and I couldna leave her there.... The pity of it! She's been a fine bit."

Wulfrey knelt down, and slipped his hand to the quiet heart, instinctively but without hope, bent closer, gently raised one of the closed eyelids, and said hastily, "There may be a chance. Help me back home with her! Quick! You take her feet...." and he taking her under the arms they hurried back along the spit.

"She is not dead from drowning anyway," he jerked as they went. "The exposure may have killed her.... She must have suffered dreadfully."

It was no easy task to get her on board, but they managed it somehow, and laid her gently among the blankets in Wulfrey's bunk.

"Now.... Bags of hot sand, as quick as you can and as many.... Then mix some hot rum and water—not too strong,"—and Macro found himself springing to his orders with an alacrity which would have surprised him if he had had time to think about it.

Wulfrey, his professional instincts at highest pressure, drew off the clinging garment, muffled the sea-bitten white body in the blankets, and through them set to gentle vigorous rubbing, to start the chilled blood flowing again.

Macro came hurrying in with hot sand from the hearth, wrapped in linen and tied with strands of untwisted rope.

"Good! ... As many more as you can," said the Doctor, and placed them against the cold, blue-white feet, and rubbed away for dear life.

By degrees he packed her all round with hot sand-bags, Macro heating them as fast as they cooled, in a frying-pan over the fire. He placed them under her arms and between her shoulders, and never ceased his vigorous friction except to renew the bags.

Each time the mate came in, his face asked news, and each time Wulfrey shook his head and said, "Not yet," and went on with his rubbing. His own blood was at fever-heat with his exertions in that confined space. But that was all the better. His superfluous warmth might transmit itself in time to the chill white body of his patient.

Macro came in with hot rum and water, and Wulfrey poured a few careful drops between the still-livid lips, watched the result anxiously, and followed them up with more, and then resumed his patient rubbing.

For over an hour they worked incessantly, and then Macro was for giving it up as hopeless.

"'S no good. She's gone, sure," he said.

"I don't think so.... Too soon to give up anyway," and the Doctor worked on tirelessly. "If she should come round—"

"She won't."

"—She'll be starving. You might break up some hard-tack very small and warm it up in some weak rum and water," and he went on with his rubbing.

And at last, when he had almost given up hope himself, he had his reward. The mate, poking in a head deprecatory of further waste of time and energy on so hopeless a job, stood staring amazedly. For the pinched dead look of the pitiful white face had given place to a faint presage of life, like the first flutter of dawn on the pallid darkness of the night. Death had visibly relaxed his chill grip. There was a tinge of colour in the parted lips, and the white teeth inside had come together.

"She lives," said Wulfrey softly. "Her heart is at work again. Warm up that rum and water," and when it came he administered it cautiously in drops again, and this time they were visibly swallowed.

"Have the warm mash ready," he said; and even as he spoke the blue-veined lids fluttered, but so feebly as hardly to lift the long dark lashes from the white cheeks. And through that narrowed window the recovered soul looked mistily out on life once more.

He gave her still a little more hot rum and water, and when the warm mashed biscuit came fed her slowly with that, and she swallowed it hungrily if unconsciously.

Then, well satisfied with his work, he piled more blankets on her and left her to herself.

He had had many a fight with death, but none closer than this. The snatching of a life from the cold hand that was closing on it was always a cause for rejoicing with him. And this life, by reason of its comely tenement, had appealed to him in quite an unusual way.

Who she was, and what manner of woman, was still to be learned. For the moment it was enough that she had been within an ace of death and was alive again, and that she was unusually good to look upon.

XXV

When the Doctor had had a plunge overboard to restore the vitality he had expended on his patient, they sat down to eat, and the mate was inclined to enlarge somewhat exuberantly on the morning's work,—upon his own share in it especially.

"A wonderful fine piece of goods for any man to drag out of the water. I'm doubting if you'd have seen her if you'd bin there, Doctor. Just happened to lift my eye that way, and the white of her caught it, and in I went. Not that I thought she could be living, you understand. She felt like Death itself when I carried her ashore in my arms—"

"She'll be distressed for lack of clothes when she's ready to get up. But that won't be to-day anyway. Do you think you can light on any out yonder?"

"Lit on some last time I was there, but left 'em 'cause they were no use to us. That lot'll mebbe be gone, but there's plenty more for the finding. I'll see to it to-morrow."

"She will be grateful to you, I'm sure."

"She should, for if it hadn't bin for me she'd be tumbling about on yon spar still, and dead by this time, I'm thinking."

"She couldn't have stood much more, that's certain. I was near losing hope myself at times."

"Wouldn't have believed she'd ever come back if I hadn't seen it. It's being a doctor made ye keep on so."

"One feels bound to keep on while there's a possible chance left. In this case one couldn't but feel that there was a chance, if only a small one. We've done a good day's work to-day."

"Ay," said the mate, and presently, "I'm thinking I'll go out there today to get her some clothes. They'll need a lot of drying, you see."

"Can you do it before dark?"

"I'll do it. Ye'll see to her."

"I'll see to her all right. A little more food and then the longer she sleeps the better. If she'd lie where she is for a couple of days it would be all to the good."

"Then I'll go," but he came back to bend down into the little companion-way and say, "If she's asking, ye'll tell her it was me pulled her out the water."

"I'll tell her."

When, presently, Wulfrey went to see how she was going on, he found her sleeping quietly the sleep of utter exhaustion, and as he stood looking at her it seemed to him that she grew more beautiful each time he saw her.

The long wet tresses, whose clamminess he had carefully disposed behind the rolled-up blankets which served as a pillow, were drying to a deep warm brown. As they carried her in he had thought her hair was black. It was very thick and long. The texture of her skin, now that the coursing blood had obliterated to some extent the pinch and the bite of the sea, was fine and delicate, he could see, though suffering still from the salt.

The pink fingers of one hand had pulled down the blankets round her neck as though she had craved more air, and the soft white neck was smooth and white as marble. The one ear turned towards him was like a delicate little pink shell.

All these things he noted before his gaze settled on the quiet sleeping face, and lingered there with a strange new sense of joyous discovery and unexpected increase, as one might feel who suddenly unearths a hidden treasure.

He wondered again who she was and whence she came. Of gentle birth, he was sure. It showed in every feature of the placid face,—in the strong sweet curves of a not too small mouth,—in the delicately-turned nostrils,—in the soft level brows,—in the long fringing lashes which, with the shadows left by her sharp encounter with Death, cast about her closed eyes a misty enchantment full of witchery and allurement. He wondered what colour her eyes would be when they opened.

A wide white forehead, somewhat high cheek-bones, and a round well-moulded chin, added a fine dignity to the sleeping face. He stood so long gazing at its all-unconscious fascination that he feared at last lest the very earnestness of his look might disturb her.

So he picked up her only earthly possession, and leaving her, sleeping soundly, in sole charge of the ship, paddled across to the nearer shore, washed the salt out of her dainty single garment in a fresh-water pool, and spread it in the sun to dry, and then went after rabbits for her benefit when she should waken ravenous.

Returned on board, after a glance at his still-sleeping patient,—who lay so motionless that, but for the slight, slow rise and fall of the blankets over her bosom, one might have deemed her dead,—he set to the making of as tempting a soup as rabbit and rice could furnish, and regretted, more sorely than ever before, his lack of salt and seasoning.

Then he sat waiting for her to awake and for Macro to come home. If she did not wake of her own accord before sunset he decided to wake her himself. Sleep was without doubt the best of all restoratives, but Nature craves sustenance, and she was almost certainly starving. She would recover strength more quickly still if her system had something to draw upon.

Then, too, they had no light but that of the fire. If she woke up in the dark she would be sorely exercised in her mind to know where she had got to. It would be better to satisfy her, mentally and bodily, while still there was daylight to see by.

So, when the sun shone level through the western portholes, he went softly to where she lay, still sleeping soundly, and after watching her again for a moment, he placed his hand gently on her forehead.

She frowned at the touch and moved uneasily among her blankets. Then the heavy eyes opened and she lay staring wonderingly up at him, evidently trying to piece past and present together, and to make out where she was.

"Where am I? ... Who are you?" she jerked, in a voice that would have been rich and full if it had not been a little hoarse and husky. And the pink fingers grasped the blanket and drew it up under the rounded white chin.

"You are quite safe on a ship. I am a doctor. I want you to eat some warm soup and then you shall sleep again as long as you can. Here is your night-rail, washed and dried; perhaps you would like to put it on. I will go and fetch the soup."

When he came back presently she was visibly more at ease with her frills about her neck. She raised herself on her left elbow, and he placed the tin pannikin of soup in front of her, together with some broken biscuit.

"Can you feed yourself?" he asked.

"Oh, yes—if I had a spoon."

"I am sorry to say we have no spoons."

"No spoons?" and she stared at him in vast surprise.

"Perhaps you can make shift to drink it out of the pannikin. You see—"

"What a very odd ship—to have no spoons!" she took a sip of the soup and screwed up her lips. "Would you get me some salt, if you please? This soup—"

"I'm sorry, but we have no salt either. You see—"

"No salt?" and she shot another quick amazed look at him. "Mon Dieu, mon Dieu!" at which Wulfrey pricked up his ears. "Whatever kind of a ship—you did say a ship, did you not? Where is it going to?"

"It's not going anywhere. You see, it's practically a stranded ship though it's really afloat—"

She put her hand to her forehead and rubbed it gently, and then clasped it tightly, with her thumb at one temple and her fingers at the other. "I think my head is swimming yet," she said simply. "I cannot follow what you say."

"You'll understand as soon as you get on deck. This ship is bottled up inside a lake on an island. It has been here for probably thirty or forty years—"

"And you—have you been here all that time?"

"No, we were wrecked as you were, I suppose, on the banks out there. We managed to get ashore and found this ship to live on."

"Who are 'we'?"

"The mate of the ship and myself. We were the only ones saved. It was he saw you in the water and went in after you and brought you ashore."

"It was good of him. I will thank him. Where is he?"

"He's out at the wreckage trying to find you some clothes."

"He is a good man.... How long have you been here?"

"About three months."

"And no one has come to you in all that time?"

"You are the first. Now"—as she finished the soup—"take a good drink of this,"—some weak rum and water warmed up in another pannikin, over which she choked and coughed and wrinkled up her pretty nose distastefully. "Then you will go to sleep again, and in the morning I hope you will be all right."

"But there is so much I would like to know—"

"When you have had another long sleep. Are you quite warm?"

"Quite. That horrid stuff was like fire."

"You were cold enough when we found you. In fact we believed you were dead."

She shivered and nestled down among the blankets with a wave of colour in her face.

"I will sleep," she said quietly, and the Doctor left her to herself.

XXVI

It was almost dark before the mate pitched his cargo up on to the deck and came groping up the side after it.

"What luck?" asked Wulfrey, as he came up to help him.

"Brought all I could lay hands on, but I wouldn't like to say they're right kind of things."

"She'll be glad of them whatever they are."

"Has she come round?"

"I wakened her to take some soup and biscuit. Now I hope she will sleep till morning."

"And you told her it was me brought her ashore?"

"Yes, I told her that. She will thank you herself."

"Did you find out who she is and where she hails from?"

"Not yet. There'll be time enough to learn all that. My only desire was to get some nourishment inside her. She'll be building up now all the time she's sleeping."

"An' she's a good-looking bit of goods, eh?" asked the mate, as they sat eating.

"Very good-looking, I should say, and pulling round quickly. A gentlewoman without doubt."

"And how can ye tell that now? There's many a good-looking hussy that's not gentle-born."

"Undoubtedly," said Wulfrey, looking across the fire at him. "But this isn't one of that kind. She's a lady to the finger-tips."

"Ah—too fine a lady to live on a ship with the likes o' you and me, mebbe," growled the mate. "All same, if't 'adn't bin for me her leddyship ud be no more'n a little white corp tumbling about out yonder in its little white shift."

"Quite so," said Wulfrey, on whom this insistence on his sole claim to the salvaging of her was beginning to pall. "And if it hadn't been for me your bringing her ashore wouldn't have been of much service to her. So suppose we say no more about it. We'll divide the honours."

"If I hadn't brought her ashore ye couldn't have brought her round," growled the mate.

"Six of one and half a dozen of the other."

"No six of anything. Ye can't deny I brought her ashore."

Wulfrey lit his pipe and went up on deck, wondering what was working in the curious fellow's brain now.

When he went down again he found that Macro had opened his bundles and spread their contents out to dry, and had turned in. He just glanced at the varied assortment, and then, not to disturb his patient by going anywhere near her, spread some blankets in the room next to the mate's, and turned in himself. But he lay awake for a long time, wondering if the introduction of this new element into the limited circle of their lives was like to make for peace or otherwise.

XXVII

Wulfrey was up early, after a restless night, anxious to see how his patient fared. It was such a morning as usually followed their storms—clear and bright and sunny, with a pale-blue wind-swept sky, and a crisp breeze that tipped the green of the waves outside with white.

The first time he went softly in she was still sleeping, and with much satisfaction he noted the improvement the food and rest had wrought in her. Her face had filled out, the cheek-bones were less prominent, the dark circles round her eyes were not nearly so pronounced as before, though he imagined the long dark lashes and level brows would always lend a sense of depth and witchery to the great dark eyes themselves. The slight salting and roughening of the skin would speedily cure itself under the application of fresh water. She was almost herself again.

Their fire, on its bed of sand, was never allowed to go out. The supply of wood was unlimited and always, in the depths of the heap of white ashes, was a golden core of heat only waiting to be fed. So he set to and prepared coffee for her, and some flour-and-water biscuits, and when he went in again she was awake. She turned her head and looked at him, and his heart beat quicker than was its wont.

Her eyes, he perceived, were very dark blue, almost black, and looked the darker for the dark fringing lashes. They were very beautiful eyes, he decided, and very eloquent,—there was something of apprehension in them when first they met his, but it vanished when he spoke.

"You are better, I can see. You slept well?"

"I have only just wakened. You are the doctor."

"Yes, I am the doctor. I have got some coffee for you and some biscuits. I will get them."

"You are very good," as he came in with them and she raised herself on to her elbow again. "Did your friend get me any clothes? I feel quite well, and I would get up."

"He brought a whole heap of things. They have been spread out all night, but I'm afraid they'll never dry properly till they are washed in fresh water."

"And have you fresh water?"

"Oh, plenty,—Ashore there, in pools. If you can select a few things I will go across and steep them. They will soon dry in the sun."

"You are very good," she said again, and sipped the coffee and glanced up at him with a somewhat wry face. "No, you have no sugar on this strange ship—nor milk. Nor a brush, nor a comb, I'll be bound. Nothing but—"

"A brush and a comb we can provide at all events, and of exceptional quality. They belonged, I believe, to His Royal Highness the Duke of Kent."

"Edward of Kent?" she asked quickly. "Why—how...."

"Some ship, bringing home his belongings from Canada, must have been wrecked here. We have found quite a number of his things."

"Well, he would not mind my using them," she said quietly. "He is of a pleasant temper, quite the nicest of them all"; and as she finished the coffee and biscuits, "If you could find me ... a brooch—no, you will not have a brooch! ... a large pin or two,—but no, you will not have any pins! ... Let me see, then,—a sharp splinter of wood—"

"I can get you all the splinters you want. Might I ask—"

"To pin some of these blankets about me, do you see,—so that I may get up. And if you would get me that royal brush and comb—"

He trimmed up half a dozen sharp little skewers and left them with her, together with the brush and comb, and plunged overboard for his morning swim.

The mate was sitting by the fire at his breakfast when he went down again.

"Well?—how is my lady this morning?" he asked.

"So well that she is getting up."

"Them clothes all right?"

"She will pick out what she wants. But they'll never dry with the salt in them. I'll rinse them in one of the pools as soon as she says which."

"There's more mebbe for the finding—" and then they heard the door of her little room open and she came into the cabin to them.

The mate jumped up and stood staring as if she were a ghost; and even Wulfrey, who had already made her acquaintance, eyed her with surprise, and was confirmed in the idea that had been growing in him that there was foreign blood in her. He doubted if any Englishwoman could have made so brave a showing out of such poverty of material.

Fastened simply with her wooden skewers, she had one blanket draped about her as a skirt, and another covered her shoulders, with a high peak behind her neck, like a monkish cloak. And inside this rough calyx the fair white column of her neck rose out of its surrounding frillery like the stamen of a flower from its nest of petals. Her abundant hair, combed and brushed, but still lacking somewhat of its natural lustre, was coiled about her head in heavy plaits.

Though her garments were only rough blankets they were so disposed about her person that she stood before them tall and slim and graceful. Her eyes and face were all aglow at the novelty of her situation. Her feet were bare.

She sailed up to the mate with outstretched hand.

"It was you who brought me ashore out of that terrible sea," she said, and her voice was no longer hoarse and husky. "I thank you with all my heart."

Macro ducked his head but never took his eyes off her.

"Gosh! Ye looked very different then, miss," he jerked. "We scarce expected ye'd ever come round like this."

"I am the more grateful. But—what a wonderful room you have!"—as she looked round at the mate's barbaric hangings. "Silks and satins!—and such gorgeous colours!"

"There's bales of them about, miss, and you're very welcome to them. They'd look better on you than them blankets."

"But the blankets are warm, and the dreadful chill of the sea is still in my thoughts all the time. Now I would go on deck and understand about this strange ship of yours," and Macro hastened to lead the way and Wulfrey followed.

"But it is truly amazing," she said, as she gazed round at the sandhills and the spit, at the tumbling waves beyond, and the unruffled waters of the lake.

"And another ship! Who lives there?"

"No one. There is not another soul on the whole island but we three," said Wulfrey.

"It sounds dreadfully lonely."

"It is not so lonely as the sea."

"No, it is not so lonely as the sea. The sea is dreadful, and oh, so-o-o cold when you are dying in it slowly, an inch at a time," and she shivered again at the recollection.

"You must try to forget all about it."

"I shall never forget it. That is not possible. The memory of it is frozen into my soul. What noise is that?" she asked, listening intently with her hand uplifted.

"It's a great cloud of sea-birds that haunts the island. All the wrecks come ashore at that end, and they live there most of the time."

"It is like the wailing of lost souls."

"Right, miss!" broke in Macro. "That's what it is. They're only birds, mebbe, but there's the souls of the dead inside 'em, an' sometimes they're fair deevils when they come screaming round in a storm."

"I could believe that,—the souls of the dead without a doubt."

"Suppose we turn to something pleasanter," suggested Wulfrey. "Perhaps you will choose out the things you think most suitable from all that the mate brought over from the wrecks?"

"From the wrecks?" ... and she glanced at him doubtfully with a little shiver. "It does not sound too nice."

"We will bring them up. You will see them better here," and they spread the deck with Macro's latest importations.

"Mon Dieu, mon Dieu!" murmured she, as she turned them over with curious fingers, and held them up to adjudge their style and make. "But they are things of the days before the flood! ... They are too amazing! ... They are wonderful beyond words!"

"Could ye no alter them to your needs, mebbe?" suggested Macro hopefully.

"Perhaps—with needle and thread and scissors. But have you these?"

"Mebbe I can find 'em for ye. There's the cargoes of hunderds o' ships out there. Ye can find a'most anything if ye look long enough. And mebbe there's newer things if I can light on 'em."

"And some shoes and stockings, think you? I would be very glad of them. It feels strange to go with bare feet."

"I'll find 'em if there's any there."

"It is very good of you. I thank you. Could I perhaps come too?"

The idea evidently appealed strongly to him. He looked at her eagerly, and hesitated, but finally said, "It's no easy getting there. There's over six miles' walk through the sand, then near a mile of wading up to your neck in the water, and sometimes a bit of a swim, all according to the tide. Some day, mebbe, I'll mek a bit raft to tek ye across from the point there—just to see what it's like. But ye want these things and I'll get along quicker alone."

"I thank you all the same. It will be for some other time then," and Macro let himself down on to his raft and paddled away to the spit. She stood watching him till he landed and set off at speed towards the point.

"He is truly good-hearted," she said, as he disappeared. "He is not all English?"

"He is from the islands off the west coast of Scotland, but he confesses to a strain of Spanish blood also."

"And why confesses? It is not, I suppose, his own doing. One confesses to a fault. Is a strain of foreign blood a sin in your eyes then, Monsieur le Docteur?" she asked, with pointed emphasis.

"By no means. I should have said he rejoices in it."

"We English—British, I should say,"—with a fleeting gleam of a smile—"are too apt to look upon all foreigners as of lower breed than ourselves, which is quite a mistake and leads to much misunderstanding. Every nation has distinctive qualities of its own, is it not so?"

"Undoubtedly. And unless one knows them by personal experience one should not pass judgment. I must confess to being nothing of a traveller."

"How came you here?" she asked abruptly.

"I was bound for America—or Canada, with the intention of settling out there. It looks now, according to the mate, as though this strip of sand has got to suffice us for the rest of our lives."

"Really?" ... with a startled look. "Is there no getting away then? Does no one ever come here?"

"None but dead men, if they can help it, apparently. You were an exception to the rule. So were we. We have none of us any right to be here alive."

"If I had some shoes and stockings, and some proper clothes, I believe I could be quite happy here," she said. "That is if one has not also to starve."

"There is no need to starve. The island is over-run with rabbits. There are fish in the lake here if only we could catch them, and out there among the wreckage are all kinds of things—casks of pork and beef, and coffee, and rum, and flour—enough to last us for hundreds of years."

"It is a most excellent retreat."

"If one were sick of the world. But you surely are too young to have arrived at that stage."

"One may be young and yet be sick of one's world.... Sometime I will tell you.... Now, if you please, I will take a few of these things and you will show me your pool and I will wash them—"

"Oh, I'll do all that for you—"

"Not at all. Besides, with your permission and if you will leave me quite alone, I would like also to wash in fresh water. I too shall never feel quite dry until I have done so."

He assisted her down to the other raft, through a break they had long since made in the side for that purpose, and paddled ashore. There he showed her the pool they had set apart for washing, and told her he would come back for her at whatever time she chose.

"In two hours, please," and he went off into the sand-hills.

But his mind stubbornly refused to interest itself in rabbits. He dropped down on the sunny side of a hummock and let his thoughts run on this most surprising addition to their company. What could possibly explain her,—young, beautiful, of undoubted birth and breeding, yet ready to renounce the world, of which her twenty years or so had apparently given her a surfeit, and to welcome the chance of a hermit life?

It was a puzzle beyond any man's understanding. All his thinking led him only towards shadowy possibilities. And these the thought of her sweet face and clear frank outlook rejected instantly as libels on her fair fame, which he, with no more knowledge than he now had, yet felt himself prepared to defend with all his might against the whole world. If that girl was not all that she seemed and that he believed her to be, he would never trust his own judgment again.

All the same, it was very amazing, and she filled his thoughts to such an extent that the rabbits hopped fearlessly about him as he sat thinking of her; and it was long after the two hours before he came to himself, and rewarded their temerity by knocking a couple on the head and striding away back to find her.

She was sitting waiting for him, with a fresh-water brightness in her face, her hair coiled loosely round her head, and her washing still drying in the sun. She hastily bundled up her things at sight of him and came along to meet him.

"I began to fear you had forgotten me," she said.

"Very much to the contrary. It was our dinner I came near forgetting," and he dangled the rabbits before her. "You feel better for the fresh water?"

"Oh, very much better. And now I am hungry. When does your friend come back?"

"Not till evening as a rule. If he can lay hands on what you want he may come sooner to-day."

"And you—do you never go out there with him?"

"Oh, sometimes. But it doesn't attract me as it does him."

"Why then?"

"We are differently made, I suppose;—which is perhaps a good thing. He delights in finding things out there. I go out only for necessaries."

"What does he find—besides strange old clothes?"

"Oh, heaps of things—treasure. There are the cargoes of very many ships out there. They have been accumulating for hundreds of years, I suppose."

"And it does not attract you?"

"Not in the slightest."

"You are, perhaps, rich."

"I have enough, and I have my profession,—and little chance apparently of making any use of either."

"Ah..." and presently, "As to that, am I wrong then in thinking that if you had not been here I would most likely not have been here either?" and the wind and the sun had whipped a fine colour into her face.

"You would, perhaps, not be very far wrong."

"I remember it dimly, and in broken bits, like a horrible dream,—the crash, the terrible noise of the waves, the shouting and the screaming. It was the Captain himself who tied me to that mast when everything was going to pieces. And when the waves washed over me, and I felt myself slowly dying, I would have loosed myself if I could, to make an end. It was terrible to be so long of dying. And the cold of the sea!—oh, it was a horror," and she shivered again at the remembrance... "Then I died.... And then—long long afterwards—I found myself coming slowly back to life, and beginning to get warm again, with prickly pains like pins and needles all over me—"

"That was your blood beginning to flow again."

"—I felt warm hands rubbing me—rubbing, rubbing, rubbing. They must have rubbed for years, and, all the time, I was slowly coming back. They were very warm and soothing. And at last they rubbed me back to life."

"What was the name of your ship?"

"The 'Ben Lomond,' from Glasgow to New York, and the Captain was John MacDonald. It was a large ship and full of passengers. It is terrible to think of them all gone but me.—Oh, terrible!—terrible!"

"Might I ask your name—since we are like to be neighbours for the rest of our lives?"

"I am Avice Drummond," she said, with a quick glance at him. "And you?"

"Wulfrey Dale."

"And the mate?"

"Sheumaish Macro,—or Hamish, I'm not sure which."

"It is the same. He is a good man?—to be trusted?"

"I have no reason to think otherwise, but I have only known him since we landed here. He is chock full of superstition—"

"That is the Highlander in him."

"A bit hot-blooded too, and apt to boil over."

"That is the Spaniard."

"And he's crazy after the spoil out yonder."

"The Highlander again. It is, as you say, perhaps just as well you do not care for it, or you might have quarrelled."

"He is welcome to it all as far as I am concerned."

"I am of his country. I can understand how he feels. It is the old riever spirit in him finding its opportunity."

XXVIII

He was vitally conscious of her proximity to him as they paced through the soft sand towards the raft. The sight of her pink toes popping in and out from under her blanket-skirt quickened his blood. He knew without looking when she glanced round at him now and again, as when he had asked her name.

He had not thought that the feeling of a woman's eyes upon him could stir him to such an extent, no matter how wonderful they might be in their depths of eloquent darkness. He knew all about women,— physically, organically, professionally, and still held woman in reverence. Experience had taught him also that in reality he and his fellows knew very little about them beyond merest surface indications,— that there were in most women, perhaps in all, deeps beyond man's sounding, heights beyond his attainment,—a general elusiveness mysteriously comprehensive of feelings, instincts, passions, emotions, nerves, moods, humours, vapours, which a wise man accepted without expecting ever fully to understand.

That this shapely girl in her swathed blankets should affect him to such an extent that he was actually conscious of a superb new joy in living, of an absolute rejuvenescence, of a vitalising of all his energies, was a very great surprise to him. He could feel the blood running redder in his veins. His heart beat more briskly than it had done since he landed on the island.

But after three months of nothing but Macro and rabbits and screaming birds, it was not to be wondered at after all, he reasoned to himself. Life had been running on a low level. There had been nothing to lift them above the mere satisfaction of their bodily necessities. Eating, sleeping, getting through the days had sufficed them.

And here, into that rough husk of a life, had suddenly come a soul, to animate them both to higher things, even though it were no more than the ministering to her more delicate necessities.

Even Macro was feeling it, and was toiling out yonder, not for himself but for her. Without doubt life was immensely more worth living than it had been two days ago.

It was a joy even to cook for her, though he had always detested the preparation of food. To know beforehand what one was going to eat was sufficient to reduce one's appetite. To superintend a meal through all its stages, from raw to ready, put anything beyond the mere filling of an internal void out of the question.

But cooking for himself and cooking for her were matters of very different complexion, and he found himself considering culinary enterprises which surprised him greatly.

"You will let me help," she said, when they had climbed on board, and she saw him setting to work on the rabbits.

"Can you make biscuit?"

"If there is anything to make it with," so he provided her with flour and water and a frying-pan, and tackled his own repulsive job, looking forward to the best-made biscuit they had had since they came ashore.

"You have no butter—lard—dripping—fat—nothing?" she asked.

"There is some fat pork. We stew it with the rabbit as a rule."

"Get me some and I will render it down and we shall have much better cakes. Men never know how to cook unless they are trained to it. You have no seasonings of any kind—no? Nor salt?"

"Not a scrap."

"We might find something on shore there. I saw many little plants. We will search next time we go."

Yes, indeed, even the repellent cooking took on quite a new aspect and became a joyous pastime in her company, and they presently sat down to such a meal as he had not tasted since he left Liverpool. Many a more abundant one he had had, but none with such a flavour to it, and that was due entirely to the deft white hands that had helped to prepare it.

Meals hitherto had been in the nature of necessary nuisances. He and the mate had often sat eating without a word between them, and with perhaps less enjoyment in it than the rabbits out there among the sandhills. But, henceforth, meals would be feasts full of delight because of this stranger girl, whose presence would be salt and savour and seasoning to the poorest of fare.

"And he—the mate,—when does he eat?" she asked suddenly, after they had begun.

"Not till he gets back,—at night-fall as a rule. It's a good long way, you see, and he likes to spend all his time working."

"I hope he will find me some shoes,—and some needles and thread. Then I shall feel much happier.... And you really think we shall never get away from here?" she asked, quite cheerfully.

"If we could prevail on Macro to think of building a boat, instead of amassing treasure-trove, we might at all events try it. Nova Scotia is but a hundred miles away, he says,—"

"So close?"

"But he seems to think it a risky voyage, and so far we have come across no tools with which to build. You see, they are not things likely to come ashore."

"For myself, I believe I could be quite content to live here," she said again.

"For ever?—Never to get back to the larger life of the world as long as you lived?"

"Ah—that! ... I do not know.... It is a very hollow life after all, that larger life of the world."

"To grow old here," he said thoughtfully, emphasising his points with slowly nodding head. "To be the last one left alive perhaps.... To be all alone, sick, starving, dying slowly in the dark, unable to lift a finger...."

"I would drown myself if it came to that. It sounds horrible.... Perhaps, after all, we had better build the boat and get away."

"But I don't know that we can. I know nothing about boat-building even if I had the tools, and Macro won't turn to it till he has raked through the wreckage, and that will take him about a hundred years. It grows with every storm, you see."

"We must make him."

"And the tools?"

"We must find them."

"Two difficult jobs, perhaps impossible ones. You might perhaps prevail on Macro, but even he can do nothing without tools.... But, if I may venture to say so—it is surely early days for you to have discovered the hollowness of life, and to feel ready to spend the rest of it on a sandbank. Life should hold more in it than that for you."

She looked meditatively across at him for a moment, then seemed to make up her mind. "It is natural you should wish to know.... I will tell you.... It is a somewhat sorry story, but I think you will understand.... My name told you nothing?"

"Nothing—except that it was a very pretty name."

"I feared it would. It is natural, I suppose, to imagine that the whole world knows of one's misfortunes. Have you ever heard of the Countess d'Ormont?"

"The name is familiar to me in some way," he said, staring at her in surprise at the trend this was taxing.

"But I cannot recall—"

"And the Comte d'Artois—"

"Of course!" he nodded. "Now I remember—"

"The Countess d'Ormont was Margaret Drummond, my mother. My father is Charles Philippe, Comte d'Artois, brother of the poor King, Louis, whose head they cut off; and I hate and detest him for his treatment of her.... She is dead, my poor dear one! ... She believed at first that she was properly married to him, and I have no doubt she was—in London. He is a poor thing, but he was very fond of her, for a time.... I was born at Chantilly. It was before his quarrel with the Duc de Bourbon, and we lived in Paris and elsewhere according to his caprice. When my mother learned all the truth, and that in Paris she was not legally his wife, it broke her heart, I think. I never remembered her but as sad and troubled. Except on my account she was not sorry to die, I know. I was in Paris all through the Red times, and saw—oh, mon Dieu,—the horrors of it all!—things I could never forget if I lived to be a thousand.... In London we were all very badly off.... But he liked to have me with him, and poor Mme de Polastron was very good to me, but she was a strange, strange woman.... Her death was a great blow to him ... and a great loss to me. He was really very badly off there, and I did not like the people he had about him,—de Vaudreuil, de Roll, du Theil, and the rest, and I made up my mind to seek my own life elsewhere. And that is about all."

"And you have friends in America—relatives perhaps?"

"My mother's people, in Virginia. They have prospered there.... The new life out there, where all men are equal, appeals to me. Now you understand why I would not have cared very much if Mr Macro had not brought me ashore and if you had not rubbed me back to life. I seem to have no place in the world. I hate the aristocrats for what my mother suffered at their hands, and I hate the others for the terrible scenes I passed through as a child. These things are stamped into my heart and brain for ever. And that is why this lonely island, far away from it all, seems better to me than any place I know."

"You would grow tired of it."

"I could never grow as sick of it as I did of what I have left. It is not perhaps a very full life, but neither is it hollow and heartless. You I can trust, and Mr Macro also. It is lonely, but it is sweet and peaceful—"

"Wait till you see it in a storm."

"Storms are nothing when you have seen Paris drunk with blood. Ach!—the horror of it!" and she flung out her hands in a gesture full-charged with terrible memories, and then pressed them over her eyes as though to blot it all out.

"Well, we will do all in our power to make things comfortable for you, for as long as we have to stop here.... For your sake I hope it will not be long. Life should hold more for you than this," said Wulfrey, and mused much on the beautiful stranger and her strange history, and wondered what the future held for them all.

The mate came back when it was growing dark, very tired and in none too good a humour at the poverty of his finds. The results of a hard day's work, so far as he disclosed them, were a number of rusty sail-maker's needles which he had found in a chest, and half a dozen pairs of shoes, sodden almost out of semblance to leather.

Miss Drummond, however, was delighted and thanked him heartily.

"You will lend me a knife, and out of some of your beautiful silks I will make a new dress. I shall like that better than wearing any of those ancient ones which belonged to the dead."

"You're very welcome, miss. I broke into more'n a score of chests and boxes and not a blessed stocking among the lot. And them shoes are pretty bad, but they were best I could find."

"I will rub them with fat and they will return all right, and the needles will come bright with sand. I shall do very well now. Thread I can get from a piece of your linen. I thank you very much. Now you will eat some of my cakes."

"Best cakes ever I tasted," he said with a full mouth. "Takes a woman to cook properly. And best day's work I done since I got here, fishing you out the water."

"Perhaps—I am not yet sure, but I thank you all the same. When will you begin to build a boat for us to get away in?"

"Ah! ... Building a boat needs tools. What for do you want to get away so quick? You're but just got here."

"At present I am content. But—for always? I am not sure."

"Doctor, there, is always wanting to get away. But he knows we can't build a boat without tools. An' I put it to him—has he so much as set eyes on a tool out yonder since we come ashore?"

"I can't say I have, but then I haven't seen as much of the wreckage as you have. There may be any amount of—"

"Oh, ay, there mebbe! But so far we haven't struck 'em, an' it's no good talking o' boats till we got the tools."

"We will look for them," said The Girl confidently.

"Oh, ay, ye can look for 'em, and mebbe sometime a boat'll come ashore ready-made, or one that we can make shift to patch up. Meantime we've got all we want here and there's plenty more for the getting out yonder. So be content, say I, miss, for by rights the Doctor and me ought to be two clean-picked white skeletons out there on the pile, an' you ought to be a little white corp tumbling about on yon spar for the birds to peck at."

"Are there skeletons out there?" she asked with a shiver.

"Heaps."

"I think I will not go. I have seen so much of Death. I would forget it for a time."

"Ye'll meet him sure if ye try to get across from here in any boat we could build," growled the mate, and filled his pipe and his pannikin.

XXIX

Next morning Macro went off as usual to the wreck-pile, and Miss Drummond set to work on her dressmaking. Wulfrey hoisted up out of the hold for her such pieces of silk and linen as she required, and scoured a couple of the smallest needles with sand till they were usable. Then, with the sharpest knife he could find among their stock, he cut out on the deck, under her direction, various lengths and designs which to him were meaningless, but replete with possibilities from her point of view.

But when, presently, she saw him preparing to go ashore for water and rabbits, she threw down her needle and said, "I will go also. You will not mind?"

"On the contrary, I shall mind very much. I shall feel honoured by your company. It is a pleasure to have someone to talk to again," and he helped her down on to the raft, and thought how much less interesting shoes were than little naked feet.

"Do you not then talk much with Mr Macro?"

"Sometimes, and sometimes we hardly spoke all day."

"You quarrelled?"

"Hardly that, but ... well, we had not very much in common, you see. His mind was always full of his discoveries out there, and one got rather tired of it at times."

"I do not think I shall like him as much as I thought."

"Why that? I'm sorry if I have said anything that seems to reflect on him in any way."

"I am used to judging for myself. It is a look that comes into his eyes at times,—like a horse when it is going to bite. No,"—with a decided little nod,—"I shall not like him as much as I hoped; and I am sorry, for I ought to feel grateful to him for pulling me out of the water."

"I'm glad you are feeling grateful for being alive, anyway," he said, with a smile. "That is better than being doubtful about it."

"It is better to be alive than dead. And if we have to live here all our lives—very well, we must put up with it. And if you and he die, and I am left all alone, and get old and sick, as you said yesterday, I will make an end of myself. I was thinking about it all night except when I was sleeping."

"I'm sorry to have troubled you so. We will hope for better things. Anyway I have no intention of dying for some time to come, if I can help it."

"You must not," she said, with sudden deep earnestness. "I count it God's good mercy that you are here, for I can trust you."

"I am used to being trusted," he said quietly.

"I know. I can see it.... If I had been all alone ... with nobody but him ... But, no! I could not..."

"I don't know that there is any harm in him."

She sat nodding her pretty head meaningly.... "You have not seen men loosed from all restraints as I have. I was but a child and did not fully understand. But I see their faces and their eyes still, fierce and wild and hungry for other than bread. When men are answerable to none but themselves they become wild beasts and devils."

"It is a hard saying."

"But it is true. I have seen it."

"And women?"

"They are as bad, but in a different way. Oh, they are terrible."

"And you and I and Macro here? To whom are we answerable?" he asked, to sound her to the depths.

"He is answerable to you," she said quickly. "You and I are answerable to one another, and to God, and to ourselves—to all that has made us what we are. I do not think you could trespass outside all that, any more than I could."

"I do not think I could. I am honoured by your confidence in me."

He helped her ashore, and they filled the buckets at the pools, and then she expressed a wish to see something more of this sandbank where they might have to pass the rest of their lives.

So they threaded their way among the hummocks to the northern shore, and, at the first green valley they came to, she went down on her knees and examined carefully the nestling growths on which the rabbits fed, and found among them certain pungent little plants which she thought might serve for flavouring, and they gathered enough to experiment with.

The firm smooth tidal beach, with the ripples creaming up it in sibilant whispers tempted her to bare feet, and she handed him her shoes and splashed along as joyously as a child.

"It is a most delightful island," she said. "I do not think I would ever tire of it."

"Oh, yes, you would. It is all just the same, you see. You can walk on and on like this and round the other side for forty or fifty miles, and every bit of it is just like the rest."

"I think it is beautiful."

"It gets monotonous in time. The only diversion is the pile of wreckage down yonder. That is constantly changing and growing."

"And discovering more skeletons! It feels odd to think that I should have been one myself if you two had not happened to be here."

"I'm sure it feels very much nicer to be comfortably clothed with flesh," and glancing at her supple grace and entrancing bare feet and ankles, he found himself profoundly grateful for the facts of the case. The thought of her as a skeleton was eminently distasteful to him.

"Yes, it is better. Dead bodies and bones have always had a horror for me; but not the simple fact of being dead, I think.... I do not think I would be afraid to die—if it were not very painful. But ... well, the thought of my dead body is horrid to me. I would not like to see it."

"You're not likely to be troubled to that extent anyway."

"No, one is at all events spared that. But why do you talk of such unpleasant things when the sun is shining and the waves are sparkling? Tell me about yourself. All you have told me so far is that you are a doctor, and that your name is Wulfrey Dale. I never heard the name Wulfrey before. And that you were going out to Canada when you were wrecked here. Why were you going out?"

He would have liked to be as frank with her as she had been with him. But that was impossible. Another woman's good name was too intricately interwoven with his story, and the whole matter was so open to misjudgment. If he tried to explain he must either label that other woman as murderess or himself as an incapable doctor, and he chose to do neither. He wished she had not asked, but found it only natural that she should desire to know all about him.

"I have nothing much to tell," he said. "I come from Hazelford, in Cheshire. My father had the practice there and when he died I succeeded to it. But the wander-spirit seized me. I wanted a larger sphere. The new world called, and I came,—as it turns out to a still smaller place—"

"But we are not going to stop here all our lives. We must build that boat and get away."

"We will live in hope, anyway, but for that we are dependent on Macro, and he's not an easy man to drive."

"We will see," she said confidently. "How do you catch your rabbits?"

"Every one of these little valleys is full of them. As soon as you appear they all bolt for their holes and in the panic they tumble over one another and you pick them up."

"I am always sorry to kill things, and they are so pretty," she said, as they crept cautiously up the side of the nearest hummock. "But they are very good and I suppose one must eat."

"Or starve. Now—see!" and he jumped down into the hollow, which scurried into life under his feet, and came back in a moment with a couple of rabbits which he had already knocked on the head.

"Poor little things!" she said, stroking the soft fur.

"They were dead before they knew it.... Our lake ends there," he said, pointing it out to her from where they stood on top of the hummock. "But the island goes on and on, all just the same as this as far as you can see."

"It looks very lonely ... but I like it," and she sat long, with her hands clasped round her knees, gazing out over the wandering yellow line of sandhills, and the slow-heaving seas which broke in white-fringed ripples along the beach.

"And you left no ties behind you there in England?" she asked suddenly, showing where her thoughts had been.

"No ties whatever. Friends in plenty, but nothing more. When my father died I was quite alone in the world."

She nodded fellow-feelingly, and they sauntered back in a somewhat closer intimacy of understanding and liking for one another.

XXX

Macro had had a good day out there, and returned in the best of humours with himself and as hungry as usual.

As he ate he enlarged on his finds, and when he had finished his supper he piled the fire with light sticks to make a blaze, and spread them out for Miss Drummond's inspection.

He had evidently lighted on the personal baggage of some person of quality. There were rings and brooches and pins and bracelets, of gold and silver, set with coloured stones, a couple of small watches beautifully chased and studded with gems, a small silver-mounted mirror all blackened with sea-water, two gold snuff-boxes with enamelled miniatures on the lids—quite a rich haul and very satisfactory to the craving of his spirit.

The Girl examined them all carefully, and Wulfrey, watching her quietly through the smoke of his pipe, thought she handled them somewhat gingerly and distastefully, and understood her feeling in the matter. And now and again he caught also a glimpse in the mate's black eyes, as they rested on her, of that which she herself had felt and resented.

It might be only the unconscious continuation of the gloating proprietorial look with which he regarded his treasures, which still gleamed in his eyes when they rested on her as though she herself were but one more of them. But whatever it was it was not a pleasant look, and Wulfrey was not surprised at her discomfort under it. He was as devoutly glad that he was there as she could be. Alone with this wild riever, in whom the cross-strain of his wilder forebears was running to licence in its sudden emancipation from all life's ordinary shackles.... It would not bear thinking of. Yes, he was truly glad he was there. And then he remembered, with another grateful throb, that if he had not been there, neither would she have been. For the mate most assuredly would never have brought her back to life.

"Some of these are of value," she was saying. "But they are rather pitiful to me.... Some dead woman has treasured them and she is gone. Perhaps you came upon her skeleton out there.... But they are not all real stones—"

"And how can ye tell that now?" asked Macro gruffly.

"I can tell at once by the feel of them. That now"—pointing to a heavily-gemmed bracelet—"the emeralds are real, the rubies are real, but they are all small. The white stones are not diamonds, but very good imitations. They look almost as well, but they are not diamonds. If they were that bracelet alone would be worth some hundreds of pounds."

"Deil take 'em! And you can tell that by feeling at 'em?"

"I can tell in a moment. You see I have handled many jewels—some of the finest in the world, and I have seen very many imitations of them."

"The deil ye have! How that?"

"I have lived among those to whom they belonged, and I am very fond of precious stones."

He went away to his own cabin and came back presently with a good-sized bundle done up in blue velvet, and opened it before her. Wulfrey was surprised at the extent of his treasure-trove. For these were only his most precious possessions. He knew that he had in addition considerable store of silver articles which he had been allowed to examine from time to time.

If Macro's idea had been to dazzle her with his riches he must have been disappointed. For she greeted the display with a depreciatory "T't—t't!"—and said presently, as she picked out a piece here and there for examination, "It looks like a peddler's pack.... And it makes me sad to think of those to whom they belonged...."

"They've no further use for them. And there's no telling who they belonged to. They're for any man's getting now," said Macro defensively.

"I suppose so. All the same ... For me—no!" with a most decided shake of the head.

"Are they good, or is there false ones among them too?"

"Many are good," she said, passing them rapidly and somewhat distastefully under her delicate fingers, "but not by any means all.... You have laboured hard to accumulate so much."

"Harder than ever I worked in my life before, but it suits me fine."

"But what good is it all unless you can get away from here and turn it to some good use?"

"We'll talk of that when I've got all I want, mebbe."

"You are like a miser then, ever accumulating and loth to spend."

"Just that! Ye see I never had siccan a chance before,—nor many others either. Ye wouldna care for a ring or two, or mebbe a bracelet or a brooch?"

"Oh, I could not. It is good of you to offer, but ... no, I thank you. They would always make me think of the skeletons out there. Poor things!"

"They don't hurt, and they're aye laughing as if 'twas all a rare joke," which made her shiver with discomfort and draw her blanket closer round her neck at the back.

"Well, well!" said he, with a hoarse laugh, as he made up his bundle again. "Folks has queer notions. Ef 't 'adn't been for me—"

"And the Doctor," she interposed quickly.

"Ay—and the Doctor there—"

"I know," she cut him short, "and it is very much nicer to be sitting here by a warm fire than tumbling about on a mast out there. I appreciate it, I assure you."

Perhaps it was to restore the balance of his spirits, which had suffered somewhat from the discovery that his treasure was not all he had thought it, that made him apply himself more heartily than usual to the rum cask that night. By the Doctor's advice any water they drank from the brackish pools was mixed with a few drops of rum. Macro always saw to it that a cask was at hand, and he himself took but small risks as far as the water was concerned. But he could stand a heavy load, and as a rule it only made him sluggish and uncompanionable.

This night, however, as he sat dourly smoking, and taking every now and again a long pull at his handy pannikin, it seemed to set him brooding over things and at times he grew disputatious.

Miss Drummond had turned with obvious relief to the Doctor and said, "These things do not interest you?"

"As curiosities only, not intrinsically. I never had any craving for jewelry!"

"It is a feminine weakness, I suppose, though I have known men who outvied even the women in their display."

"We have simpler ways in the country, and more robust."

"Mebbe you're right, and mebbe you're wrong," growled Macro, as the result of his cogitations. "I d'n know, an' you d'n know, an' Doctor, he d'n know, an' none of us knows.... They're mebbe all right... What the deil wud folks want mixing bad stuff wi' good like that?"

"It is done sometimes to make a larger show, and sometimes as a matter of precaution," said Miss Drummond quietly. "Those who have valuable jewels are always in fear of having them stolen. They have imitations made, and wear them, and people believe they are the real ones. It is commonly done."

"An' is it a thief you wud call me for taking these?"

"These are dead men's goods and dead women's, and you do not know whose they were, so it is not stealing. But, for me, I do not like them."

"An', for me, I do. An' more I can get, better I'm pleased."

"Each to his taste, and you are very welcome to them all. Now, if you please, we will forget all about them, and speak of pleasanter things," and she turned to Wulfrey and began questioning him as to his knowledge of London, which was not nearly so extensive as her own.

The mate smoked and drank and glowered across at them. More than once Wulfrey caught his glance resting balefully on The Girl. More than ever was he thankful that he was there to look after her.

XXXI

"No," said The Girl to Wulfrey, as she sat busily sewing at her new dress on deck next morning, "I do not like your mate as much even as I thought. Do you know what I would do if you were not here?"

"What would you do?"

"I would go and live on that other ship, or else among the sandhills."

"Either would be very uncomfortable. I am glad I am here."

"He looks at me as though I were another piece of his treasure-trove, especially when he is getting drunk. If he had tried to wrap me up with the rest in that blue bundle of his I should not have been very much surprised."

"He brought you ashore, you see."

"Well? What use would that have been if you hadn't brought me back to life?"

"Not much, I'm bound to say. But I imagine he considers it gives him first claim on you."

"First claim?—for what?" she asked quickly.

"Oh, on your regard, your gratitude,—"

"My gratitude, if you like. My regard—that goes only where I can respect and esteem. And for him—neither. If he were never to come back again from over there I would not in the least regret it."

It was as inevitable that these two should instinctively draw closer to one another, as that their doing so should create something of a breach between them and the mate, and that he should feel and resent it.

Except the untoward circumstances of their lot there was practically nothing in common between him and them. His outlook and aims were as different from theirs as were his habits and upbringing. Yet it did seem preposterous to them that three persons, situated as they were, should not be able to live together in peace and good-fellowship.

To the ancients, without doubt, the gods would have been apparent behind the slow-drifting white-piled clouds, and behind the storm-wrack and the mists, laughing at the perverse little ways of men, and watching with interest the inevitable tangle produced among them by the advent of a woman.

Since the year one, two have found themselves good company and the coming of a third has led to mischief. And yet even that depends on the spirit that is in them. More than once, since he landed on the island, Wulfrey had found himself wishing Providence had sent him honest Jock Steele for company, and that it was the mate's bones that were whitening out there in place of the carpenter's.

Whether he himself would have fared so well, if he had not stuck out his leg at risk of his life and helped the mate on to his raft, and so had come ashore alone, he was not sure. And again, whether, if he had been alone, he would ever have sighted The Girl on her mast, was doubtful. If they had much to put up with In Macro, they had also much to thank him for. And so—to bear with him as well as they might and give no occasion for offence if that were possible.

But it was no easy matter. They were having a spell of fine weather which enabled him to go out to the wreckage every day. And every night he came home ravenous, and ate and drank and afterwards sat smoking with scarce a word.

If they enquired how he had fared he growled the curtest of answers, and showed plainly that their polite interest in his doings was not desired by him. He showed them none of his finds, but sat smoking doggedly, and occasionally gazing through his smoke at The Girl in a way that distressed and discomforted her.

But there was nothing in it that Wulfrey could openly take exception to. Even a cat may look at a queen. The look in the mate's black eyes was akin to that with which the cat favours the canary, when he licks his lips below its cage;—if he only dared!

Still, they were free of him during the day, and the discomfort of him at other times but drew them closer together. But Wulfrey, watching the man cautiously, saw in him signs and symptoms that he did not like, which bade him be prepared for a possible change for the worse in their relationship.

For one thing, he was drinking more heavily than he had ever done since they landed, and the drink and the brooding of his black thoughts might well hatch out unexpected evil to one or other of them. As he lay there of a night, smoking and drinking, with a face of gloom and smouldering fires in his eyes, he was more than ever like a sleeping volcano which might burst forth in flame and fury at any moment.

But for the lurking possibilities of trouble, the cool way in which he devoted himself to his own private concerns, and left them to attend to all the irksome little details of the common life, would have had in it something of the humorous.

Miss Drummond was indignant and was for leaving him supperless when he came home of a night.

But Wulfrey rigorously repressed his strong fellow-feeling therewith, and determined that no provocation should come from their side. So they continued to make ample provision for all, and the mate helped himself as if by right. If, however, good-feeling on the part of the maker has anything to do with the compounding of cakes, as The Girl averred, those she made for the mate must surely have lacked flavour, for her views on the matter were most uncompromisingly expressed, both by hands and tongue, as she made them.

"Does he look upon us as his servants, then?"—with a contemptuous slap at the innocent dough.—"To do all his work without so much as a 'Thank you'?"—another vicious slap. "—And to be glowered at as if one were a rabbit that he wanted to devour!"—cakes pitched disdainfully into a corner till the time came to cook them.—"No!—for me, I wish he would stop out there among his skeletons and trouble us no more."

Her little tantrums at thought of Macro gave Wulfrey no little amusement. The vivacity of her manner as she delivered herself, blended as it was of Scottish frankness and French sparkle, made her altogether charming. He soothed her ruffled feelings, however, by his own eulogistic appreciation of the cakes she provided for their own use, and it was then that she explained to him how intimately the character of a cake is associated with the feelings of its maker.

Matters came to a head a few days later, when the commissariat department began to run low in certain essentials.

"We're almost out of flour and pork, Macro," Wulfrey said to him, as the mate was preparing to set off as usual one morning. "Will you bring some back with you?"

The black-faced one hesitated one moment, and then cast the die for trouble.

"Well, you know where to get 'em," he growled.

"Yes, I know where to get them," and Wulfrey braced himself for the tussle. "But—"

"Well, then—get 'em, and be — to you!" and he leaped down on to his raft and set off for the shore.

XXXII

Wulfrey watched the mate's retreating figure for a minute or two and then turned quietly to The Girl.

"Are you prepared to trust me completely, Miss Drummond?" he asked.

"Absolutely. What is it you want me to do?"

"We cannot go on this way. He is becoming insufferable. Unless you have anything to say against it, we will take possession of the other ship—you and I, and leave him here to himself."

"Yes—let us go. When shall we go? Now?"

"We must make it habitable first. It is as empty as a drum, you know."

"All the better, since we are overcrowded here with that man. It is to get away from unpleasantness that we go."

"We shall need fire,—that means sand for a hearth; and wood—we have heaps here; and cooking things—we will take our fair share, and our blankets. Everything else I can get out yonder."

"Allons! Let us go at once and get them."

He looked carefully round the horizon. "The weather will hold for a day or two still, I think. Today we had better lay our foundations—sand, wood and so on. Then tomorrow we will go out to the pile and take our cargo straight to the other ship."

"What do we do first?" she asked, abrim with excitement.

"We will take a load of wood across at once and then go for sand. We will leave the cabin open to air it and light a fire."

She was as eager as a child going to a new house, and when presently he helped her up over the side of the other schooner, she tripped to and fro delightedly, and could hardly wait till he forced back the rusty bolts of the cabin hatch with a piece of wood, so impatient was she to inspect the new home.

"I like it better than the other," she said, as they stood in the little cabin.

"Why? It seems to me just about the same."

"The man of gloom is not here. It makes all the difference."

They got their wood on board, and he tumbled it down the fore-hatch, which was easier to handle than the main. Then they went ashore, filled a bucket with fresh water, got half a dozen rabbits and a supply of the pungent herbs.... "Why so many?" she asked, and he said quietly, "I don't want to hit him below the belt,"—at which she laughed—"We can afford to be generous. The breach will be wide enough as it is."

Then they loaded the raft with sand, and getting back to the ship, arranged their hearth, and with his flint and steel succeeded at last between them in lighting a thin chip, which he ceremoniously handed to her and begged her to start their fire.

And as she knelt and applied it, and coaxed and blew till the cheerful flames shot up with a crackling shower of sparks, and the thin blue smoke streamed up the companion-way, still kneeling she waved her hands above it and said, "Light and warmth and comfort and peace! God bless the fire!" and he endorsed it with a hearty "Amen!" and thought he had never seen a fairer sight.

When the mate got home that night, he was somewhat surprised to find a supply of food and no objections made to his helping himself. He chuckled grimly, and showed by his face and manner that he considered the matter settled on eminently satisfactory lines.

They made no enquiries as to his doings and he volunteered no information. Wulfrey and Miss Drummond talked together as if he were not there. He lay and smoked, and drank, and glowered at them.

In the morning he set off as usual, and when they had taken their blankets and their fair share of cooking-utensils across to the 'Martha,' and got them all stowed away, Wulfrey turned to The Girl and said, "Now I will go out to the store-house yonder and get all I can lay hands on."

"I will come too. Perhaps I can help. I am very strong, and I would rather go with you than wait here alone. But I do not wish to see any skeletons if you can manage it."

"We will try to keep clear of them,—if you are quite sure—"

"Have we got to swim, as that man said?"

"I may have to. You need not. I will go out to the pile and make a raft, and take you across on it. And all that will take time, so the sooner we're off the better."

They paddled across to the spit and hurried along to the point, as nondescript a pair as could well be imagined in disrespect of clothing, but in all else that mattered—in all the great essentials that make for vigorous life—in health, good looks, and high and cheerful spirit—pre-eminently good to look upon.

For work on the wreck-pile the less one wore the better; and so he was clad in one simple but sufficient garment, which consisted of a long strip of linen wound many times round his waist and falling to the knees like a South Sea Island kilt. And she wore one of the prehistoric woman's sarks which Macro had brought over from the pile, and a similar, but slightly longer, kilt which swung gracefully a foot or so above her ankles as she walked.

He carried an axe in his hand, and had a knife at his back, in a seaman's belt which he had unhooked from its owner's body out there on the pile one day; and his face was somewhat grave and intent, since he was considering the possibilities of Macro's violent rejection of the situation he had himself created, and the consequences that would then ensue. But her bright face was all alive with the spirit of adventure and the novelty of this new departure.

"We look like Adam and Eve turned out of Paradise, and setting out to conquer the world," she laughed excitedly. "What would your friends think if they saw you so?"

"What they thought wouldn't trouble me in the slightest. If they understood they would understand. If they didn't it would not matter. We are doing what has to be done in the only way to do it. See the birds out there!"

"Are those really all birds? I thought it was a cloud whirling about," and she stood and stared in amazement.

"Listen and you'll hear them,"—and every now and again the south-west breeze brought them the thin strident wailing of the hungry myriads as they swooped and fought for their living.

"They sound horrid," said The Girl, with a sudden shadow on her face. "It is like the wailing of lost souls, as he said. Do they never attack you?"

"We have had more than one fight with them. But you can always escape by slipping down into a crack or jumping into the sea. Where did you learn to swim?"

"We had a cottage in the Isle of Wight for a year, when first we came from France, and I grew very fond of the water."

"Do you see Macro over there?" as they came to the end of the point. "He's hard at work. We'll tackle a different part. If you will sit down here and rest, I will get across and be back as soon as I can."

"Could I not come with you?"

"I don't know how deep the channels may be. Sometimes we can wade across, sometimes we have to swim."

"I don't mind. It can't make me any wetter than if I have to jump in because of the birds. And I have been wetter still."

"Very well. It will save much time," and they waded out alongside one another,—The Girl catching her breath at times with spasmodic little jerks of laughter, as she stepped into unexpected depths or a wave came higher than usual;—and he, intent as he was on the business in hand, yet mightily cognisant of her proximity and the penetrating and intoxicating charm of it.

When, at one sudden plunge, she gasped and clutched wildly at his bare arm, her touch sent the blood whirling through his veins. He took her soft wet hand, which was all of a tremble with excitement, in his strong and steady one, and she gripped it tightly and drew new strength from it.

Out on the great pile of wreckage in front, but somewhat towards their right, they caught glimpses now and again of Macro—a wild dark figure silhouetted against the pale-blue sky behind—as he climbed to and fro, and stood at times, and swung up his arms and his club and smashed his way through to the desire of his heart.

Wulfrey worked round to the left, and so came upon a channel which they had to swim. He fastened his axe into his belt at the back and they struck out together. He watched her anxiously at first, but was satisfied. She swam well and knowingly; they soon touched ground again, and another wade and another short swim brought them to the pile.

The Girl had been regarding it with curious eyes and ejaculations of wonder.

"But it is amazing!" she jerked, when at last they clung to a ledge of the chaotic jumble of flotsam and jetsam. "I never saw anything like it in my life."

"That's just as well. Now we'll climb up here, and you will rest while I gather wood and rope and make a raft. Then we'll see what fortune sends us."

"Whatever are all those?" she asked, when they had worked their way to the top, and stood looking round.

"Those are the bones of the ships that have perished here. There are hundreds of them half-buried in the sand."

"It is the most amazing sight I ever set eyes on," she said again, and sat and gazed at it all while he worked busily at the raft.

"Now," he said, climbing up to her again at last, "We will look for necessaries first and take anything else we come upon that may be useful. Those barrels are pork, but they are too heavy for us to handle—"

"Couldn't you break one open?"

"Then the birds would be on us like a shot. Some of them have got their eyes on us already," and he pointed to them swooping watchfully round. "We did that once and had to fight and run for it. Maybe we'll come across some smaller ones before we're done. Here's a small cask of rum. We'll make sure of that," and he rolled and carried it to their landing-place, and they scrambled on.

"These barrels are biscuits. Some of it may be good. We'll bring the raft round for it. Those small casks are flour. It's only good in the middle. We'll come round for one of them presently. We want some coffee. We're sure to come across some sooner or later."

"What is it like?"

"Small square cases about so big."

"Oh, I wonder what's in this great case."

"We'll soon see," and he smashed at it with his axe. "Hardware. We'll add to our stock since it's here."

"And this? Oh, I wish I had an axe too. I want to break open every box we come to," and he laughed out at her quick surrender to the riever spirit.

"Why do you laugh at me then? It would surely be helping you."

"I know just how you feel, and now you know just how Macro feels."

"I know just how he feels. It must grow upon one. I don't want any of the things, but still I would like to break open and find."

"We'd better stick to business. When we've got all we come across that will be of service I'll hand you the axe and you can smash away at anything you like, except your toes.... No doubt what's in that box anyway,"—for the ends of rolls of silk were sticking out of it. "I expect Macro has been over this ground already. Shall we take some?"

She picked out several rolls, saying, "They may come in useful, even if it's only to make our cabin as fine as his," and he stacked up the silk along with a raffle of rope, which was always to the good.

They scrambled to and fro, so busily smashing open cases and discussing their contents that they took no note of the birds gathering above them in ever-increasing numbers. Their ears had grown accustomed to their raucous clamour, and the fact that it had grown louder had not troubled them. But suddenly—they were delving into the side of a huge crate of blankets at the moment—the sky was darkened as by a cloud, and Wulfrey, glancing up in fear of a change in the weather, jerked out a sudden exclamation which made her jump. Then he crushed her roughly down into a narrow black chasm between the blanket-crate and another, and dropped in after her, just as the cloud, grown bold by its increase, came swooping down upon them.

Never in her life had she imagined such a nightmare experience. The bristling confusion of the wreckage, the shimmering blue sea beyond, the very light and peace of day itself, all were blotted out in an instant, and in their place was nothing but a prodigious whirling and swooping of vari-coloured feathered bodies, snaking necks, cold beady eyes, pitilessly craving them as food, cruel curved beaks keen to rend and tear, and a hideous clamour of wild wailings. The flutter and beat of myriad wings set the whole atmosphere throbbing, till the blood drummed furiously in The Girl's ears and her head felt like to burst.

She shrank down on something that crackled and subsided under her, feeling herself terribly bare to their assault. Wulfrey reached out an arm and groped for a loose blanket and dragged it over them and so hid the nightmare from her. His arm was bleeding when he drew it in.

"They will go presently when they find there is nothing to eat," he said into her ear.

"They looked as if they would tear one to pieces," and he could feel the shudder that shook her.

"They would try if they got the chance."

"They are awful.... Oh, listen!"—as the rest of the cloud, sure that such a clamour portended food, whirled round their shelter, brushed it with wings and feet, shrilled their needs and their disgust more loudly than ever, and swept away to seek more satisfying fare elsewhere.

The sound of them drifted away at last, occasional stragglers still swooped down to make quite sure there was not a scrap left, but presently these followed the rest and Wulfrey climbed up and looked about him.

"All right," he said, and reached down a hand to her. "I think they've gone after Macro," and he hauled her up into the light.

"Your arm!" she cried.

"Only scratches. No harm done.... What is it?" for she was staring with tragic face into the hole out of which she had just come.

And looking down into it he saw that he had flung her bodily on to what had been a skeleton, but was now only a confused heap of brittle bones.

"I'm sorry," he said, "but there was no time to pick and choose."

"It's a horrible place. Let us go home!"

"We'll go at once as soon as we've found some coffee ... and I would like another knife or two.... Look in that chest. Macro has opened it for us.... And if you find any tobacco, I'll thank you," and he rooted rapidly through one broken-open seaman's box, while she did the same by another.

"Tobacco—I think," she announced presently, ... "and a knife and a tinder-box."

"Another knife" was his find. "And we'll take these two coats—"

"Whatever for?"

"Well—if any of those screaming deevils, as the mate calls them, should come after us as we go back, you feel them less through a coat than on your bare skin."

"I don't think I'll come again."

"Oh, it's quite easy to avoid them, you see. And they soon go if they find nothing eatable."

"Hideous things! ... Will those cases be coffee?"

"I think so.... We'll chance one anyway.... And those small casks are rice. We're doing famously. Is there anything else you would like?"

"Heaps of things—spoons, forks, plates, stockings—"

"Here are stockings—" and he delved into his chest again.

"Truly—but twenty sizes too large. These boxes all seem to have belonged to men. Let us get home before those awful birds come back."

So they returned to the raft and pushed it slowly along the pile, from place to place, where the various portions of their cargo stood awaiting them, and Wulfrey wrestled manfully with casks and barrels and boxes in a way that would have astonished himself mightily three months before. And The Girl, eager to help as far as she could—brushing shoulders with him as they hauled and lifted, their hands overlapping at times, their bare arms in closest contact as they struggled with the insensate obstinacy of dead weights,—was very conscious of the play of the corded muscles in his arms and back, and the energy and determination of the quiet resolute face. And she was at once grateful and exultant in the knowledge that all the powers this man possessed were at her service, and that, if occasion should arise, they would be expended for her to the uttermost and without hesitation.

She experienced sensations entirely new to her. She found them good. They quickened her blood and stimulated her mind. She had seen much of men, more perhaps than most for her years, but men of a very different type,—unmuscular, powdered and peruked and befrilled, with airs and graces and velvet coats which hid the lack of virility within, and did duty for it to the world at large; men of wealth and highest culture and too often of meanest heart, self-seeking, intent only on their personal satisfactions, self-forgetful only in the pursuit of ignoble ends.

In every particular so different from this man. She had met but very few men whom she felt she could trust implicitly. Some of the most apparently sincere had proved the least worthy. And they were the most dangerous. They drew your trust, and so disarmed and then most treacherously betrayed you. Oh, she had seen it, time and again, and so her mind had come to look on men in general as beasts of prey, to be dreaded, and avoided except in the most open and superficial fashion.

But this was a man of another world. She had met none like him. He roused her and soothed her as none of those others ever had done, as no man before had ever done.

She had seen men as good-looking, perhaps, but in a very different way. Would they have looked as well, stripped of their trappings? She doubted it. And never a man among them could or would, she was sure, have handled these obdurate barrels and boxes as this man did. Truly they seemed to object to removal from their lodging-places as though they were endowed with minds of their own.

And she had trusted him implicitly, from the first moment she had looked into his eyes, and recognised that it must be he who had drawn her back out of the closing hand of death.

"Better put that on," said Wulfrey, dropping one of the coats over her shoulders, when they had got everything aboard.

"Why? I am quite warm."

"We have done our work now till we get to the spit. No good chilling in the wind. We're going to sail home," and he slipped on the other jacket, and proceeded to rig up a sail and a steering plank as he had seen the mate do.

The Girl broke into a laugh at the change for the worse produced in their appearance by the jackets.

"You looked like a Greek or a Roman before," she said. "Now we both look like gipsy tinkers."

"Fine feathers—fine birds?" he smiled, as they hauled out past the end of the pile and began lumbering slowly homewards.

"Those awful birds!" and she glanced anxiously round for them, but they were busy a mile away and troubled them no more.

The Girl was glad enough of her old coat before they reached the spit, in spite of its demoralising effect on her appearance,—glad even to snuggle down among the blankets, for, after the hard work of loading, even the south-west wind began presently to feel cool.

Then came the discharging, and the transporting of their heavy weights to the smaller raft on the lake, which could not take more than half their cargo at a time. So he took her and a portion across to the 'Martha,' and she undertook to have supper ready by the time he got back with the rest.

And surely she wrought pleasanter thoughts even than usual into her cooking that day, for it seemed to him, when in due course he sat opposite to her on the other side of their fire, that he had never enjoyed a meal so much in his life, deficient as it was in many things that he had always regarded as needful.

"We have done a good day's work," he said, as he lit his pipe at her request.

"I wonder what he will say about it."

"We will not let it trouble us. He has only himself to blame."

"I wonder if you and he would have quarrelled if I had never come."

"We certainly would if he had taken the line he has done. As long as he did his fair share of the providing I did not mind. But the position he took up was an impossible one."

They fell into reminiscent talk of that great outer world which seemed so remote, and from which, for all they knew, they were now for ever cut off. She had many strange recollections of her earlier life in France, some very terrible ones of the times of the Red Deluge, very mixed ones of the later times in England.

It was amazing to him to sit in that bare cabin of a deserted ship, on an island shunned by all, listening to her familiar talk of men and women who had been but names to him, until her intimate knowledge of them made them into actual living personages.

Her outlook on life had been very much wider than his own. She had lived among the scenes and people of whom he had only read in the news-sheets. He was immensely interested, both in the things she talked about and the way she talked about them. His questionings towards a clearer understanding on points which were to her matters of simplest elementary knowledge amused her not a little. And he got many a self-revealing glimpse into that strange past life of hers, from which she was so contented to escape, but which was yet so full of colour and contrast and vivid actuality that, in spite of all its discrepancies and disillusionments, it had assumed for her a certain glamour which she averred it had never worn at the time.

"Wait a moment," he would say, breaking into her flow of reminiscence, "'Monsieur' is—?"

"The Comte de Provence, the late King's brother, my uncle. My father, the King's next brother, the Comte d'Artois, is 'Monseigneur.' He has become terribly devout since Mme de Polastron died. The abbè Latil is his heart and mind and conscience. In his way he was fond of me, I believe, but since I came to understand the wrong he did my mother, I have detested him. And I have no doubt he was not sorry when I broke away. I was a perpetual reminder, you see—"

"And there is another Countess d'Artois?"

"Oh, yes,—Marie Thérèse of Savoy, but she is too awful,—a quite impossible woman, one must say that much for him. If ever a man had good excuse for seeking his pleasures elsewhere, he had. She was terrible. She had no more moral feeling than a cat."

"And Madame Adélaide—? Let me see—who was she?"

"My great-aunt—poor old thing! Those atrocious Narbonnes lived on her and turned her round their fingers."

"And Madame Elizabeth? It is terribly confusing."

"Not at all. It is all as simple as can be. Madame Elizabeth was my aunt, my father's sister. She was very sweet. Poor dear! They cut off her head, though she never harmed a soul since the day she was born. She was very good to me. If she had lived I do not think I would be here. She was not like the rest. I could have lived happily with her."

And so she chattered away,—about the late King—her uncle also,—and of the Duc d'Orleans,—"always a self-seeker, and intriguer, with a very sharp eye on the way things might turn to his own benefit. Oh, I am glad they took his head off. It was righteous retribution."—And of the Queen— "She did foolish things at times, but she meant no harm, and, mon Dieu, how she suffered!"—And of Lafayette, and Talleyrand, and many and many another.

And it was indeed passing strange to lie there listening to it all—she clad in her blankets, for the night air had a chill in it, and he in the sea-damaged coat and small clothes of a gentleman of the Duke of Kent's suite, while between them the thin blue reek of the drift-wood fire on its hearth of sand stole up through the half-closed companion-hatch to the lonely night outside.

XXXIV

"We shall have a visit from our next-door neighbour presently, I expect," said Wulfrey, when The Girl came out of her cabin next morning. "Will you mind stopping below while I dispose of him?"

"But why?"

"He puts things coarsely at times, and he will probably be in a very bad humour at having to get his own meals ready."

"I don't mind him."

"Nor do I, except on your account. But I shall feel happier if you are out of sight and hearing."

"Oh, very well. But nothing he could say would trouble me in the slightest."

So, after breakfast, she sat down on the cabin floor to her sewing, and he lit his pipe and went up on deck carrying his axe. He closed the companion-doors and hatch very quietly—but she heard him—and went forward into the bows, which, since the usual wind blew from the south-west, was the nearest point to the 'Jane and Mary.'

It was a long time before the mate showed any signs, beyond an extra rush of smoke when he made up his fire to cook his breakfast. But he came up at last, caught sight of Wulfrey, and stood scowling across at him for a time. Then he dropped down on to his raft and came wobbling, with quick angry strokes, across to the 'Martha.'

"So that's it, is it?" he growled, with a grim look on his dark face.

"That's it," said Wulfrey coolly.

"And you think you've got her all to yourself?—what you've been plotting for ever since I hauled her ashore."

"Are you speaking of Miss Drummond?"

"I'm speaking of that girl. 'Twas me hauled her ashore an' she's my right if she's anybody's."

"There it is, you see. She is nobody's right but her own. And neither she nor I are your servants, to prepare your food and see to your comfort while you dig treasure out of the wreckage. So we have decided to fend for ourselves and you can fend for yourself."

"Ah! You think so, do you? We'll see about that."

"We undertake not to go aboard your ship if you give your word not to come aboard ours."

"See you — first!"

"Thank you! Then now we know how we stand, and will act accordingly."

"Ay, now you know."

"And will act accordingly," emphasised Wulfrey once more. "I must ask you to keep off," as the mate paddled alongside and reached up a rough hairy hand to the side. "I'm sorry it's come to this, but I won't have you on board."

"Won't, eh?" and as he reached up the other hand and prepared to mount, Wulfrey picked up his axe and held it threateningly above the clinging hands, which straightway loosed their hold amid a volley of curses.

"— you! You'd maim me! — me, if I don't pay you for this! The girl's mine. I found her. I'll get her over your dead body if needs be."

"Ah! And who found you? And where would you be if I hadn't helped you on to the raft yon first night? Tell me that, will you? By the same rule you're mine, and all you've got is mine."

"— you for a — sea-lawyer!" foamed the mate, his dark face and eyes all ablaze, his shaking fists hurling curses beyond the compass of his tongue.

Wulfrey, eyeing him professionally, said to himself, "Too much rum. He'll have D.T. if he doesn't slack off—or a fit if he does much of this kind of thing."

The mate thrashed back to his own ship with furious strokes and climbed aboard, and Wulfrey, having watched him safely up the side, went down to The Girl.

"He is very angry," he said quietly.

"He did not whisper. I couldn't help hearing him. What will he do next?"

"We can only wait and see. We shall have to be on our guard, but we won't let him trouble us. He is drinking too much."

They saw nothing more of him all that day, not even his head above the bulwarks. Wulfrey surmised that he was probably treating his wrath with rum, and plotting mischief, or maybe he was lying dead drunk in his cabin. They themselves were well provided in all respects, but he had good reason to know that stocks across there were running low, and that before long the man of wrath would have to go abroad to make up his deficiencies, and that would give them the opportunity of getting in fresh water and rabbit-meat.

He could only hope the mate would not postpone his journey too long, for the weather seemed like changing. There was no sun visible, not a speck of blue sky, but in their place a wan-white opaqueness which looked portentous and might mean anything.

Wulf spent most of the day on the alert, leaving the deck only for meals, and popping up even in the middle of them to make sure that all was right. But Macro made no sign.

There was no knowing, however, what a furious, rum-fuddled man might attempt. His crazy jealousy and anger might stick at nothing, and Wulfrey looked forward to a watchful night as a necessity.

And, as he paced the deck, he ruminated on the handicap imposed by virtue on an honest man when fighting roguery. Here was Macro at liberty to sleep without fear of assault, to go ashore for water and fresh meat, and to the wreckage for everything he wanted, assured in his own mind that no one would rifle his stores, or fire his ship, or play any other dastardly trick, in his absence. While they, if they left their stronghold unguarded for an hour, must be exposed to all these things, and constant watchfulness would be necessary to prevent them.

It was not a pleasant prospect and he did not see how it was going to end. At the same time he did not see what other course had been left to them, and he was determined to go through with this, cost what it might.

The thought of striking down this man with whom he had lived in fellowship, even in fair fight, was abhorrent to him. The thought of being struck down himself made his blood run cold on The Girl's account. Both possibilities must be avoided if possible. The latter at all hazards. If it came to the mate suffering or The Girl, the mate would have to go without compunction.

XXXV

The night passed without disturbance, the morning found them swathed in dense white mist which hid one side of the ship from the other.

"He did not come again?" asked The Girl when they met. "I am ashamed to have slept so soundly. I intended to take my fair share of the watching."

"There was no need. I bolted the doors and slept at the foot of the stairs. It's all cotton-wool outside. You can't see a couple of feet. He won't venture out in that, if I know him. But we need water. I'll go across after breakfast and get some."

"I shall come too. I wouldn't stop here alone for anything."

"All right. Our only difficulty will be in finding the shore and getting back to the ship. Fog is terribly bewildering."

"If you can find the shore we can get back all right," she said, after thinking it over.

"How?"

"We have that heap of rope you brought over. Could we not untwist some and make a cord? Then if we tied one end to the ship and carried the other ashore we could feel our way back by it."

"It will take a lot of untwisting. We're quite two hundred yards from the shore. But it's worth trying."

So they untwisted rope till their fingers were sore, and tied the pieces together till he judged they had enough, and presently they embarked noiselessly on their raft and paddled in the direction in which he believed the shore lay, The Girl paying out the string as they went.

This weird envelopment of dense white mist was a new experience for her. She could barely see the water a foot or two away. The string slipped through her fingers and vanished into the fog-wall. Dale, sweeping the water with his oar, loomed dim and large just above her.

They went on and on, but found no shore.

"The string is nearly all done," she said at last.

"Then we're going wrong," he whispered. "Don't speak loud, we don't know how near we may be to—" and, as if to confirm his fears, a great black bulk appeared in the clammy white above them, and Wulfrey hurriedly checked their way and backed off into the fog again.

"'The Jane and Mary,'" he whispered, when they had put a space between them and it. "We've been circling round. The shore must be this way, I think—" and the cord slacked in The Girl's fingers as he struck off to the right, and in due course they made the beach with cord to spare.

They tied the precious guiding-line to the raft and set off with their buckets, Wulfrey trailing his oar behind him so that by its mark in the sand they might grope their way back. In his belt he carried the only weapon he possessed, his axe, which, as matters stood with the mate, he deemed it advisable always to have at hand.

Keeping along the edge of the lake till he judged they were opposite the ponds, they struck inland, and managing to keep a straighter course than on the water, came at last to their goal.

They filled their buckets and were returning on their trail, bending every now and again to make sure they were right, when, with an abruptness that startled the buckets out of their hands, a dark figure loomed up on them out of the fog and they found themselves face to face with the mate.

He had heard them coming and was ready. Wulfrey had barely time to drop his oar and pluck out his axe when the other sprang at him with his weapon swung up for the blow.

It was very grim. Of all fighting-tools the axe is the most brutal—after, perhaps, the spiked club and the scythe-blade tied on a pole, which are only fit for savages. It is cumbersome and ungainly. It admits of little skill either in attack or defence. Its arguments are final and convincing, and its wounds are very ghastly.

The Girl could barely make out which was which, so thick was the veiling fog. But that did not matter. She sprang in between the two dark figures with arms outspread, at imminent risk of receiving both their blows, crying, "No!—You shall not! You shall not!"

The mate hurled oaths at her. She thought he was going to strike her down. And past her, at Wulfrey,—"— ye! It's like ye. Steal her first, then hide behind her!"

With one big black hand he gripped her blanket cloak and whirled her away into the mist, and came plunging at Wulfrey, who stood with poised axe and eyes that watched his every movement.

The mate played round him for an opening. Out of the corner of his eye he saw The Girl groping about for the oar. He rushed in to end it with one crushing blow.

But Wulf was ready for him and he was the cooler man. As the mate's axe came swooshing down straight for his shoulder and neck, his own swung round, caught the other full in the blade with its own stout back, and with a ringing click sent it flying, with such a shock to the arm that had held it that the mate believed it was broken. He ducked with an oath and disappeared into the fog.

The Girl came panting up, her face all sanded with her fall, her eyes ablaze. "Did it reach you?"

"Not at all. I'm all right."

"The brute! I feared he would kill you."

"He did his worst.... What were you going to do with that?"—the oar she had picked up.

"I was going to smash him on the head with it, but I couldn't find it at first."

"Two to one!"

"I don't care. I'd have killed him if I could."

"What about our water?"

"It's all spilled."

"We'll go back for more. He won't come back. I doubt if he'll find his axe in this fog. Which way now?" and he stood puzzling, for force of circumstance and much trampling of the sand had lost them their clue. "You cast round that way for the mark of the oar, but don't go far. I'll try this side. Call if you find."

"Here!" she cried, almost at once, and he followed her voice into the fog and found her standing on the line.

But so confused were they that even then they had not an idea which way to follow it.

"Which way?" she asked, staring down at the groove under her feet.

"This, I think.... I don't know," and he stood perplexed, "There is nothing for it but following it up and seeing where we come to."

So they picked up their buckets, and he took the oar, and they set off again,—and came out at last, not on the green undergrowth which flourished round the ponds, but on the bare shore of the lake.

"Now we know where we are at all events. Dare you stop here while I go back?"

"No," she said with a shiver.

"Come along, then!" and they turned and went back, and he discoursed of fogs as they went. "Nothing like a fog for absolutely confusing one's sense of direction. I've known people wander for hours on a common, round and round, quite unable to get anywhere. And one soon gets into a panic and common sense goes overboard."

She had not had much experience of fogs, but expressed herself vehemently on the subject, and so they came to the ponds, and back, in time, to their raft. And Wulfrey was mightily glad to see it again, for the idea had been troubling him that Macro might have found it, and set it adrift, or gone off to their ship to find solace there for his discomfiture ashore.

"I wonder where he's got to?" he said anxiously.

"I don't care. I wish he'd get lost in the fog and never come back."

"You feel strongly," he said, with a smile at her vehemence.

"Yes, I like or I dislike, and both to the full."

The guiding-line led them safely home, and glad they were to get there, for the chill of the fog and the treacheries it held were enough to weigh down the staunchest of spirits.

XXXVI

Their experiences in the fog had occupied many hours, and the unusual strain had left them both somewhat lax and weary. By the time they had prepared and eaten their much-delayed meal, and were enjoying the after-rest, the thick whiteness outside had turned to chiller gray, and the comfort of a blazing fire was eminently agreeable.

Wulfrey closed the companion-doors and hatch, all except the narrowest crack through which the smoke could escape, lit his pipe, and lay at ease, watching the many-coloured tongues of the dancing flames and The Girl who sat gazing dreamily into them on the other side, and wondered how it would have been with them all if Macro's vicious blow had got home on his neck.

She was very good to look upon as she sat there in the flickering half-darkness. The gracious curves of her supple young figure transformed the bare little cabin into a Temple of Youth and Beauty.

The dusky glamour of her hair, the shadowy beauty of her dark soft eyes, the level brows and wide white forehead which gave such strength and dignity to her face—they all held for him an arrest and an appeal such as he had never before experienced.

She had made herself a robe out of a piece of the crimson silk they had brought over from the pile. It was hardly a dress, for it swathed about her in flowing folds rather than fitted to her. But he thought he had never seen so becoming a garment. It was sheer delight to lie and look at her.

But it was a sufficiently difficult problem that faced him. In his present state of mind, the mate seemed determined to make an end of him the first chance that offered. Was there any reasonable hope of a change for the better in him? Were they to live in a perpetual state of defence till one of them went under?—all the advantages of unscrupulous attack being left to the enemy. Was it reasonable? If not, what was to be done, and how?

The man had suddenly become a deadly menace. He was no better, in his unprincipled cravings, than a wild beast. If that girl fell helpless into his coarse hands.... And she knew it and looked to him for protection.

And protection to the utmost of his powers she should have.... Was he justified in slaying the man? ... In view of the deadly intent of this latest attack he thought he was. But whether he could bring himself to it, if the chance offered, he was not by any means sure.... The deliberate killing of one's fellow was a serious matter.... In self-defence of course one was justified.... As to the law—it seemed as though the mate was right in his belief that they were destined to spend the rest of their lives—some of them at all events—on this bare bank of sand, where none ever came who could help it, and where no law but that of Nature obtained.... But there was a higher law. "Thou shalt not kill." ... Yes, it would be very much against the grain of his life and conscience, but it might have to be....

He sat up suddenly, listening intently.

"What is it?" asked The Girl, startled out of her own reverie.

He raised his hand for silence.

"I thought I heard a cry," and he got up, and went up the steps, and opened the door and stood there straining his ears into the clammy darkness. The fog lay thicker than ever. It was like listening into the side of a bale of raw cotton. The faint glow of the fire below died against the opaque wall in front. It could not have been seen a yard away.

The Girl stood on the stairs close behind him.

"I must have been mistaken," he murmured, "or perhaps it was a seagull,"—when, just below and almost alongside them, there came the violent sweep of an oar used as a paddle, and a wild spate of curses like the furious outburst of a panic-stricken brain.

Wulf slipped noiselessly down for his axe and stepped up on deck. If he went past, well and good. If he ran into them—

There came a sudden bump against the side of their ship and the sound of a fall on the raft.

"— ye, ye — rotten old coffin! I've got ye at last, —!" and right up out of the fog under Wulfrey's nose came two clammy black hands clawing nervously at the bulwark.

"You can't come aboard here, Macro," he said quietly. The grimy hands loosed with a startled oath and the mate dropped back on to his raft.

"—! That you again? — you! I thought.... Then my — craft must be over there. —! I'll do for you yet, my cully!" and the oar dashed into the water again and he cursed himself off into the darkness.

"You could have killed him," gasped The Girl at his side, through her chattering teeth.

"I could—but I couldn't."

"We shall have no peace while he lives."

"I fear not. Still—I couldn't cut him down in cold blood like that. What would you have thought of me if I had done so?"

"I should have said you had done well."

"I know you better."

At which she shook her head. "You don't know what horrid thoughts whirl about in my mind. No man really knows what a woman thinks," and the frank dark eyes regarded him solemnly.

"I know you better than you do yourself."

"I doubt it," with another shake of the head. "But, even then, it might have been best,"—with a shiver— "It sounds horrible—but—"

He could understand all her feeling in the matter. In her place he would have felt just the same. The man was a hideous menace—to her especially—and there would be no security for them while he lived. But all the same....

"Let us get back to the fire," he said quietly. "He won't come back tonight. Poor wretch, he's probably been paddling about all day looking for his ship and he's half crazed with it."

"I don't think I am bloodthirsty by nature," she said, with her hands pressed tight to her eyes, when she had sunk down before the fire again. "But I fear that man with all my soul, both for myself and you. He will kill you if he gets the chance. If he kills you I shall kill myself. It is better that one should die than two."

"I agree, but I don't want to have the killing of him if I can help it."

"Killing is horrible," and she shivered again, "But being killed is worse ... and to fall into the hands of a man like that would be even worse still. What will be the end of it all?"

But that was beyond him, and their hearts were heavy over it.

XXXVII

"Is it often like this?" asked The Girl depressedly, on the third day of mist.

"I'm afraid there's a good deal of it. We've had it three or four times since we came. It may be worse in the winter."

"I wish we could get away."

"I wish so too, but I don't see how we're to manage it ... unless, sometime, a boat washes ashore among the wreckage. And even then ... without Macro to manage it..." and he shook his head unhopefully. "... In the meantime I count it marvellous gain that you should have come—"

And at that it was her turn to shake her head. "I don't know. I seem to have brought more harm than good."

"It has made all the difference in the world."

"Yes, it has set you two by the ears and put you in peril of your life. That is not a good work."

"Your company more than compensates. Besides, we should probably have got to loggerheads in any case, and without anything like so good a reason."

"It would have been better, I think, if you had let me go when I was so nearly gone, and not rubbed me back to life."

"I thank God that you came," he said weightily. "Without you we might have sunk into savages, caring only for the lower things. You lift me without knowing it."

"You couldn't sink into a savage. He is one naturally. And I am becoming one, for I am all the time wishing he were dead."

"He must be having a bad time, unless he brought over provisions that last time, and I doubt if he did. He's probably living chiefly on rum. And that won't bring him to any better frame of mind, I'm afraid."

"To think," she mused, "that three people cannot live on an island big enough to hold thousands, without quarrelling to the death!"

"The trouble is not of our making, so we need not blame ourselves."

"Yes, it is. I began it by coming ashore. You ought to have let me stop out there—"

"You are very much better here."

"—And you continued it by bringing me back to life. You ought to have let me die."

"Very well. I accept all the blame and rejoice in it," he said, with a smile. "It is just the fog getting into you. You'll feel differently about it when the sun comes out again."

"Sun? I don't believe we are going to see it again. I don't believe it ever shines here or ever has done since the world began. It is an island of mist ... and we are just vapours—"

"Macro's not anyway. I wish he were. He wouldn't trouble me in the slightest then. He's a solid strong mixture of Spanish buccaneer and Highland robber, with a touch of volcano to keep the mixture boiling."

But the chill of the mist was upon her and nothing he could say availed to cheer her. So he hauled out the rolls of silk they had brought over, and set to work decorating the cabin with them, and interested her out of her depression by the purposed mistakes he made.

It was the ravelling off of a long thread from one of the pieces of silk he was cutting, that showed him the way to a new employment for her and the possibilities of a welcome addition to their meagre larder.

"Do you think you could twist two or three of these into a fishing-line?" he asked her. "I've seen heaps of fish in the lake. We might try for some."

"And hooks?"

"If you could spare me one of your big needles I think I could make something that might do."

She went at once and got him one, and then set to work on the line, and he could hardly get on with his own job for watching her.

She was so eminently graceful in all her movements. Her tall slender figure, supple, shapely, and all softly rounded curves without a discoverable abruptness or angularity anywhere about it, lent itself with singular charm to her present occupation. After thoughtful consideration of the matter, she unrolled one of the pieces of silk the whole width of the cabin, then picking out a thread, she fastened the end of it to the woodwork and travelled along the side of the piece, bending and releasing it as she went. The same with two more threads.

"Three ply will be strong enough?" she asked, straightening up and looking across at him.

"Let me see what three ply feel like," and he went across and watched her while she twisted the threads tightly together with deft soft fingers.

"I should think that would do," he said, running it between his finger and thumb. Their hands met, and the touch of hers sent a quite unexpected thrill of physical delight tingling through his veins. He did not dare to look full at her for the moment, lest she should see it in his eyes. But he was conscious to the point of pain of her close proximity,—somehow conscious too—and that quite unconsciously and without any reasoning on the matter—that, in the twinkling of an eye, she was no longer simply a beautiful and charming girl, but had become for him the most beautiful and charming girl in all the world.

His heart felt suddenly too big for his body. He could have taken her in his arms then and there, and crushed her to him, and smothered her with hot kisses. And he could no more have done it than he could have brained her with his axe. For she trusted him implicitly, and he was himself.

He took a deep breath to give his heart more room, and bent to examine her twist.

"It will do splendidly," he said, and she glanced quickly at him and wondered what had made that curious change in his voice. "How will you keep it rolled tight like that?"

"I've been thinking. If I greased my fingers with some of that pork fat as I roll it, and roll it very tight, it will probably keep so. How long will you want it?"

"As long as you can make it without too much trouble."

"I can make it the full length of that silk as far as I see."

"That will do admirably.... If I can make as good a hook as you have made a line we will have fish for dinner," and he went back to the fire, where, with his axe and his knife and two rusty nails lashed together at the top to act as tweezers, he was endeavouring to bend a portion of her needle into a hook.

At the cost of some burns and cuts he managed at last to make something distantly resembling one.

"It looks horrid," said The Girl when he showed it to her. "I shall be sorry for the fishes if they get that into them."

"So shall I. But we'll not let them suffer long if they give us the chance."

She was as eager as a child with a new toy to put their work to the test. So he cut some small pieces of pork and embedded his hook in one, and dropped it into the bed of mist over the side.

And she leaned over, with her shoulder unconsciously against his,—but he felt it, and rejoiced in the feel as keenly as ever Macro did in his treasure-trove—and peered anxiously down at the line, of which she could see but a couple of feet, and waited impatiently for results.

He put it into her hand, saying,

"If anything comes of it you shall have the honour of catching our first fish," but he held on to the slack behind.

"It's jerking," she whispered breathlessly, "Oh, I'm sure there's something on it..." and as she let go the line he gave it a jerk on his own account, then drew it quickly in and a plump astonished fish lay jumping and twisting on the deck. It was over a foot in length, very prettily coloured, dark blue with many cross-streaks and silvery below.

"Mackerel, I think," he said, and promptly knocked it on the head, to end its troubles and allow him the further use of his hook.

"The poor little thing! I'm so sorry," she said, looking mournfully down at the iridescent beauty. "I don't think I like fishing."

"You'll think better of it when it's fried."

"I couldn't touch it," with a vigorous shake of the head.

So he asked her to go down and make some cakes, and then caught another fish of a different kind the moment the bait reached the water, and a couple more for breakfast next day, and was thereby much reassured as to the future of their larder. He cleaned two of his fish and fried them with some pork fat as soon as she had made her cakes, and proceeded to reason her out of her prejudice.

"You have eaten fish all your life, haven't you?" he asked.

"Ye-es."

"Well, every fish has had to be caught before you could eat it. They generally leave them to die. But even that is probably only similar to our drowning, which is said to be about as pleasant a way as there is of going."

"It's horribly cold if you're lashed to a mast,"—with a reminiscent shiver. "And being rubbed back to life is just as bad."

"And we are more merciful, because we kill them at once."

"It's horrible to think that everything we eat, except things that grow of course, has got to suffer death for us."

"But you have always eaten these things without being troubled about it."

"The killing has never been brought home to me so closely before."

"It's Nature's law, you see. Everything feeds on something else. These fishes feed on smaller things. And how do you know that when you cut a cabbage or a potato—"

"How I wish I had the chance!"

"So do I, most heartily. But how do you know they don't feel it just as much, in their own dull way, as the pig did from which we get our pork?"

She shook her head and sighed. "We can't get away from it, I suppose," and tasted the fish and found it good, and ate quite heartily though with an appearance of protest.

"You see," he said. "Some fishes lay millions of eggs at a time. If they all grew up the sea would be choked with them, as the earth would be with animals if they weren't killed off. Besides, unless I am mistaken in my recollection of our old parson's reading, all these things were expressly provided for man's sustenance, so we are only doing our duty in eating them."

"All the same, I think I will let you do all the catching and killing."

"Of course. That is the man's proper part in the family economy. He is the bread-and-meat winner. And the wife's—the woman's, I mean—is to see to the cooking," and he occupied himself busily with fish-bones, and felt like biting his tongue off for its involuntary slip.

"If you had lived on pork and rabbits for months you would find this fish delicious," he said presently, to break the odd little silence that had fallen on them.

"It is very good. I wonder you never caught any before."

"I did try, but my tackle was too rough. The fish would have none of it. It is your clever line that has done the trick."

"I am glad to be of some use, though I can't help being sorry for the fish."

And if he had dared he would have delighted to tell her of what infinitely greater use she was to him in other and higher ways.

XXXVIII

Wulfrey was awakened in the night by the sounds he had come to recognise as the accompaniments of bad weather. The ship was humming in the wind and straining and jerking restively at the rusty cable which he was always expecting to give way. He wondered sleepily what would happen to them if it did. Wondered also if The Girl was frightened at the changed conditions, or whether she would understand. He slipped on some clothes and went into the cabin, to reassure her if necessary.

The fire was a bed of white ashes and a rose-gold core in the centre. He piled on some chips and the flames broke out with a cheerful crackle. The door of The Girl's little passage way opened an inch or two, and he caught a glimpse of her startled eyes shining in the fire-light.

"I was afraid you might be disturbed by the storm," he said.

She went back for a moment, and then came out with her blanket skirt and cloak swathed about her, and sat down by the fire.

"It woke me, and I cannot get to sleep again. Oh ... what is that?"—as a shrill scream pealed out just above the opening in the companion-hatch.

"It's only those infernal birds. They always come screeching round us in bad weather."

"I had just been dreaming that that horrid man came across in the night and murdered us both. It was such a relief to see you alive again."

"No fear of his venturing out in this weather. Those screaming birds get on his nerves. He'll be sitting drinking, and cursing them in the most awful Gaelic he can twist his tongue to. This weather will probably last a couple of days. Then it will slack up, and just when you're thinking it's all gone it will come back worse than ever. Fortunately we've got— By Jove!"—and he ran hastily up the companion, unbolted the door and ran out on deck. The gale came whuffling down on the fire and scattered the white ashes in a cloud, and set the silken drapery of the walls rustling wildly. The shrill clamour of the birds sounded very close, and The Girl sat anxiously wondering.

He came back in a minute, empty-handed and disconsolate. "I just remembered my fish. I left two up there for breakfast, but the birds have had them. They're as thick on the deck as bees on a comb, hoping for more."

"Is that all? I was afraid that man was coming and you'd heard him."

"It means living on pork till the storm passes."

"That is nothing. We shall enjoy the other things all the more later on."

"I'm wondering all the time how Macro is getting on—" he said, pulling out his pipe and filling it.

"Why trouble about him? He would not trouble about us if we were starving."

"I don't suppose he would.... I suppose it comes of my being so in the habit of helping people through their bodily troubles."

"It is wasted on him. He would not let you help him if you could."

"I don't believe he would, unless he were helpless.... I wish he'd never come ashore."

"But in that case I would not be here either, and you would have been all alone for the rest of your life."

"Then, after all, I'm glad he came ashore."

"I wonder if you would have gone mad in time with the loneliness of it," she said musingly.

"It would be horrible to be all alone for all the rest of one's life, but I don't think I would have gone mad. I've no doubt there are books to be found among the wreckage out there. Still ... for the rest of one's life!"—and he shook his head doubtfully. "As things are, however...."

"As things are?" she queried, after waiting for him to finish.

"As things are, I am quite content to stop here for the rest of my life, if that has to be. But that won't stop my doing my best to get away if the chance offers.... And you?"

"If we were delivered from that man I could be content here also.... But I do not say for all my life. That sounds terribly long.... But for that man it would be a welcome retreat from a world of which I had had a surfeit."

He wondered much if she were heart-whole. It seemed almost incredible to him that she could have lived that strange life of hers without some man wanting and touching it. So fair a prize, to go wholly unclaimed and undesired! But never, in all her talk, had she said one word that pointed to anything of the kind. Rather had she held up the men she had met to derogation and contempt. Surely, if there had been anyone to whom her heart turned and clung, some evidence of it would have shown itself.

From all she had said, from all her little unconscious self-revelations, and the wholesome judgment he had formed of her in his own mind, he could well believe that, in that whirlpool of a world in which she had lived, she had come to hold most men in doubt and all at arm's length. And the thought was agreeable to him.

When the slow day broke, dim and clangorous with the gale, they dallied over a meal, talking of many things to pass the time, and then went up on deck, and with a brandished stick he ridded the ship of the clustering birds. They shrieked threateningly and came swooping at him on the wings of the wind, with hungry beaks and merciless eyes. But here he was at home and would not suffer their invasion, and finally they gave it up and fled to the sandhills, cursing him shrilly as they went.

"Oh, there's one gone downstairs," cried The Girl; and running down after it, he found a great black cormorant squawking fearfully round the cabin and dashing itself against the walls in its wild attempts at escape. At sight of him it grew frantic, but finally found its way out of the hatch again, almost upsetting The Girl in its passage, and then tore away to tell its fellows of the awful place it had been in, which smelt so good but was so much easier to get into than out of. Wulfrey had to open one of the lee ports and let the gale blow through to get rid of the smell of it, and then he went up again to The Girl.

They watched the great rollers thundering on the beach beyond the spit, rocketing their white spume high into the grim black sky, and lashing over at times into the lake. And when he called to her to look the other way she watched with amazement sandhills of size melt away before her eyes and re-form themselves in quite different places.

"But it is past words!" she cried into his ear.

They stared long too at the 'Jane and Mary' of Boston, but saw no sign of life aboard of her except the birds that clustered there unmolested.

"It is a most amazing place," she said, when they went down again, as she dusted the saltness out of her hair with her hand. "Is it often like this?"

"Very often in the winter, I should fear. We've had our best weather since you came."

"I don't think I want to live all my life here," she said dejectedly. "I love the sun."

And he would dearly have liked to tell her that he did the same, but that for him she made more sunshine even than the sun itself.

Instead, he prosaically set her to the making of more fishing-lines, in case of accident to the one they had, and he himself hammered away at more hooks, burning and ragging his fingers out of knowledge, but producing hooks of a kind somehow.

XXXIX

The gale slackened on the third day, and Wulfrey was actually relieved in his mind at the sight of Macro hurrying ashore on his raft, after fresh meat, and, from the fact of his buckets, water, which he had probably been too careless, or too drunk, to secure during the storm. For the thought of his possibly lying there alone and foodless had not been a pleasant one, good reason as he had for disliking the man.

For themselves, he baited and cast his hooks, and landed half a dozen fish as fast as he could haul them out. Their fresh meat supply would have to wait until Macro went out to the wreckage and their minds could be at ease as to the safety of their headquarters. The sea outside was still too high for any possibility of his going that day, and fortunately, thanks to their new source of supply, they could wait with equanimity. Water they had caught in plenty in the buckets slung under the scuppers.

"He's alive at any rate," said Wulfrey, when he went down to breakfast.

"So much the worse for us," said The Girl.

"He's been fasting, I should say, by the way he has gone off after rabbits. We ate our first ones raw, I remember."

"Savages!"

"Savage with hunger. We had had nothing to eat but shell-fish and sea-weed for days."

"Horrible!—raw rabbit and sea-weed!"

"We had no means of making fire, no shelter. We slept out on the sands, and were glad to be simply alive."

"I'm truly thankful you had risen to a higher state before I came."

"So am I. We were not good to look at. We were as men who had died out there among the dead ships' bones and been born again on this sandbank, lacking everything. Fortunately for us the years that had gone before had been unconsciously making provision for us, and here were houses ready-made and waiting, and out there more than we could use in a lifetime."

They saw the mate return after a time with his supplies, and he never showed head again all day. Wulfrey let The Girl keep a look-out, and tried himself to get some sleep, in anticipation of the night-watch which he saw would be necessary.

"He will probably go out to the pile tomorrow," he said. "He must be out of flour and probably of rum. Then we can take a run ashore ourselves. When he gets back he will probably be too tired to be up to any mischief."

"I wish he would tame down and let us have peace, or else go and get himself killed," she said anxiously. "We can't go on like this for ever."

"I'm afraid he won't oblige us either way. We can only hang on and hope for the best, and keep our eyes open."

His watch that night passed undisturbed. In the morning, as he expected, Macro set off for the wreckage; and, taking some food with them, they went ashore for a long day's ramble.

"It is good to feel the width of land under one again," said The Girl, fairly dancing with delight. "I am very grateful for the ship, but truly it is small and cramping."

"Sandhills are good for play-time, but you'd miss the ship when bed-time came. It's cold work sleeping on the sand."

"Almost as bad as sleeping on a broken mast. Which way shall we go? You are quite sure he has gone to the wreckage?"

"Quite sure. I watched him out of sight. Besides, I am sure he had to go."

"Then let us go the opposite way, as far as we can, and we'll stop out all day long and behave like children. I'm going to walk in the water," and she kicked off her shoes and lifted her blanket skirt and tripped along in the lip of the tide, and he did the same, enjoying her enjoyment.

A watery sun shone feebly through a thin gray sky, the air was still heavy with moisture, the water in which they were walking was warmer than that of the lake. On that side, the island curved like the concave side of a great half-moon. The pale yellow sand stretched on and on as far as their eyes could reach.

"I would like to bathe," said she exuberantly.

"Wait till we get beyond the end of our lake, then you can take this side and I'll go across to the other. You won't go out too far? There may be under-currents that would carry you out."

"I'll be very careful. And you must not come back for an hour... Oh, what are those? ... Dead men?"

In a tiny dent in the long sweep of the curve, made by the sandhills running almost down to the water, were half a dozen dark objects lying on the dry sand and looking for all the world like dead bodies. He had never seen any jetsam of size on that side. The drive of the storms and drift of the currents landed everything on the western spits and banks. Still there was no knowing.

"Wait here!" he said, and set off towards them. And she followed close at his heels.

But before they had gone many paces, one of the bodies set itself suddenly in motion and began to shuffle towards the water.

"Seals," said Wulf, who had never set eyes on a live one in his life, but had a general idea of what they were like.

Before they could reach them, all had flopped away except one, which, when they drew near, raised its head and eyed them piteously and made an effort to rise.

"It is sick or wounded," said Wulf. "Poor beast! Its eyes are like a woman's in—" He bethought himself and bit it off short. He had seen just such a look in many a woman's eyes.

"We won't disturb her," he said, and led the way round to give her wide berth.

"Oh—look! Oh, the little darling! How I would love to cuddle it!" whispered The Girl, for there, on the other side of Mrs Seal, with her front fins clasping it protectingly, was a late-born baby sucking away for dear life.

The Girl's face was transfigured,—ablaze with intensest sympathy and the wonderful light of mother-love. The mother's eyes followed them anxiously, the fear in them died out as they backed slowly away, and she bent her head to her baby and seemed to say, "Thank you so much! You understand, and I am very grateful to you."

"I am so glad we saw them. I like the island better than ever I did before," said The Girl. "What a dear little thing it was! And she was just delightful," and all day long she kept referring to them and to her joy at the sight of them.

They went on again, mile after mile, and whenever he glanced at her, her face was still alight with happiness, and unconscious smiles rippled over it in tune with her thoughts. So inborn and unfailing is the mother-feeling in all true women.

"Now, if you wish to bathe, here is a good place. I will strike across to the other shore and will come back in about an hour. Don't go too far out!" and he strode away across the hummocks.

Under cover of the nearest sandhill she loosed her slender garments, and sped like a sunbeam across the beach and into the water; and her face, as it came up from the kiss of the sea, was like a sweet blush-rose all beaded with morning dew, than which no fairer thing will you find. And as she swam and dived and splashed in the lucent green water, like a lovely white seal, her bodily enjoyment and her mental exhilaration flung wide her arms at times, as though she would clasp all Nature's joys to her white breast, and her eyes shone with a brighter light than had the mother-seal's, and a seal's eyes are deeply, beautifully tender and bright.

She laughed aloud at times, though none but herself could hear it, in the pure physical joy of living and being so very much alive. She was happier than she had ever been in all her life before. And one time, as she lay afloat with her arms outspread, she looked up at the pale sun in the thin gray sky, and all inconsequently said, "Yes—he is good. He is good. He is good," and her face was golden-rosier than ever when she was conscious that she had said it aloud.

She was sitting in the side of the sandhill, combing her hair with her fingers, when she heard his distant hail. And she climbed the hill and waved to him that he might come.

"I don't need to ask if you enjoyed your bathe," he said, as he came up. "I can see it in your face."

"It was delightful. I would like to bathe every day."

"Two days ago?" he laughed.

"No, days like this. Oh, it was so good! And now I am hungry. Let us eat."

So they sat in the wire grass of the hill-top and ate their frugal meal, she with her wonderful hair all astream, the ends spread wide to dry on the sand; and he, clean, and strong, and brown, as fine a figure of a man as she had ever met, though his raiment was nothing to boast of. And he said to himself, "She is the most wonderful girl I have ever seen. I would like to kiss her hair, her hands, her feet."

And she, to herself,—"He is good. He is good. He is good."

And, buried deep in both their minds, yet fully alive, was the thought that it might be that all their lives would have to be passed on that lean bank of sand—together.

XL

On their way back, Wulf lingered behind for a moment or two and came along presently with rabbits enough for their requirements, but did not obtrude them on her notice.

"It has been a day of delight," she said, as they drew to their ship. "Let us do it again.... I wonder if that man has got home."

"Not yet. I can see his raft on the spit. Just as well we're here before him."

"If only he were not here at all—"

"Even the original Paradise had its serpent."

"This one cannot beguile this woman at all events."

It was almost dark when they saw Macro's laden raft lumbering slowly across to the 'Jane and Mary.'

"He won't starve," commented The Girl.

"Nor go dry. I see at least half a dozen kegs there. He's making provision for bad weather. The gale may blow up again during the night. See the birds whirling about over there."

"Will you have to watch again?"

"Safer so, though the chances are the kegs will keep him quiet for a time. He's probably been on short allowance the last day or two."

"It is monstrous that you should have to. I wish—" and the petulant stamp of her stout little brogue conveyed no suggestion of a blessing.

"Time may work for us," he said quietly. "He is our thorn in the flesh—"

"He's a whole axe if you give him the chance."

"I won't, I promise you. I cannot afford to give him any chances," and she knew that in that his thought was wholly for her.

Wulf dutifully patrolled his deck when it grew dark, though he acknowledged to himself that the precaution was probably unnecessary, for this night at all events. Still, he was there to protect The Girl and he would suffer no risks.

It was possibly the distant sight of him, tramping doggedly to and fro in the wan moonlight, that set Macro's rum-heated passions on fire. Wulf heard him spating curses as he tumbled over on to his raft and came splashing across. He went quietly to the companion-way and closed the door, then picked up his axe and stood waiting, with a somewhat quickened heart at the thought that the next few minutes might end the matter one way or the other.

"— you, you white-livered skunk! Come out and fight for her like a man if you want her," was the mate's rough challenge, supplemented by a broadside of oaths, as he drew near.

Wulf stood looking quietly down at him. Words were sheer waste.

"D'ye hear me? Come down an' fight it out like a' man, an' best man takes her, — you!"

He bumped roughly against the side and picked up his axe. Curses foamed out of him in a ceaseless torrent, and he made as though he would come swarming over.

"Keep off," said Wulf. "If you try to come aboard I'll cut you down."

"Come down then and fight it out if you're half a man, — you! What right have you to her, I'd like to know, —!"—he picked up his oar and whirled it round at Wulf's head and it splintered on the hard-wood rail.

"Get back to your ship, man, and don't make a fool of yourself," said Wulf. "I won't fight you. If you try to come on board here I'll make an end of you."

"Ye skunk, ye! Ye— white-livered cowardly skunk!"—etc. etc. etc.—to all of which Wulf made no reply, which provoked the furious one more than any words he could have flung at him.

He remained there, hurling abuse and invective at the steady-faced man up above, till the night air cooled the boiling in his brain. Then he seized his splintered oar and thrashed away home. Wulf quietly resumed his sentry-go, watched till all was quiet on the 'Jane and Mary,' and then went down.

To his surprise The Girl was sitting by the fire. He had supposed her in bed, had hoped she was fast asleep and had heard nothing of the bombardment.

"He has gone?" she asked.

"Yes, he has gone home to bed. I was hoping you were asleep."

"Asleep! ... And you did not kill him?"

"He gave me no chance. He invited me on to his raft for a fight—"

"I heard it all."

"I'm sorry. He is hardly suitable for a lady's ears."

"I feel myself a terrible burden to you."

"But you are not. Very much the reverse. You are—" he began impulsively, and stopped short. It was too soon to tell all that she was to him.

"I am a bone of contention. I bring you in peril of your life—"

"And I thank God I am here to protect you. Now, take my advice and go to bed. I will bring my blankets and lie at the foot of the stairs here."

The next day passed without any sign of the mate, beyond the thin blue smoke that floated up from his hatchway.

Wulf surmised that he was making up his leeway in the matter of food and drink, and would probably not be over-eager for battle for the time being. Nevertheless he relaxed no whit of his vigilance, and after watching on deck for half the night slept the rest at the foot of the companion-way as before.

Contrary to his expectations, the gale did not work itself up again, but the sky was still low and dark and full of thin smoky clouds hurrying along towards the north-east, and he was not at all sure that they had done with it yet.

On the following day, to their great satisfaction, Macro set off early for the wreckage, and when they had watched him out of sight they went ashore for a ramble, and to get water and fresh meat.

The Girl must of course make straight for the place where they had met Mrs Seal and her baby, but, to her great disappointment, there was not a sign of them.

"And I did so want to see them again," said she. "She would have known us by this time and not been afraid. Perhaps she would even have let me touch it."

"They are much happier in the water," he said, with a smile, for her face made him think of a child who had lost its toy.

She would not be satisfied till they had searched far along the shore, but nothing came of it, and she was disconsolate. The day was not cheerful and she would not bathe. They filled their buckets, and he caught some rabbits and they returned early to the ship.

Her humours appealed to him, even though he could not possibly understand them completely. Everything she did, and the way she did it, and indeed everything connected with her, was coming to have a vital interest for him.

He could not know how the anguished fear in that mother-seal's eyes had touched her heart, how she had yearned to pick up that sleek little baby and fondle it in her arms, how she had been hoping and longing to see them again, how great her disappointment had been. She felt bereft and went off early to bed.

Wulf lay smoking and thinking till night fell, and then went up to do sentry. He paced the deck till midnight, saw no sign of movement aboard the 'Jane and Mary,' and went below and was soon sound asleep.

He woke once with a start, believing he had heard a footstep. Then a ripple clop-clopped against the side of the ship and he lay down again satisfied.

He was awakened again by a hand gripping his shoulder, and, starting up, found a ghostly white figure bending over him, and The Girl's voice in his ear,

"There is something wrong. Can you not smell it?"

For a moment he imagined her dreaming. Then his nose warned him that she was right. There was something unusual in the atmosphere.

Even when their fire was no more than a heap of gray ashes with a golden core, and one of their lee ports was open, the faint, not unpleasant smell of wood smoke hung about the cabin. But this was quite different,—an acrid, pungent smell as of burning fat. He glanced at the fire and raked his mind for an explanation of it.

"It is worse in my room," she said, and he went quietly to the sacred little passage off which her sleeping-apartment opened.

Yes, it was worse there, and what it meant he could not imagine.

"You have not been burning anything?" he asked.

"Nothing. The horrid smell wakened me."

He turned and ran up the companion-steps, with a vague idea that something in the hold might have caught fire, though how that could be was beyond him. There was nothing there but their reserve stores, and certainly nothing that could take fire of its own accord. Besides, it was two days since he had been down there, and he never took a light, as the hatch, when shoved askew, gave all that was needed.

He fumbled the bolts of the little doors open, but the doors seemed jammed. He pushed. They remained firm. He made sure of the bolts again and put his shoulder to the doors. They resisted all his efforts.

"Good Lord!" he said, in something of a panic. "What's all this?"

He brushed hastily down past The Girl again, groped for his boots by the side of his blankets, pulled them on, and picked up his axe, with the certainty in his mind that something wrong was toward and it was as well to be fully armed.

Then he smashed away at the woodwork till it was in fragments, and he could climb up through the bristling splinters and over an unexpected plank that had somehow got across the doors and prevented their opening.

The first thing he saw when he got on deck was a faint glow about the main-hatch opening, and smoke pouring out of it. Running to it, a glance showed him a fierce fire roaring somewhere down below. A cry of dismay at his side told him that The Girl had scrambled up after him.

"The buckets," he jerked, and she sped back, tearing skin and garment on the splintered doors, while he sought and found a length of rope.

His voice was steady again, though his hands shook with agitation, as he slipped one end of the rope through the handle of the bucket and held the two ends, while the bucket hung in the bight and so could be released instantly by loosing one end of the rope. He filled both buckets and with a hasty, "Hand them down to me and fill again as I throw them up," lowered himself into the hold.

The fire was burning fiercely against the after starboard bulkhead, which, as it happened, was the one nearest The Girl's sleeping-cabin. Their lighter stores had been moved from their usual places and heaped about it and were blazing furiously. The bulkhead itself was on fire, but had apparently only just caught.

Wulf flung his first bucketful at it, and it answered with a hiss like a snarling curse, and showed a red-starred black blotch amid the crawling yellow flames.

He tossed the empty bucket up on deck, and gave the bulkhead another dose with his second, and as he tossed that one up the first came dangling down filled again.

"Good girl!" he shouted exultantly, to reassure her. "Plenty more! We shall do it all right," and the full buckets came dangling down as fast as he could empty them.

A score or so of bucketfuls ended it, and he climbed up, black with smoke and streaked with steam and sweat, and very grateful to be in fresh air again.

The night was just thinning towards the dawn. The Girl was sitting on the coaming of the hatch in a state of collapse, her wet garment clinging clammily about her, her head in her hands, her slender figure shaken with convulsive sobs. His anger boiled furiously at thought of the malice that had planned her suffering—her possible death. Love and pity swelled his heart for her. She looked so utterly forlorn and broken with the fight.

"It is all right, dear!"—he could not help it, it slipped out in spite of him. "Come away down to the cabin. You are shivering. You are wet through and torn to pieces. You have done splendidly, but it was an upsetting piece of business all round. Come!" and he put his arm under hers and drew her up.

She was so limp, however, that he had almost to carry her, and the feel of her unconscious sobs under his enfolding arm quickened his blood again.

At the companion-doors he had to release her and go back for his axe. A stout plank had been cunningly bound against the doors by a rope tied round the companion. His lips tightened sternly as he chopped the rope through and the plank fell to the deck.

He carried her gently down and laid her on his blankets, put some sticks on the fire and blew them into flame, and set on the kettle, which was fortunately full. By the time he had made some coffee and dashed it with rum, she had recovered herself and was sitting up in the blankets with one drawn closely about her.

"That was an unnerving business," he said, as he handed her her cup. "I'm afraid you had the worst of it. You have a lot of scratches—and your hands! Oh, I am truly sorry—"

"It was the rope," she said quietly, looking at the rasped rawness of them. "It was all horrible. How did it get on fire?"

"It was a deliberate attempt on the part of that wretch to make an end of us."

"No!"—and she gazed at him in blankest amazement.

"Without doubt. He blocked our doors here with a plank and a rope, and then started the fire down in the hold."

"Is such wickedness possible?"

"To a madman living chiefly on rum anything is possible."

"He deserves to die."

"Richly. He deserves no mercy. The thought of cutting him down with an axe was horrible. But after this—"

"There is no safety for us while he lives."

"I'm afraid there isn't."

Sleep, he knew, would brace her unstrung nerves better than any thing else, so, after bathing her hands in luke-warm water and anointing them with some of the rendered pork fat she kept for her cooking, he induced her to go and lie down in her bunk. Her other scratches she said she would attend to when she could see them properly.

Then he went on deck and drew up a bucket of water and washed off his own stains, and afterwards smoked many pipes as he pondered the unpleasantly weighty subject of Macro. For that matters could go on like this was out of the question.

XLII

He had cakes made and breakfast all ready long before she came out of her room, still visibly feeling the effects of the night's proceedings.

"I am stiff and sore all over," she said, lowering herself carefully to her seat on the floor. "And you?"

"Sorer in mind than in body."

"What will you do?"

"I shall go over presently and tell him that now he must look out for himself. I will end him, the first chance I get, as I would a wild beast."

"He will try to kill you on the spot."

"He won't get the chance. I'll see to that."

"I shall go with you."

"No."

"Yes, indeed. My heart would thump itself to pieces, waiting here all alone."

"He is dangerous, and he has a vile tongue when it runs away with him—"

"I do not care. It is no more dangerous for me than for you. No—no—no!"—as he was about to argue the matter,—"I cannot be left behind," and nothing he could say could move her.

They saw no sign of life on the 'Jane and Mary,' not so much as a whiff of smoke from the companion-hatch.

"Perhaps he fled when he saw his horrid scheme had failed," suggested The Girl hopefully.

"Not very likely, I'm afraid, but we can go across and see. Won't you be good now and take my advice—"

"I'll be good, but I won't stop here alone."

So perforce he took her with him on the raft, and paddled quietly across to the other ship.

But before they reached it she lifted a warning finger for him to stop paddling and listen. And on their anxious ears there broke the strangest medley of sounds conceivable, and chilled them in the hearing. Wild bursts of laughter, cut short by yells of rage or sudden screams, as of one in mortal fear,—hoarse shouts, torrents of oaths, dull flailing blows which sounded like fists on wood, and, through it all, the never-ceasing yells and screams.

"He has gone mad," panted The Girl, very white in the face, and looked at him with wide anxious eyes.

"Delirium tremens,"—with an understanding nod. "He could stand more than most, but a man cannot live on rum alone," and he paddled slowly towards the ship, his face knitted with doubts as to what he should do.

He was in two minds. If he left the man to himself he would inevitably die in the end, for he had unlimited liquor on board and would turn to it at once, like a hog to its mire, as soon as this bout ran its course. On the other hand, every fragment of professional instinct in him impelled him to the rescue.

Never in his life had he withheld aid from one in extremity. And yet it seemed monstrously absurd—to drag a man back from death solely for the purpose of letting him do his best to kill you, the first chance that offered.

And he had more than himself to think for. Suppose he saved this wretched man, and was worsted by him later on, what of The Girl? She would have reason enough to blame his pusillanimity, and he himself would curse it with his last breath.

But was it fair fighting—to see your enemy in a hole and make no effort to save him? Old-time Chivalry would never even have argued the matter. It would have helped the enemy out, handed him his weapons, and courteously awaited the renewal of the combat. Ah—times were changed.... And this man was compound of treachery and malice.

Thoughts such as these whirled through his brain before he had covered the short space to the other ship.

"Wait here!" he said to The Girl, and climbed through the well-known hole in the side,—and she followed him close in spite of his frowning objection. She had not come thus far to be out of the critical moment.

He ran down to the cabin, and went straight to the mate's door. The dreadful sounds,—the shouts and yells and cries of fear, the furious oaths, the wild thumping blows—filled the cabin with horrors. Even in that anxious moment The Girl was cognisant of a dreary, dirty, repulsive look about it which had not been there before. It was more like the den of a wild beast than a living-room. Some of the silken hangings were torn down, the one or two that were left hung by single pegs. It looked as though a maniac had chased his mad fancies round the room and sought them behind the draperies.

Wulf, gripping his axe, opened the door into the passage, looked in, then went in. And The Girl drew near, to be at hand in case of need, and stood shuddering.

"Keep off! Keep off, ye blank-eyed deevils! —! Wi' your bloody beaks and tearing claws.... Keep off! Keep off — ye!" and the black fists, all bruised and bleeding, whirled and struck at the roof and sides of the bunk as he fought the birds the rum had bred in his brain. Then, as they beat him down in a pestiferous crowd, he gave a shrill scream and doubled himself over In a heap in his bunk, with his hands clasped over his head to save it from their attacks. Then up again, shouting and fighting for dear life, and down flat again with a scream, cowering in uttermost extremity of terror, while oaths dribbled out of him like water out of a spout.

Wulf came out and closed the door, and pushed her brusquely up the stairs to the deck.

"You should not have come down," he said sternly. "This is no place for you," and then, seeing how white her face was, he added more gently, "There is no danger—except to him. He is fighting for his life with the birds. I can do nothing for him—except get rid of all his rum. He would turn to it the moment he comes round, and it is poison in his present state."

He went down again and rooted about everywhere, found two kegs in the cabin under the torn hangings, and another in Macro's room, with a spigot in it. He carried them up on deck, staved in the heads with his axe, and emptied them overboard. In the main-hold he found three more and did the same with them.

"When he gets through, his throat will be like a lime-kiln. There is a bucket of water down there. I will put in it the coffee we left from breakfast and leave it in his cabin. It will be the best thing for him if he will drink it. But he'll be crazy for rum— I'll take you back and get the coffee. I'm sorry you came."

There was strong disapproval in his tone, but she did not resent it. After all, his thought was entirely for her in the matter.

"You're sure he won't fly at you?" she asked anxiously.

"He's much too busy with the birds. Besides, I shall not touch him or speak to him. It is best to leave him to himself. We will leave some food by him also," and she obediently let herself down before him on to the raft.

"It does seem absurd—" she began impulsively, as they joggled along.

"To keep him alive so that he may try again to kill us,"—he nodded. "I know. But there it is, as the country-folk say. However, he won't live long if he keeps on at the rum. As soon as he gets better he'll go straight out to the pile to get more, unless he's too weak. It's terribly wasteful work, what he's at, and no food to work on."

"Whether it's wrong or not, I cannot help wishing he would die," she said passionately. "It is too dreadful."

"I don't want his blood on my hands if I can help it," he said briefly. But he felt as she did.

XLIII

After carrying supplies to the mate, he came back for her, and they went ashore for fresh water, and he providently secured a couple more rabbits.

The Girl was very quiet, depressed, and very unlike her usual bright self. But he was not surprised. Her anxiety for the future was enough to account for it, and there was, besides, the reaction from the strenuous upsetting through which they had just passed.

Each morning he went across to see how the sick man was getting on, and she let him go alone, but followed him with anxious eyes, and stood in the bows watching till she saw him safely on his way back.

On the third day they took advantage of the enemy's enforced inactivity to go out to the pile and make good the losses caused by the fire. And all the time they were away The Girl was in a state of dire anxiety lest he should have discovered their absence and got across and fired their ship. But to her great relief it was there all right when they got back, and showed no signs of visitation.

On the fourth morning Wulf found his patient sufficiently recovered to be spoken to plainly as to the future, and he did not mince matters. While he spoke, the mate lay watching him through almost closed eyes, just one narrow line between the heavy lids catching the light from the port and imparting a singularly sinister look to the haggard face. The veiled eyes watched him cautiously, charged with what?—suspicion? hatred? treachery? All these, Wulf imagined. But they gave no sign. They were like the eyes of a snake, of a caged beast being rated by its keeper.

"Your dastardly attempt on us failed," said Wulf, to the steely glint of the black soul behind the narrowed lids. "And now,—understand! You are outside the pale. Leave us alone and we leave you alone. Interfere further with us and I will kill you as I would a dangerous beast. Now you are warned, and your blood be on your own head."

The other made no sign. The narrow gleam of the dark eyes out of the rigid impassivity of the dark face was more bodeful than a torrent of curses.

As he left the ship, Wulf picked up and took with him the only two axes he could find. Magnanimity had its limits, but it was wasted here.

"Well?" asked The Girl anxiously, when he returned.

"He is almost himself again, but very much weakened of course. I have given him final warning that if he molests us further I shall kill him."

"It would have been simpler to let him die."

"Simpler—yes, but I could not bring myself to it. We'll fight him fair if fight we must."

The weather still kept dull and gray and heavy, with a reserve of menace and malice in it akin to that of the mate. The sky was veiled with ever-hurrying clouds. The sea was smooth, with something of treachery in its sullen quietude, as though it were only biding its time to break out again and do its worst.

The following morning, to their surprise, they saw Macro start out early for the wreckage. And Wulf, watching him grimly, said, "He's after his poison. And now he'll probably drink himself to death. It's amazing the hold it takes on a man. He won't trouble us much longer."

They spent the day ashore, but the vivacity and enjoyment of that other day were awanting. Perhaps it was the cheerless weather,—the physical and mental strain of these later days,—the thought that their devil was loosed again,—anyhow, a subtle sense of foreboding. Whatever it was it weighed upon their spirits, and a long tramp up the beach, in forlorn hope of meeting Mistress Seal again, did not succeed in raising them.

"What is it, I wonder?" said The Girl. "Something is going to happen, I know. I have felt like this before, and always something dreadful has followed."

"But you never knew what, beforehand? Perhaps you have the gift of prevision,—the second sight."

"I may have, but it doesn't go so far as to explain things. I just feel anxious for it to be over and done with."

"What?"

"What's coming, whatever it is."

"We must be extra careful for a time, till you are sure the trouble is past," he said, with a smile, but he felt the weight on his spirits as she did.

Physically, however, their long tramp did them good, and they returned home with famous appetites.

"I wonder if he's back yet," said The Girl, as they were paddling to the ship. There was no doubt as to where her fears centred.

"I don't see the raft. We'll see better from the deck," and when they had climbed aboard they looked at once towards the spit and saw the mate's raft still lying there. He was not back yet.

They ate, and rested, and until the darkness swallowed the spit, the raft still lay there.

"He's staying late," said Wulf. "Maybe he's broached a keg and taken too much. It would be what I would expect from him under the circumstances."

He patrolled the deck, after she had gone to bed, listening for the sound of the mate's oar. But he heard nothing, and at last made up his mind that the fellow had probably waited too late and had made himself snug out there for the night, though, for himself, the idea would not have commended itself. There was little danger, however, of his coming across in the dark, so he went down and slept soundly at the foot of the companion-steps.

All the next day they were on the look-out for him, but he did not come.

Wulf had told her of his idea that he had probably found means of passing the night out there, in which case he would no doubt put in another long day rooting for treasure. So that it was not until night had fallen again, and the raft still lay waiting on the spit, that he decided in his own mind that something was wrong.

"I shall go across to the pile in the morning to find out," he said, as they sat by the fire.

"I shall go with you."

"I would very much sooner you stopped here."

"And suppose it was all a trick on his part. He may be hiding in the sandhills. He would watch you go and then come out on me. No," with a very decided shake of the head, "I go with you."

So, in the morning, they set off, walked along the spit to the western point and waded and swam to the wreckage, keeping a keen look-out for first sight of the mate.

"Those hideous birds!" panted The Girl, as the skirling, squabbling crew swooped and hovered over the far end of the pile.

"We'll keep as far away from them as possible," and they crept up at a distance, and he proceeded to make a raft, since a supply of further stores was needed to make good their losses by the fire.

So far they had come upon no signs of Macro. From the top of the pile they looked carefully all round, but beyond the usual smashed boxes and cases there was nothing to show that he had ever been there.

"Where on earth can he have got to?" said Wulf.

"Perhaps he's fallen into the sea, or down into some crack," said The Girl, not unhopefully.

"It is always possible. He might not recognise how the fever had pulled him down."

They loaded their raft without any interference from the birds, beyond the blood-curdling clamour of their angry disputations. They were quite ready to go, but still the whereabouts of the mate was a mystery, and Wulf was loth to leave it at that. He might be lying broken in some crack. If he had come to some sudden end it would be best to know it, if that were possible, so that their fears—on their own account as well as his—might be at rest. On the other hand it was quite impossible to rake over the whole pile. That would be a good month's work.

A grim idea shot suddenly into Wulf's mind, as he stood looking keenly round from the highest point he could clamber up to. It came at sight of the birds whirling and clamouring round the end of the pile. Suppose ... oh,—horrible! ... yet it might very well be.

"What is it?" asked The Girl anxiously, for his lips and face had tightened ominously at his thought.

"Nothing, maybe. I'm going over there to see...."

"Can you see anything of him?"

"No."

He poled the raft along the edge of the pile towards the hovering cloud of birds.

"Now, I'm going to swim along here and climb up. I want to see what they're at. You will be quite safe here."

She glanced at him with a startled look, fathoming his grim thought instantly, and it blanched her face for a moment.

"They may turn on you," she jerked.

"They seem too busy."

He let himself down into the water and swam noiselessly along the side of the pile, and she stood watching anxiously.

When he reached the outskirts of the whirling cloud he found a sodden crack, and drew himself in, and disappeared from her sight. Her heart kicked till it felt like choking her. Her face was strained, her eyes wide and fearful. She felt horribly alone.

Inside his niche, Wulf climbed cautiously, the curdling clamour very close. Now and again a feathery fiend with eyes like glass and reddened beak swooped past his hiding-place, with a shrill cry of warning to the rest at sight of him, or it might be of invitation.

He got his eyes above the top at last, in spite of pointed attentions from angry outsiders, scanned the spot where the shrieking crew centred most thickly, and dreamed of what he got a glimpse of there for weeks afterwards.

— The remnants of what had been a man, all pecked and scratched and torn to shreds,—white, clean-picked bones showing through fragments of his clothing, myriads of squawking birds, of all shapes and sizes, clustered on it like bees on a comb, hustling and fighting one another with shrill screams and thrashing wings and red beaks. It was only when, through some unusually bitter struggle, the mass writhed and rose for a moment, only to settle more closely the next, that he could see. Not far from the body was a broached keg which the birds had overturned in their strife. It explained everything to him.

He dropped back down his cleft, sick at the sight, grateful for the clean feel of the water. He plunged his head under and spat out the feeling of it all. Then he made his way quietly back to The Girl, and she had no need to ask what he had found. He nodded, and climbed up on to the raft and pushed quickly away.

"You are sure he is dead?" she asked, after a time.

"Horribly dead," and told her no more till later, and then not very much. "It is strange to think of it all," he said, in conclusion. "He always feared the birds. In his delirium it was the birds he was fighting. And the birds got him at last."

The manner of his death shocked and horrified them. But the knowledge that the menace of him had passed out of their lives was untellable relief.

BOOK IV

LOVE IN A MIST

XLIV

The effect of the mate's death on The Girl's spirits was visible at once. The cloud had lifted from her face before they got fairly home. Her eyes shone untroubled, though a look of horror and disgust came into them whenever they rested on the swirling gray cloud behind them. In her very movements Wulf noticed a new and gracious freedom.

And his judgment did her no injustice in the matter, nor imputed it, in any slightest degree, to mere exultation over a fallen enemy. For he knew to the full in what terror of the dead man she had lived, and how the fear of him, both for herself and himself, had lain like a weight on her soul and darkened all her outlook.

He felt as she did about it. He could not regret the fact of the man's death, but the manner of it gave him poignant distress.

In spite of their hard work they had neither of them much appetite for food that night. They turned in early and slept as they had not slept for long, without fear and without strain. The darkness was no longer pregnant with ungaugeable terrors. The dawn was like the beginning of a new life to them.

Wulf, indeed, saw again that night, and many a night thereafter, the horror of the clustering birds and that over which they bristled and fought. But he woke each time to the immeasurable relief of the man's death. That had been essential to their own safety, but he thanked God with his whole heart that it had not been by his hand that he had had to die. For that he never could be sufficiently grateful. He had played him fair and more than fair. He was dead, and their consciences and their hearts were alike at rest.

They woke next morning to the close folding of the mist, and he had to set to work at once making good the broken companion-doors to keep it out of the cabin as much as possible.

Being but a poor carpenter, the only way he could do this was by nailing a blanket to the top of the hatch and pegging it down tightly to the top step. But he foresaw that the next gale would blow his stop-gap to pieces and destroy their comfort below. So did the dead man's deeds live after him, and it was not the only one.

They were sitting at their mid-day meal, when the thick silence of the mist outside was rent by a shrill frightened scream right above their heads, and almost simultaneous with it a heavy thump, and then, on the deck above them, blows and screams and the sound of some large body tumbling to and fro.

The Girl sprang up with a white face and scared eyes and a word of dismay. Wulf picked up his axe and burst through his carefully adjusted blanket at the top of the companion. Then she heard the chop-chop of his axe on the deck, and the fall of something into the water, and he came down laughing at the start it had given him also.

"It was the biggest bird I ever saw," he said. "It had banged itself against the mast, I think, and was flopping all over the place. I chopped its head off and pitched it overboard. It must have measured six feet at least from tip to tip of its wings. It gave you a start."

"I was just thinking of that man and how different everything was now he is gone, and then that horrid scream—"

"Yes, it was enough to make anyone jump."

"It seemed to me for a moment that it was his spirit come back to trouble us still, as he had done while he lived."

"It won't come. Unless it's got inside a bird, as he always said. You must try to forget all about him."

"It is not easy. But, whether it is wicked of me or not, I thank God he is dead."

"And I thank God that he did not die by my hand. I shall never cease to be thankful for that."

"We shall never be able to build a boat now," she said presently, following out the natural train of her thought.

"I'm afraid not,"—with a doleful shake of the head. "Unless you have had any experience in such things."

"And so we may have to pass the rest of our lives here."

"It is better to consider how very much worse off we might be. For myself.... Besides, one never knows. Some unexpected chance may turn up."

"And you can bear to think of living on and on and on here till—the end?"

"I can bear to think of it very much better than I could a short time ago.... No cloud is black on both sides. Look on the bright side. Either of us might have been here alone. That would have been terrible—"

"I should have been dead."

"But instead of that we are two, we have comfortable shelter, the mighty blessing of fire, food enough to last us as long as we live—

"It sounds like that man in the Bible—the man who had his barns full, all he wanted to eat and drink, and so he made merry. And that night he died, if I remember rightly."

"We are not boasting. We arrived here lacking everything, and everything has been provided for us. We have reason to be grateful. Even Macro was necessary. He showed us how to turn the wreck-pile to account. If I had come ashore alone I doubt if I would ever have gone out to it again. It did not attract me.... And—he found you and brought you ashore."

"And that was the beginning of the end."

"No—the beginning of better things. We will hope the end is a long way off yet."

"I wonder ... and what it will be," said she thoughtfully.

And he wondered if in her heart there was any sweet white seed of hope akin to that which was striking its roots so deeply in his own,—and if not, if it might be possible to plant it there.

XLV

This new life, free from the shadow of perpetual menace, was full of rare and delicate charm for both of them, differing only in quality and degree according to that wherewith Nature had endowed them.

One root-thought was inevitable to both their minds—that here were they two, cut off from the rest of the world, probably for the term of their natural lives. Here, as far as they could foresee, they two must live, alone,—together; and here, in the end, they must die; their living and their dying alike unseen and unknown except by their Maker.

In his heart the white seed of the greater hope was striking deep and strong, filling his whole being with a new and exquisite delight before even it had had time to shoot and flower.

Exile for life on that barren strip of sand, which with Macro as sole fellow-sufferer would have been barely tolerable, assumed a very different aspect with Avice Drummond as his companion; and with her as sole companion, an aspect of supremest joy and expectation. It was no longer a thing to look forward to with foreboding, or at best with dull and hopeless acquiescence in the inevitable. The shadow had suddenly lifted. The desert had suddenly blossomed like the rose. The future smiled shyly as does the dawn with promise of the day.

But this new great hope, and the sense of it all in him, were of so fine and delicate a nature that he hardly dared to whisper it even in his inmost heart, lest she should see some sign of it and take fright, and all his hope vanish like smoke in a gale.

She was so fair and sweet, so charming and gracious, so pre-eminently and perfectly desirable. It was highest and keenest delight—delight so keen that at times it had in it the elements of pain—simply to watch the play of her face, so eloquently responsive to the quick emotional soul within,—the large dark eyes so clear and frank, so unreservedly trustful of him.

He would sooner die than forfeit one iota of the honour her faith conferred on him. And that great springing hope of his must be carefully covered and concealed, until such time as he should discover in her eyes the outlook of a hope responsive.

It would come. It would come, he said to himself—in time—when she should have come to know him still better and to trust him still more fully—to the uttermost.

For the ultimate goal of his desire was, in the manner of its possible attainment at all events, somewhat nebulous to him, though it set the whole distant future ablaze with rosy fires. In the nature of things, circumstanced as they were, such ultimate attainment, if ever it were reached, could be reached only by the treading of unusual ways. And to require that of any girl—and especially of a girl such as this, high-born, intelligent beyond most, and deeply versed in the great world's ways—was asking of her more than any true man, truly loving, could bring himself to ask,—unless to both their hearts no other thing were possible,—unless the barrier of Circumstance left no other possible hope or way.

And for the proving of that, Time held the keys and must have his say.

He wondered often, and with keenest anxiety, if her heart could possibly have come through all the strange experiences of her previous life unchallenged, unassailed, unwon. Seeing that she was what she was it seemed to him almost impossible.

She was to him so compact of goodness and beauty, so fashioned to bewitch, that he could not imagine any man impervious to her grace and charm. What manner of men could they be who, consorting with her daily and on terms of equality, had failed to capture a heart so made for loving?

He recalled in minutest detail all she had told him of her past life and friends and acquaintances, figured them all in his mind, weighed them jealously in the scales of his own devotion, and could not discover one trace of emotion towards one or another, but rather of aversion towards all.

Again and again she had expressed the joy she had felt at the prospect of her escape to a freer and larger life. It was, of course, not impossible that that feeling might but hide some heart-breaking disappointment of the earlier times. But he did not think so. She was to him truth personified, though still a woman. He believed in her absolutely, as a man should in the woman who holds his heart. So far as assurance could go,—without the definite question which he longed to put but did not yet dare, lest the hopeful anxiety of his present state should be turned to hopeless regret,—he felt fairly safe in building on a rosy future.

How she regarded himself he could not surely say. But she trusted him and that was a good foundation for his building.

And she? Well, that is our story!

XLVI

That thick white bank of mist clung to them for the best part of a week. But, freed from all fear of treacherous assault, it troubled them little.

Once they had to go ashore for water, but got back safely by means of their guiding-line, and as they pushed through the fog they recalled that former time, when the mate's grim figure fashioned itself suddenly out of the clammy whiteness and brought them near to a disastrous end.

For the rest they had no scarcity. The fish bit as well in the fog as in the clear, and they had pork and flour for weeks to come.

In their narrow confinement to the ship, their intimacy and knowledge of one another grew with the days. She talked well, and he was an excellent listener, and led her on and on to tell him of the past and all that had interested her in it, and mused on all she said, and sought in it enlightenment as to her heart's freedom or otherwise.

Once, when she had been roving at length through her earlier days, she broke off suddenly with, "But, mon Dieu, I am doing all the talking! Now, tell me of yourself!"

"I have so little to tell compared with you. Shall I tell you of school-days—of college—of the hospitals—of my patients and their ailments?"

"Tell me why you left it all to seek the new life."

"For very much the same reason as you did, I imagine. I was living in a groove and I wanted something wider and larger."

"And now you are sorry."

"So very sorry that if I had the chance again, and knew beforehand all that was to come, I would jump at it like the fish to our hooks," as he hauled one aboard and knocked it an the head. "And you?"

"Ye—es, I think I would have come also. Not perhaps if I had known I would have to float about on that mast. It was so terribly cold,"—with a shiver. "For the rest, I have no regrets, but it is perhaps too soon to say. In ten years hence I may have come to be sorry."

"Ay—ten years hence!" he said musingly. "Many things may happen in ten years. There's a fish on your hook," and she hauled it in and let him dispose of it.

As they sat at supper that night the blanket which supplied the place of companion-doors began to flap, and, going up to look, he found the mist whirling away before a gusty breeze.

"It's going to blow," he told her, "and when it's blown itself out we may have a spell of fine weather again," and he proceeded to block the opening with some planks he had chipped to size as well as he could with his axe.

The wind was rising rapidly, and before they turned in for the night the birds had all come in and were whirling and screaming round the ship, and lighting on it as was their custom in bad weather. But they had grown accustomed to their clamour and both slept soundly.

Wulf was shaken back to life in the dead of the early morning by a restive jerk of the ship at her rusty anchor-chain, followed by a momentary sense of the unusual. And while he lay sleepily considering the matter, his bunk heeled slowly over—over—over, and rolled him right against the side of the ship. The sound of a heavy fall, somewhere beyond, made him scramble out very wide awake, full of wonder, but dimly perceptive of what must have happened. The rusty chain had evidently parted, the ship had drifted ashore broadside on, and the force of the wind had caused her to heel over. The sound he had heard was, he feared, of Miss Drummond's falling out of her bunk.

He flung on some clothes and clawed his way out to the cabin. The floor of it was tilted up at such an angle that he had to claw his way up by the side wall as best he could.

"Are you hurt?" he cried, outside The Girl's door.

"Bruised a bit. Whatever has happened?"

"The cable has parted and we're ashore on our beam-ends. No danger, I think."

"I'll be out in a minute."

Then he became aware of a smell of burning, and found that the sand hearth with its core of fire had slid downhill and was smouldering among the silken draperies, which were beginning to break into flame.

He crawled back and tore them down and bunched them tightly together, then scooped up handfuls of sand and smothered every cinder he could see.

Miss Drummond's door opened just as he had finished.

"Stop where you are," he cried. "I'll come up for you. Everything's on the slope. I think we'd better sit on the floor and let ourselves down by degrees."

Outside, the wild screaming of the birds mingled eerily with the rush and howl of the gale. It was still quite dark. He could not see her, but groped about till he felt her blankets, then found her hand and eased her carefully down the slope, and they crouched side by side in the angle made by the floor and the side of the ship.

"Will she go down?" she asked quietly.

"Oh, no. No fear of that. We're aground. But whether she'll ever come straight again I don't know. Did it pitch you out of your bunk?"

"Yes. I woke with a crash on the floor, and could not imagine what had happened."

"I hope you didn't break yourself."

She was silent for a moment and then said, "I'm afraid I did break something, but I couldn't—"

"Broke something? What?" he asked hastily.

"My arm feels numb and queer. I fell on it."

"Let me feel it," and, kneeling in front of her, he groped till he found it, and felt it with anxious gentle fingers.

"Good Lord, it's broken!"

"I'm sorry, but I couldn't help it. You see"—

"Your right arm too! Don't move it!"

He groped about for another length of the silken hangings, tore it down, and wound it tightly round her arm. "That will keep it in place," he said. "The moment it is light I will make splints and set it properly. I am truly sorry you should have suffered so."

"Better me than you. It might have been worse. What made that chain break, I wonder? We've had worse storms than this."

"It was bound to give sooner or later. It was very old and rusted. Its time came, I suppose, and it went. Sure you have no other damages?"

"Only bumps and bruises. I felt as if the side of my face were crushed in, but I don't think it is."

"Were you in the top bunk?"

"Yes. I liked to look out of the window in the mornings."

"That's a good big fall to take unawares."

"Yes, I fell out like a sack and woke on the floor. What shall we do if she doesn't come right side up again? We can't live all upside down like this."

"There's always the other ship to fall back on ... unless her chain's broken too."

"I like our own much the best."

"But not if she stops like this.... And even if she straightened up she would heel over again in the next gale. I'm afraid we'll have to move."

"I shall always see that man's black face about the cabin, glaring at me as he used to do as if he wanted to eat me."

"If we have to go we'll give it a good cleaning, and fresh hangings, and make it to your taste."

So they chatted quietly, while the gale and the birds shrieked in chorus outside, and the waves of the lake thumped scornfully on the exposed bottom of the ship.

As soon as he could see, he rooted about for axe and knife, and chopped up a board and made a set of splints for her arm. And, though he grieved for the pain she must have suffered, he could not but feel a huge enjoyment in ministering to her.

The mere touch of her firm white flesh was a rare delight and made his fingers tingle. He did his best to think of her only as a patient, but found it impossible. She was so very much more to him than any ordinary patient ever had been or could be.

But for her suffering, he felt inclined to bless the breaking of the rusty cable. It brought them closer than ever before. It threw her more than ever on to his care. With her right arm prisoner she would be able to do but little for herself. She had not been able to dress herself properly, but had simply swathed a blanket about her night attire, leaving the broken arm free. But even so, her natural taste and capability had so arranged it, even in the darkness and moment of danger, that she looked like a Greek goddess, he said to himself, with one arm in a sling. One can make allowances for him.

As the light grew stronger he saw, to his distress, that her face had also suffered sorely in her fall. The whole right side was badly bruised and discoloured.

"Is it very bad?" she asked, as she saw him looking at it. "It feels sore and my head hums like a bee-hive."

"You got a bad bump there. I will get some salt water and bathe it. Our fresh will all be gone in the upset, but I'll sling a bucket under the scupper-hole and we'll have enough for some coffee presently. When you've had some breakfast you will go and lie down in my bunk. If you could get a good sleep it would be the very best thing for you. Does the arm hurt much?"

"Not so much as it did, but I don't think I can sleep."

"You will when you lie down. You've had a bad shaking up. I'm truly sorry that all the penalties have fallen on you."

"It's a good thing you didn't break yourself too. Suppose we'd broken all our arms!" and she laughed a wry little laugh.

He crawled up the slope, and wormed himself through his barricade, and came back presently with a bucketful of water, found a piece of soft linen and insisted on bathing her face, under plea that she would joggle the broken arm if she tried to do it herself.

Then he scraped together at the foot of the slope sand enough for a small hearth, split some wood and kindled a fire, but found it necessary to open one of the ports to leeward to let out the smoke. When he did so he found the water within a foot of it and could only hope they would heel over no more. He proceeded to make cakes and coffee, and then fried some salt pork, and anointed the bruised face with the fat of it, and she found it soothing.

When he had cut up her meat for her, and she had managed to eat a little, he helped her into his bunk, the upper one because it was airier and allowed more head-room, and covered her with blankets and told her to go to sleep. And then, since there was nothing more to be done, he crawled up the slope and got her blankets off the floor of her room, and made up a bed for himself in the angle at the foot of the slope. He lay for a time listening to the gale, and pondering the possibility of its doing them any further damage, and fell asleep with the matter still unsettled.

XLVII

When he awoke it was close on mid-day, unless his appetite misled him. He prepared another meal and then tapped gently on The Girl's door. Receiving no answer he peeped into the dim little room and found her still sleeping soundly, her head in the crook of her left arm, from which the wide sleeve of her night-dress had slipped down,—as fair a picture as man could wish to look upon, in spite of her bruised face and broken arm.

He stood watching her for a moment with bated breath, and recalled that first morning when she came ashore and he had doubted if he could recover her; and he thanked God again for the dogged obstinacy which would not let him accept defeat so long as smallest hope remained.

She moved, opened her heavy eyes, and lay quietly looking at him, just as she had done that other time, and for a brief space there was no more recognition in them than there had been then.

"What is it? Who are you?" she asked, and he suffered a momentary shock. But for reply he laid his cool strong hand—rougher than it used to be, but vitally sensitive to the feel of her—on the broad white forehead, and found it hot and throbbing. That did not greatly surprise him. There was sure to be a certain feverishness after such an experience. And he would have given much for five minutes' root round his old dispensary.

He had nothing,—nothing but common sense, and his professional knowledge, and Nature's simplest remedies. He went out quietly and got cold water and soft linen, and bathed the throbbing forehead and then laid the wet bandage on it.

"That is nice," she said softly. "What a trouble I am to you!"

"Oh, frightful!" he smiled, as he changed the cloth for a fresh one. "You see how I resent it. Has the arm been hurting?"

"It hurts at times, but my head is the worst, and I feel bruised all over."

"But no more breakages?" he asked anxiously.

"I don't think so, just bruised and stiff and sore."

He hesitated for a second. She was so very much more to him than simply a patient.

"Will you let me remind you that I am a doctor? The very best cure for all that is gentle rubbing. If you will allow me I will undertake to reduce the pains by one half."

"Then please do, Doctor, for I ache in every bone."

And he drew off all her blankets but one, and through it proceeded to massage the aching limbs, and had never in his life found greater enjoyment in his work. He even ventured to treat the throbbing head in the same way, drawing his fingers soothingly over the white forehead and up into the masses of her hair.

"There is virtue in your fingers," she murmured drowsily, and before he had done she was sleeping soundly again. Then he laid another wet cloth on her forehead and left Nature to do her share in the good work.

It was fortunate that she had little appetite for the next few days. The cakes he made for her, and water, scrupulously boiled and cooled and flavoured with coffee, amply satisfied her; and he, himself lived on pork, fish and fresh meat being unobtainable.

For four days the gale bellowed round them, but being to leeward, and protected somewhat by the heeling of the ship, they felt it less than if they had been on an even keel, and it never kept The Girl from sleeping.

Much of that time Wulf spent in an endeavour to obtain salt from sea water, the lack of it being one of their greatest deprivations. As the result of many boilings and the careful scraping up of the slight encrustations on his pans, he managed to get a little, and exultantly let The Girl taste it as a great treat; but it was a long and slow process.

The default of her right arm made her very dependent on him in many little ways, but never was service more tactfully rendered or more delighted in by the servitor. And every service, so rendered and accepted, made for increased knowledge on both sides, and so for closer intimacy.

Never, in all her contact with the greater world, had she met any man in whom she felt such implicit confidence as in this man. Never, since that first time her wondering eyes met his, when his strenuous exertions had dragged her back from the dead, had he by word or deed or look, raised one shadow of fear or mistrust in her mind. In everything, to the extremest point of death itself, he had proved himself a simple, brave, and honest gentleman.

And as she lay there helpless, with the gale howling outside and the broken waves of the lake clop-clopping in the strakes under her ear, she had much time to think of him and all he had done and was doing for her, and all her thought was warm and grateful.

"I am a dreadful burden to you," she would say. "And you are very very good to me."

And he would answer her, with the smile she liked to provoke, "But for your suffering in the matter I would tell you how grateful I am to that rotten chain for giving me the opportunity. I count it a privilege as well as a pleasure."

And when he had left her, she would think at times how it might have been with her if it were not this man but the other with whom she had been left alone. And she would shiver at the thought, and then remember that if the other had been alone she would not have been there, for he could never have drawn her back from the dead as this one had done.

And she thought also at times of their fight with the other in the fog, and followed that idea up and shivered still more. For if the mate had killed this man it would indeed have gone hard with her. Ay, she had much to be thankful for, and thankful she was.

And as to the future.... It was all vague and dim, as the future always must be, but she had no fear of it, because she trusted this man so perfectly.

Vague and dim it might be, but it was shot with rosy gleams.

Whatever he might ask of her she would hold it right because he asked it. She had found him worthy. She would trust him completely, ask what he might. Yes, ... ask ... what ... he ... might.

XLVIII

"The sun's coming out," was his cheerful announcement, one morning when he came in with her breakfast. "And here's some fish for you at last."

"The sight of it makes me hungry."

"That's the best news you've given me for four days. There's some salt for you in payment," he said, with full pride of accomplishment.

"Salt is a great treat. Have you left any for yourself?"

"Oh, I've got some. I'm going to set up a regular salt factory as soon as you're about again."

"I would like to get up and go on deck when I've had breakfast. Surely the ship is not so tilted as it was."

"Not quite so bad, but I'm afraid it will never come quite right side up again. It's hard and fast on the shore at present. I could wade across."

"I must see it. I will get up as soon as I have had my breakfast."

"Can you manage?" he asked doubtfully. "You must keep that arm quiet, you know."

"I'll try anyway. If I get stuck I will call," and in due course she called, and he found that she had managed to get her blankets round her, and that as gracefully as ever in some marvellous fashion, but she had doubted her power of getting out of the bunk in its lopsided state without his help.

He stepped up on to the lower bunk, and worked his arms under her.

"Now, if you wouldn't mind steadying yourself with your usable hand on my shoulder—so! There you are!" and he lifted her gently to her feet on the floor. "Now, hang on to my arm.... But your shoes?—you had better have them on. In your own room of course. Wait and I'll get them," and he climbed up and got them, and put them on and tied them for her. "I've pegged some slats across the slope for better foot-hold. You can't slip," and he got her safely out on to the deck.

"It is delightful to be in fresh air again," she said, as she drank it in. "I wish the good weather would last for ever."

"We'll hope for a good long spell anyhow. Doesn't it feel odd to be so close to the shore? We'll have rabbit for dinner. You must almost have forgotten what it tastes like."

"I can still just remember," she laughed.

"I'll get up some blankets and tuck you into this corner, and then I'll go and get some and some fresh water. Our raft's blown ashore and the other one also. I shall have to wade."

He made her comfortable in the corner, got his buckets and a stick, and dropped over the side.

She lay watching him as he waded ashore, saw him stop for a moment to examine the raft, and then, with a wave of the hand, he set off for the pools, swinging his buckets jauntily.

Were there many such men in the world, she wondered, and why had she never met any of them before? The men she had met were so very different. They were as a rule so elusive and evasive that you never quite knew what they were driving at ... except that it was certain to be for their own satisfaction and advantage ... and that unless you were always on your guard it was likely to turn out ill for you ... a queer world, and life was a puzzle past comprehending.....

She was glad to be out of it ... even on this sandbank.... Life was sweeter here, and certainly very much simpler.... Well, perhaps a little too severely simple in some respects.... But one could not have everything.... Thank God, again, that it was this man who was with her and not that other!...

She saw him coming at last with his full buckets, and presently made out a couple of rabbits hanging round his neck.

"The birds are having a great time out yonder," he called to her. "Lots of new wreckage, I expect, and they've been fasting. I must get across as soon as I can and see if the storm has brought anything for us.

One never knows,"—he had come alongside, and lifted the buckets and tossed the rabbits on to the deck. "I'll fasten the raft to the chain there"—and he hauled himself along on it to the bows.

She heard a smothered exclamation, and presently he climbed up and came along the deck with something in his hand.

"What is it?" she asked.

"What do you make of that?" and he handed her the link of the rusty cable which had given way and let them drift ashore.

She turned it over in her fingers. Just where it had opened, the metal glinted in the sunshine, and just above that there was a patch that looked like grease. She shook her head.

"Don't you see?—it's been filed enough to weaken it, and there was grease on the file."

"And you think—" with a shocked look.

"Undoubtedly. No one else could have done it. But what his idea was, I can't make out. Just to make trouble, I suppose. Of course if the wind had come the other way, as it has done once or twice, we might have blown right down the lake. It was a mean trick. I wonder when he did it."

"I am more thankful than ever that he's gone."

"So am I.... I've been thinking we'd better move across there as soon as possible."

"Must we? I have grown so fond of this old ship."

"But we can't live on the slope like this. Besides, if a gale did come the opposite way we might have trouble. I'll go over presently and begin cleaning. When I've finished you'll find it much more comfortable than this."

"I shall always like this the best."

"I was thinking as I went over to the pools that it might not be a bad idea to build some kind of a house on shore. I can get timber enough for a hundred. You see, we don't quite know what winter may be like in this place, but it's pretty sure to be a time of storms."

"Can you build a house?"

"One never knows what one can do till one tries. This is a great place for bringing out one's unknown faculties. I've done a good many things I never expected to do, since I came here."

"It might be a good plan. Can't it wait till I can help?"

"We'll see. We must do like the ants and squirrels—work hard while it's fine and get in our supplies for the winter. We are mighty fortunate to have such a store to draw upon."

He spent all the rest of the day slaving like a charwoman on the 'Jane and Mary,' and The Girl lay in her nest watching him, as he went up and down, now flinging rubbish overboard, then hauling up buckets of water, and sluicing and mopping, with every now and again a cheery wave of hand or mop in her direction, and long periods below devoted, she did not doubt, to the doing of more of those things which he had never done, or expected to do, until he came there. And her heart was very warm to him, knowing that it was not for his own comfort but for hers that all these great labours were toward.

She saw him busy on deck, bending and bobbing up and down, and once she caught the gleam of vivid colours, and wondered what he was at. He was a long time below after that, and then he went ashore for a load of sand, and when it was getting dark she suddenly caught glimpse of his head in the water as he wound up the day's work with a very necessary swim.

He came across on the raft all aglow, but visibly tired and hungry, and greeted her with a cheery, "I think you'll find it all to your liking. I've swabbed away every trace of the former tenants and everything is fresh and new."

"I wish I could have helped."

"Oh, but you did, by sitting quietly here and getting better, to say nothing of a wave of the hand now and then."

"That was not doing much when you were working like a—"

"Like a nigger. I looked like one too till I'd had that swim. Now I'll get supper ready, and tomorrow we'll flit, and you'll be able to walk about on an even keel without any danger of falling."

He helped her down to the cabin and their very close quarters at the bottom of the slope, and set to work preparing their evening meal. And the more incongruous his occupations and the more menial his tasks, the more The Girl's heart warmed towards him.

XLIX

In the morning, as soon as they had eaten, he got the raft round to the lower side of the ship, ruthlessly hacked out a section of the bulwarks so that she could step down with the smallest possible exertion, and took her across to the new house.

Getting her on board without shock to the broken arm was not so easy. He moored the raft, stem and stern, and braced it tight so that it could not move. Then he built on it a pyramid of three empty boxes, forming steps up which she could climb high enough to grip his strong hand teaching down through the gap in the side and so be drawn safely up on to the deck, which he had swabbed with sand and water till it was cleaner than it had been for years.

"It is nice to be able to walk on the flat of one's feet again," she said, and he led her down below to a cabin gorgeous as an Eastern room with drapings of amber silk and blue, and every bit of woodwork scoured as clean as elbow-grease could make it.

"It is delightful," she said fervidly. "How you must have slaved at it!"

"And how I enjoyed doing it!"

There was a new sand hearth, nicely banked up between planks pegged upright on the floor, and a pile of wood on it ready for lighting. He lit a match with his flint and steel, and handed it to her as before, so that she might start the first fire in the new home.

"You will take your old room," he said. "Then if we should topple over again you won't be able to fall out of your bunk. Now I'll go back and bring over all our belongings. I made a complete clearance here, except some of the stores which we can use," and before mid-day he had everything transferred and stowed away.

He spent most of the afternoon weaving in and out of their rusty cable lengths of the least-rotten rope he could lay hands on, in order to strengthen it and stop its chafing as much as possible. But below water he could not go beyond a foot or two, and the lower links he had to leave to Providence.

As he worked, The Girl paced the deck, rejoicing in its horizontality, and came each time to lean over the bows and watch him and say a lively word or two. And, if any had been there to see, it would have been difficult to believe that two such cheerful people were, to the very best of their belief, condemned by an inscrutable fate to imprisonment for life on this lonely sandbank,—to a confinement as solitary in some respects, and in the prospect of escape as hopeless, as that of the Bastille itself.

But—they were together; and Adam and Eve, cast out of the Garden, could still make a home in the wilderness and turn the joys that were left them to fullest account.

L

He was up betimes next morning, and had fish for their breakfast before she came out of her room, and, moreover, had made cakes and full provision for all her needs during the day.

"I shall go out there at once," he said. "You will not mind being left? I want to get in everything we shall need for the winter as soon as possible."

"I am sorry not to be able to help, but I shall be quite all right here. You will..." she began, with a quite novel access of timidity, and finished with a rush,—"you will be very careful. I am rather fearful of that horrid wreckage. If you never came back—"

"I will be very careful, and I will certainly come back—laden, I hope, with good things," and he went off on the raft, and she stood watching and waving her hand at times when he turned, until he disappeared along the spit. And as he went his heart beat high, for he did not believe that her fears were chiefly for herself, although she had made it appear so.

He found the wreckage considerably altered. The gale had swept it bare of all traces of their previous peckings and nibblings, and had piled and stuffed it with tempting-looking new plunder. And with things less attractive. Whatever had been left of the mate had disappeared, hurled down probably into some black crack. But, during the day, in various crannies he came on no less than three drowned men, partly dressed in what appeared to him naval uniform, anyway not in the usual slops of the merchant service. And they set him thinking how narrow, yet how sharp, was the dividing line between themselves and the outer world.

He built his raft as usual and toiled all day, smashing his way through scores of boxes, cases, seamen's chests, and rooting in them as eagerly as ever did the mate, but with a different spirit within him.

First he gathered indispensable stores, and practice had by this time so perfected his eye that he could tell almost at a glance what a cask or box contained, how long it had been afloat, and what damage its contents were likely to have suffered.

Many odd, and some extraordinary and incomprehensible, things his hasty search brought to light. It was indeed an absorbing inquisition into, an endless revelation of, the ruling passions and frailties of the human heart.

Little hoards of money and jewelry were his commonest finds, pitiful now in view of their uselessness to those who had gathered them. But he would take from the pile nothing but what it rightly owed them, means of life and the tempering of its hard conditions, and he left all these untouched. Tobacco and pipes, and flints and steel, were lawful plunder.

One brass-bound chest he broke open and found great store of women's clothing, rich with lace and finely wrought even to the eyes of a man. The Girl might find that useful and he began to make a selection, with the eyes of her delight dancing before him as he did so. Then with a start, and a sharp breath of amazement, he straightened up for a moment, crammed everything back into the chest, and hauled it to the edge of the pile and hurled it into the sea. For there, at the bottom, wedged tight among all these delicate draperies was the body of a new-born child, strangled at its birth, as he knew by the look of it.

Bundles of letters, papers which might be of highest import to waiting friends, anxious heirs, business houses, he found in places, but left them as they were.

He came on another box containing women's clothes, of plainer material and simpler make, and rooted carefully after the character of its owner before deciding to take some back for The Girl. It seemed above suspicion, and he rejoiced to be able to supply some of her more pressing needs. Clothes for himself the wreckage had always been generous of, but to come upon two chests of women's things in one day was extraordinary. They had at times searched far and wide and anxiously, and never lighted on one.

He got back with his load, and in two journeys from the spit got it all on board, before it was too dark for his reward in The Girl's exuberant joy at the things he had brought for her.

"Shoes! ... stockings! ... Some proper needles and thread! ... and oh, but I am glad to see these other things! ... I was washing some of my things while you were away, but it was not easy with one hand ... And another brush and comb! ... and scissors! If we can clean them I can cut your hair for you."

"I shall be grateful. I feel like a savage. I'll clean them all right."

"And did you make any strange discoveries?" she asked, while they sat at supper, as one asks news of the outer world from a traveller.

"Oh, heaps. Jewels and money, and papers, letters and so on—"

"They might be interesting,—in winter days."

"I had not thought of that. I'll bring you an armful tomorrow."

"You will go again tomorrow?"

"I must go till I think we have enough for the winter's siege. There may be weeks when I can't get out there. This storm brought in a mighty pile of stuff and it's best to get it while it's in good condition. Do you want more clothes if I can find them?"

"A woman never has too many," she laughed. "But don't waste time searching for them. I can manage very well, especially now that I have needles and thread."

"I just smash open each box as I come to it. One never knows what one may come upon. Their contents are as different as their owners. I have been trying to imagine them from their belongings."

He wrought at the pile for many days, and she filled in the time at home by evaporating endless pans of water over the fire to get the salt, and managed to accumulate quite a fair supply.

He brought over for her amusement a great bundle of written papers which she was too busy to delve into at the moment, all her time being given to salt-making. And then one day he returned exultant with some great lumps of rock salt, such as cattle love to lick, and her little efforts were like to be put in the shade. But he averred that her salt was infinitely the finer to a cultivated taste and they would use it only on very special occasions.

He brought her too a quantity of oatmeal in cases, and—treasure-trove indeed—a dozen cans of the oil used for ships' lights. He searched in vain for a lantern, but felt sure he could turn that oil to account in some way during the long winter nights. From the marks on the cases in the neighbourhood of these discoveries, and the superior quality of some of their contents, he thought a warship must have gone down not very far away.

His belief was confirmed by finding other unusual supplies in the same place, and he worked at it for days until there was hardly a case or box or barrel which he had not tapped.

One of his greatest finds was a handful of spare tools, in a chest that had probably belonged to a ship's carpenter—an auger, a gimlet, a chisel, a screwdriver, and a small piece of sharpening hone. And that same day he lighted on an unpretentious little box, stoutly made of deal, which had swelled with the water to the partial protection of its contents. A glance inside showed him how great was this treasure, and he carried it at once to his raft and bestowed it with care.

When he opened the little deal case on deck that evening The Girl gave a joyful cry, "Books! Oh, but I am glad, and the winter nights will not be long! Let me see them all quickly.—"Poems," by Robert Burns. "Life of Samuel Johnson," by James Boswell. The Book of Common Prayer. "Decline and Fall of the Roman Empire," by Edward Gibbon, Vol 1. "The Vicar of Wakefield," by Oliver Goldsmith. "Tristram Shandy," by Laurence Sterne. "The Castle of Otranto," by Horace Walpole. The Annual Register—one, two, three volumes. "Tom Jones," by Henry Fielding. "Clarissa Harlowe," by Samuel Richardson. Cruden's Concordance. Hymns by Rev. Isaac Watts, D.D. A Bible. One, two, three volumes of sermons. John Bunyan's "Pilgrim's Progress" and "Holy War," and Foxe's "Book of Martyrs"! Oh, we shall do famously. Now what do you make of the owner of this fine thing?" she challenged him merrily.

"A parson, I should say. They are the greatest readers. But that is easily seen," and he turned to the fly-leaves of several of the volumes and found them all inscribed with the same name, 'James Elwes, Esq. M.A. Fellow of Brasenose College, Oxford.'

"Good Mr Elwes! I am sorry he is drowned, but I am grateful to him for taking his books with him when he travelled, and leaving them behind him when he went. That is the greatest find yet," said she.

"We won't despise the lower things. All the same I'm glad to have the books."

"They will be a wonderful help. Let us dry them at once. They are more precious than jewels," and he got her soft cloths, and they carefully mopped up and wiped over every volume and promised them they should be set in the sun to complete their cure on the morrow.

"And those horrid birds?" she asked, as they worked. "You had no trouble from them?"

"They were all too busy elsewhere. There is grain enough floating about there to feed a city. They will be plump and happy birds for some time to come. They were too busy even to quarrel and they never so much as looked my way."

LI

As though exhausted by its late violence, or needing rest before renewing it, the weather continued mild and open except for occasional mists.

Thanks to her own caution and Wulfrey's assiduous attention, The Girl's arm was going on well, and she was looking forward eagerly to being an active member of society again.

"You see, I have never been laid up in my life before," she said, "and it is unnatural to me. A dozen times a day I have to stop that wretched arm when it wants to do something."

"A very little longer and it shall do what it wants, within reason. Let me rub it again for you."

"You are a great believer in rubbing," she said, with reminiscent smiles, as she surrendered the arm to him, and he rubbed it gently and tirelessly to keep the sinews and muscles from stiffening.

"I have found great virtue in it, and great reward," he smiled back.

He took her ashore almost every day, and they rambled far along the northern beach and enjoyed the soft autumnal days to the full. But all the time his thoughts were on the coming winter whose rigours he had no means of forecasting. And so, like a wise man, he made such provision as was possible for the worst.

He set her to gathering and drying every herb she deemed suitable for seasoning purposes. And he himself caught very many fish and split them open and dried them in the sun as he had read was done elsewhere. He tried some rabbits in the same way, but they did not take to it and had to be used for bait.

And, after a few days' rest from his exertions at the wreckage, he set to work on building a house on shore, in case anything should happen to the 'Jane and Mary,' or they should find solid ground preferable to water during the winter gales.

He had for a long time past secured every nail he could knock out of the old timbers, and regarded them as most precious possessions. The finding of the auger and gimlet opened up wider possibilities. Where nails are scarce, a hole and a peg may take their place. Wood he had in superfluity, for the remains of every raft that had brought cargo from the pile lay strewn about the spit, in some cases hurled half-way across it by the waves that broke there in the storm times.

Where best to build was a matter not easily decided. They would need all the sunshine obtainable. But all the heaviest gales came from the south and west and from these they wanted shelter. And they must be within easy reach of the fresh-water pools and not too far from the ship, where their supplies would be mostly stored.

After much discussion they fixed on an odd little hollow—a mere cup in the centre of three sandhills of size, which stood close together and moreover were well matted with wire-grass and looked too solid to whirl away in a gale as the smaller hills constantly did.

To the south-west of these stood the largest hill in the neighbourhood, and this would break the force of the gales in that direction. The water-pools lay out in the sandy plain just beyond this hill.

Wulf entered on the building of this first house he had ever attempted, with the gusto of a schoolboy.

"I feel about fourteen," he laughed, as he detailed his ideas to her.

"So do I,—except this wretched arm, which is one hundred and five."

"We'll soon have it back to fourteen. You see, if I can carve out the sides of those three smaller hills, and back our house into each of them, it will make immensely for solidity and warmth. No gale can blow through a sand-hill, though they do waltz about now and again. But these seem fairly well set and fixed. I'll start on it tomorrow. I wish I had a spade and a saw. I can chop out some kind of a spade from a plank, maybe, but, lacking a saw, the house will be a bit rough, I'm afraid."

"That doesn't matter as long as it stands up and keeps us warm."

"Oh, I'll guarantee it will stand up and keep you warm."

"Can you make a chimney?"

"I've been thinking of that. I will run four boards up through a hole in the roof, and we must try to induce the smoke to go up. There is no clay here, you see, nor stone,—nothing but sand."

The site settled, he set to work at once rafting his timber across the lake from the spit, and then hauling it across the sandy plain past the fresh-water pools, and this gave him a full week's hard labour. Some of the lighter planks he let The Girl drag across, since she insisted on having at all events one hand in the work. The heavier ones were as much as he could handle himself. In his rest times, and after supper of a night, he whittled pegs till he had an ample supply, and sharpened his axes with the bit of hone he had found in the carpenter's chest.

With his axe he hacked out a rude spade from a plank, and trimmed the handle and the point with his knife; and then he set to work on his three sandhills, cutting down the side of each where it rounded down into the cup-like hollow, and flinging the sand into the cup itself to make a level floor.

The building of such a house was entirely new to him, but he had brains and he bent them all to every problem that presented itself, and never failed to find the way out. For instance,—the space he wished his house to occupy between the sandhills was quite twelve feet in width, and his planks ran mostly to six or eight feet only. There must therefore be a row of posts in the middle, with one or more beams on top as a ridge-pole, from which he could carry side pieces to the walls six feet away on either side, and he had foreseen some difficulty in fixing these posts absolutely rigid in the yielding sand. If they wobbled or gave in any direction his roof would be in danger.

But before he began carving down his sand-slopes he had settled that point. He selected his uprights, the longest and strongest in his stock, chopped them to size, and to the end of each pegged stout flat cross-pieces, boring the holes with his auger and driving home the pegs with the back of his axe. These he set up in a line in the middle of the hollow, standing upright on their cross-piece feet. Then, as he carved down his slope, every spadeful of sand buried the cross-pieces deeper, till, when he had finished, they were under two feet of well-trampled sand and he looked upon their rigidity as a personal triumph.

That was surely as extraordinary a house as was ever built by a man who knew nothing whatever about building. It took him five full weeks and he enjoyed every minute of it. And so did The Girl, for she sat in the sun, watching all his cheerful activities with envious eyes because she was so unable to share them, discussing points with him as they arose, giving suggestions and advice which he always adopted when they chimed with his own, and approving heartily of all he did.

"I wish I could help,"—how many times she said it, and thought it very many more. "It is disgusting to have to sit and watch while you work like a—like a galley-slave."

"Galley-slaves don't build houses—not such houses as this anyway. There never was such a house before," he laughed. "Besides, you help more than you know by simply sitting there and approving of it. 'They also serve,' you know, 'who only sit and watch.'"

"Who says that?"

"One John Milton,—not quite in those words, but the meaning is the same. As a matter of fact, he had, I believe, just gone blind when he said it and was feeling rather out of it. Your arm will soon be all right again. It's doing famously."

Truly a wonderful house, not so much because of the quaint way in which its difficulties were surmounted or evaded—which alone might have given an ordinary builder nightmares for the rest of his life, but more especially by reason of the rose-golden thoughts which swept at times like flame through hearts and minds of both watcher and builder as they wrought. If all those glowing thoughts could have transmuted themselves into visible adornment of that rough little home no fairy palace could have vied with it.

For ever and again—and mostly ever—in his heart—helping the auger as it bored and the axe as it hammered the pegs well home—was the thought that was radiant enough and mighty enough to transform that desolate bank of sand into a veritable Garden of Eden;—"If no rescue comes, here we shall live—she and I—together,—one in heart and soul and body, and here, maybe, we shall die. But death is a long way off, and Love lives on forever. I would not exchange my Kingdom for all the Kingdoms of the earth."

And perhaps he would permit himself a foretaste from the cup of that intoxicating happiness, in a quick caressing glance at her as she sat in the sand nursing her arm; and at times she caught those stolen glances, for her eyes found great satisfaction in his tireless energy and visible enjoyment in his work.

And she knew as well as if he had told her in words,—nay better, for, without a word, the heart speaks louder than all the words in the world when it shines through honest eyes,—she knew all that possessed him concerning her, and she was not discomforted thereby.

She trusted him completely. She had never felt towards any man as she did to this man. Whatever he willed for her would be right. Her whole heart and soul rejoiced that he should find such hope and joy in her. She was wholly his for the asking, but she knew he would not ask it all until he was satisfied in his own mind that he was right in asking and she in giving.

She felt like a wounded bird, sitting below there, while her mate built their nest up above. But not, she said to herself, like their island birds, for they were harsh and cruel, with cold hard eyes, and ever-craving hunger in place of hearts.

That wonderful house, when at last it was finished, would have given no satisfaction to the soul of any ordinary builder, but to these two it was a monument of hard work and difficulties overcome.

It contained one room twelve feet square in front, with two smaller rooms opening out of it at the back. The roof sloped slightly from ridge-pole to side-walls and was made in four layers—boards side by side below, then thick sheets of crimson velvet, an outer shield of overlapping planks, and a thick coat of sand and growing wire-grass over all. He was hopeful that it would withstand the heaviest gales and rains the winter might bring. The walls were of stout boards backed up against the sandhills, with new sandhills thrown up in the intervening spaces, and inside they were draped with more crimson velvet, of which they had a large supply. The floor was of planks. The door had been a troublesome problem, and, lacking hinges, had to be lifted bodily in and out of its place. The bay-window alongside it was the cabin skylight from the 'Martha' and this, and the square smoke-shaft of four stout boards above the sand hearth, they regarded as crowning achievements.

Emboldened by success, and finding enjoyment in the development of a craft of which he had never suspected himself until now,—experiencing too, to the very fullest, the primal blessing of work, he evolved an arm-chair for The Girl, out of a barrel that had once held salt pork, and when its asperities were softened and hidden under voluminous folds of red velvet she assured him it was the most comfortable chair she had ever sat in.

And, for his part, he knew that no girl ever sat in any chair that ever was made who could compare with her.

Beds too he made with some old sail-cloth fitted to rough frames, and a table, and their furnishing sufficed, though he promised to add to it during the winter.

The Girl's arm was well again, though he still urged caution in the use of it, and kept a watchful eye on it and her; and never had he felt himself so full of the joy and strength of life. When the house was finished, they brought over a supply of stores and lived in it for a time, and turned the waning autumn days to account by long ramblings all over the island, in anticipation of the days when ill weather might coop them strictly within narrower bounds.

There were no discoveries to make in land or sea or sky, scarcely any in themselves. He felt assured in his own mind that she was not unaware of all that he felt for her. The fact, the great undeniable fact, that she did not seem to resent it, was a deep joy to him.

Their good-comradeship had known no cloud. She was as charmingly frank and gracious as ever. She talked away without reserve or constraint of that strange past life of hers, which, in every smallest particular, was so absolutely the opposite of this one. And never once did she display any hankering after Egypt, rather seemed to regard this as the Promised Land, or at all events the doorway to it.

Ever and again the possibilities of rescue or escape came to the front in their discussions, but grew less and less as the weeks went by. He had been seven months on the island, and she four, and save herself, in all that time no other living soul had come to it,—unless, as the mate had so strenuously held, the bodies of those discomforting sea-birds were occupied by the souls of drowned sailor men.

"And you, you know, were a miracle," he would remind her. "The chances against you were about a thousand to one—"

"And you were that one."

"It was not that I was thinking of—"

"I never forget it."

"This place is undoubtedly shunned, as Macro said. It is known as a death-trap. No ship comes here except in pieces. No man comes until he is dead. And so, our prospects of rescue or escape are very small, I fear. For your sake I wish it were otherwise."

"Have I shown signs of discontent, then? I assure you I have never been so ... so content to wait and hope. It is the most delightful holiday from the world I have ever had.... Sometime perhaps we shall look back upon it as the wide dividing line between the old world and the new ... and between the old life and the new."

"A line is black as a rule."

"It may be light," she said, and waved her hand expressively towards the shimmering golden spear which the setting sun sent quivering over the water right up to their feet, as they stood watching it on the beach.

"If we could only walk on it!" she said softly, as the red disc swelled and sank and disappeared amid a glory of tender lucent greens and blues and glowing orange, with a line of crimson fire on the edge of every hovering cloud, and a heavenful of crimson flakes and splashes smouldering slowly into gray above their heads.

"It points the road, but we cannot take it," he said quietly, and they turned and went back to the house.

There were times when she thought he was about to tell her all that was in his heart concerning her. She could see it in his face and eyes and restless manner. And she was ready to respond.

There were times when it was almost more than he could do to keep it all in. He believed she knew. He hardly doubted her response.

But he said to himself, with set jaw and a firmer grip of his manhood,—"She has known me just four months. She is here helpless in my hands. I may not press her unduly, for she might feel that she could hardly say me nay. Her very helplessness must make me the more careful and considerate."

And more than once, when the desire of his heart was leaping to his lips, he jumped up abruptly and went out into the night and strode away along the beach. And there he would pace to and fro under the quiet stars, with the black waves swirling up the shore in long slow gleams of shimmering silver, till the peace of it all passed into his blood, and presently he would go quietly in again, with face and heart toned down to reasonableness.

And when he went out so, The Girl would smile to herself at times, as one who understood. And again, at times the smile would slowly fade and she would sit thoughtful. But, if she wondered somewhat, and found him beyond her complete understanding, she liked him none the less for his restraint.

She was quite happy in their present fellowship, but she knew it could not continue so, indefinitely. A man always wants more. The woman gives.

She felt towards this man as she had never felt towards any man before. Without a word spoken, she was satisfied as to the integrity of his intentions, as she had never been of any of those who had approached her in that old life, and she had been approached by many. But the coinage of love about the Court had grown as debased as did the paper money of the Republic later on. Whispers of love had become but fair cloaks for foul deeds. This man had whispered nothing, but she understood him and held him in honour.

And she was in no hurry. His love would not burn out, or she was much mistaken in him. The flame repressed burns brightest in the end.

And then ... and then.... Well, she sometimes laid hold of the future by the ears, as it were, and held its changing face while she peered intently into it, and endeavoured to read there all that it might mean for her.

Sooner or later he would open his heart to her—and that would be the first change. Their relationship would of necessity become closer and warmer. She would welcome that. It would bring great happiness to them both.

And then—later on—sometime—when all hope of rescue or escape had left them ... he would ask still more of her.... That was inevitable.... And in her heart, hiding behind a thinning cloud of doubt, which had, when first it came upon her, been tinged with dismay, she knew he would be right, and that in consenting, she would do no wrong, although it must run counter to all her normal views of right and wrong.

She faced it all squarely and honestly,—Courtship properly ends in Marriage. If by this accident of their strange fate the regular marriage rites prescribed by the law of the land could not take place, they would have to content themselves without them. It was inevitable.

Elemental views of right and wrong were indeed tap-rooted in her heart and safe from bruising. But she recognised that circumstances alter cases and that normal views were out of place here.

And as to the law of the land—what country claimed this bank of sand she did not know. It was a No Man's Land, outside the pale of all laws save God's and Nature's.

With no man she had ever met, except this man, could she have imagined herself considering possibilities such as these. But with him she would feel as safe and happy as if all the archbishops and bishops in the land had performed the ceremony. For, after all, it was only man's law and man's ceremony; and God's law and Nature's were mightier than these.

With such thoughts in her—deep thoughts and long—she could wait quietly, and she veiled her feelings for him lest he should deem her of light mind and too easily to be won.

Now and again, induced perhaps by some adverse humour of body or atmosphere, a plaguy little fear would leap at her heart and nibble it with sharp teeth,—could it be that he had ties in the old life of which he had never dared to hint,—some other woman—to whom he was bound by honour or by law?

He had told her much, and yet not very much. Had he told her all? Did men ever tell all? He had told her much, but there was room in what he had not told for anything—for everything.

But surely he had one time said that he had left no ties behind him,—that he was alone.

If there should be anything of the kind it would explain his self-restraint, his quiet service, the looks he could not wholly check, the words he did not speak.

That his heart had gone out to herself she could not mistake. But that was not incompatible with ties elsewhere that might keep them apart.

But fears such as that could not hold her long. They had sprung up, in spite of her, once or twice when he had jumped up and left her alone, and gone out into the night to pace the beach. But when he returned, quieted and all himself again, they disappeared at once, and her heart was at rest. Wrong and this man had nothing in common, she said to herself. She felt as sure of his honour as of her own.

LII

"This weather cannot last much longer," he said, one night as they sat talking after supper; he with his pipe, which she never would permit him to sacrifice on her account, pronouncing the smell of it homely and comfortable, in spite of his apologies for the varied qualities of his tobacco. "We must be somewhere near the end of October."

"It is either the 21st or 22nd or 23rd," she said very definitely.

"You have kept count?"

"Except the time I was on the mast and before I came to life again."

"Two days probably."

"I imagined so. In that case it is the 21st."

"And we must be ready for November and bad weather. Would you sooner stop here or go back to the 'Jane and Mary'?"

"We could not be more comfortable than we are here. But I will do whatever you wish."

He glanced at her through the wreathing smoke of fire and pipe, for nothing they could do would make it all go up the chimney.

Would she say as much if he asked her more? he wondered.

Was she ready to be asked? Or was it still too soon?

If he told her all that was in his heart, would he startle her out of this most pleasant companionship?

She sat gazing quietly into the fire of scraps of old ship's timber. Those leaping tongues of blue and green and yellow and crimson flame were a never-failing joy to her. Many a curious thing had she seen in them, and thought many strange thoughts to the tune of their merry dance.

She was winsome beyond words when she sat so, with the lights and shadows playing over her face, and about the misty dark eyes in which her clear soul dwelt and shone without disguisements.

Suppose he said to her—here and now,—"Avice, dearest, do you know what you are to me? I cannot possibly tell you in words, but—do you know?..." And she said "I know,"—and said again, "I will do whatever you wish...."

Ah—God! ... If that could be he would ask no more of life.... One word from her and this bare bank would be swept with golden fires; in the twinkling of an eye it would become a Paradise for him and her to dwell in....

If he sat there looking at her it must out. He could not keep it in. And why should he? Why not tell her, here and now? ...

He got up quietly and strode out into the night. A smile hovered in the corners of her lips, as, without looking, she caught sight of his face. Then she rose also and stole out after him.

She was causing him pain when she wished him only joy. His thought, she knew, was all for her. She would think and act for them both. If he had sat there like a pent-up volcano for another second the hot lava would have come rushing out. She had felt it all in the air. Her heart too was so full of expectant joy that the tension was akin to pain.

It was very dark, with only throbbing stars in a velvet sky and the white gleam of the foam along the beach. She did not know which way he had gone, but he would come back presently, all himself again. She sank down into the side of a hummock and waited.

He came at last, slowly, heavily, with bent head.

He stopped quite close to her, where the way led to the house, and stood looking out over the darkness of the sea. Then he heaved a great sigh and turned to go back to the house.

"God!" she heard him mutter. "If I dared but tell her!"

She rose swiftly out of her form and caught him by the arm, with something between a laugh and a cry, "Tell me, then!"—and the mighty arms of his love were round her, gripping her to him till she was squeezed almost breathless.

"Avice! Avice!—and you knew! Oh, thank God for you!"

"Of course I knew," she gasped. "And I want you as much as you want me."

"Thank God for you, dearest!" he said deeply. "We will thank Him all our lives. He has given us with a full hand.... I have nothing left to ask Him ... except your fullest happiness, now and always."

"And I yours. You are my happiness. You give me Heaven."

"God requite me ten times over if ever you rue this day. I have longed for you till my heart was sick with the pain of longing—"

"Foolish! Why did you not tell me before?"

"I could not. Until I knew.... Placed as we are, you see, it felt like forcing you.... You might not have felt free to say no.... It might have put an end to all our comradeship...."

"You don't know me. I'd have said no quickly enough if I hadn't wanted you. But I do, and you make me very happy."

He led her into the house and held her there at arm's length in the firelight, as though he could hardly believe it all true, and looked deep into the dark eyes and rosy face and kissed it rosier still.

And the blue and yellow and green and crimson flames danced their merriest, as these two sat hand in hand watching them, and talking softly by snatches with long sweet silences in between.

LIII

"I was so afraid there might be some other to whom you were bound," she said, as she lay there in the firelight, with her head against his arm and his right hand smoothing her hair, that wonderful hair which had been to him as the aureole of a saint and was more to him now than all the gold in all the world.

"There is no other, my dear one. Not a soul on earth has any claim on me except that of friendship.... It was inevitable that we should both have that fear. Four months ago we did not know of one another's existence—"

"Isn't it wonderful?" she murmured. "I wonder if we had never met if you would have found someone else—"

"Never anyone to fill my heart as you do. I cannot even imagine it."

"And if I should have found someone else?"

"That is possible, but no one who could feel for you all that I do, or could want you as much as I do. You are to me the one supreme good," and the clasp of his arm told her even more than his words.

"You do not ask me if I had any ties in the old life," she began.

"You would not be lying in my arm like this if there were. I know you too well."

"That is true and I thank you. It is good to be taken on trust. But indeed there were none. The men one met there—faugh!—they were masquers, puppets, dandies;—some had brains, but few had hearts, and they were most dreadful liars. Such talents as they possessed were devoted to finesse and intrigue, and the turning of everything to their own satisfaction and advantage."

"Thank God you are out of it all."

"Yes, I do thank God,—for the shipwreck and everything else, but chiefly that He sent you here to meet me and took that other one away."

The weather held still for a few days, and he spent them in providing for her future comfort in every way he could think of.

He chopped logs enough to last them through the winter, and piled them in stacks about the house. He got over from the ship supplies in abundance. As the result of much labour and many failures he constructed a primitive lamp out of the silver mug from which Macro used to swill his rum. He distorted a beak out of one side of it, and contrived a wick which passed through a hole in a piece of beaten copper, and if the light was not brilliant it was at all events steadier to read by than the dancing flames.

He had lighted quite by accident on Macro's hidden hoard in the hold of the 'Jane and Mary.' He was rooting in a corner there for his knife, which had worked out of its sheath at his back as he hoisted out provisions, and found it sticking point downwards in a plank. As he pulled it out, the plank gave slightly, and lifting it he found, underneath, the useless treasure.

He wanted none of it, was indeed loth to touch it, but, on consideration, took out two more silver mugs for their daily service and half a dozen gold pins and brooches for Avice's use, since she was always needing such things and regretting her lack of them.

The long spell of mild soft weather—which had come at last to have in it a sense of sickness and decay— broke up in the wildest storm they had yet seen.

The birds came whirling in in a shrieking cloud, but the wind out-shrieked them. It shrilled above their heads in a ceaseless strident scream like the yelling of souls in torment. It shook their protecting sandhills and made their house shiver right down to the buried cross-pieces of its pillars. It picked up the smaller hummocks outside and set them waltzing along the shore. It heaped a foot of new sand on their roof and sent a cartload of it down the chimney.

But their position had been well chosen. The more the sand piled on their house and against it, the tighter it became. Then the rain came down in sheets and torrents, but no drop came through, except down the chimney, and that Wulf presently plugged with a blanket and let the smoke find its way out through an inch of opened door, which he had purposely placed to leeward, as all their great storms came from the south and south-west.

But the change of atmosphere was bracing, and with solid sand under their feet, and assured of the safety of their house, they welcomed it and felt the better for it.

After the first day's confinement he must out to see, and she would not stay behind. So they rigged themselves in oldest garments and fewest possible and started out.

They were drenched to the skin in a second and whirled away like leaves the instant they forsook the cover of their hollow.

Avice was being carried bodily towards their nearest shore. He feared she would go headlong into the sea and started wildly after her. He saw her throw herself flat and grip at the sand, but she was broadside on to the merciless wind and it bowled her over and over, and rolled her along like a ball. It carried him along in ten-feet leaps. He flung himself down beside her, put his arm round her, wrenched her head to the gale, and they lay there breathless, she choking hysterically with paroxysms of laughter.

It took them an hour, crawling like moles, to get back to the shelter of the hills. He would have had her go in, but she would not hear of it. They could hear the booming thunder of the great waves on the spit even above the wind, and she must see them.

So they set off once more, flat to the sand, and worked round in time to the breast of the great hill near the fresh-water pools, and lay in it, safe from dislodgment unless the hill went too.

They could only peer through pinched eyes, and then only with their hands over them, into the teeth of that wind, but, even so, the sight was magnificent and appalling. The grim gray sky and the grim gray sea met just beyond the spit, and out of that close sky the huge gray waves burst, high as houses,— whole streets of houses rushing headlong to destruction. They curved gloriously to their fall with a glint of muddy green below and all their crests abristle with white foam-fury. Right out of the sky they came, right up to the sky they seemed to reach, flinging up at it great white spouts of spray like flouting curses, towering high above the land, crashing down upon it with a thunderous roar which thinned the voice of the wind to no more than a shrill piping.

Their own land-locked lake was lashed into fury also. The flying crests of the outer waves came rocketing over in wild white splashes. He was not sure that some of the waves themselves did not cover the spit and come roaring into it. The 'Jane and Mary' danced wildly to her cable. He wondered if it would hold. The 'Martha,' more than ever on her beam-ends, was being pounded like a drum.

"Did you feel that?" he shouted in her ear, and she nodded, with a touch of fear in her wind-blown face. For, under the impact of one vast mountainous avalanche, the very ground on which they lay seemed to shake like a jelly, and the whole island shuddered.

"It cannot wash it all away, can it?" she gasped, when they had wormed their way back to shelter.

"It never has done yet anyway," he said cheerfully, as he squeezed windy tears out of his smarting eyes. "Now, dear, change all your things at once. We are wet through to the bone."

"It was very wonderful. I wouldn't have missed it for anything. But I'm glad we're ashore," and she slipped away into her own room.

That was the first of the winter storms, and there were many like it. But they bore them equably. They were in splendid health, the weather at its worst was never very cold, indeed the gales were more to their taste than the smothering chill of the frequent fogs. They had all they needed,—food and fire, and light and books, a weather-tight house, and one another.

If they lacked much of what their former life had taught them to consider necessary, they had more than all that former life had given them, and they were happy.

LIV

Between the storms and fog-spells, they tramped to and fro discovering the changes wrought in their island, and many a strange thing their wanderings showed them.

One great gale which lasted a full week strewed the south-west Point with wreckage as thickly almost as the great pile beyond. Their hearts ached at thought of the still greater loss it represented, of which the proofs were never lacking. The chaotic bristle was studded with the bodies of the drowned, and the sight sent them home sorrowfully, yet marvelling the more at their own deliverance, and still more grateful for it.

"We are miracles, without a doubt," said Wulf gravely, as they went back home. "No one else gets here alive, you see.... I was the first miracle. Macro was the second," and he told her what she had not known before, how he had contrived to save the mate, and of his regret that it had not been old Jock Steele the carpenter, who would have been a blessing to them instead of a curse. "And you are the third and best miracle of all," he said, clasping her arm more tightly under his own. "God! what a difference it has made!" he said fervently. "Alone here one might go mad. In time one most certainly would. See how good a work you are accomplishing by simply remaining alive. Instead of being a melancholy madman you make me the happiest man on earth. Oh, the God-given wonder of a woman! Truly you are the greatest miracle of all, and He has been good to me."

"And to me. If you had not been here I should have been dead and we would never have met. Perhaps He sent us to one another."

"I'm sure He did, and all our lives we'll thank Him for it," and so the sight of the dead but put a keener edge on their gratitude for life and their joy in one another.

The next big storm washed the point clean again. All had gone, wreckage, bodies, everything, and the great pile beyond bristled higher than ever.

"Do you notice anything strange?" he asked her, as they stood looking out at it.

"There seems more of it."

"And not a bird to be seen. They've all gone for the winter, I expect. We shall not see them again till next year."

"I am glad. They are evil things. Our Paradise is sweeter without them," and he kissed her for the word.

The weird forces of the gales, however, afforded them many surprises.

Tramping round the further end of their lake one day, they saw changes in the great stretch of sand that ran out of sight towards the eastern point. What had been a level plain was scored and furrowed as by a mighty ploughshare. It was like a rough sea whose tumbling waves had in an instant been turned into sand—league-long grooves with high-piled ridges between, and in the hollows the watery sun glinted briefly here and there on shining white objects sticking out of the sand.

"Bones!" said Wulf in surprise, as they stood looking into the first hollow, and he jumped down and picked up a human skull.

"Horrid!" said Avice. "And there's another, and another over there. It's a regular grave-yard."

"A battle-field, I should say," as he examined them one after another. "This is very curious. This fellow was killed by a bullet through the head. Here's the hole. And this one's skull was split with an axe or a sword. This one also. I wonder what it all means...."

"Pirates and murderers. That's what they look like."

"I shouldn't wonder.... Here's an ancient cutlass."

"And what's this?"—rooting at something with her foot.... "An old pistol! ... and the hilt of another sword! ... I wonder if they were the men who lived on our ships."

"Maybe. But I think these things are older than the ships.... Why—the place is thick with them," as they wandered on. "There must be scores of them, and more still underneath the ridges, no doubt.... There was no lack of life here at one time evidently—"

"And death!"

"Yes, and death without a doubt. A good thing for us, perhaps, that customers such as these don't frequent it now."

"I'm glad we live at the other end. You haven't found any bones there, have you?"

"Not a bone! They're not very cheerful company. Let us hope the next gale will cover them up again."

Further on, in another trench, they found one side of a boat, mouldered almost into the similitude of the sand in which it had been embedded for very many years. And, further along still, Wulf thought he could make out the stark ribs of ships like those on the outer banks at their own end of the island. But they were very far away and held out no inducement to closer investigation, and Avice had had enough of such things for the time being.

There were spells of bad weather, when, for days at a time, they scarcely ventured out except to get in wood or fetch water from the pools, which always meant a thorough soaking.

But they were completely happy in one another's company, and ever more grateful for the Providence that had cast their lot together.

The days slipped by without one weary hour. Shrewder and subtler proving of hearts and temperaments could hardly be conceived. But they stood the test perfectly, never thought of it as such, found in their present estate nothing but cause for joy and deepest thankfulness.

The depth and warmth of his love for her expressed itself in most devoted service and tenderest care, and hers for him in so frank and implicit a confidence that he felt it an uplifting honour to be so favoured. Indeed the man who could have betrayed so great a trust must have been lowest of the low and basest of his kind.

"I can't help wondering sometimes whether we would have felt like this to one another if we had met in an ordinary way, outside there," she said musingly, one night, as she lay in the hollow of his arm, watching the coloured flames.

"Yes," he said emphatically. "For you laid hold of my heart as soon as I set eyes on you. It got tangled first in the meshes of your hair, and in your long eyelashes, and the thing I wanted most was to see what your eyes were like. They were wells of mystery."

"And—they were right?" she laughed softly.

"They were exactly right and just what I had hoped. Large and dark and eloquent and tender and true and—"

"Dear! dear! If I had known such an inquisition was going I should have been afraid to open them."

"Ah, you didn't know me, you see."

"I didn't know you, but I knew I was all right as soon as I saw you. I knew I could trust you.... How strange and wonderful it all was!"

LV

One strange and terrible experience they had when the winter was almost over, and it came within measurable distance of making an end of them both.

Depending on their reserve stock of flour on board the 'Jane and Mary,' they had used freely what they had on shore. When he opened the other he found to his dismay that it must have been more damaged at first than he imagined. It was nearly all mouldy and smelt badly. He had run short of tobacco also, and so decided to go over to the pile for supplies on the first possible day.

The worst of the storms seemed over. They had occasional brisk gleaming days in between times, and on one such, after seeing that Avice had all she would need in his absence, they set off along the northern shore.

She wanted to go out with him, but he dissuaded her from that. The crossing would be very different from what it was in the summer and he would not have her exposed to it. Besides, he intended to make only a short job of it, just get what he wanted, and be back almost before she knew he had gone. She was so loth to be parted from him, however, even for that short time, that she insisted on walking with him to the point and said she would sit there and wait till she saw him on his way back.

So she sat down in the sand and drew her blanket cloak about her, and watched him wade and swim and at last scramble up on to the pile. He waved his hand to her and then set to work constructing a raft as usual.

She saw him climbing to and fro among the wreckage, smashing away at casks and cases, and then, to her dismay, he and the pile and the gaunt wrecks beyond disappeared completely, wiped out by a bank of mist that had come sweeping in from the sea. The sun still shone up above, but intermittently. Dark clouds came rushing up out of the south and presently it too was hidden. The wind blew gustily and increased in violence every minute.

She wished he had not gone. She could do no good by stopping there, but she did not care to go home. Behind her, on the southern shore, the waves were beginning to break with the short harsh sounds that portended storm.

Perhaps he would leave his work and swim across. He would know she was waiting for him. She must wait till he came. She drew her blanket over her head and sat there, huddled up with her back to the wind, and hoped and prayed. For, if this sudden storm should work up into a gale and last, she would be full of fears for his safety.

Suppose he should be drowned! What that awful pile would be like in bad weather she dared not think.

She prayed wildly for his life,—"Oh God, spare him to me! He is all I have! Spare him! Have pity on us both! Spare him! Spare him!"—over and over again the same ultimate cry, for her mind was closed to every other thought but this, that the man she loved more than anything on earth was out there in peril of his life.

She stayed there, drenched by the rain and flailed by the wind, till it began to grow dark, and then she crept wearily home like a broken bird.

Grim fear gripped her heart like an icy hand, but she would not despair entirely. He was so strong and capable. He might have tried and found it impossible to get back. He might come in at any minute.

If he were here the first thing he would have told her was to change into dry clothes. She changed, and made up the fire and put on the kettle. He would be cold and hungry when he came. She must be ready for him.

Out there on the wreckage, Wulf had been so hard at work that he noticed no sign of change in the weather, till the clammy mist swept over him and blotted out everything but the box he was delving into.

The winter storms had wrought great changes in the pile. It seemed thicker and higher and more chaotic than ever, bristling with new stuff which he would have liked to investigate, in case it should contain anything that would add to Avice's comfort.

But first, to find some decent flour, and, as it happened, there seemed fewer barrels about than usual, and most of them had suffered in their rough transit. The search for a good one took time. Such as he found were gaping and he did not trouble to open them. However, he discovered one at last, opened it to make sure of the goodness of its heart and then turned to seek tobacco.

It was then that the fog swept down on him and chained him to three square feet or so of precarious foothold. Trespass beyond that limit might mean a broken limb or neck, for the surface of the pile was seamed with ragged rifts and chasms, in which the tide whuffled and growled like a wild beast anticipating food.

So he rooted away in the chest he had just smashed open, lighted on a supply of tobacco to his great satisfaction, and then sat down where he was, to wait till the fog cleared. But this, he perceived, was not one of their usual clinging fogs which enveloped one like a pall of cotton-wool. It drove on a rising wind and sped past him in dense whirling coils that made his head spin. He thought briefly of mighty spirits of the air trailing ghostly garments in rapid flight. Down below him, in the black rifts and along the sides of the pile, the water was yapping savagely, as if the wild beast would wait no longer.

When the last of the fog tore past him in tattered fragments, he found to his dismay that the sea between him and home was beyond any man's swimming,—every channel raging and foaming, and the banks between boiling furiously in the rising tide and the rush of the south-west wind. The raft he had made had already broken loose and started northwards on its own account. It went to pieces on the nearest bank, as he watched, and swept away in fragments.

There was nothing for it but waiting. So sudden a storm might pass as quickly as it had come.

For himself he had no great fears. The pile had stood a thousand storms, and worse ones than this. But he was filled with anxiety on Avice's account. She would imagine the worst when he did not come, and her suffering would be great. Thought of her troubled him infinitely more than fear for himself.

He tried hard to make her out on the beach, though how to reassure her he did not know. But the sky was overcast and the atmosphere murky with sweeping showers, and he could not even see the point.

He was wet through with his swim, and the wind, though not cold in itself, was so strong that it chilled him. He searched about for shelter, and coming on a huge case which presented a solid back to the weather, he stove in the front and found it contained fine lace curtains. He hauled out a sufficiency, which the wind whisked playfully away. Then he crept into their place, grateful for so much, and lay and watched the strange writhings and contortions of the pile under the impact of the gale and the rising tide.

The wind would go down with the tide probably, and then he would make another raft and get home as quickly as he could with his flour. For, great as Avice's anxiety would certainly be, they were still short of flour, and it would be better to take it with him than to have to come back for it. The wreck-pile in a gale was a decidedly unpleasant experience, and its behaviour most extraordinary. He had never imagined a dead conglomeration such as that capable of such antics. When the tide was at its height the whole mass writhed and shuddered through all its length and breadth like some great monster in its death agonies. The rifts and chasms gaped and closed like grim black wounds or hungry mouths. Strange and awesome sounds broke out all about, groanings and creakings, ragged rendings and grindings, as the component pieces lifted and settled regardless of their neighbours. When the tide went down it was more at ease, and the only sounds were the waves snapping at the sides and gurgling and rushing in the depths below.

He did not find it very cold. Sheltered from the wind, the heat of his body in time made a warm nook round him in the heart of the curtains. But he was never dry. And before it got too dark, when he saw it would be impossible to get away that night, he crept out and crawled precariously to and fro till he lighted on a small cask of rum. He carried it to his shelter, knocking in the head with his axe, and it kept his blood warm through the night. But it was a terribly long night, chiefly because he was thinking all through it of Avice, and her fears for him, and her suffering.

To his bitter disappointment, morning showed no signs of abatement or relief. It brought another wild gray day without a glimmer of hope in the sky.

He had eaten nothing for more than twenty hours and was feeling empty and ravenous. The tide had risen and gone down again in the night. Before the pile began its writhings and contortions again he must eat. So he crept out and foraged till he found a barrel of pork, and bashed it open and carried back to his nest a big chunk which he ate raw and washed down with rum.

All that day the gale held. He hardly dared to think of Avice and yet could think of nothing else. At times, under the impulse of his fears for her, he was tempted to leap into the sea and try to battle through to the point. But when he studied the chances of it, common sense prevailed. Adventure into those boiling currents meant death as surely as if he cut his throat on the pile.

If he could only let her know that he was alive.... If he had had his flint and steel he would have tried to set something on fire—even if it were his nest—on the chance of her seeing the smoke and understanding it. He searched eagerly for another tinder-box, but could not light on one.

It was an anxious and gloomy man that crept into the heart of the curtain-case that night; but he slept, in a way and brokenly, in spite of it all, for Nature knows man's limits, and when he goes beyond them she steps in at times and takes command.

LVI

To Avice, also, that first night was one long horror.

She made up the fire and sat waiting for him to come. He would know in what a state of despair she would be and he would certainly come. She was sure he would come—if he could. If he did not it was because he could not. And ... if he could not....

The wind shrilled eerily outside. It sounded cold and heartless ... pitiless ... like messages from the dead ... warnings of evil. It got on her nerves and set her shivering. She crept to her room at last and dropped hopelessly on to her bed, and lay there sorely stricken.

In the gray of the morning she ate mechanically, and hurried away to the point for sign or sight of him. But it was all she could do to make out the pile itself, like a bristling rampart in the dull dim distance. As to distinguishing anything on it, that was out of the question.

She wandered about there all day long, with her eyes strained on the pile like one bereft, and only crept back when night shut it out and drove her home.

She was satisfied in her own mind now that he was dead. If he had been alive he would certainly have come. Well, she would not be long in following him.... Without him she had no desire to live ... even if she could struggle on alone, which was very doubtful ... better to join him quickly than to drag on miserably all by herself on that lonely bank, and go crazy in the end.

She sobbed herself asleep, her last wish that she might never waken. She had eaten nothing since the morning, and then only a hasty scrap that had no taste in it. The fire had gone out.... It did not matter. She would go out herself as soon as might be.... A woful end to all their golden hopes and happiness.

Morning found her still lying spent and hopeless on her bed, comatose, neither asleep nor awake, simply careless of life and even of the fact that the wind had fallen at midnight and that the new day had broken soft and clear.

Then, in her dream-weariness, she heard a voice in the outer room—or thought she did—but all her senses were dulled except the sense of loss and heartache. People, she knew, heard voices when they were going to die.

"Avice!"—the voice of God calling her—the sweet voice of death. She was ready to go.

"Avice! Where are you?"—and a tapping on the wall of her room.

How like Wulfrey's voice! Perhaps he was permitted to be the messenger,—a gracious thought—a joyful thought.

She rose painfully, stiff with weakness and long lying, stumbled to the doorway, stood leaning her hands against the sides, and peered, white-faced and awe-stricken, through the curtains into the room. Then, with a broken cry, she threw up her hands and fell forward into Wulf's arms.

When she came to herself she was lying on a blanket outside the house and he was bathing her forehead and kissing her. She lay looking up at him in wonder, out of eyes almost lost in the mists and darkness of her suffering. She raised a hand and touched his face.

"Are you real? Are you alive?" she whispered doubtfully.

He proved it with hot kisses. His eyes swam with pity for her sufferings. Her face and eyes told him all the story.

"By God's mercy we are both alive, dear. It might have been otherwise.... You have suffered sorely."

"I thought you were sent for me ... the angel of Death. And it was so good of them to send you and not a stranger.... But it is better to have you alive," and happy tears welled weakly out of her eyes and rolled down the white cheeks.

"I believe you have eaten nothing since I went. Lie still and I will get you something," and he jumped up and went inside, lighted the fire quickly, and presently was sitting by her side, feeding her with warm rum and water, for she was icy cold, and some bits of the cakes she had made three days before.

"You ought not to have starved yourself like that," he remonstrated.

"I was sure you were dead and I had no wish to live.... You will never go out there again...."

"Not in the break of a storm anyway. We must go to the storehouse sometimes, but we'll make sure of our weather in future."

"I wouldn't have minded if I'd been with you."

"I would. It was ghastly out there in the night," and he told her how he had lived in the big case of curtains, and how the pile heaved and writhed like a wounded sea-serpent under the tide and the gale. And how he had brought back some flour after all, though it had been no easy job as there was no wind to help him.

"It is dear flour," she said. "It nearly cost us our lives. I would sooner live on raw meat another time."

LVII

That was their sorest trial of the winter. Often, over the fire of a night, they talked of it and told one another all there was to tell of their feelings and their fears, and their love burned the brighter for its tempering.

But Avice was soon herself again, and as the Spring quickened all about and in them, the bitterness of the experience gradually faded out of their recollection and only the brightness was left.

And then there was so much to interest one everywhere that the days were hardly long enough for all there was to see and do.

First, seals—mothers and babies galore. Those sandy beaches of the northern coast seemed a favourite basking place and nursery, and Avice could creep along behind the sandhills, and crawl up among the wire-grass, and peep over, and she never tired of watching them. There was something so human in the way the babies snuggled up to their mothers when they were hungry, and still more in the way the mothers looked down at their nurslings.

And the baby-rabbits. They were almost as entrancing as the seals, but far shyer and more difficult to spy upon.

For the simple lifting of a head among the sparse tufts of grass set the hollow below alive with tiny bobbing white scuts, whose terrified owners tumbled over one another in their anxiety to get below ground. Avice would not hear of rabbit-meat in those days. She said the very thought of it made her feel like a cannibal.

And lastly,—birds. They were coming back in flights. The eastern point seemed their chosen ground, but closer at hand stray families were found, and importunate babies were being fed by the cold-eyed mothers with whom, a few months later, they would be waging the fierce battle for food. But Avice never took to the birds as she did to the seals and rabbits. She could never forget what they would grow into—brigands and fighters and cold-blooded raucous screamers at all times.

Now and again they lived on the 'Jane and Mary' for a week by way of a change, and fish was always obtainable whether they were afloat or ashore.

The clear fire of their love waxed ever stronger, devoured the days and weeks and months, and refined and fused them all into golden memories without one smallest speck of alloy. More devoted lover never woman had, nor man a sweeter mistress. Never was princess of the blood—without a bar across her scutcheon—held in loftier esteem or shown it more gallantly. Never, in word or act, did he offend her sense of right in the smallest degree; yet she could set his heart leaping and his blood racing by a touch—and she knew it.

Sometime,—when he believed it right—she knew he would ask more of her. It was inevitable. She had known it from the beginning. And she had no fear of it. Love such as theirs knows nothing of fear.

They were not playing at love. They loved with all the white fire of passionate devotion which loses sight of self in the one beloved. For better, for worse; in life, in death, she was wholly his. With the ardour of the Spring in her blood, and the love-light in her eyes, she waited for him to speak.

LVIII

Time came when, according to her calendar, he had been there full twelve months and she just about nine. And as to prospect of escape, or further addition to their company, they were in exactly the same position as when they came.

Whenever they discussed that matter, she said, "Still, I came ashore alive."

And he always said, "You were the miracle. Besides you were nine-tenths dead."

She wondered when he would ask the next step of her, and how he would do it. Her answer was ready—herself. Still, something of extra fragrance—something ineffably sweet and delicate—would cling to it for ever, or be for ever just that much lacking, according to the manner of his asking.

But she believed his great love would choose the proper chord and strike it with strong and gentle fingers.

And it did.

They were sitting in the firelight one night, when a more than usually pregnant silence fell on them. The depth of their feeling for one another expressed itself not infrequently in these long delicious pauses in their talk, when that which was in them was all too sacred for words. Her Northern blood, of which she was proud, prevailed as a rule over the Gallic strain, which she held in light esteem, and made for undemonstrativeness in any outward display of feeling. But she felt to the depths, and when she did permit the brakes to slip, the wheels struck sparks.

He also was more doer than talker. Hence those long sweet silences, when she lay with her head in his arm in the coloured firelight, and the gentle play of his hand on her hair was more to them both than all the words in the world.

But this night there was more in the silences that fell on them. In both their hearts the high-charged thoughts and feelings of many months were converging to a point. The quickening of the Spring was in their blood.

His hand slipped suddenly down from her hair and clasped on both of hers where they lay in her lap. His voice as he spoke was deep with emotion. It thrilled her to the depths. She felt the hot pulses in his hand leaping and throbbing. His words were very simple, as became a matter so vital. Deepest feeling needs no garnishment.

"Dearest, you have honoured me with your trust and love"—Her hands turned and clasped his fervently.

"Every hair of your head is precious to me. I would not knowingly offend your feelings in any smallest thing.... We are here, cut off from our kind, it may be, for ever.... We are as alone here with God, as Adam and Eve were in The Garden.... You make my Paradise. You can perfect it.... Will you?..."

And for answer she put up her arms, and drew down his face, and kissed him passionately, and clung to him as if she would never let him go.

"I thank God for so precious a gift," he said, clasping her to him so that she felt his heart pounding inside as furiously as her own.

"Heart ... soul ... body ... all yours!" she whispered, and he kissed her hair, because her face was hidden, and clasped her closer still.

"It is the ordained crown of our love," he said presently, when their first blinding whirl of emotion was over. "I cannot see that we offend any law of man's, for here we are beyond the law. God's law we are surely keeping.... And, so as not to act on simple impulse I have thought that we would let another month go by before..." and he kissed her rosy face again.

"But why?"

"Perhaps you have not thought it all out as I have—"

"But I have ... I knew it must be so...." and the joy in him was very great.

"All the same, dear, we will not enter into that high estate without your very fullest consideration.... And if you should find any reason or instinct against it I shall abide by your decision."

"I am all yours. I shall not change."

"From what the mate said I imagine this island may pertain to Nova Scotia. It is possible that Scottish law runs there.... We can take one another for man and wife and place it on record...."

"How?"

"We have books with fly-leaves. Among the sand-hills you will find all the quills you want. The birds are some use after all.... Anyone can make a pen ... and ink we can always get even though it is red.... All we need for a good Scots marriage is a pair of witnesses."

"Seals, rabbits, birds...."

"They cannot testify.... All we can do," he said thoughtfully, "if, by God's mercy, we ever leave this place is to regularise ourselves by proper marriage ashore as soon as we land. But the prospects of getting away seem very small, I'm afraid."

"We have been very happy here. We can still be very happy here," she said contentedly.

So amazing is this great power of Love in covering all deficiencies of outward circumstance.

LIX

The days slipped past, and each day he watched her quietly for slightest sign of compunction, or retraction. And if such had come to her, sore though he might have felt, and bereaved of the perfect unfolding of the fair flower of their love, he would have choked the feeling down, trampled on it, buried it so that she would have seen no sign of it in him. For he recognised to the fullest what a mighty thing this was that he was asking of her.

But she understood him perfectly, fathomed his fears, was on the look-out for his quietly-questioning looks, and met them with clear full-eyed serenity and a face rosy at times with anticipation.

"You need not fear for me," she laughed softly, one night as she lay in his arm before the fire. "I shall not change."

He clasped her closer. "I could not blame you if you did. From every worldly point of view you would be right—"

"What have we to do with worldly points of view? We are out of it all. We are here alone, and like to be. And we are doing right in our own eyes."

"I would risk my soul on what seems right to these pure eyes," and he bent and kissed them warmly.

"Ten more days!" she murmured, and nestled closer, with her head on his breast so that she could feel the strong beating of his heart.

"It says 'Avice!—Avice!—Avice!'" he said quietly. "It is full of Avice," and she pressed still closer.

So the great day came, the greatest day either of their lives had known.

Wulf had found sleep impossible. His heart, full-charged, felt like to burst its mortal bounds. He rose quietly in the dark and went out into the soft twilight of the dawn—to greet the coming of the perfect day. And she, as impossible of sleep as he, heard him in spite of all his caution, and laughed softly to herself for very happiness in him and in herself. And when he had gone, she thanked God for this great gift of a true man's love, and for that in herself which responded to it so fully.

She had not a doubt nor a fear. The smallest of either would have barred her from him. But there was not the smallest shadow between them. Their hearts were one. It was meet and good that their lives should be one also. Wulfrey paced the beach out there and found the silent darkness soothing to his bounding senses.

It was late April. The air was sweet and fresh. The sea just breathed in its sleep and no more. The water rippled silently up the hard sand with scarce a murmur. The darkness of the eastern sky thinned as he paced and watched. There came a soft suffusion of light there. It throbbed and grew. A faint touch of carmine outlined a cloud above it. The darkness seemed to fade and melt out of the sky. All the tiny clouds above him turned their faces to the east and flushed rose-red with the joy of the new day.

He climbed a hill and caught the first golden gleam of the rising sun. His eyes shone, and his face. In his eyes two suns were reflected. But there was only one sun. And they were two and now were to become one. The Perfect Day had dawned.

And just as she, lying in her bed with her face in her hands, had thanked God for His goodness, so he. He flung his right hand up towards the sun in the brightening sky and said deeply, "My God, I thank Thee for this day and most of all for her!"

And, down below, he saw her coming out of the house towards him.

He sprang down to meet her, caught her hands, and looked right down through her eyes into her heart, and was satisfied.

LX

Arm in arm they paced the beach till the sun was well up, and their bank of sand shone in the flood of golden light as it had never shone before,—fresh and sweet as if but new-created.

A light wind had come with the sun. The small waves came hurrying in as though they were invited guests. At sight of the wedding-party they broke into crisp white laughter, curled themselves over in league-long sickles of tenderest lucent green, and raced up the sands to their feet in long soft swirls of liquid amber, laced with bubbles and edged with creamy foam.

"They haste to the wedding, to pay their tribute to the only bride they have ever set eyes on," said Wulf, as they stopped to watch them. "And each one is glad to give his life for a single peep at her."

"Foolish little waves," laughed she. "I am going to make their very close acquaintance presently. How beautiful the sea is this morning!"—as her eyes travelled out to the wide blue sweep beyond, with its dapple of purple shadows.

"The most beautiful sea and the most wonderful morning that ever was," he asserted heartily. "But it is only a beginning. There will be many more like it. And still better."

"I am so glad it is so sweet a day. A dull one would have troubled me."

"But it could not possibly have been anything else."

"Oh, but it could."

"In mere outward accident perhaps. But I've got the sun inside me. I wonder it doesn't show through."

"It does," she laughed joyously. "You are all aglow."

"And never man had better reason. I would not change places with all the kings of all the earth rolled into one."

"Nor I with all the queens. We are happier here by far with nothing but ourselves."

"Ourselves, and our Love, and infinite Hope. Now let us go and eat. My bride must not starve. That would be a bad beginning. Did you sleep?"

"Not a wink. I heard you go out."

"And I was pluming myself on not having made a sound."

While she was making cakes he busied himself making a pen out of a quill he had picked up on the beach, and she smiled when she saw what he was at.

"And the ink?" she asked.

"I've got it all ready. I always carry some with me in case of need," at which she knitted her brows prettily and looked puzzled.

After breakfast she said, "Now you must leave me for a couple of hours. I am going to thank the waves for their good wishes and then I shall go to the fresh-water pool."

"You will be very careful.. You won't get yourself drowned."

"I will be very careful. And you!"

"I will go across to the spit. But when we are wed—"

"Yes—then!" she nodded rosily, and he kissed her and went off past the fresh-water pools, and splashed through the narrows that joined their lake to the smaller one, and so to the shore and into the sea, for the last time alone.

He waited till he was sure she had done with their bathing-pool, and then ran across and plunged into it, for the salt water braces, but sticks and never makes one feel so clean as fresh.

She was still busy with the princely brush and comb when he came on her, and his heart leaped again at her fresh and radiant beauty.

She had clothed herself all in spotless linen, swathed about her in that marvellous fashion of which she held the secret to perfection. To his rejoicing eyes she appeared half angel, half Vestal Virgin, yet all bewitching human girl, and, best of all, his bride.

"Be thankful you're a man, and delivered from this," she said, her eyes shining through the glorious veil at his visible joy in her.

"I'm thankful I'm a man, but I wouldn't have you relieved of that for half the world. I glory in it," and he bent and kissed it. "For a moment I thought you were an angel."

"Perhaps I am."

"I know you are. But, thank God, you're human too! Men don't wed with angels.... I must go and dress myself also," and he disappeared into the house.

When, in due course, he came out, gallantly clad in a long blue coat with flap-pockets, and figured vest, and white silk knee-breeches, and stockings to suit, she first stared and then laughed.

"My faith, but we are fine!" said she. "But, in truth, I like you best as I have known you best. Do you marry in a dead man's clothes?"

"Not if I know it. Sooner in my rags. But, to the best of my belief, these belonged to your friend the Duke of Kent. Macro would have them, but little he dreamed of the high use to which they would be put. I borrow them for the occasion. His Highness would make no objection I am sure."

"I am sure he would not, and they become you well. But still I like you best as I have known you best."

"I will doff them presently. But you are so like a queen that I did not like to come to you like a beggar."

In his hand he had brought the Prayer-book, with the quill in a certain place.

He stepped up to her and lifted her hand to his lips.

"You do not repent you of this we are about to do?"

"I shall never repent it," she said, with dancing eyes.

"Please God, and as far as in me lies, you shall never have cause to repent it.... We are here, our two selves, with none to witness this that we do but God.... We are doing what we believe to be right for our own great happiness and well-being.... It would suffice, I believe, for a Scots wedding, simply to declare ourselves man and wife. But I have thought it would please us both to do something more. We are not entering upon this new estate lightly or without due thought.... It will, I know, be to both our minds and comforting to both our hearts, to think that in our loneliness here we have done all we could to supply the deficiencies for which we are not to blame."

He spoke with very great emotion. She rejoiced in this fresh evidence of the heights and depths of his nature and his essential goodness of heart, though indeed she had not needed it.

Her great dark eyes, fixed on his, were abrim with happy tears.

"So," he continued, "We will read together the Form for the Solemnization of Matrimony in this Prayer-book, and then we will inscribe on the front leaf of it the fact that this day we have become man and wife. We will sign our names to it, and we can do no more to comply with man's law.... Is that your will, my dear?"

"Yes."

"Then here we will kneel and wed," and down they knelt in the sand, with a clear sky and bright sun above, and the blue sea that held them captive dancing and laughing in front; and holding the book between them he read the Service aloud in a deep and reverent voice.

Parts of it were of course somewhat incongruous to their situation, but he would not slur or miss a word. The statement that they were gathered together in the face of this congregation almost provoked her to an explosion. For out of the corner of her eye, as she followed his reading, a slight movement on the side of an adjacent sandhill showed her a rabbit, sitting up and watching them with critical attention, and it looked to her just like the frowsy old female in black she had seen hovering about the skirts of a wedding in a London church.

And there were parts that brought the colour to her face, though she was familiar with them. Applied to oneself they seemed to hold new point and meaning.

However, he read bravely on. No one interfered to show any just cause why they should not lawfully be joined together, nor had either of them any confession of impediment to make.

At the "Wilt thou—?" he answered heartily, "I will." And waited for her to do the same when her turn came.

When it came to—"Who giveth this woman to be married to this man?"—he answered boldly,—"God."

Then they took hands and plighted their troth, reciting the words in the book.

But when it came to the putting on of the ring there came an interlude not provided for in the Marriage Service.

He had duly provided a plain gold wedding ring.

"Where did you get it?" she asked with a look of surprise.

"I found it among Macro's treasures."

"It must be some dead woman's, then. I would sooner not. Can we not leave that out? Will it make any difference?"

"No, dear. It will make no difference to our being truly wed."

"Then please go on without it."

So they left the ring out and read on to the end together.

He closed the book and drew her to him as they knelt, and kissed her as his wife.

"Now," he said, lifting her up. "We will put on record the most wonderful thing that has ever happened on this island, and then we will go home and prepare the marriage-feast.... I wonder now if James Elwes, M.A., late of Brasenose College, Oxford, is aware of the high use to which his Prayer-book is being put,"—as he pointed to the name inscribed on the fly-leaf, and turned over to the blank on the other side.

"Do you think they know?"

"I do not see why not. But as we never knew him, nor he us, it is possible he is not present."

And suddenly those words at the beginning of the Marriage Service assumed a new and mighty significance for her. "In the face of this congregation" might mean more than she had ever dreamed of. Perhaps her mother had been there— If she had, if she should be here now—it, was somewhat startling to think of—she would be glad, for she would know how good and true a man this was.

But he was busily writing, and at the sight she cried, "Oh!"—for the writing was red and the ink was drawn from a little jag he had made in his arm.

"In blood," she said, with a touch of dismay.

"It could not be put to better use," he laughed. "It is all at your service ... to the very last drop.... How begin better than by setting down here that we are one till death?"

"What you said made me think that perhaps my mother had been with us—"

"I am sure she was, and mine too.... They will both approve, you may be sure.... Here is what I have written—

"'I, Wulfrey Dale, do hereby declare that I have this day taken Avice Drummond to be my lawful wedded wife.' And for you, 'I, Avice Drummond, do hereby declare that I have this day taken Wulfrey Dale to be my lawful wedded husband.' Now I will sign.... And you will sign there ... and I will add the date as far as we know it ... and our present place of abode—Sable Island."

He held the book till the writing was dry, then kissed her signature. "It is the first time I have set eyes on your handwriting," he said. "It is like yourself—clear and strong and true ... Mistress Dale,"—with a smiling bow, as he handed her the book,—"your marriage-lines! You will like to keep them."

"And the pen, please," she said, holding out her hand for it, and wrapping it and the book in a fold of her white robe. "These will be more to me than all the treasures of the world."

He put his arm round her and they went slowly home—man and wife.

BOOK V

GARDEN OF EDEN

LXI

Happy? If all newly-married folk could find such happiness as was theirs, what a wonderful world it would be!

From every worldly point of view they had nothing. They were outcasts, paupers, dependent for the food they ate and the clothes they wore, on Nature and the caprice of the sea. Yet, having nothing, they had everything, since they had one another.

If he had rejoiced in her before, and loved her with a love akin to pain in the repression he subjected it to, he loved her now a thousand times more, and she filled him with a joy that knew no bounds. Time, he said to himself, would not suffice for all their love, it would fill eternity.

The days were never long enough for them. In this new joy of life and perfected fellowship they forgot their years at times, and were like a pair of children, endowed with the freedom of time and space and hearts attuned to the most perfect enjoyment of these new attributes.

They made long journeys and explored every inch of their territory—sleeping out at times in the side of a sandhill under the soft summer night. And those were wondrous times.

—To lie there flat on their blanket, side by side, chin in hand like children, his arm about her, and watch the red sun sink into the water at the end of his fiery trail, while all the sky above burned crimson right into the east behind them.—To watch, with bated breath, the rabbits creeping out to feed and frolic about them, all unconscious of their presence.—To lie and watch the colours fade slowly in the darkening sky, and the stars come out till the whole dark dome was a never-failing marvel of delight.—Or, on the other shore, to lie and watch the moonbeams dancing on the sleeping bosom of the sea.—To feel oneself oneself in the midst of it all—a part of it all—the height and the width and the immensity and wonder of it all.—To feel his arm enfolding her, and all that that meant to them both.—To feel the warmth of life, and all the mighty joy of it, throbbing in her slender body as he drew her closer.—To know, as he knew, that God lived and had given her to him, and that she loved him with every fibre of her being, as he loved her....

Happy? At times, so full was her heart that she wondered if such happiness was right for mortals to enjoy, and so, if it could last.

And when she shared that with him, as they shared everything in common, he reasoned her back to comfort.

"Happiness and health are life's proper conditions," he asserted, with such hearty conviction that her doubts hid their heads. "Sorrow and sickness come of trespass, somehow, somewhere, somewhen, though it is not always easy to trace them back to first causes. But, without doubt, people were meant to be as healthy and happy as it is possible for them to be."

"But I have known people suffer who, I am sure, never did any wrong—none, that is, deserving of suffering such as they had. In fact," she mused, "it seems to me that the good people suffer most and the wicked prosper."

"That is as we judge. But we see only the outsides of things and we are purblind at best. Nature has certain laws, and God has certain laws—though a parson could tell you more about these than I can. And if those laws are broken the results have to be borne, and sometimes they run on and on and fall on innocent people."

"It doesn't seem very fair."

"The laws cannot be altered for individuals or exceptional cases. Fathers sin and the children suffer. But the blame is the fathers'."

"Yes," she nodded, and perhaps she was thinking of her own case.

"So you've no need to fear being as happy as you can," he added quickly. "God meant you for happiness, and truly, I think we have more certainty of it here than we might have had elsewhere."

"I am sure of it and I am happy," and she nestled still closer under his folding arm.

But they had their strenuous working times as well, and enjoyed them equally. He developed his new-found capacity for carpentering. Made her more chairs and a table, added to the comfort of their house in many ways. And she kept it all in perfect order, and attended to the cooking, and proved herself a most admirable housewife and helpmate.

They were down almost to fundamentals. Their life—partaking as it did of the development of the ages, and so of the wider freedom of thought and feeling, was the life of the ancients and not far from idyllic.

The hunter went forth to the chase—though it was only rabbits—and the fisherman to the lake, and brought home his spoils to his waiting mate, and they ate of them and were content.

They enjoyed the most perfect health, and for society they had one another and desired no more—at all events, no outsiders.

They had storms and mists and spells of dull weather, but their house was proof against all assault from without, and warm and bright with their abounding love. They had fire and light and books and themselves, and always in time the sun shone out again, and they enjoyed it the more perhaps for its frequent defaults.

They had their trying times too. Stores had to be replenished from the pile, and, after that dreadful experience before they were married, she would not be left behind.

"I do not care what happens if we are together," she said. "The worst that could happen would be nothing compared with that other time," and he could not gainsay her.

So whenever he had to go she went also, and they chose their day with care and made a picnic of it, and came home laden with spoils.

Only once they got caught by one of those swift-travelling mists which seemed to spring from nowhere. It swept over them just as they were preparing to leave, and in the twinkling of an eye they were prisoners, bound clammily to the pile till it should pass. For in that close-clinging bank, as thick as wet cotton-wool, all sense of direction was gone in a moment. They could not see a foot before them, the pile was pitted with death-traps, a step might be fatal.

They had both come lightly clad, for the day had been warm and the wreckage claimed unhampered limbs.

Fortunately they had come upon a case of blankets during their operations.

"Sit you down here," he said, as he felt her shivering under his arm, "And I'll get you some blankets."

"You won't get yourself lost?" she asked anxiously.

"Not if you will keep calling to me," and he crawled away in search of the case, while she sat calling, "Wulf ... Wulf ... Wulf," and he answered her, "Avice ... Avice ... Avice," and at last a shout, "I've got it."

And presently his muffled "Avice ... Avice ... Avice," drew near again, and he loomed through the fog like a creeping ghost, and taking her arm they crept together from blanket to blanket, which he had spread as a guide, till they came to the case itself. He hauled out more of its contents till there was room inside for both of them, and they crawled into their nest and in time got warm and comfortable.

The fog showed no sign of lifting, so before it got quite dark he crawled out again, she calling to him as before, and found a cask of rum, of which there was always plenty about, and one of pork, and on these they supped as best they could.

The writhing and creaking of the pile, as the tide rose and fell, caused her some alarm. But he explained it all to her, and after a time she fell asleep with his arm about her, and they were wakened to a clear bright morning by the shrieking and squabbling of the birds over the barrel of pork, which he had left standing open.

The barrel itself and all the pile adjacent seemed suddenly to have sprouted feathers. It was alive with fiercely-beating wings and jerking feathered necks and squirming feathered bodies, and cold hard little glassy eyes, and cruel rending beaks, and shrill angry cries.

"How hideous they are!" she said, shrinking back into the case.

"It is the great fight for life. They seem always hungry."

The barrel stood on end. The fortunate ones among the feathered pirates wormed themselves in, and tore and rent at the food, regardless of the shrill expostulations of their fellows and the beaks and claws that tore and rent at them in turn, till the barrel itself was lost under a seething mass of shrieking, fiercely-struggling birds. They pecked at one another's glassy eyes, they struck wildly with their wings, they clawed with somewhat futile feet, and all the time screamed at the tops of their voices as though they were trying who could scream the loudest.

"I wish they'd empty it and go," said she, and he wrenched down a slat of wood and leaned out with a blanket over his head and arm, and succeeded at last in tipping the barrel over, and pork and pirates rolled out together.

It was all cleaned up in five minutes and the cloud drifted away after other prey. The disappointed ones swooped round the empty barrel for a time, and some of the bolder, or more hungry, or least intelligent, came fluttering at the opening in the blanket-box as though set on fresh meat at any cost, and he had to beat them back with his slat. It was only when a score or more were flopping brokenly about the pile in front of the box that the rest grew tired of so losing a game and sped away to join the main body. As soon as the way was clear, he helped her out of her nest and they got to their raft, and eventually safely home.

But that was only an incident, though it confirmed her dislike and dread of the pile. She still always insisted on going with him when he had to go, and at such times they laboured long and hard, and got in supplies enough for many weeks, and so went out there as seldom as possible.

LXII

So, working, wandering, bathing, reading, hunting, fishing, eating, sleeping, with hearts and minds stripped bare to one another and every thought in common, they lived that first golden year of their married life, and grew into still closer fellowship and communion, into still clearer understanding of one another, into still greater love,—although, at the beginning, all this would have seemed to them impossible. But there are always heights and depths beyond, and will be, until the final heights are scaled—and doubtless even then also.

And now, to one such depth and height they were drawing near, with a touch of not unnatural fear on her part, as to an experience unknown and invested with all the possibilities of life and death, and new life.

He cheered her with his own great confidence; and her reliance on his professional knowledge, and the love he bore her, comforted her mightily. But they both knew full well that, given all the knowledge and love in the world, the certain issue of this great matter still lay beyond the utmost power of man; and it sent them to their knees and brought them nigher heaven than ever in their lives before.

It also set her very busily to work on tiny garments, which she had to contrive as best she could from her very scant materials. And it set him to the making of a cradle out of a very carefully-cleaned and sand-scrubbed pork-barrel, which turned out an immense success and filled him with great pride of accomplishment.

She was in the very best of health, without a trouble on her mind, and rejoicing more than ever in his joy and pride in her. And these and the free open-air life they led all made for good. He would not permit her a despondent thought, though as the time drew near she not seldom, for his sake, assumed a braver and more cheerful aspect than her heart actually warranted.

But all went well, and within a day or two of the anniversary of their wedding-day, their son, Wulfrey, was born and proved himself at once a true Islander, lusty both of lung and limb.

Prouder and happier father and mother, and more wonderful baby, it is safe to say that island never saw. And if their days had been full of delight before, the coming of Little Wulf filled them quite three times as full. For there was Little Wulf's own happiness, which was patent to all,—and his mother's rapture in him, and his father's,—and his father's mighty joy in them both,—and her joy in his joy,—and so on all round the compass;—and deep below and high above and all through it all, their unbounded thankfulness for safe deliverance from peril.

If he had admired and loved her as a maid, and loved and rejoiced in her as a wife,—as mother of his child he found himself at times dumb with excess of delight. He could only sit and watch, with worshipful eyes, and newer and deeper thoughts of that other Mother, and of The Child whose coming had transformed the world.

She got out the treasured old Prayer-book, and they read over him as much as seemed applicable to his case of the Ministration of Private Baptism of Infants, and then inscribed on the fly-leaf, under the record of their marriage, his name, Wulfrey Drummond Dale, and the date of his birth as nearly as they knew it—with the same pen as before, in the same red ink, and from the same glad source.

And now indeed their days were full, and their nights, for Master Wulfrey had an appetite that brooked no waiting, and he ruled that household with a lusty pair of lungs against which even equinoctial gales strove in vain.

But it was all part of the price of their joy in him, and they paid it joyfully; and he repaid them tenfold by simply being alive and permitting them to watch his vigorous kickings as he lay naked on a blanket at their feet in the sunshine.

Avice was speedily herself again, herself and so very much more. In his rejoicing eyes all her beauty was clarified, dignified, emphasised manifold, in a way that he would not have believed possible.

It was his turn now, in spite of all his philosophy,—and at times hers again also—to marvel at all that had been vouchsafed them, and to wonder, with a fleeting touch of fear, if happiness so great could possibly last.

The sense of the mighty responsibility their love entailed was upon them. Suppose, by any dire misfortune, he were to be taken away,—what would happen to them? He believed her capable of rising to the occasion for the boy's sake and doing man's work in his place, but it would be a desperately hard fight for her. Suppose they should be taken from him—either, both. God!—he could spare the boy best, but it would be terrible to lose either.

And suppose, thought she in turn, either of themselves should be taken! Suppose they should both be taken!—Well, in that case the poor little fellow would linger behind but a very short time. They would soon all be together again.

But such black thoughts, natural as they were, inevitable almost, still partook, to both their minds, of basest ingratitude and lack of trust. And yet they did high service, for, when they came upon them their souls went down on their knees, and there they found strength and joyousness again.

Little Wulf—but they very early began to call him Cubbie, it seemed so appropriate—fulfilled all the promise of his advent. He was a marvellous child. He crawled vigorously at nine months, and headed straight across the soft yellow sand for the water, like a true Islander, born of freedom and the open air and the sunshine, the moment he discovered this new power. And they followed him, foot by foot, with beaming faces, as he wallowed along like a well-developed white frog, digging his little snub nose into the sand at times, but gurgling and laughing all the same, and struggling on without a look to right or left, intent only on the water in front.

At the lip of the tide, where it came creaming up the beach in long soft swirls of amber, laced with bubbles and edged with filmy foam, she was for snatching him up. But Wulf stayed her. He wanted to see what the boy would do.

He was no stranger to cold water, but he had so far met it only in a tub, never in such quantity as this. He crawled on along the wet sand and the soft swirl came rushing up to welcome him. It was quite two inches deep. It filled him with astonishment and took away his breath. Everything under him seemed on the move. He stiffened for a second on his front paws, gave a huge bellow of amazement, tried to grab the back-streaming water with both hands as a cat pounces on a mouse, and then set off after it at top speed, and was swung up into the air by his delighted father, and held there, kicking and crowing, and striving still after the enchanted water below.

"He'll do," laughed Wulf. "He'll swim as soon as he can walk. The first native! And a credit to the Island!"

Golden days! If the first year of their married life was all pure gold, this second was gold overlaid with jewels of rare delight. Every moment of it was happiness unalloyed. The boy throve mightily. Avice was in the best of health and spirits, and to the eyes of her lover grew more beautiful with every day that passed.

What more could the soul of man desire?

LXIII

Their Wulf Cub was fifteen months old, and could swim like a fish, and run like a free-born savage, and talk in a jargon of his own which was yet quite understandable to his parents, when his sister Avice came on the scene. She took after her mother, and her father vowed there never had been such a lovely child born into this world before.

Their patriarchal life flowed on, deepening and widening, as it went, and so far without any break in its smooth-swelling current. The great gales, to which they had grown accustomed, piled up ever-increasing supplies for them. Within certain narrow bounds they knew no lack, nor would they though they lived there for a hundred years. On great occasions the wreckage even yielded them luxuries of the commonplace which in the former life they had looked upon as ordinary adjuncts to a meal and accepted perfunctorily, without a thought of special thankfulness. But here they were rarities, priceless delicacies to be held in esteem and made the most of. Apples for example. Once their western point was strewn thick with what seemed a whole ship-load of delicious red apples. They had probably been packed in frail barrels or cases which the waves made short work of, and the birds were fortunately away. They spent days carrying them up above tide-level and then transporting them home, and revelled in apples for weeks till their stock went bad. Another time it was potatoes, which they had not tasted for over three years. Wulf declared it was almost worth while to have been denied them so long, to find such new relish in them now. Avice regretted, for the children's sakes, that they could not have them all the time.

And that set him to planting a quantity in some of the damp bottoms by the water-pools. They came up all right, but the rabbits cleared the green shoots as fast as they appeared. Upon that he fenced off a patch with some of his superfluous raft timber and planted more, and succeeded in raising a small crop, but they were a degenerate race, lacking the good soil which had gone to the making of their ancestors.

Curiously enough, that fact started into expression trains of thought that had been latent in both their minds.

He had come in exultantly with his first fruits of the potato-patch, Cubbie at his heels proudly bearing one in each hand, and Avice cooked them rejoicingly and pronounced them excellent.

"It will be so delightful to have potatoes again," said she.

But he was critical of his own production, as the author of a work—even though it be but a potato—may be allowed to be. "They have neither the texture nor the flavour of the original stock," he said. "I suppose they need better soil than our old sandbank can afford them,"—and his eyes happened to fall on Cubbie munching away at a potato, and hers lighted on the dark little head in her arm. The same thought pricked both their hearts and their eyes met with understanding.

As with potatoes—so with children. He and she, growths of the larger world, had found unlooked-for happiness through the accident of their transplantation to this outer isle. But they brought with them the strength of heart and mind that had come to them through contact with that other world. In many respects it was a vain and hollow world. The change had made entirely for their good and happiness.

But—these little ones! ... Were they to be condemned for ever to the sweet narrow groove of this island life, which to their father and mother, by reason of the wonder of their love, had been like Paradise?

To the children no such transformation, no such veritable transfiguration of life as had been theirs would be possible.

They could, indeed, teach them all they knew themselves—all the essentials at all events. They could train their hearts and brains to highest things. But in time the children would feel what the island life entailed and denied them—what their lives were missing. The higher their development the keener would be their regrets.

"Dear," he said, clasping her closer, as she lay in the hollow of his arm before the fire that night, "I know what you are thinking. It came on me, and it came to you, when I was criticising those degenerate potatoes."

"I suppose it must have been lurking somewhere in my heart," she said quietly. "But it all came on me with a rush as you spoke. You and I desire no better. It has been wonderful ... perfect happiness. But for them...."

"Yes," he said soberly. "For them it would be different. For them we desire the very best. And here they cannot get it."

And so they were face to face with the mighty problem which thenceforth must of necessity be constantly in their minds and hearts.

For themselves, all that the outside world could give them could add no whit to their perfect content and happiness.

But for the children's sakes ... how to cross that treacherous hundred miles of sea which barred the way to the wider—in some respects wider,—to the larger—in some respects larger,—to the questionably happier life, which yet these newcomers must prove for themselves, as was their right?

They discussed it quietly and at great length that night, but could see no way out, and for the moment he could find no further comfort for her than this—and yet it was much,—"Providence, which has done so much for us," said he, "may in time do this also. Meanwhile the Island life is all to the good for them. They are splendid little specimens, and if they run wild and free for some years they will reap the benefit all their lives. We will hope and pray, and puzzle our brains for them."

Hope they did. And pray they did. But no amount of brain-puzzling afforded them any solution of their difficulty.

Nothing in the shape of a boat had ever come ashore, and he had neither the tools nor the skill to build one. And if he had done he would not have dared to risk his wife and children in it for so doubtful a voyage.

Wild ideas came upon him of constructing a raft stout enough for such a journey and venturing on it himself, leaving Avice and the children, fully provided for, to await his return with succour. But he knew she would never hear of such madness, so sent it to limbo with the rest.

He took to lighting huge fires of timber from the pile, as he had done more than once before, but the wood burned brightly, with splendid crackings and spittings which set Master Cubbie dancing with delight, and the volume of smoke was trifling. It occurred to Wulf also that no matter how dense a smoke he could raise it would, if seen at all, be probably taken only for the cloud of sea-birds which were doubtless known to mariners and avoided like death itself—when avoidance was possible to them.

That every ship that could do so kept well away from their notorious bank was evident, for they had never set eyes on a single sail since they landed. Of course their ordinary range from the level could not be more than four or five miles, he supposed; and even from their highest hill, which he reckoned to be sixty to eighty feet, they would see but twice as far;—and nothing came so close to Sable Island as that if it could help it.

Still wilder ideas he had,—of tying messages to some of the birds' legs—but they were such a vicious set that he knew they would get rid of them at once,—of nailing messages to boards, to empty casks, to anything that would float—but he knew they might float for a score of years and never be found, even if the seas did not strip them within a week.

He was reduced at last to that certainty of knowledge which it is always of highest benefit to man to attain,—that in this matter he was as helpless as a child in arms. He could do absolutely nothing that was of the slightest avail. And so he was thrown back upon, and led and lifted up to, that complete and perfect trust in a Higher Power which is the measure of a man's understanding of the great lesson of life.

LXIV

They had been five years on the Island. Little Wulf was three, Avice two,—as healthy and handsome youngsters as the world could show.

Life had been all joyous to them. All the year round, except just now and again when unusual drift of ice came rustling and grinding about their island, they trotted about with almost nothing on. They swam before they could walk, and now were in and out of the water a dozen times a day, and so they regarded clothing of any kind as a hindrance to pure enjoyment and freedom of action, and their mother judged it well to insist on no more than the most reasonable minimum.

They never lacked friends or company, though truly the friendship was mostly on their side and provokingly lacking in mutuality. Rabbits and seals, especially baby-rabbits and baby-seals, were the chiefest objects of their young affections, and they were sorely disappointed at the small response their proffered friendship evoked. On crabs this could be enforced by capture and imprisonment, but they found them cold-blooded, impassive playfellows, of altogether too-retiring dispositions, and only to be stirred into display of their natural abilities by provocation. Sea-birds were just as bad in a different way, and fishes were altogether too elusive until you wanted to eat them, when a baited hook did the trick in a moment.

That wonderful father of theirs, however, managed to capture a pair of baby-rabbits, whose mother he had unfortunately knocked on the head for dinner before he perceived the mischief he was doing. The babies were welcomed with shrieks of delight and were like to be killed with the expression of it. The youngsters spent hours flat on their stomachs watching them in their boarded enclosure alongside the house, and more hours foraging for them the sweetest and tenderest herbs the hollows could yield. And presently the captives became friends, and were so comfortable in their narrow estate that they had no desire for a wider, but galloped about after their owners wherever they went, and sat anxiously twisting their noses on the beach when the irrepressibles found it necessary to wallow and frolic in the water.

At times, for a change, they lived aboard the 'Jane and Mary' for a week or two, but Mistress Avice always had a very reasonable fear of one or other or both of the children tumbling overboard, and so the greater part of their life was passed ashore, with the sand-house as headquarters and all the rest of the island as playground.

That a life so circumscribed should never have grown monotonous tells its own pleasant story. But the youngsters had known no other life with which to compare it, and their elders, who had, found it fuller and sweeter in its pastoral simplicity than any the great world had ever offered them.

Every moment of their day was occupied, if not with work, then with enjoyments. The elders had to provide for the youngsters, and these again for theirs; and when every single thing must be drawn from Nature or from an accommodating but distant wreck-pile, such provision takes time and forethought.

When the day's work was completed they all bathed and rambled far and wide, and it was on one such ramble, when they had gone as far along towards the eastern end of the Island as small legs could carry, that the end came—as suddenly as had come the beginning.

They were sitting on the sunny side of a great sand-hill, eating and resting after their journey,—resting, that is, so far as the elders were concerned. The youngsters, who had found walking tiring, or perhaps tiresome, found no fatigue in scrambling to the tops of sandhills and sliding down the smooth soft sides with shouts and shrieks of laughter.

A cessation in the sport drew their father's and mother's eyes to them. They were both standing on the hill-top gazing eagerly out to sea and chattering to one another.

"Seals probably," said their mother. From where they sat they could not see the shore for an intervening ridge. And seals were always a mighty attraction to the children.

But when they began dancing excitedly on their hill-top their father called, "What is it you see, Cubbie?"

"Somefing, dad! Somefing funny."

"Somefing funny!" repeated little Avice eagerly, and the elders got up lazily and slowly climbed the hillside to see what it was.

"My God!" said Wulfrey, as his eyes cleared the top first, and he turned and kissed his wife joyously.

"Thank God!" she breathed deeply, as her eyes also lighted on that which was coming.

For there, not half a mile away, was a white boat manned by blue sailors, leaping towards the shore as fast as eight lusty oars could drive her, and out beyond her, probably three miles away, was a white-sailed ship of size.

Wulfrey shouted and waved his arms. The children immediately did the same, and the regular rise and fall of the oars stopped suddenly as every eye in the boat turned on them. There were men in the stern with gilt on their hats. Then the oars fell-to again and the boat came bounding on. Wulfrey and Avice picked up each their namesakes, and plunged down the hill and ran round the ridge to the shore.

With a final lunge the boat came up the beach, and a tall man rose in the stern and asked, "Who, in heaven's name, are you, and what are you doing here?"—while nine pairs of eager eyes raked over the little party.

"I am Dr Wulfrey Dale, of Hazelford in Cheshire. This is my wife—and our children. We have been here five years."

"Good God! Five years!"—he was ashore by this time, and the rest tumbled hastily out and stood about them, the burly sailors listening with one ear and trying to make up to the children, who gazed with wondering awe at the only men they had ever seen except their father. "How on earth have you lived? ... Five years! ... Not all of you," he said with a smile.

"Not all of us. The children were born here. We were afraid we would all have to live and die here. I thank God you are come. What brought you?"

"We've been sent to prospect with a view to a lighthouse here. There has been an outcry about the number of wrecks—"

"Ay, there are hundreds over yonder," said Wulfrey, pointing westward. "They have kept us alive, but the cost to others has been heavy."

"And where do you live?"

"Come and I'll show you—or will you take us along in the boat? It's good four miles over that way."

"Boat'll be easiest. Sand's heavy walking. How long can we count on this weather?"

"Oh, for a week at least. It's our best time of year."

"You will take us home?" asked Avice eagerly, when they had climbed into the boat and were swinging along parallel to the shore, the children staring in a vast silence and with rounded eyes at the bearded sailor-men and their amazing ways.

"As far as our service permits, madame, we will do anything and everything you wish. We return to Halifax in Nova Scotia, but once there you will have no difficulties."

"That is where we want to go," said Wulfrey.... "Better keep out a bit here. There are ridges below there.... Now if you will turn in."

"What's that? A ship?" asked the tall man, and all eyes shot round to the bare poles of the 'Jane and Mary' snowing over the sandhills.

"A schooner, land-locked in a lagoon. That was our first home. Now we live ashore."

"And you've been all alone all that time?"

"We had one companion, the mate of the ship.... He died four years ago. Since then none have come but the dead.... We can get in here, I think."

The boat ran softly up the beach again, the sailors carried out Avice and the children, and they all struck up through the sandhills to the house.

John Oxenham – A Concise Bibliography

God's Prisoner (1898)
A Princess of Vascovy (1899)
Under the Iron Flail (1902)
Barbe of Grand Bayou (1903)
Bondman Free (1903)
Hearts in Exile (1904)
John of Gerisau (1904)
A Weaver of Webs (1904)
White Fire (1905)

Giant Circumstance (1906)
Profit and Loss (1906)
The Long Road (1907)
Carette of Sark (1907)
In Christ There Is No East or West (1908)
Pearl of Pearl Island (1908)
The Song of Hyacinth (1908)
My Lady of Shadows (1909)
Great Heart Gillian (1909)
A Maid of the Silver Sea (1910)
The Coil of Carne (1911)
The Quest of the Golden Rose (1912)
The Gate of the Desert (1912)
Bees in Amber (1913)
Broken Shackles (1914)
The King's High-Way (1916)
All's Well (1916)
The Fiery Cross (1917)
The Vision Splendid (1917)
High Altars (1918)
Hearts Courageous (1919)
The Wonder of Lourdes: what it is and what it means (1924)
The Hidden Years' (1927)
Gentlemen - the King! (1928)
God's Candle (1929)
Hearts in Exile (1930)
The Splendour of the Dawn (1930)
The Man Who Would Save the World (1930)
The Pageant of the King's Children (1930) (with his son Roderick Dunkerley)
Cross-Roads: The Story of Four Meetings (1931)
A Saint in the Making (1931)
Christ and the Third Wise Man (1934)